W9-CQK-628

Praise for

THE QUEST FOR THE GOLDEN PLUNGER

"The Quest for the Golden Plunger is a rare breed of book – a YA comedy that's heartwarming, hilarious, and deep with meaning at every turn. A fast, fun, and fearless tale, reading this book made me wish I hadn't dropped out of Cub Scouts, or, rather, that I attended camp with this bunch of rambunctious adventurers as my guides. Jackson Dickert is a master storyteller."

—Grant Faulkner, Executive Director of National Novel Writing Month and author of *Pep Talks for Writers*

"Take the attitude from the Sandlot, throw in the charm of Moonrise Kingdom, and polish it off with a balance of absurdity that would make anyone's inner delinquent give a devilish grin, and what you have is *The Quest For The Golden Plunger*. A delightful tale of youth, exploration, and comradery, Jackson Dickert has written a story that will make even the meanest old coot think fondly back to their days away at camp."

—Daniel Greene, Author, Creator, and Disheveled Goblin

"The Misadventures of the Adventure Rangers is a humorous, edgy, and surprisingly deep exploration of teenagers learning to work together in the face of overwhelming adversity. I could only stop laughing when the author slipped in moments that made me pause to reflect on my own youth."

—B.K. Bass, author of *What Once Was Home*

First published by Campfire Publishing LLC 2021

Copyright © 2021 by Jackson Dickert

All rights reserved. No part of this publication may be reproduced, stored or transmitted in any form or by any means, electronic, mechanical, photocopying, recording, scanning, or otherwise without written permission from the publisher. It is illegal to copy this book, post it to a website, or distribute it by any other means without permission.

This novel is entirely a work of fiction. The names, characters and incidents portrayed in it are the work of the author's imagination. Any resemblance to actual persons, living or dead, events or localities is entirely coincidental.

Designations used by companies to distinguish their products are often claimed as trademarks. All brand names and product names used in this book and on its cover are trade names, service marks, trademarks and registered trademarks of their respective owners. The publishers and the book are not associated with any product or vendor mentioned in this book. None of the companies referenced within the book have endorsed the book.

THE QUEST FOR THE
GOLDEN PLUNGER

THE MISADVENTURES OF THE ADVENTURE RANGERS

JACKSON DICKERT

Campfire Publishing

KNOXVILLE | BOSTON

For everyone except the adults who still think Charizard is the coolest Pokémon. There are hundreds of others at this point. Pick a different one. I believe in you.

For everyone who hasn't fed their Nintendogs in over ten years. I'm sure they're fine. Probably. Maybe. (You should check on them.)

For everyone who still feels like they're lost in the woods.

1

A RANGER IS USEFUL

"See you in Valhalla!" Uncle Ruckus shouts as his avatar blasts an RPG at the alien warship.

"Coms! Coms!" Turbo Cakes yells.

Boom.

I mow down a group of aliens with an automatic grenade launcher. A notification pops up in the lower-left corner of the screen: *Do-Over just got a Penta-kill!*

"Turbo, if you yell 'coms,' you aren't helping the situation. Just take off the headset and wait for him to stop screaming," I say and toss my own headset onto the beige couch cushion.

"Do-Over, don't go radio silent. Die, you prickless alien bastards!" the tinny sound of Uncle Ruckus's voice blares out of my headset.

Turbo Cakes's shrill voice replies, *"Uncle Ruckus, I swear to God, if you don't stop screaming right now!"*

My mom always wanted me to play the piano, but the gaming controller is my real instrument. Bobbing and weaving on my couch, I obliterate alien after alien. Uncle Ruckus is fifteen and not old enough to be anyone's actual Uncle. It's just a nickname. Turbo Cakes is a sweet kid who isn't quite sharp enough to dish out insults, so he settles for being the target. Both my friends take a death ray to the face and die, but not me. I tune out my friends' argument and try to focus on the game. I am owning. Even Mozart with his precious piano would be proud.

Then, my internet starts hiccupping.

I snatch the squalling headset back up and shout into the mic, "Guys, I'm lagging, cover me." The internet cuts out. Bright blue aliens taunt me while my character is frozen in place. Thank you, Concast.

"Crap." I throw my controller at the wall. It bounces off and sends my leaning Jenga tower of Xbox games crashing to the floor. There's an instant pang of regret in my heart as I stoop to pick them back up.

I roll the controller back and forth between my hands as I pace the room, trying to calm down. My foot crunches *Lead Space*'s plastic case. Of course the game had to come out the day before we go to summer camp.

I stare down the little "M" on the cover. I can still hear that mocking tough-guy voice from the commercial say, "Play the deadliest game of the summer. Rated M, for mature." The splash art on the game's cover is badass. Blue aliens with guns on their tails fire off lasers at the buff G.I. Joe rip-off characters. One of the muscle-heads is shielding a shirtless chick from the gunfire, and a little tagline reads, "She's humanity's last chance!" I glance back at the frozen, flickering TV. *What's so mature about pixelated blood and boobs?*

Turbo Cakes, Uncle Ruckus and I are all about to be freshmen in high school, so we can't buy M-rated video games. We also can't buy alcohol, see R-rated movies, or drive cars. That's why I slip the newest violent games into Dad's grocery cart at the store when he isn't looking. I'm one hundred percent confident he notices, but he never says anything. I think he feels bad for me being an only child with parents that are never around. There's an unspoken understanding: he buys me video games and keeps the fridge stocked, and I won't bug him or Mom. They're tired a lot.

It's more complicated than that, though. When people are tired all the time, there's something wrong with them. My parents used to be really outdoorsy. They'd go hunting together for entire weekends. One weekend they came home with over thirty ticks on each of them. I was eight. They got sick from the tick bites and they've never been the same since. I don't blame them or anything. But I miss them.

My headset crackles, "... *getting killed out here! Turbo, Do-Over, where'd you go?!*"

I smirk, dash across the room, and sweep up my controller. My full weight bounces onto the couch and my anxieties instantly dissipate. The Raysword gaming headset settles around my ears. My character barely moves before a swarm of death lasers disintegrate all my gear, tissue, and bodily fluids—leaving nothing but a pile of bones. The puff of red dust from my character's body doesn't even look like blood. A little tag in the lower left corner of the screen taunts me: *Congratulations, Do-Over. You just won a Darwin Award.* Lame.

Uncle Ruckus sighs into the headset. "Man, we almost won that time. But no, you had to lag out, and Turbo Cakes had to go try to sneak a peek at his sister in the shower."

I look around the room, trying to change the subject and keep my temper reigned in after such a humiliating death. A half-packed duffel bag catches my eye, so I speak before Turbo flips his lid at Uncle Ruckus's last comment. "Lay off, man. This is the last time we'll get to play games for almost a week. Have you guys packed yet?"

Uncle Ruckus snorts. "Dude, I haven't unpacked from last year. At this point, I'm too afraid to open my garbage bag of stuff to get out my gear; it's gonna reek."

Turbo Cakes says, "I got a suitcase, backpack, and a drawstring knapsack filled with first aid stuff. I'm worried I forgot something. After all, an Adventure Ranger is always ready." Turbo is your typical by-the-book Ranger. He's a stickler for the rules, always over-prepares for campouts, and his nose is stained brown from the amount of ass he kisses when it comes to any kind of authority figure.

Thunk.

I roll my eyes, "Did you just hit your mic saluting? You're sitting at home, not in an Adventure Ranger meeting."

"*A Ranger is always ready,*" Uncle Ruckus mimics. "I'm just gonna rough it, I think. Except for my prank supplies. And maybe my cell phone so I can look at Turbo's sister's nudes."

Sounds of protest tumble out of Turbo.

Uncle Ruckus talks over Turbo's exclamations, "Graduating high school did her two huge favors if you know what I—"

Boo doop. The sound chimes in my headset, and a notification pops up on the screen: *Turbo Cakes has disconnected.*

A message from him appears: *Go to hell, Ruckus. I'm gonna get some sleep. See you idiots tomorrow.*

Uncle Ruckus dies laughing. "It's so easy getting him to rage quit. It's not even fun anymore. And easier than his sister, if you know what I—"

"Remember that new kid? At the troop meeting last week?" I interject.

"Yeah, kinda dopey-looking, blonde buzz-cut, kinda skinny, but also fat," Uncle Ruckus says, sounding thoughtful.

"That's called average, moron."

"Yeah, that's it." Uncle Ruckus snaps his fingers. "Shovel looked like your average moron." He explodes into raucous laughter.

"Why are we calling him Shovel again?" I ask, raising my voice over his obnoxious laugh.

"I don't know. He kinda seemed like a tool. You know... Shovel, tool? Also, I feel like shovels aren't very smart, like they got a low IQ and everything?"

My mouth drops and I feel my eyelids squint. "No shit, Sherlock. It's a shovel. It doesn't have a brain."

"Exactly, he seems like he's got no brain." Uncle Ruckus snaps his fingers again. I don't have to see him to know he's shooting finger guns.

"That's not what I s—"

Uncle Ruckus cuts in, "And that's Uncle Sherlock to you, bud... Wonder if we could get him to eat dirt? I bet Hawkins'll make him at some point."

Anger wells up inside me. "I swear, if you give Hawkins the idea, I'll make *you* eat dirt."

"Woah, chill," Uncle Ruckus says. "I'm only joking around. You don't need to get so mad all the time. Actually... There's something I haven't told you."

My temper wilts and compresses into a weight in the pit of my stomach, "Yeah?"

"Well, I told Turbo last week but... I just didn't have a good opportunity to tell you. It's been really cool getting to know you and Turbo and becoming friends over the last two years in the Adventure Rangers." Uncle Ruckus takes a deep breath. "I'm moving to San Francisco in a few weeks. This'll probably be the last time we'll all be at summer camp together."

My head lolls back to rest on the couch cushion. Deep breath. My school counselor's voice pops into my head: *When you feel like you're going to lose control, look around the room and try to find something for each color of the rainbow.*

5

At the time it seemed like stupid advice. But credit where it's due, it works. Red... Like my hair. I always cheat with that one.

"It's nothing personal, obviously," Uncle Ruckus nervously continues. "It's just that, you know, my home situation is complicated."

Orange... Like my favorite t-shirt.

"I'm gonna miss you guys a ton."

Yellow... Like my character's gun.

"It's just, I want to go live with my Uncle Mark. We'll still be able to play games and stuff together, though."

Green like my controller. Blue like my walls. Indigo is a fake color. Violet like my bedspread. Deep breath.

"No worries, man. I get it," I say. "I wish I could get away from home too. Let's just focus on making this week the best week of camp ever. Camp Winnebago isn't much of a home away from home, but I still look forward to it every year. There's nobody else I'd rather get lost in the woods with than you and Turbo Cakes." Uncle Ruckus doesn't say anything. This would usually be welcome because he never knows when to shut his mouth. But now? Talking about serious stuff? It makes me uncomfortable. "I think I'm gonna get some sleep too. Morning comes early and all that. See ya."

Boo doop. With that, I disconnect from the chat. The mess of games on the floor catches my eye. *I'll take care of it when I get back home.* I leave the TV on and lay in bed listening to the gentle *boo doop* of the Xbox across the room every time Uncle Ruckus gets an in-game achievement.

* * *

EARLIER THAT NIGHT...

SUNDAY, MAY 31ST, 2015. 8:53 PM.

Shovel went through the Adventure Ranger Handbook one more time, going down the entire checklist of things he might need. He had everything except a pocketknife—he wasn't allowed to have one of those yet.

"Hey, Dad?" Shovel called.

His dad's head appeared in the doorway wearing a bucket hat with fishing lures and hooks all over it. "What's going on, sport?"

Shovel frowned at his Adventure Ranger branded backpack. "I don't know if I want to go. I don't really know anyone."

Shovel's dad fiddled with the hand crank radio in his hand. His voice sounded far away. "Sure, sure, I totally agree." He looked up. "Did you know I went to this camp every single summer? I must've gotten a dozen Ranger patches there. Way back when I was a kid, they called me The McTerminator! What's your nickname again?"

"Shovel."

"Great nickname; shovels are useful. Listen, son, you're going to have a great time. We both are. Let's just feel it out for a few days, and if you don't like it, we can leave."

Shovel looked at his dad. "Really?"

"Sure, sure. I'm going to finish getting my fishing stuff together. Nighty night, son." And with that, The McTerminator turned off the lights and closed the door.

The door cracked open, "Don't forget extra socks and underwear." He pulled it shut again.

Shovel sat in the dark for a moment before putting a few extra pairs of tighty-whities into his black leather suitcase. The glow-in-the-dark constellation stickers on his ceiling gave off enough light to see by. He put on his Adventure Ranger uniform and crawled into his twin bed. He opened his Nintendo DS, booted up Nintendogs, and fed his virtual pets for the last time of the week. With the stylus, Shovel gave each dog a treat and took the time to scratch each one behind the ears.

The Buzz Lightyear alarm clock glared the time at him. Feeling guilty, Shovel gave each puppy another biscuit from the 989 treats in his inventory. Noticing the number, he grabbed the lock-journal from his bedside drawer and used a tiny key to unlock it. He flipped through the pages until he got to the most recent ledger entry. He clicked the light at the end of his pen. Bending its rubber body, the light aimed at the paper while Shovel wrote. *5/31/2015: Go to the store, need more treats.* Using the calculator in the game, he figured out how much ten more dog biscuits would cost. Under the first line, he scribbled, *Buy ten treats, three dollars, will have 999,996 dollars left after.*

Shovel closed the journal, picked up the game, and craned his neck toward the screen to whisper the list of names, "Goodnight Bubbles, Toffee, Moose, Nibbles, and Cujo. I left some toys to play with, so be good."

With the same care a supermarket manager might take to bag a carton of eggs, he closed the device and plugged in the charger. Shovel laid on top of his sheets in his itchy khaki uniform, Ranger hat, and shined leather boots. He stared up at the glowing ceiling. The night he got the stickers he stayed up naming every star, but he forgot them all by morning. It didn't seem right to give the stars all new names, so he never did. The boy squinted at the luminescent shapes until they blurred.

"What does it mean to be useful?"

2

A RANGER IS COOL

PRESENT

MONDAY, JUNE 1ST, 2015. 2:04 PM.

"Oh my God! The trailer is gone!" Hawkins exclaims in a rehearsed tone for the third time during the four-hour drive. Turbo Cakes twitches next to me, and I give him a pat on the knee to assure him the trailer is, indeed, still hitched to the back of the restored church van. Though, not restored enough if you ask me. The windows don't even open. I'd be asking for my money back.

Church vans are like something out of *Doctor Who*. It looks like a normal size from the outside, but inside there's five rows of scratchy seats the color of mop water. Shovel and Treb, the two youngest kids in our troop, sit in the front row. Treb's pretty quiet, so I haven't talked to him much. Shovel, on the other hand, has such a smooth brain that if you tell him gullible is written on the ceiling, he'll first stare at the ceiling deep in thought, then squint as if to magnify a too-small font.

Then there's Turbo Cakes, me, and Tri-Clops in the second row. Tri-Clops is... probably the weirdest guy in our troop, and that says a lot. I keep my distance from him as much as possible. Next, Uncle Ruckus is stretched out with a whole row to himself. Behind him is Hawkins. He's an asshole. The cool, older guys—Ducky and his two friends—sit in the very last row. I don't actually know that much about them. Just that they're almost eighteen, so they always get the back row. That's the rule.

Uncle Ruckus, whose acne-mottled face makes him look like a teenage Freddy Krueger, uses his best tattle-voice, "Mr. B, Hawkins is taking the Lord's name in vain again!"

Shovel not-so-casually explores the interior of the van with his eyes. Like a broken bobble-head, the new kid's blond, buzz-cut head swivels around to gawk at the trailer for the third time during the four-hour drive.

I shrink down in the seat, knowing what comes next as Hawkins dives two seats forward, swinging his arm straight over my head toward his target. The most impressive part about the whole thing is the finesse with which Hawkins swings, missing every other kid crammed in their seats like sardines to land a hit on Shovel's tiny bicep, the same place it struck the last three times.

Wap.

Turbo Cakes reacts late and covers his head with his hands as Hawkins sits back in his seat. Uncle Ruckus lets out a sound of satisfaction as he stretches his legs across his solo seat. He enjoys conflict of any kind.

"Ouch!" Shovel squeals, throwing his arms up to ward off further blows. He turns around in the seat and gets on his knees, his head inches away from the ceiling. Tears well up in his eyes as he thrusts a finger over my head at Hawkins. "You jerk! You..." he hesitates, then juts the finger further and adds, "ass!"

Mr. B slams on the brakes.

I brace myself against the seat in front of me with my legs so I look unfazed by the sudden shift in acceleration.

Turbo lurches forward against his seatbelt and Uncle Ruckus jams his hand against the back of our seat, trying to look chill.

Shovel lets out a yelp and—still on his knees and facing the rear—hugs the seat for dear life.

Four seconds later, we stop. The weight of the trailer jostles behind the van, doing its best to follow Newton's first law on the gravel road. As soon as it does, we all scramble to buckle in. All except Turbo Cakes, who snaps his seatbelt against his chest with a smug look on his face.

Without air-conditioning, the inside of the van is a hotbox of chicken nuggets and Axe body spray failing to cover up teen body odor. As stocky, red-faced Mr. B glares at us, I try to avoid his gaze, turning to keep everyone in my periphery.

I don't respect the man, but I respect the thick, trimmed black mustache on his lip. It dances as Mr. B says, "We've got half an hour left to drive. Don't make me bury one of you in the backwoods." Mr. B has been Troop 99's leader ever since the old leader, his dad, died a few years back. He's hard on us sometimes, but he wants the best for us. Even if it means burying a few Rangers in the woods from time to time.

Everybody, even Shovel's dad in the passenger seat, nods.

Mr. B adds, "Hawkins. Put the seatbelt on. Also, I'm tired of the trailer game."

Hawkins throws his whole head into an exaggerated eye roll, but none of the older guys notice his efforts. He tries all kinds of antics to impress them, so it wouldn't surprise me if they're ignoring him on purpose.

Mr. B continues down his shit list. "Shovel, if I hear another curse word out of you, you'll be cleaning the new bathrooms at camp for the whole week. Treb..."

Treb looks up from his *Encyclopedia of Medieval Siege Weapons*, dark hair obscuring his eyes.

"It's been two hours," Mr. B continues. "Finish. The. Chicken. Nuggets. Our Class A uniforms are going to smell like they were ironed by the Hamburglar."

Reluctantly, Treb puts the half-eaten chicken nugget he had been nibbling on for a good forty-five minutes in his mouth and begins a slow chew.

Mr. B points, "Whatever you don't eat, I'm throwing out when we get to camp. The next Ranger on my radar cleans the bathrooms tonight. What are we going to earn this year?"

"The Golden Plunger," everybody drones.

The Golden Plunger is Camp Winnebago's most coveted award, given every summer. There's no actual prize, it's just bragging rights. But there's nothing teenage guys love more than a good dick-measuring contest. Metaphorically, obviously.

With that, Mr. B throws the vehicle in drive, hits the gas, and the van once again bumps down the makeshift road. Individual trees blur into woodsy pastels as they streak past outside the window.

We all shut up. Nobody wants to clean the bathrooms. Not to mention, I'm pretty sure we're running out of breathable oxygen in the van. The air is hot and thick. The van shudders as Mr. B nails a pothole in the road. Under such miserable conditions, I can't help but think I'd make a great astronaut.

Mr. McNitt, Shovel's dad, twists in the passenger seat to address the Rangers. "Come on guys, thirty minutes. We're almost there. Let's get off to a good start. I know Troop 100 usually wins the Golden Plunger, but this could be our year!"

Mr. McNitt's too-cheery words hang over us. He's one of those dads I can't help but feel bad for. He's balding, single, and has way too much camp spirit. It's hard not to cringe every time he opens his mouth.

12

The tires kick up pieces of gravel that ping off the trailer and do Shovel a belated favor—continually reminding us of its presence.

Plink.

Mr. McNitt leans back in his seat as Shovel whines, "But, Dad. He hit me!"

"That's the game, son. They play every trip." Mr. McNitt lowers his voice as he turns back to look Shovel in the eye, but it doesn't make a difference in the silent car. "You're new to this troop, bud. Let's try to fit in, huh? What if you try to get Hawkins every once in a while? Then you can punch *him* in the arm."

Plink.

Hawkins snickers.

Shovel's brow furrows as Mr. McNitt turns back to the front. "Eyes on the prize, fellas. Golden Plunger."

Plink.

A bead of sweat rolls down my cheek. It gets absorbed by a stray strand of crimson hair which I brush behind my ear. "You'd think they could afford a nicer van."

Plink.

"How are you wearing that?" I ask, half-twisting to look behind me.

Uncle Ruckus gestures to his oversized, inside-out, splotchy black hoodie. "What, this?"

Plink.

"It's comfy stuff, my man. This right here is the big spit," he says.

Hawkins leans forward, his thin nose curled into a sneer. "Does your family even own a washing machine? You look stupid wearing that thing inside-out. I can't *believe* the troop lets people in who don't even go to St. George's Academy. Maybe if you weren't a leech, they'd have the money to fix the air conditioning."

Turbo's head droops onto my shoulder. I don't know how he can just fall asleep like that. On my left, Tri-Clops sits in the window seat entranced with a ball of yellow, crusty foam in his hand. He's spent the entire car ride hollowing out the seat in front of him.

"Yeah, or maybe if some of us treated it better," I say.

The van hits a pot-hole, Turbo Cakes's head slips off my shoulder, and he jerks awake. Drool seeps from the corner of his mouth onto my khaki uniform.

"Sorry," Turbo Cakes murmurs, swiping the glob of spit off my shoulder and using it to style his moussed, black hair. It looks the same once he is done playing with it.

I want to detach my shoulder. "Awake from your shortcut," I observe.

Turbo stretches and his little oval face yawns wide, "Always makes the drive go by faster." His eyes focus on Tri-Clops picking seat stuffing out of the hole in front of him. "What a waste of a window seat..." Turbo Cakes says. "You might wanna stop. This van's a relic. You're destroying history."

Tri-Clops hisses at Turbo, then keeps on picking. I can't help but stare for a second at the huge brown birthmark in the center of his forehead, for which he was so aptly nicknamed.

"Yeah, okay," I say. "That's it for me. I'm going to sit with Uncle Ruckus." I clamber over the seat, "I can't take sitting in row number two anymore."

Plink.

Ruckus holds up a fist, "Ha. Number two. Nice."

I bump it.

Turbo plays his trump card. "At least I *have* facial hair." Like Vanna White revealing a clue on Wheel of Fortune, his fingers slide down a lone black hair jutting out from his chin. "Talk to me when you weigh more than ninety pounds soaking wet, Do-Over. This baby is ni—"

"9.398 centimeters long," the whole van drones in unison.

Turbo Cakes wilts. "It's eight repeating..."

Plink.

"You got a disease, Turbo," I say.

"Tell that to AIDS face over there." Turbo Cakes points at Uncle Ruckus. He's been a little *too* quiet. He doesn't look so good either. I guess Mr. B's threat really spooked him.

Uncle Ruckus rolls his eyes, "Yeah, everybody make fun of the guy with acne. Claps for you, bud." He claps for emphasis. "That's such low-hanging fruit. That's like calling Do-Over fire crotch. It's too easy. Turbo, if you can't play nice, we're gonna put you down for another nap. I brought my special chloroform hanky." A soiled Kleenex appears in his hand, then he blows his nose and shivers.

"Do you have a cold?" I ask.

"N-nah dude. I'm good..." Uncle Ruckus pulls the front of his sweatshirt so it makes a big tent. He tucks his legs and arms inside, looking much more comfortable now. We pass a sign and Uncle Ruckus emphasizes the vowels "Camp Winn-eh-bay-goh. Who the heck names a camp after Treb's house?"

Mr. B slow-claps as he steers the van, "Uncle Ruckus! Guess who cleans toilets tonight? Bathroom duty, my friend! Look, boys. Let's read the Ranger Rules as we drive past." Each sign outlines part of the Ranger Rules and Mr. B, Shovel, and the other little Tenderboots shout-read them. Every. Single. One.

"A Ranger is..."

"Cordial! Compliant! Devout! Honest! Ardent..."

My brain initiates a defense mechanism to put itself in sleep mode. I zone out and let my mind wander instead of listening to the Ranger Rules for the millionth time in my life. Despite the lack of video games, I love

Camp Winnebago. It feels more like home than home does. The more I'm able to get away from my parents, the more I realize that there's so much more to life than sleeping the whole thing away. The only thing that slows me down at camp is… well, everything. Kind of. I'm afraid of a lot of stuff. Not actually afraid, more like aware of all the things that *could* happen. Like, I don't want to get a tick and get sick like my parents. I don't want to swim in the murky lake. The mandatory swim test is easily my least favorite part of camp. I fail it every year. But once that's over, it'll be a whole week away from home. Just me and the guys.

Mr. B stops in Camp Winnebago's parking lot with one last *Plink*.

"I know you guys are sick of hearing about the rules," Mr. B says, "but I want to win the Golden Plunger this year. I'll only say this one more time: if anyone thought breaking the rules and bringing electronics was a good idea, let's go ahead and hand them over once we get to the campsite. We need good behavior to win."

Or I can not hand over my phone and play games on it every night. The choice is simple. Sorry, Mr. B.

Mr. B tells Mr. McNitt, "Stay put, Joe. Watch them," and heads into the Administration Building.

Shovel squints. "What's that place?"

"That," Uncle Ruckus points with his middle finger, "is pretty much the Mordor of camp. Nothing in there but rules, paperwork, and punishment."

"I don't remember any paperwork in Mordor," Shovel mutters, face scrunching in concentration.

"And that." Uncle Ruckus rotates his hand palm-side toward his face, finger pointing up. "Is the ceiling."

Ha. Nice one.

Shovel looks up at the ceiling. He gives a slow nod at the truthfulness of the statement and turns to face the front of the van.

I'm half tempted to tell him to check again for gullible, but it's not worth it. Poor kid's already been whapped on the arm enough times, no point in embarrassing him even more.

Everything is still. We're parked in the middle of a sparsely populated gravel parking lot. The Administration Building sits on the far end of the parade field next to the Infirmary. There's some old guy who looks like a hobo Santa milling around the field, picking dandelions poking up in the otherwise perfect plain of grass. Past the parade field is Cardiac Hill. I can't remember anybody *actually* having a heart attack climbing it, but every time I go up it I feel like I'm going to have one, and I'm only fifteen.

Shovel breaks the silence, stifling a laugh. "Hey, Hawkins, I think the trailer is gone." Shovel's nostrils flare, and a half-smile flicks back and forth across his pale, pre-pubescent face.

Hawkins rolls his eyes, not turning around to look.

"Screw this," says Ducky, the oldest, toughest, and muscliest guy in the troop.

The Hierarchy of Coolness goes into effect as each age group waits for their elders to exit. The back row of seats populated by the "men" in the troop, like Ducky, move to get out first. Hawkins will go after them. Myself, Uncle Ruckus, and Turbo Cakes will get out after him. The little kids—Treb and Shovel—plus Tri-Clops will be next. We all know the drill and wait our turn to escape the van.

Everyone except Shovel, who slings the sliding door open and jumps out as soon as the older boys shuffle around in the backseat.

Does this kid want a target painted on his back from the moment he steps out of the van on his very first campout? Who does he think he is? He won't last the day.

After Shovel, each Ranger waits his turn to explode out of the van. We breathe deeply, thankful to be free of the Ronald McDonald meets Blazing Phoenix scented cell on wheels.

Shovel is kicking gravel around with a dopey grin on his face. *Maybe he doesn't even know he did something wrong?*

"Dude," I say, "you're gonna get your teeth kicked in."

Shovel's restless feet stop and his smugness wavers.

I continue, "If you don't respect the older guys, they're going to get pissed. Have you learned about graphs in school?"

Shovel nods.

"Okay, well, imagine the y-axis is coolness, and the x-axis is your age." I demonstrate each axis with my arms. "There is a perfect linear equation for the age to coolness ratio." I draw an imaginary diagonal line in the air in front of Shovel's blank face.

"Get it? You're just a little kid. So, you aren't cool. So, you exit the van *after* everyone older than you. That's after Ducky's gang, after Hawkins, after the freshmen," I gesture to myself and my friends, "and you get out with the nose pickers over there living out *Lord of the Flies*." I conclude, sweeping my arm to include Shovel, Treb, and Tri-Clops.

Shovel's eyes track to Tri-Clops, who is balling up seat-foam in his fist.

"He's older, yeah, but he's an outlier," I explain. "Outliers are really bad. It means you're weird. This stuff isn't an exact science. Just don't be weird, and don't die, and one day you'll be cool."

I pat Shovel's head and go stand with my friends. Mr. McNitt is still sitting shotgun reading the *Ranger's Life* magazine. Maybe he's missing some brain cells and likes the van's hotbox? I can't help but wonder if Shovel is a chip off the old block; that maybe he'll never be cool. Looking at his dad, there's no *way* that guy was ever cool.

"What was that all about?" Turbo Cakes gestures toward Shovel, who is staring up at the sun like he's trying to figure out its color. Well... At least he'll be protected by his disability if he ends up blind. Maybe it's for the best this way—nobody picks on blind kids. Probably.

"Just trying to help him survive the first week, at least," I say.

"I don't think it worked." Uncle Ruckus nods toward Shovel.

I watch in horror as Shovel dances up with a stupid-ass smile on his face and punches Hawkins in the arm. Hawkins spins, spit slinging from his mouth in a snarl.

"Gonna bruise, Hawkins?" calls Uncle Ruckus. "I've seen Treb close books harder than that."

Treb doesn't notice the jab. He's too busy half-cradling his book as he attempts to coerce what looks like a half-dozen chicken nuggets into the already-full pocket of his khakis.

"Shut up," Hawkins spits. He shoves Uncle Ruckus into me and stomps back over to Shovel. *This kid is so stupid, why didn't he run when he had the chance?* Hawkins delivers two punches to the already-forming bruise on Shovel's bicep. "You don't get to punch if I don't look, *retard*."

Hawkins starts walking away when Shovel sputters, "But you did look. You looked at the trailer as soon as you got out of the van. I saw you." A chorus of exclamations erupts from the group of older boys; a mish-mash of ooh's, cuss words, and other unintelligible sounds come together to play one of Bach's unreleased symphonies: *Masses, Humiliations, Hawkins.*

"You're an outlier, Hawkins!" Shovel yells.

I smack a palm to my face. Shovel doesn't get it. He doesn't know when to stop. I crack my fingers to see everyone else look at each other, their faces asking a silent, "What?"

The summer sun glints off the rows of aluminum sheets drilled into the side of the trailer. Each dent and imperfection serves as reflective jump-off points for the rays of light seeking to photo-bleach the eyes of all those who look at the giant tin can.

Shovel sniffs. "You looked. I saw you."

Hawkins whirls, grabs Shovel by the scruff of his uniform collar, and jerks him to face the trailer attached to the rear of the van.

"Let me explain. The point of the game..." Each word flicks off Hawkin's tongue like boiling venom. "...is to trick little idiots like you into thinking the trailer came loose from the van *while* it's driving. You see the trailer? All your stuff is in there." Hawkins jerks Shovel's collar forward, forcing him to take a step toward the van. "If it came detached, all the stuff would be gone. So. The. Point. Of. The. Game." He forces Shovel to take a step with each word until he is inches away from the trailer. "Is not to look when the van is *moving*. What am I supposed to do, live my whole life without looking at the trailer again?"

Hawkins is hunched over, jutting a finger into Shovel's red, wet face. He jerks Shovel's collar again, smooshing his face against the shiny metal trailer. I feel the heat radiating off the glorified dumpster on wheels even from where I'm standing. Bright red letters above Hawkins's head read, "Troop 99, Property of the St. George Catholic Academy."

"Now, I think—if you wanna be tough—we'd better toughen you up."

Shovel's chubby cheek smears against the trailer. Tiny beads of sweat sizzle as they stream down his face toward the metal sheets. Static shoots down my forearms and pools in my hands. I hate bullies.

"It's hot! Stop, stop, it's hot!"

Hawkins presses harder. "You got it, retard?"

Shovel's tears slip down his face to join the beads of sweat. They sizzle in harmony as his chubby cheek fills in the dents and imperfections on the trailer.

I shift my stance so my weight is balanced between both feet and growl, "He's only like twelve."

Turbo rests a hand on my shoulder and speaks in a hushed tone, "You good, man? Come on, calm down. You know you have a temper."

Shovel's pre-teen falsetto rises to a scream as he flails against the older boy's push, "Hawkins, stop! Please, stop. Stop!"

All the muscles in my forearm tingle. My fingers curl. The corners of my vision turn red.

"Do-Over, come on. Stop. Deep breaths. Try to calm down."

Hawkins grins. "You little dipshit tard-monkey."

Rage builds inside as my trembling right hand picks up a fist-sized rock and I brush off Turbo. Ready to unleash my fury, I creep up behind Hawkins. My hand grips the rock tighter, knuckles turning white.

"Hey, boys!" Mr. McNitt gets out of the car.

Everyone freezes.

My hands drop to my sides. The rock hits the ground. It stands out in the gravel lot.

Shovel, his cheek an angry Van Gogh painting, pulls away from Hawkins as his dad walks up.

Mr. McNitt surveys the group. "Never seen y'all so quiet before. Out of the way, boys, let me get the trailer open." He makes his way through the crowd and unlocks it. "I know I can trust Moon Rangers. Go ahead and get your stuff and head down to Campsite 21. Tenderboot, Bear, and Pine Rangers, stay here." Mr. McNitt throws the trailer doors wide. Ducky's two friends, Tyler 2 Electric Boogaloo and iBall, swarm the sleeping bags and luggage as they tumble to the ground.

Amid the commotion, Ducky—who has so much testosterone at seventeen he's already showing signs of male pattern baldness—leans down to Hawkins. Ducky wears a bandanna over his bald spot, and his beard is an unkempt mess. He's the spitting image of John Cena dressed up like a badass pirate.

"Next time you look at the trailer, and you don't play right," Ducky reveals his clenched teeth, "*I'll* punch you. And watch your damn mouth." With his two hundred pounds of muscle, he pushes past Hawkins to pick up his pack.

I stare at my shoes like I've never seen them before as Ducky walks past. Yikes, a threat like that is enough to scare the shit out of anybody.

Hawkins hefts his stuff onto his shoulder and blends in with the rest of the older guys under Mr. McNitt's lax eye.

Mr. McNitt says, "I know I don't have to tell y'all, but please, walk down the hill."

The older Rangers were already out of earshot and halfway across the parade field.

Mr. McNitt walks past his crying son toward a porta-potty against the Administration Building as he preaches to the already-gone Rangers. "It's a steep mile downhill. If you run, you'll fall, and you probably won't stop rolling until you hit the lake, and even then…" He closes the porta-potty door as his lecture continues, now muffled.

The other Adventure Rangers stand around socializing. But Uncle Ruckus, Turbo Cakes, Shovel, and I—none of whom go to St. George's Catholic Academy—stand off to the side.

Uncle Ruckus pats Shovel on the head. "You're gonna die, dude." He eyes me. "Well, both of you, probably. You gotta watch that temper, Do-Over."

I push past the sixth-grader to watch the older guys retreat into the distance and begin the descent down Cardiac Hill. I feel rather than see Shovel walk up next to me.

He asks, "Why do you guys let Hawkins be so mean?"

Turbo Cakes pipes up behind us. "The old guy named Hawkins before him was worse than the new Hawkins is. Every troop needs an asshole, and he's ours, I guess. Whenever the last Hawkins left the troop, we had no asshole."

"Speak for yourself," Uncle Ruckus says, sucking on a hoodie string. "My asshole has always been intact. If you're missing yours, that explains why you're always so full of shit."

Poor Turbo Cakes. Uncle Ruckus never lays off the guy. To be fair, though, he kind of sets himself up for it.

"Cute," Turbo Cakes replies with a bead of sweat rolling down his forehead. "How can you wear that over your uniform? It's hotter than Hell out here." He casts a nervous glance at the glaring letters on the trailer.

"I feed on your weakness and use it to keep my body temperature low," Uncle Ruckus says.

We all stare at him.

Emotionless, Uncle Ruckus's eyes fix on Turbo Cake's as he slides a pair of sunglasses over them and says, "Cool as a cucumber." He pulls on the other sweatshirt string and puts it in his mouth.

My face gnarls in disgust. "You're a weird dude sometimes." I swat at the strings in Uncle Ruckus's mouth. "You freaky little outlier. That's nasty."

"Anyway..." Turbo Cakes draws out the word and leans against a bulletin board. "Without the old Hawkins, the new Hawkins kind of just stepped up and donned the mantle, and we've called him Hawkins ever since."

"And he's been a jerk ever since," I say. "Now that you've royally pissed him off, we'll *all* suffer for it *all* week." I slump to the ground. "Thanks."

I throw a piece of gravel at the trailer.

Plink.

By the time Shovel's dad comes out of the porta-potty, we've raked all the gravel in a six-foot radius into a tiny mountain. Mr. McNitt saunters up to the vending machines outside the Administration Building.

"I've never been camping before," Shovel offers.

"Don't care." Uncle Ruckus shoots him a pair of finger-guns and puts his sweatshirt string back in his mouth.

"You gave me my nickname, right?" Shovel asks.

"Mmm-hmm," Uncle Ruckus adds a garnish of grass to the mountaintop.

"Why did you pick Shovel?"

Uncle Ruckus, Turbo Cakes, and I exchange a glance. I don't approve of the nickname, but it's easier to just let Uncle Ruckus have his fun and stay out of his sights. He's not really a bully, just a dick. But now Uncle Ruckus has to squirm his way out of the Shovel nickname hole he's dug. Might be best if Shovel finds out. It'll be good for everybody. Shovel gets thicker skin, and Uncle Ruckus might ease up.

"Because," Turbo Cakes hesitates before continuing, "of that game you like to play so much. The one with all the blocks and you dig with a shovel?" Each word tumbles out a little faster than the one before.

"Oh." Shovel looks perplexed, then smiles. "Cool!"

Turbo Cakes is too good for this world. Leave it to him to bail out Ruckus even after he gives him shit all day. Oh well, probably better this way.

Shovel squints. "How about him? Why's he called Treb?"

Treb is sitting next to Tri-Clops in the van, looking at the encyclopedia together. A chicken nugget teeters on the edge of Treb's pocket, and he offers the one he's nibbling on to Tri-Clops, who gratefully eats the whole thing in one bite.

Before Uncle Ruckus spouts anything hateful, I say, "It's because he always has that book about knights and castles on every campout. He never puts it down."

"I don't get it," Shovel says.

"Trebuchet," Uncle Ruckus blurts. "It's short for trebuchet, you moron."

Wow. He almost made it through that sentence without being an asshat.

"Oh, okay. What about—"

"Even you aren't dumb enough to be confused about Tri-Clops's nickname. Did you *see* that *thing* on his forehead?" Uncle Ruckus asks, letting one of the spit-saturated strings fall from his mouth.

"Right." Shovel says, reaffirming his suspicions with a nod. "Is everyone's nickname that simple?"

"No," I say.

"Well, how about yours, Do-Over?" Shovel asks.

My heart pangs. Images of rocks and bloody noses blur through my head.

"Kid," Turbo Cakes says, "asking a lot of questions about someone's nickname is a good way to get beat up. All right? There's just some stuff guys don't talk about, and nicknames are one of 'em. Once you've been around longer than one campout..." He tilts his head. "Then maybe we'll tell you about our nicknames. You joined last week. Either figure it out, wait, or ask and risk death."

"Seems like a weird rule..." Shovel mumbles.

"I got snacks and Coke." Mr. McNitt has an armload of sodas, Pop-Tarts, and Skittles.

Uncle Ruckus's head snaps up. "Thank God, a nice kilo is going to make this campout so much more bearable. You generous man, I didn't have you pinned as a cartel guy. I can't imagine why you would offer free—oh, you mean like the drink." He concludes with a frown.

"Sorry, no white powder here, Adventure Rangers. Pass 'em around, will you, Ruckus?"

"That's Uncle Ruckus to you, sir."

"Just seems weird to call somebody a third of my age 'Uncle,'" Mr. McNitt says.

Uncle Ruckus cracks open his Coke. "Seems weird to offer drugs to minors."

Mr. McNitt passes out drinks to all six of us. "Good thing we got rid of those older guys, huh? Would've been another twenty dollars, probably."

Turbo Cakes fingers the Coke's lid with distaste, "Does this man not know about proper hydration?"

"My dad doesn't know what?" Shovel pipes up through a mouthful of Skittles. Mr. McNitt looks up at his son and saunters over to us.

"Know," Turbo Cakes says in a long breath, "about Shovel's injury. He's got a sunburn already!" He points at Shovel's cheek.

Mr. McNitt frowns, "Son, I thought I told you to put on sunscreen."

"Gee, Mr. McNitt," I say, an idea forming. "He looks pretty bad; maybe we should take him to the Infirmary?"

Mr. McNitt squints at his son and adjusts his glasses. "Well... Maybe... But I don't know where—"

"Don't worry, Mr. McNitt!" I interject. "We know where it is. We'll take excellent care of him, won't we?" Turbo Cakes and Uncle Ruckus nod. They grab the younger boy by his sweaty arms and hoist him to his feet. Shovel chugs the rest of his soda, grabs another pack of pop-tarts, and follows us like a good little Tenderboot. "All good, Mr. McNitt," I assure him.

We half-drag, half-carry Shovel down the parking lot until we're out of sight.

* * *

THE PREVIOUS NIGHT...
SUNDAY, MAY 31ST, 2015. 10:36 PM.

Uncle Ruckus cackled at the little notification that read, "Do-Over has left the party" in the corner of his TV screen. The condo walls rattled, causing dust to flit down from the popcorn ceiling. Tiny specks settled around the rim of a day-old, green soda. He stretched, grabbed a sharpie, and changed the name on the can. Uncle Ruckus took a big glug of flat Mountain Poo and grabbed the bulky black garbage bag from last year.

Holding his breath, he stuffed the concentrated Uncle Ruckus reek into a different garbage bag, tied it with a knot previously unknown to mankind, and sat back down on the discolored orange shag carpet in his room. His eyes lingered on the rolls of toilet paper and special chocolate. Man, this summer was going to be *epic*. The game un-paused and Uncle Ruckus resumed his warmongering. Faint yelling crept through the floor. He ignored the sounds along with the smell seeping out of his garbage bag of camp gear. If everything went according to plan, Uncle Ruckus would be in San Francisco in no time. He'd miss his friends, sure, but he couldn't stand living with his dad anymore.

Coated with orange chip dust, the buttons crunched every time he unleashed a barrage of gunfire. He turned up the volume on the TV and drowned out the rest of the world.

3

A RANGER IS INJURED

We walk past the Administration Building and are almost across the parade field when Uncle Ruckus asks, "What's the deal? Why do we care about dude's ugly mug?" He jerks his head toward Shovel.

"I don't know about you guys," I say, "but I would much rather sit inside in the cool air than sit in a gravel parking lot with the rest of those morons."

"I don't mind it," Uncle Ruckus says with a grin.

Turbo, his khaki uniform drenched through with sweat, asks, "How do you do it? We're out here dying of heat stroke, and you're dancing around like Snow White. In the sun. In a *black sweatshirt*."

We step onto the porch of the Infirmary, Shovel in tow. Even though it is the first day of camp, there is already a line of Rangers sitting outside, waiting their turn to see the doctor. A plastic cooler next to the door gives off a gentle chill, condensation dripping off in rhythmic beads.

Plip, Plip, Plip...

Uncle Ruckus says, "Told you, I grow more powerful from the suffering of others. I'm like... The *Devil*!"

I notice a look of shock flicker across a nearby Ranger's face from his place in line. He had to be the youngest kid in the whole camp. His uniform is creased as if it came straight from the store. With the official Adventure Ranger boots, knee-high wool socks, and matching sock garters, he's a pristine example of a proper Class A uniform. The too-tight neckerchief fastened around his neck with a Camp Winnebago woggle didn't do him any favors either. His backpack is overflowing with merit patch books. Like the other sixth-graders who haven't hit their growth spurts yet, the kid looks like a chipmunk. The eyes on his chubby face widen and lock on Uncle Ruckus.

"*Ay, Dios mio! El Diablo!*"

Uncle Ruckus wags his tongue at the boy, and I push him inside the Infirmary.

We step into the little wooden building and the air conditioning wraps us in its loving arms. That's as far as we get before we are stopped.

"What's wrong with you four?" A woman whose name tag reads 'Holly' is sitting in a dark green Ranger troop leader uniform behind a desk. She puts down her copy of *The Prisoner of Azkaban* and gives us a hard look. "I got a whole line of tummy-aches, homesickness, and appendicitis out there, so hop in line."

"Well, you see," I start, stepping aside so she could see Shovel, "our friend here—" I didn't get to finish. After the fight with Hawkins and eating all that junk food in the hot sun, I don't think any of us *actually* considered how lousy Shovel might be feeling.

His skin is pale, he's sweating even more than Turbo Cakes, and his cheek is an angry red.

"You look like a dead zombie!" Uncle Ruckus blurts.

Shovel gives him a quizzical look, an expression we—and Holly, apparently—know all too well. We take a step back as Shovel blows chunks on the floor.

"You brought this poor baby in here without a *bucket?*" Holly demands.

Turbo turns to Uncle Ruckus. "I thought all zombies were dead?"

"Nah, dude. Think about it. Death, re-animation, re-death. Dead zombie." He claps and points at the speckled floor tile. "See those dots? Hey, look, Shovel! The cherry pop-tarts you ate in the car before we stopped at McDonald's!"

"Not the time, Ruckus," I insist.

"Uncle Ruckus," he corrects. "Don't forget the name. I'm the big spit. Well," he considers the puddle on the floor, "I guess *that's* the big spit. Somebody get this man to the bathroom so he can try to call Captain Ahab on the Great White Telephone."

Holly hits the "call" button on her walkie-talkie. "One of you come into the back to stay with your friend." She waves her hand. "Buddy system and all that."

Shovel stares at his puke. "Like looking in the mirror, huh, Ruckus?"

Uncle Ruckus beams like a proud father. "Atta boy, get in there! You paying attention, Turbo Cakes?" He throws his arm around Shovel. "*That's* a way better insult than pizza-face. I'll be your Infirmary buddy."

Shovel gags. "Please don't talk about pizza."

Uncle Ruckus makes a face and reels his arm back in, "Forget I said that."

A tall doctor with dark curls glides into the room to escort Shovel to the back. I'll admit it: She's hot.

Doe-eyed, Turbo Cakes stares after the doctor. "Dibs. Too slow fellas." He steps around the puddle on the floor and hurries after her and Shovel.

"Dang," I say, "Did you see the way she took Shovel back there? I like an older lady in charge."

Uncle Ruckus says, "She's sexy. I got eyes." He turns to face Holly, "But what about us, Ms. Holly? I'm feeling pretty sick."

"You two get to clean up." Holly tsks as she walks away.

I follow Uncle Ruckus's lead and yell down the hallway, "I think I'm gonna puke, too!"

The doctor didn't come back.

Neither did Holly.

Uncle Ruckus thumps my head. "Smooth, dude. You scared her off. Nothin' hotter than a scrawny freshman getting ready to spew lipshit all over the place." Without an adult to corral him, Uncle Ruckus picks up an ophthalmoscope off Holly's desk and peers through it at the sludge on the floor. "What do you think it means?"

I wave my arm in a circle. "I think this swirl here means Shovel dies an early death."

"I concur. At the hands of Hawkins, no less."

"But what kind of death?"

"Hmm... My interpretation leads me to believe a concentrated poison causes his dick to fall off."

"Madame Ruckus, you always see the worst."

Holly returns with a bag of powder, a broom, and a dustpan. She dumps the powder onto the vomit, holding a rag over her mouth and nose. "Don't breathe any of this stuff in."

She stands to leave, but squints her eyes at the floor. "Y'all seen *Harry Potter*? It kind of looks like the bad omen dog, The Grim. You don't look so good either." She points at Uncle Ruckus. "If you need to hurl, use the trash can."

Holly leans the broom against the desk, grabs *The Prisoner of Azkaban*, and takes refuge inside the office behind her.

Uncle Ruckus and I look at Holly's office door, then each other, then back to Shovel's chunderchuck.

"I think she could be right actually," I mumble, reaching for the broom.

"It's *The Grim*!" Uncle Ruckus fluctuates his voice for effect. His body wracks with a shudder.

"Was that a shiver? At your own impersonation? It wasn't *that* good."

"It..." Uncle Ruckus hesitates, "it was a powerful scene." He doubles down on his story. "Gives me the heebie-jeebies." His face is pale, like it's twenty degrees colder than it actually is in here.

"The *heebie-jeebies*? Who even are you? You said you were too old for those movies—literally last week. You're still shivering!"

"I'm f-fine." He grabs the broom and eyes the dubious mixture on the floor. "It's just freezing in here. T-that's all, Do-Over. I need to move around a little."

"*Freezing*? I thought you were Uncle Diablo. Don't you thrive on the suffering of others and all that? We're in the *Infirmary*; this should be like your yellow sun or something, right? There's suffering all around us." A moan drifts in from the back of the building. "Come on, man, what's up?" I give Uncle Ruckus a sharp poke in the belly. Something bursts.

Liquid soaks his uniform, hoodie, and pants. Uncle Ruckus yelps and flings something out of his sweatshirt. It *splats* against the floor.

Plip, plip, plip...

The steady drip of water is the only sound until Uncle Ruckus throws his hands up and shouts, "What the hell, man?!"

"You bastard! You had an *icepack* under your shirt that whole car ride, and you didn't bother to share? Or tell me? We sat outside under the sun in ninety-degree weather for almost a full *hour*. Don't you think you ought to tell your best friend?"

"First of all," Uncle Ruckus shoves the broom at me, "you aren't my best friend. The three of us agreed there would be no best friend pairs. All right? Second of all, I didn't have it the whole ride. I filled it when we stopped at McDonald's this morning. It was too hot in that van."

"You could have shared, or at least told me your idea so I could do it too."

The door bursts open. Two Adventure Rangers—Ducky and his friend iBall—are holding Hawkins in a two-handed seat carry. Blood drips down Hawkins's face. His whole arm is bleeding, too. In fact, there's almost no bare skin unscathed on his arms. Gravel bits and leaf litter cling to his sticky, red wounds. His legs are even worse off. A jagged tibia is jutting out below his knee with a tourniquet fashioned from Ducky's bandanna tied on his thigh.

I gag.

Uncle Ruckus makes the sign of the cross. "*Ay, Dios mio!*"

"Holly!" Ducky yells.

Holly bursts out of her office and takes in the scene. "Compound fracture! Multiple open wounds and lacerations!" she shouts down the hall. "Looks like a Hill K.O. coming your way, doc! Come with me, boys. Come, set him down here." She gestures to a gurney and tears open a packet of gauze.

Ducky and iBall crunch across the dried vomit powder as they set the unconscious Hawkins down and wheel him into the back.

"Holy shit... Holy shit..." I say.

The line of boys outside peer in through the open door. They see the trail of blood on the floor and the suspicious powder at Uncle Ruckus's feet. Turning to face them, he looks pale, shivering, and dripping wet. *Plip, plip, plip.* The water hits the floor, adding to the pool of blood.

"That's him! *El Diablo!*" The young boy from earlier exclaims to the other "sick" Adventure Rangers. "It's the devil! He fed off the suffering of the hurt dude and ate him alive! Look at all the blood!" He points at the blood on the floor.

It *does* look like it's dripping off Uncle Ruckus.

"And look!" Chipmunk kid points at the dried vomit powder on the floor. "He burned the other two alive, leaving nothing but ashes behind!"

Without skipping a beat, Uncle Ruckus began ululating gibberish in a low tone, volume escalating with every guttural syllable. The huddle of boys stumbles backward, unable to take their eyes off the madman in front of them. His chanting reaches its peak, and Uncle Ruckus unleashes a blood-curdling scream that morphs into maniacal laughter. The junior Adventure Rangers don't stick around to hear the laughter part.

They run away squealing:

"The Devil is here!"

"At Camp Winnebago!"

"Run for your lives!"

Their screeches fade into the distance.

Uncle Ruckus grins from ear to ear.

I stare at him cockeyed. "Dude."

"What?"

"Why do you have to be so weird? The Devil? Come on, man. Adventure Rangers is a *Christian* organization. You could get in trouble. And since when do you speak Spanish?"

He shrugs. "Guess I picked it up somewhere."

The empty hallway pulls my gaze like a magnet. "I almost didn't recognize Hawkins at first."

"Eh, bloody ugly is still ugly."

My nostrils flare. "Dude, how can you say that? He looks pretty bad. Don't you ever quit? Shit's serious. He's really hurt."

"Because, *dude*, the guy is a major asshole and he had it coming to him. Maybe Turbo Cakes is wrong? What if we don't need an asshole?" Stepping to the other side of the vomit pile, Uncle Ruckus cocks his head. "'Sides, I think we were reading this wrong. If you look at Shovel's upchuck from this angle it kind of looks like your mom's boobs." He shrugs. "Seems like a good sign to me."

I let out a puff of air and crouch to sweep, "'Yo' momma' jokes are beneath you; you can do better than that." Clenching my teeth, I try not to imagine tiny particles of Shovel barf drifting into my mouth and lungs. There're probably all kinds of funky diseases you can get from middle-schooler barf. "Will you freaking help me? It's your fault he threw up anyway."

Uncle Ruckus is holding the busted Ziploc bag, that same stupid smile on his face.

I trace his gaze. "No, no way, not a chance in hell."

Holly strides down the hall, walking a safe distance ahead of Shovel, with Turbo Cakes lagging far behind. "You two better be almost done cleaning that up."

Dropping the broom and pan, I rise to greet Holly.

She says, "Praise the Lord for puke-absorbing powder." Holly meets my eyes. "Your friend is going to be fine. Dr. Cassandra says 'Shovel' can't get in the lake until that queasiness passes. She gave him some aloe vera to help with the sunburn; try to remember both cheeks next time with the sunscreen. Other than that, just dehydration, excitement, and heat exhaustion. Try to stay in the shade and drink water instead of sugary drinks," she adds with a stern look.

"Thank you, ma'am," I say. "Do you know anything about that guy that just came in? He's in our troop, so we should tell our troop leader if he's okay."

Holly's face darkens. "Boys I'm afraid your friend—"

"He died, didn't he?" Uncle Ruckus nearly shouts. "Yes! Dibs on his matches and bug spray!" Eyes hopeful, he looks up, still holding the dustpan of dubious powder.

"No," she says, "he's not going to die. But we called his parents, and your friend's dad is coming to get him right now. It doesn't look like he's going to get to stay at camp this week. I'm sorry, boys." She passes off Shovel—who is clutching crackers and a bottle of water close to his chest—and says, "Please tell your other friends to be more careful." Holly sits down and resumes reading her book.

"You good?" I ask.

Shovel nods.

"Hey, what's with you?" I turn to Turbo Cakes, who is staring down the hall.

No response.

"Guess you saw Hawkins too, huh?" I stammer.

When no response came again, I poke Turbo Cakes in the small of his back, half-expecting to feel something pop under his uniform. "Dude."

Turbo Cakes jumps. "What?!"

"Nothing, sorry! Jeez, what's with you?"

"Did you see how beautiful she was?" Turbo Cakes shuffles backward, unwilling to tear his eyes away from getting one last glimpse of Dr. Cassandra.

I rub the back of my neck. "Christ."

"Yes?" Uncle Ruckus asks, standing now.

"I thought you were the Devil," I mumble, scanning the floor.

"Depends on the situation, dear Do-Over."

I can't keep the surprise out of my voice. "You cleaned up all the barf powder?"

"Yeah, I did. Because I'm a good friend. Some might even say the *best* friend. Shovel, are you done going to Europe with Ralph and Earl in a Buick?"

"Going to...What does that even mean?" I immediately regret the question. He knew I'd fall for the bait.

Uncle Ruckus stands up straight, thumbs in his belt loops. "It means liquidating his assets. Hurling his hash. He leggo his Eggo. Decorated with fluorescent Christmas cheer. A technicolor tribute to Disney." For whatever reason, Uncle Ruckus salutes at that last one.

"I'm so sorry, Ms. Holly—" I start.

"Honey, I got three boys."

Uncle Ruckus is undeterred. "The Brooklyn mating call. The Jersey yodel. Thunder-chunder-chucking pavement pizza!" He shoots finger guns, and looks at Shovel, "The Ruckus mirror special!"

Shovel gives him two thumbs up. His lips peel back in a smile to reveal the gap between his two front teeth.

Ducky appears from the back and heads out the door. I usher a still-talking Uncle Ruckus, Shovel, and Turbo out behind him and back into the sun.

"I almost forgot." Uncle Ruckus cracks the door open and pops his head just inside the Infirmary. He speaks two words. "Buckbeak dies!" He slams the door before she can reply and jogs to catch up with us.

"Sup, Ducky?" Uncle Ruckus asks, slowing to the group pace.

Ducky grunts, "Passed the rest of the troop on my way up. They dropped off their stuff and said to meet at the waterfront." He jerks his thumb back toward the Infirmary, "Hawkins tried to run down Cardiac

Hill. I lost my favorite bandanna because of that moron. Had to use it as a tourniquet. iBall stayed behind with him. Buddy system and all that.

"Anyway. We were headed down to the campsite to drop off our stuff and started talking about a few years back when Donnie DiAngelo tried to run it." He hesitated. "Donnie went home more stitches than Donnie. Then all the other guys started saying how *no one* could ever run Cardiac Hill. They say, 'Hey, Duck, it's your last year, why not give it a shot?'

"I told 'em no, they started hollerin' about how I should be Chicky instead of Ducky. So what does Hawkins the Igmo do? Takes it upon himself to show me up, probably took five steps before he had too much momentum. It's what? A fifty-degree incline? At least? Hawkins tripped, and once he hit the ground... Mr. McNitt was right. He didn't stop rollin' until he was almost to the lake. Effing moron." He shakes his head. "Had to carry his ass all the way back up here."

We all stay quiet save for Shovel, chewing his Saltines with an open mouth. "So, wait, is Hawkins gonna die?" Crumbs fire like projectiles. Shovel pops another cracker into his mouth.

We all heard Holly say he isn't going to die, but Ducky's opinion carries more weight than any medical doctor. "Nah. Don't expect him to be back at camp, but he isn't gonna die. Don't call him Hawkins no more, either. He's Try-Hard from now on." Ducky turns to Shovel. "He's an outlier now."

That probably made more sense to Shovel.

Turbo looks over his shoulder at the Infirmary. "Lucky Hawkins... He gets to spend all that time with Dr. Cassandra." He grins. "She said I could call her by her first name... But I'm still gonna say doctor before it."

We all stop at the top of Cardiac Hill.

Shovel looks down. "That hill saved my life," he murmurs mid-cracker.

I feel like Shovel's gut dump puddle was wrong; maybe we were looking too hard for a bad omen. It isn't going to be a bad summer. It's gonna be the best summer of our lives. The last one before Uncle Ruckus moves to San Francisco.

Maybe there's no bad omen, though I still hope Shovel's dick doesn't fall off.

Uncle Ruckus probably hopes it will fall off just for the shits and giggles.

I glance over at Turbo Cakes. He's daydreaming, clearly in love. *Ugh, great.*

Shovel's face is a blank slate. I imagine he's thinking only of the crackers he's eating at the moment.

Ducky allows a rare, brief smile. "Y'all ready to head down to the waterfront for the swim test?"

Shovel perks up mid-chew. "Swimming?"

We walk the whole way down Cardiac Hill with Ducky.

"This is so cool," Shovel whispers to me. "The whole camp is gonna see us walking with the coolest guy in the troop."

"Yeah... Yeah, it is cool," I say, even quieter, unable to keep the awe out of my voice.

Ducky smiles.

* * *

THIRTY YEARS AGO...

MARCH 15TH, 1986. 8:29 PM.

Joey Junior stumbled out of the arcade with his hands covering his head.

A moment later, the door swung open again and a group of Adventure Rangers spilled out. They stood in the open doorway as Huey Lewis and the News blared behind them from inside.

The smaller projectiles miss and go *plink* against the concrete parking lot. A quarter pegged Joey on the back of the head, and he felt sharp stings across his back as he scampered away from the hail of coins.

One of them yells, "Get outta here, McMasturbator!"

Joey's vision blurred against the bright red arcade lights as he watched the Rangers retreat back inside. He refused to search for the coins in the dark to use the payphone. Even if he found enough to make a call, he knew no one would pick him up now, so he started down the road toward his house.

4

A RANGER IS OBSTINATE

Oh, Jesus. They're already singing.

> *"The grand old Captain Kirk*
> *He had four hundred men*
> *He beamed them up the enterprise*
> *And beamed them down again*
> *And when you're up, you're up*
> *And when you're down, you're down*
> *And when you're only halfway up you're nowhere to be found!"*

We make it down Cardiac Hill alive, only to find the entire camp prepping for orientation. I spot Troop 100. *Ugh, those bastards.* Troop 52 is here; they came all the way from North Point in Canada. There's also the Alabama Troop, the Kentucky Troop, and The Salem Troop, among others.

"Are you guys ready?!" Journey asks. He has a goatee. Camp Winnebago and his goatee are pretty much his entire personality.

What in the name of God did we do to deserve this? They start the next part of the song as we pick our way through the singing lines of Adventure Rangers standing at attention.

Journey is standing on top of a picnic table with a megaphone in front of a projector screen with the song lyrics on it. "Faster!" he yells.

"Thegrandoldcaptainkirkhehadfourhundredmen
Hebeamedthemuptheenterpriseandbeamedthemdownagain
Andwhenyou'reup,you'reup
Andwhenyou'redown,you'redown
Andwhenyou'reonlyhalfwayupyou'renowheretobefound"

The camp explodes into claps and cheers. I feel dead inside. There's nothing more soul-sucking than being forced to sing camp songs. I just pray we missed most of it since we're late. Ducky spots Mr. B standing at the head of our troop, and we fall in line. Ducky snaps his fingers at me and points at my waist. I look down and stuff the bottom of my Class A into my pants.

Journey exclaims, "Superspeed!"

We all groan, but the Tenderboots have huge grins on their faces. Yeah, they'll be sick of it within a few days. Journey joined the Junior Rangers when he was six. He's nineteen this year, so the camp hired him onto the staff. Journey bends backward like he's in *The Matrix* as he takes a giant breath. He jerks back upright and starts the next version of the song.

"Thegrandallcapankirkhadfourhundredmenbeamedemupenterprise-

beamedemdownagainwhenyoureupyoureupandwhenyouredowndownyouredow-nandwhenyouonlyhalfwayupnowheretobefound"

They sound terrible. I'm pretty sure even Journey left out a bunch of words of the song trying to sing it so fast. Regardless, everyone slaps each other on the back and erupts into whoops and applause. Turbo nudges me and leans over to whisper into my ear. I swear I feel that creepy long chin hair tickle my cheek when he talks.

"Come on, man. Sing with us. All the administrators are watching. We might have a chance at the Golden Plunger this year."

"Only for you, dude," I say.

We sing all the way through Rattlin' Bog. It's my favorite camp song. Then we sing Grey Squirrel while Uncle Ruckus makes a big show of winking and nudging everyone around him every time we sing the word "nut" in the song. We go through every possible iteration of Little Red Wagon, and so many "repeat after me" songs that I want to die.

Finally, mercifully, Momma Hackett climbs on top of the picnic table and Journey relinquishes the megaphone. The projection switches to a zoomed-in camera view of Momma Hackett.

Her wrinkled hands quiver as she puts the megaphone's wrist strap on and speaks into it, "Thank you for leading everyone in all the camp songs, Journey. My name is Momma Hackett; I am the director here at Camp Winnebago." Her thin lips brush against the megaphone's white mouthpiece and her reddish-pink lipstick smears. "I know we're all excited to be back at Camp Winnebago this year. And I know we're all very excited about the prospect of winning the Golden Plunger!"

We all clap, throw our hands up, and cheer. Maybe we do have a chance at the Golden Plunger. It'll be like an epic goodbye present for Uncle Ruckus.

"Why do they think they can appeal to us by spray-painting common household cleaning tools gold?" a nearby Ranger complains. "What kind of simpletons do they think we are?"

"Woo! Hell yeah!" Mr. McNitt cheers. "Golden Plunger! Golden Plunger!"

Momma Hackett starts talking as we quiet down. "There are a few announcements before we get started. We'd like to thank Troop 99," she sweeps her hand in our direction, "for their gracious donation this year. We were able to use the money to upgrade one of our campsites. We hope Troop 99 enjoys the new Adirondacks we built in their campsite! With the extra money, we were able to install brand new showers in all of the campsites with hot water!"

Hundreds of Adventure Rangers and parent leaders applaud, and it takes a good minute for everyone to settle down again.

"Because of the massive turnout of Rangers at camp this year," Momma Hackett continues, "Troop leaders can find packets of rules in their campsite, and Rangers can find the rules posted on the bulletin boards in each campsite. Everyone is expected to know the rules." The air feels tense, and I lean forward in anticipation. She continues, "As a result, we're going to skip explaining camp rules during Orientation this year."

We all jump up and down and chant, "Hack-it, Hack-it, Hack-it!"

Thank you, Jesus. Usually, they do all these cringy skits about the rules. It's always painful to watch.

"Darn," Mr. McNitt mumbles. "No skits this year."

"But," Momma Hackett begins, but the rest of her words are drowned out by still-cheering Adventure Rangers. The leaders settle everyone down, and she starts again, "It is for the sake of time. We have a presentation to show you all for the sake of our new showers. The video was made many years ago, but the information is still good. Beg your pardon if it's cheesy, but it's important." She presses her lips together tight, and the lake sloshes against the shore in the distance. When she opens her mouth again, her lipstick makes a weird *thhpt* sound as she pulls her lips apart. "Camp Winnebago is bringing back an old rule this year. We made this decision in favor of our organization's Christian values, and to protect our investment in the new showers. The damage done to the showers in the years we haven't played this video have shown us this is a..." she hesitates, "necessary rule. Without further ado," she shimmies off the picnic table and sits down on the bench connected to it, "Journey, please play the video."

I turn my attention to the projector screen as retro graphics fade into it. The words are bright blue and peppered with orange polka dots. They say, "Can't Come at Camp Initiative." The older guys stiffen up—Ducky, Mr. B, and Mr. McNitt included.

"Oh. My. God," Uncle Ruckus says.

A familiar-looking teenager with a grey shirt and navy stripes walks in front of the forest backdrop on the video. He's wearing baggy cargo shorts and has a perfect blond bowl-cut. Kid's even holding a skateboard. It's like the '90s personified.

"Oh, hiya! Didn't see you there! I'm Joey. What's your name?" he asks.

Nobody makes a sound.

"Haha! Great! I love God," Joey says, closing his eyes and making fists for emphasis. "And that's why I try to make Him proud of me. I don't steal, I don't lie, and I definitely don't abuse others. Do you love God?" Joey looks directly into the camera.

Nobody answers. You know how, no matter where you are in the room, it seems like the Mona Lisa has her eye on you? Like she's staring a hole right through you, no matter if you're to the left of the picture or to the right of it? It feels like you can't avoid her sly smile and judging gaze wherever you look at the portrait from. That's what this is like. Joey is staring right at me.

"Haha! Great! I definitely wouldn't abuse my body. I signed the 'Can't Come at Camp Contract' because I love myself, and I'm a good Christian. Masturbation is a sin!"

Joey's face looks accusatory. He's *so* familiar, but I can't put my finger on it. This kid is a terrible actor though. He moves like a robot; like someone is pointing a gun at him off-camera. The video keeps playing, and I can't take my eyes off it. *Golden Plunger. Golden Plunger. Eye on the prize, Do-Over.*

"When you come at camp, it not only damages your body and your relationship with God, but also damages our utilities. Your semen is dangerous stuff." He gives a little laugh, and I swear I've heard it before. "When you masturbate in the showers at camp, it combines with all your hair and dirt and turns into sludge inside the pipes." A little cartoon graphic appears on the screen showing a pipe with a blockage. "This causes thousands of dollars in damage that the camp has to pay for. You like Camp Winnebago, don't you? Let's keep our souls and showers clean! Take the masturbation abstinence pledge today, and sign the Can't Come at Camp Contract!"

The screen abruptly turns into a blizzard of static. Stunned silence. Shovel turns to Turbo Cakes and says, "Why do they want us to be obstinate?" But Turbo is staring at the screen, left eye twitching. Even Uncle Ruckus looks too horrified to crack a joke. Unable to get an answer, Shovel turns to Mr. McNitt, "I didn't know you were an actor! That was great, Dad!"

Mr. McNitt hastily stands up and walks back up Cardiac Hill without a word.

Journey gets up on the table again. "And now for the part of the day you've all been waiting for!" He reaches down behind the table. "Behold," Journey thrusts his hand up into the air. "The Golden Plunger!" And that was all it took to make us forget about the scarring video we just watched.

The Golden Plunger sparkles in the sunlight, its virgin surface having never touched a toilet bowl. Looking at it always makes me feel poetic; the plunger holds some kind of special power to invoke something primal inside me. Inside many of us. The plunger was created for one purpose: to fuel a testosterone-driven contest for simple-minded boys every summer. There's no reward for winning it. No cash, no hoes, no violent video games. The winning troop gets bragging rights and their picture taken. But bragging rights over every other group of guys in camp is enough to turn Ranger against Ranger, mother against child, and, perhaps, even Christ Himself against humanity. 'Tis a beautiful thing.

"Are you okay?" Shovel asks. "You look like Bilbo right before he had his freak out with Frodo in Rivendell."

"We're gonna win this year," I hear myself say.

"You guys are weirding me out." He looks past me, back up the hill. "It's just a plunger, what's the big—"

Uncle Ruckus grabs Shovel by his collar. "Don't you get it, man? That plunger is everything, man. *It's the biggest spit, man.* You wanna achieve anything in your life, man? The plunger is the key." He makes a sucking sound. Ew, he's literally salivating.

I feel a tickle on my chin and wipe away my own drool. I shake my head a little. *Jeez, herd mentality makes people crazy.*

Journey sets the trophy back down behind the table, pulling me the rest of the way out of my trance. "The rules to win the Golden Plunger are the same as they've always been," he says, "but with a twist!" There is an audible, collective gasp from the camp. Journey grins. "Besides the good behavior requirement, the Alabama Troop will run the Culling this year." A chill goes out over the crowd. "As you know, the Culling is a special event created by the troop running it. The Camp Winnebago flag has also been hidden somewhere on camp grounds. Good behavior, winning the Culling, and finding the flag will all count towards winning the Golden Plunger."

"I found the flag!" Uncle Ruckus holds up a pair of boxers.

Everybody yells and moves toward Uncle Ruckus like it's Black Friday in 1996 and he's holding the last Tickle Me Elmo.

"That is not the flag!" Journey yells into the megaphone.

"Is this it?" Some kid holds up a scrap of cloth.

"No, that's garbage, don't—" But Journey gets cut off.

"I found the flag!"

"Here it is!"

Journey blares the alarm on the megaphone, and everybody shuts up. "You'll know the flag when you find it!" He's clearly losing his patience.

"Well, where is it?!"

Journey squints his eyes in disbelief. "I can't tell you. Every day we'll give out clues to help you find it. But, it could be hidden anywhere on camp property. And I can promise, it's hidden *really* well this year. It could be in the Dining Hall, at the bottom of the lake, in the woods—"

Uncle Ruckus drops the boxers he was holding and bolts into the woods. Seeing this, about a dozen other Rangers also turn and dash into the woods to begin the hunt.

Mr. B sighs, "Go get him." He nods at Ducky, then jerks his head towards the woods. Ducky jogs into the woods to corral Uncle Ruckus.

Journey tries to win the crowd back. "There's a few more things!" he says.

Everybody quiets down again. About a half-dozen Rangers stop running and give pause at the edge of the woods to hear the rest of what Journey has to say.

"Every troop who attempts the swim test gets an extra clue on where the flag is hidden."

Great. Time for me to flounder around the lake like an idiot.

"Next, the troop who wins this year gets an all-expenses-paid trip to a high adventure camp later in the summer."

I hold my breath. *Another camping trip with my bros.*

"And... Whoever wins this year gets to keep the Golden Plunger."

Those final words echo in my skull. It is the worst thing Journey could have said at that moment. We all stare at him, eyes wide.

He says, "This is the last year we're doing it."

Everybody goes apeshit.

* * *

THIRTY YEARS AGO...
MARCH 15TH, 1986. 8:04 PM.

"Terrific performance, Junior!" Joey McNitt Sr. said.

Joey McNitt Jr. shifted in his seat, resting his cheek against the cool window.

"With acting like that, the talent agency will take off in no time." Joey Sr. smacked the top of the steering wheel and began drumming his fingers.

"I don't want to do this anymore," Joey Jr. said.

The car slowed a hair.

"Sure you do, son," Joey McNitt Sr. said. "You're gonna make us all rich. We got really lucky we had an in at Camp Winnebago. This could be huge for us! I mean, you mostly, of course, but both of us."

The car swerved slightly to hit a can in the road.

Crunch.

Joey Jr. looked at his dad, "How is a tiny little Adventure Ranger camp gonna help us do that?"

"Have some faith! It's gonna help you get discovered!" Joey McNitt Sr. exclaimed.

Joey Jr. stared at the floor of the van, absently kicking the food wrappers away from his seat. He said, "I just don't like it. Did you hear what they called me after they watched the video?"

"Oh, that's just a couple of guys having fun. Come on, I think the meeting went really well tonight. Your troop leader sure seemed impressed by the video. So did some of the other Rangers," Joey McNitt Sr. said.

"Yeah," Joey Jr. said, "all the dumb little kids thought it was cool just 'cause I was on the TV."

They rode in silence for a few more minutes until they pulled into a parking lot bathed with dull, red light.

"Why are we at the arcade?" Joey Jr. asked.

"You," Joey McNitt Sr. said as he fished a handful of quarters out of his too-large corduroy pants, "are gonna go in there and play some games and have a good time."

Joey Jr.'s nose wrinkled. "You just brought me here because you heard the older Rangers say they were coming here after the meeting, didn't you?"

"Oh, did they?" Joey McNitt Sr. reached behind his son's seat and picked up a jar full of change and pushed it against Joey Jr.'s chest. "I didn't even realize. Say, son, if they are in there, see if they wanna be in a little movie too. We need some more guys to work with for this promotional stuff."

"They hate me, they aren't going to listen to me," Joey Jr. said, the jar heavy in his hands.

"Hold out your hand," Joey McNitt Sr. pointed at his son. "You're gonna go in there, talk up the movie, and get us some more actors to work for cheap. Tell 'em they get a pizza party or something kids like."

Joey Jr. stumbled out, dropping change everywhere. He knelt down and started picking up the coins as the car sped away.

5

A RANGER IS DEMONIC

PRESENT

MONDAY, JUNE 1ST, 2015. 5:16 PM.

"Joe! Has anybody seen Joe?" Mr. B whips his head back and forth as he tries to keep us corralled.

"He went back up Cardiac Hill." Ducky jerks his head back the way Mr. McNitt went. He practically carries Uncle Ruckus back by the scruff of his uniform. I'm itching to get out there and search too. Any of those other Rangers could have found the flag by now. The flag that gets us the Golden Plunger and an all-expenses-paid trip to a high-adventure camp.

Journey yells, "Line up to take the swim test!"

On a day as hot as today, the promise of the cool lake and the fear of waiting a long ass time in the heat spurs everybody into motion. We all push and shove, eventually forming some semblance of a line. It hugs the fence next to the lake and winds all the way back to the base of Cardiac Hill. We're toward the front, thank God, because this line is something Walt Disney would even be impressed by. I just want to get this over with and get out of the sun before my ginger ass gets burnt to a crisp. I hate swimming.

Turbo Cakes pokes me. "Where's Ruckus?"

"That's Uncle Ruckus to you," a voice yells.

We turn. Uncle Ruckus is the first person in line. How the hell did he manage that?

"His hearing is spooky good," Turbo mumbles.

Journey is standing at the front of the line and calls out, "Everyone get a buddy! We use the buddy system when we go swimming. If you leave the water without your buddy, we'll revoke your swim privileges."

I feel Turbo throw his arm around my shoulder, and I link mine around his too. Shovel hesitates, then cautiously sidles up to Tri-Clops behind us. I shudder. Poor Shovel.

Mr. B says, "Ducky, I won't be swimming. Go up there and make sure Uncle Ruckus doesn't cause any problems."

Uncle Ruckus actually looks a little relieved when Ducky walks to the front of the line and grabs him by the back of his uniform. Journey lets about ten buddy pairs inside the fence along with a few of their counselors. They all amble over to the uniform cubbies and take them off to reveal swimsuits underneath. Before we're able to follow, he stops the line. We have a front row seat to the first round of Rangers taking their swim test.

I feel Mr. B tap me on the shoulder. He leans down and asks, "You gonna be okay this year?"

"Yeah, Mr. B, I'm good. I just have to attempt it so our troop gets the extra clue for the flag. I'll tap out as soon as I'm in the water, and then it'll be over." I watch Uncle Ruckus and his parole officer walk down the dock.

"You can skip it with me this year; I know you don't like the water," he says, more gently than I thought he was capable of.

My face reddens, he's talking way too loudly. I just want him to stop.

"No thanks, *mom*. I'm not afraid of the stupid water," I snap, and he leaves me alone.

"Is that why they call you Do-Over?" Shovel asks. "Because you never pass the swim test?"

Deep breaths, Do-Over. Deep breaths. Rainbow time. Red, like my hair. Orange, like the sunscreen bottle in Turbo's fanny pack. Yellow, like Uncle Ruckus's bathing suit. Green, like Turbo's fanny pack... He looks ridiculous as he does a "hot dock" dance along with the rest of the pale, dorky looking Rangers until they reach the end of the dock and sit down with their feet dangling into the water. Ducky strides down the dock behind them. If he were wearing sunglasses, he'd look identical to The Terminator, but with a beard. Comparing Ducky to the rest of the Rangers makes me reconsider how much time I spend inside playing video games versus what I could accomplish in a gym.

Journey turns to us. "All right, I'm going to give you guys the same talk they're getting right now to speed things along. Since everyone started yelling 'help' as a joke last year, our lifeguards can't rely on that word anymore. If you get in the water and you need help or want to stop, yell 'pineapple.' Otherwise, we'll spend the whole day pulling you jokers out of the water."

Over on the dock, Ducky flicks Uncle Ruckus on the back of the head and we hear him yell, "Ow, help!"

The lifeguards standing by don't even react.

"Exactly." Journey continues, "All right, first off, no diving. You'll jump in the water and swim a lap down freestyle or breaststroke. You'll swim back to the dock doing the backstroke. Once you're done with both laps, you tread water for sixty seconds, and you're done. You'll get out of the water and come back inside *with* your buddy."

The row of Adventure Rangers stands up and jumps into the water, but

Uncle Ruckus hesitates a second. A smirk flickers across his face, he takes a few steps back, and does a running dive into the water. The lifeguards all blow their whistles at him as he enters the water, but it's too late—his whole body is under. Ducky's head breaks the surface from his own jump in, and he looks like he's struggling to stay afloat.

We wait, but Uncle Ruckus doesn't come back up after a second or two. My throat gets tight. One of the lifeguards jumps off his stand, grabs his lifesaving tube, and runs to the place he went under.

Then Uncle Ruckus's head breaks the water, and my shoulders relax.

"What an idiot," I say.

His face stretches into a broad lottery-winner smile. The lifeguards look pissed, like they might pull him out of the water and give his face some CPR with their fists, but he starts swimming right away, and so do all the other Rangers.

The "pineapple" announcement kind of makes sense. I mean, you displace a bunch of dorks from their natural habitat and force them into summer camp, and what do you expect to happen? Adventure Rangers used to be like football: all the cool kids did it. Now, it's a place for people to stick their weird kids to try to socialize them and make them more normal. Guess that makes me a weird kid too? Regardless, it's painful to watch a bunch of teenagers who think Fruit Snacks count as their daily value of fruit try to exercise. Which, to be totally transparent, I'm not convinced that they don't. If it tastes like grape, then it seems reasonable to assume it's got grape in it. Right?

It didn't take long for the desperate cries to begin.

"Help!"

"Please help!"

"I'm drowning!"

All the Rangers in the water flail and scream as they swim.

Shovel asks, "Aren't they going to jump in and help them?"

"Nah," Turbo says. "We do it every year."

"But... You don't have to take it if you don't want to," Shovel says.

Turbo replies, "Right. But if you want to do free swim later in the week or take any Waterfront merit patch classes, you have to pass. Unless you're Do-Over, then you're just doing it because you have a chip on your shoulder. Or for the Golden Plunger clue. Point is that everybody *wants* to swim, but we don't want to exercise in order to earn the privilege. The screaming is our form of protest, I guess."

Mr. B shakes his head. "Somewhere, Michelle Obama is crying."

"Good," I say, "That's what she gets for body snatching the Cookie Monster. Hashtag not my Veggie Monster."

I squint at the not-so-majestic bodies in the water. They're still screaming while they tread water by the dock. Everyone but Ducky, who seems to be struggling to finish his last lap.

Mr. B laughs. "All that muscle mass only weighs you down in the water."

Shovel pipes up again, "Wait, so if he's bad at swimming, why is his name Ducky?"

Turbo and I give Shovel a death glare, and Mr. B doesn't respond.

"Sheesh, sorry," Shovel says.

The Rangers all get out of the water, still screeching for help. Uncle Ruckus manages to blend in with the rest of the pasty, acne-ridden Rangers and escapes without being reprimanded by the lifeguards.

"Sup, guys?" he says, waiting for Ducky to catch up before he comes back outside the fence. Uncle Ruckus whips his hair like a shampoo model and flicks water onto all of us. Ducky looks like he wants to strangle Ruckus, but he's too out of breath to do anything other than thump him upside the head. Ducky wrings his beard out over Ruckus's head and walks inside the fence while trying to squeeze the water out of his thick eyebrows.

"Dudes," Ruckus says, shooing the Ducky beard water off his head. "Look what I found on the bottom of the lake."

He holds out his hand, and I shit you not, he is holding the scariest rock I have ever seen. I'd never have thought a rock could be scary, but it's shaped like a face with a bunch of white dots detailing its features. It looks like a screaming person, like someone in immense amounts of pain. And it freaks the hell out of me.

Turbo Cakes jumps backward at the sight of it. "The crap is that?!"

Uncle Ruckus smiles, unable to contain himself. "Did you count how many dots there are on it?" He doesn't wait for us to count, "Eighteen. There are eighteen perfectly white dots on its face."

"What's your point?" I ask, a sense of concern mounting inside me.

"Think about how you get eighteen," he says. "Six plus six plus six."

"Actually," Turbo Cakes starts in, "There are infinite ways you could get the numeral eighteen out of—"

"Just shut up for two seconds. Six. Six. Six. And look at the face! You know what this is? It's a Devil Rock." Uncle Ruckus finishes as Journey pushes him through the gate in the fence.

I can barely get the words out, "Dude, whatever you do, *do not*—"

"Next ten pairs, inside! Next ten pairs, inside! Next ten pairs, inside!" Journey's annoying drone cuts me off as the line begins pushing me forward.

Uncle Ruckus just smiles even wider at me and holds the rock up to his ear like he's listening to it talk. We tear off our uniforms and stuff them in the cubbies by the water. Then they herd us toward the dock. I look back just in time to see Uncle Ruckus standing next to the chubby little sixth-grader from the Infirmary. The kid is making a face like he's accidentally summoned the antichrist.

"Hiya," Uncle Ruckus says.

Oh, this is not going to go well, I think. But then I forget all about Uncle Ruckus as I step onto the dock. The burning sensation on my feet overwhelms my sense of fear, and I make a mad dash down the dock to sit on the edge with the other Rangers. My butt is hot, so nothing new to report there. My eyes won't look away from the murky green water. I don't hear anything the lifeguards say, I just imagine everything that could be in that water.

I can't see the bottom. Who knows how deep it is? If I drown, will they even be able to recover my body? What lives in this lake? There's shit science doesn't even *know* about. How does anyone know there isn't some giant Sharktocrab down there just waiting to pull me down to the bottom of the lake? Maybe it prefers gingers. It'll pull me down deep with tentacles and teeth into that endless void beneath me. My vision is turning white like someone spilled a watercolor across my eyes.

A lifeguard yells, "Go!" and all the other Rangers jump into the lake. Turbo Cakes splashes down into the water. *I'm supposed to do that too, right?* I lean forward as my vision pales more. I'm falling, and then I'm underwater. It's all black and green around me, but the white steadily bleaches out more and more color with each passing moment.

Muffled screams above me, "Ouch! Ow, ow, ow, damn it! Help, for real, help!" It sounds like Turbo Cakes. I want to tell him that's not what you yell. You're supposed to yell out "fruit snacks." Or something like that. But my head never breaks the surface, and everything goes white.

There's nothing anymore. Until a voice calls me from somewhere far away.

"Cookies! Omnomnomnom."

I smile. I know that voice. I open my eyes. I'm tied to a chair, my furry blue hands waving at the plate of cookies in front of me. Something shocks my whole body. A woman tsks at me.

Michelle Obama says, "No, no, no! Try again. Pick a plate."

The plate on my left is piled high with leafy green vegetables. The plate on my right is piled high with gooey chocolate chip cookies. The choice is simple.

"Me want cookie! Omnomnom!"

I gnaw at the ropes holding me down, I *will* get to those cookies.

Michelle Obama tasers me again.

"Why me no eat cookie?" I yell at her.

Michelle Obama slams her fist down on the table. The plates rattle. "I'll ask the questions around here!" she says and tasers me again.

She holds down the taser, and I hear myself say, "Cookie. Wait for me." Then everything goes black.

* * *

NINE YEARS AGO...

JULY 5TH, 2006. 1:01 PM.

"It's about time you learn how to swim. You're six years old; you're too old not to know. When I was a kid, I swam every day of my whole summer. It was great! What are you afraid of? Nothing in there is going to hurt you. I wouldn't ever let something hurt you." Dad looked over at Do-Over.

Do-Over stared into the ocean. "But what about sharks and monsters and stuff?"

"They never come this close to the shore," Dad said. "You'll be totally safe. Plus, you got those cool new floaties to help you out, right?"

Do-Over looked at the overinflated Blue Power Ranger on his skinny left bicep. Then at the overinflated Red Power Ranger on his skinny right bicep.

He nodded. "Yeah, I can do it."

"Sure you can!" Dad took Do-Over by the hand, and they started into the water.

Do-Over was scared he would mess this up. This vacation meant a lot to his parents. The waves buffeted at the six-year-old's stomach over and over again as he trudged onward.

"See, son? This isn't so bad." Dad smiled down at Do-Over.

"Yeah. Kinda salty, though." Do-Over made a face. The water was up to Do-Over's waist now, and the waves slapped at his chest. "Okay, I think I'm done now."

"Done? We aren't even that far out." Dad looked around and gestured out toward the ocean, "I mean look at this thing. Endless! How many wonders left to discover? Now, this is the real final frontier. Can you imagine going to the bottom of the ocean? What it would be like?"

Do-Over shifted his feet. It felt like the sand was trying to suck him down. It felt like quicksand, like in the cartoons. Whenever there was quicksand on TV, there were always snakes, too. Something brushed up against Do-Over's ankle and wrapped around it. Do-Over screamed and kicked his feet.

"What? What? Talk to me, son, what's the problem?"

"It's got me, it's got me!"

Dad picked up Do-Over with one arm and pulled the thing off him. "It's just some seaweed, nothing to be afraid of."

"Okay, well, I don't like it." A tear streamed down Do-Over's face. "Can we be done now? I want to go play with my toys in the sand."

Dad set him back down and got onto his knees. He pointed at Do-Over. "You can play with your toys anytime. This is the ocean. You've been begging us for months to take this trip. We're here because *you* wanted to go. This trip cost a lot of money. We're going to go enjoy the ocean now. Understand?"

Do-Over nodded. "Okay, but can I ride on your shoulders?"

"Sure thing, pal." Dad picked Do-Over up over his head and settled him on his shoulders.

Do-Over wrapped two small hands around his Dad's sunburned forehead, and they set off into the ocean. The waves were even bigger out here. The water was up to Dad's neck.

"Isn't this cool, bud?"

"Yeah, thanks for bringing me out here, Dad."

A wave several feet tall crashed in front of them, giving Dad a mouthful of saltwater. "What do you say we go back to the beach and play with some toys now, huh?" Dad turned, and as he did so, a wave slammed into the pair, knocking Do-Over into the water. He didn't know how to swim, so he was relying on his Power Ranger floaties to keep him above the water. They did their job, sort of.

The floaties stayed just above the water, but Do-Over wasn't strong enough to pull himself up. His arms flailed helplessly above the water, and his head thrashed beneath that endless blue expanse.

6

A RANGER IS CHICKEN

"Cookie," I groan.

"Aheehee!" Someone laughs beside me. "You've been sleep dreaming about cookies the whole time you were out!"

My eyes flutter open, and white light floods my vision. The old guy sitting next to me has pale white hair and a scraggly beard. Wrinkles course around his eyes, mouth, and nose like a river respecting the boulders within it. His smile goes just a little too high at both ends, but in a good way. There's a mountain of wood shavings on the Infirmary floor between his feet, which probably came from the pocketknife and log of wood he's holding.

"God," I say, drawing the sheets up with me as I sit up.

"Nope, never met the guy." The stranger flicks the pocketknife closed and extends a hand. "Moonpie," he says as I shake the leathery hand.

"Do-Over," I say. "I didn't think you were God, you know, it's just an expression."

Moonpie, far too skinny to ever score a role playing Santa, lets out another laugh, "Aheeheehee!" He opens the pocketknife, starts at the top of the log, and I watch it glide down the length of wood. The strip cuts off before the knife reaches the end. Moonpie flicks it onto the floor and starts again at the top. "Well, you was talking a lot of nonsense in your sleep, thought maybe you lost all your brain cells or somethin." The spaghetti noodle of wood comes off before he reaches the other end of the log again.

"What are you doing? Whittling or something?" I ask.

"I'm no good at whittlin', son," he says. The words kind of jumble together in pairs when he talks. "It just relaxes me, s'all. I try to get one solid strip from end to end."

"Why?" It comes out sounding harder than I meant it to.

"Well. It relaxes me. You know, like fun? Were you this slow before you tried to drink the whole lake?" His hands stop moving, and he looks right at me. If I saw his blue eyes without looking at the rest of his face, I'd have thought he was my age.

"I didn't try to drink the lake," I say. My face feels hot.

Thud.

Moonpie set the log on the floor next to the pile. "You know what my diagnosis is?" he asks.

"You aren't a doctor, are you?" I ask back.

Moonpie ignores my question. "You got the lasso phobia."

I blink hard, and my voice comes out flat, "You think I'm afraid of lassos... And that's why I almost drowned."

A muffled voice calls out from behind the curtain next to me, "He means thalassophobia. As in, you're afraid of large bodies of water."

"Turbo? What are you doing here?" I ask, unable to hide the relief in my voice. I'm not glad that he's in the Infirmary too, but it's comforting to have a Turbo around. Weird Santa seems nice and all, but nothing beats a good friend.

"I jumped into the water pencil-style," came Turbo's voice. "I actually managed to hit the bottom this year—"

"Dude, congrats."

"Thanks. Anyway, I think I hit a sharp rock or something at the bottom because my foot hurt pretty bad. I kicked back up to the surface and started yelling pineapple and every other fruit I could think of. A couple lifeguards jumped in and got me, and I guess one of 'em must have pulled you out too. After they realized I wasn't in any real danger, they kind of just passed me off to Mr. B and Ducky to bring me up here, so I missed all the excitement after that... I was real worried about you, man." His voice catches in his throat. "But I got to spend a lot of quality time with Dr. Cassandra. She bandaged up my foot and gave me a tetanus shot and everything."

"Wow," I say. "Sounds romantic."

"Yeah, it was nice. Kinda wished it was one of those shots you get in the butt cheek, you know, so she could see everything I got going on, but it was cool. I didn't cry or nothing."

A laugh slips out, and I tell him, "Glad you're alive, dude. Sorry about the lack of a butt shot."

"It's all good. On the way up Cardiac Hill, Ducky was bitchin' like crazy about how it was his fourth time going up the Hill today, so I tried to take his mind off it by asking for some advice. You wouldn't *believe* all the good stuff he knows about girls and how to get 'em to like you and everything."

"Oh, yeah?" I sip some water from the table next to me and just let him talk.

"Yeah! Like he said to call her babe a lot. So Dr. Cassandra would be all like, 'We need to give you a shot, or you could develop a serious bacterial disease. Now stop crying and hold still or we'll have to get someone to hold you down.' And I was like 'You got it, babe.' It was great, she laughed every single time I said it." Turbo sighs on the other side of the curtain, "I love her laugh."

I choke on a sip of water as I try to stifle a laugh, which makes me break into a fit of coughing. Moonpie takes the glass from me and sets it down on the table.

"Do-Over?" Turbo yells.

"I'm good," I croak.

"Whew. I thought you were dead again."

What did he just say? I squint my eyes at the curtain, as if that will help me see through it or hear him better.

"Dead a—" But that's all I get out before fake hillbilly Santa interrupts me.

"Take it easy on that water." Moonpie gestures toward the glass sitting next to me. "You probably drank half the lake." He wipes his pocketknife against his tattered jeans and snaps it shut. "I'm gonna get out of your hair now. I'll let the doctor know you're awake."

"Uh..." I look at the pile of wood shavings and the disfigured piece of wood. "Aren't you going to do something about that? Isn't the Ranger motto 'Leave no waste'?"

Moonpie scoops up the shavings and stuffs them into his pocket. "I use these for kindling when I teach the Dan Boone class to new Rangers." He grabs his mutilated log and saunters out the room.

The second he's gone, I sling the curtain next to me wide.

"Please knock next time," Turbo says with a serious face. "I might have been indecent."

I roll my eyes, "Right. Because you can knock on a curtain. How's the foot?"

Turbo Cakes wiggles his foot, "It's fine. Honestly, the tetanus shot hurt a lot more than the cut did."

"Can you walk?"

Turbo waves a hand, "Yeah, I can walk just fine. Was gonna try and play it up to stay here as long as I could with Dr. Cassandra. Why?"

"Have you seen Uncle Ruckus?" I ask.

Turbo snaps his fingers. "*That's* why I feel so relaxed here." He stretches in the bed and snuggles into the sheets. "I haven't seen Uncle Ruckus in hours."

I feel my face go pale. "Dude. The last time I saw him, he was about to start teasing that little kid."

Turbo throws his hands up. "So what? He makes fun of me and nobody bats an eye, but suddenly we're all freaked out because he starts messing with some Tenderboot we don't even know?"

My Ranger uniform—with socks, boots, shirt and all—is folded neatly in a chair across the room. I start getting dressed, and Turbo looks at me like I'm crazy.

"I just don't see the big deal," he says.

I meet his eyes and count off each point on my fingers. "He was holding a creepy ass rock that he named Devil Rock. He's at a Christian camp. He was talking to a kid who is terrified of him. Mr. B already warned him to chill with the devil stuff. And to top it all off, *we* aren't there to stop him when he inevitably takes the joke too far." I finish slipping my boots on and feel light-headed when I stand up.

"Woah, woah, easy there." Turbo sits up on the side of the bed and holds out an arm to steady me. He sighs. "Gimme a sec, I'll come with you."

"By the way," I say. "Did they tell us the first clue about the flag? They didn't say our whole troop had to pass the swim test, just that we had to attempt it."

"Sure did." Turbo grins and talks like a wizard NPC. *"Beneath the bridge between elements, the gateway to the world."*

"Wow. Lotta help that was." I say. "Now hurry up and get ready so we can keep Uncle Ruckus out of trouble."

After a long, hard-fought battle to get his sock over his bandaged foot, Turbo scribbles his apology to Dr. Cassandra for leaving without saying goodbye on a napkin. *Jeez, this is getting ridiculous.* Somebody needs to break it to him that he doesn't have a chance with the hot doctor.

We play it cool and manage to sneak past Holly, who is too engrossed in her book to notice us. When I step into the sunlight, the first thing I notice is Uncle Ruckus trudging across the parade field looking like his chin is glued to his chest—sobbing.

* * *

THREE YEARS AGO...
FEBRUARY 26TH, 2012. 6:48 PM.

Uncle Ruckus always thought Uncle Mark was a pretty good guy. Mark bought socks at Target, he cooked dinner almost every night, he changed his bedsheets weekly, and to top it all off, he wasn't half-bad at Sorcery: The Trading Card Game. It made sense, after all. Mark invented it.

Uncle Ruckus studied a card in his hand, then eyed the bowl of cauliflower on the center of the table. He was in a bad spot, no doubt, but he had a chance to make a comeback here and avoid the veggie punishment that awaited one of them.

Mark let out a slow snore.

"Would you quit it?" Uncle Ruckus snapped. "I'm trying to think here." He bent the cards he was holding back and forth.

"All right, all right. I'll stop," Mark conceded. "Just stop bending the cards. They're valuable."

"Pretty sad a grown man is worried about a kid damaging five dollars' worth of overpriced paper," Uncle Ruckus said, fingering one of the cards.

"Pretty sad a teenager with so much free time is getting whooped by a grown man at a kid's card game," Mark replied.

"My Knight of Despair hits your Great Wyrm for five damage. I activate Shackles of the Beyond and attach it to your Mongo Monstrosity. My Ladybug Squire attacks your hero and—"

Mark cut off Uncle Ruckus, "And I lose one Vital Health. Congratulations on learning the rules to the game."

Uncle Ruckus smiled and flicked a meaningful glance at the bowl of cauliflower.

Mark grabbed the smallest cauliflower off the top and tossed it into his mouth with a grimace. *Crunch.* He fake-gagged, which sent Uncle Ruckus into heaves of laughter.

"All right, bucko," Mark began, wiping his mouth. "I play Key of the Ancients to detach your Shackles of the Beyond. I sacrifice my Great Wyrm to play Greater Wyrm of the Abyss. I activate Mongo Monstrosity's ability—"

"You can't do that," Uncle Ruckus blurted. "You haven't placed three Vain Tokens onto it yet."

Mark pointed at the arrangement of cards. "True. But my Lumberwisp has control over the Whirlpool Slot. I don't need any Vain Tokens."

Uncle Ruckus deflated. He knew what that meant. He folded his cards and reached for the bowl of veggies. Picking one at random, Uncle Ruckus started eating as Mark finished his turn, and inevitably, the end of the game.

Crunch.

"With Mongo Monstrosity's Petrify Ability, your characters have been disarmed. Greater Wyrm of the Abyss sacrifices its Hatchling Eggs in order to subdue and charm your disarmed characters. I attack once with Mongo Monstrosity. Then with my Lumberwisp. Then I play Cleansing Pestilence to de-petrify my new characters, thanks very much by the way, and attack with my full board one more time, sending your Vital Health to zero," Mark concluded, out of breath.

Uncle Ruckus worked on the cauliflower while Mark scooped up the cards and put the game back in the box.

Crunch. Crunch. Crunch.

"With how much we play this game," Mark said, "you'd think you'd win more often! Maybe my nephew isn't as smart as I thought he was..."

CrunchCrunchCrunchCrunchCrunch.

Uncle Ruckus chewed faster to get out his retort in time. "Keep it up, Mark. I'll see you in jail." He popped another cauliflower into his mouth with a *crunch* and kept talking, sending pieces of vegetable across the table. "I'm pretty sure forcing kids to eat their vegetables after they lose a card game is against the Geneva Convention, or violates a gambling law, or something."

Mark's face went serious. "If you tell anyone about this," he said in a low voice, "I'll summon the Greatest Wyrm of the Satanic Reach to devour you!" He snatched a piece of cauliflower from the bowl and ate it with an emphatic *crunch*.

After the cauliflower was gone and the game was packed up, they settled in to watch the newest episode of Gossamer Blades. When it was over, the pair sat in stunned silence as an infomercial began. They sighed.

Hi, I'm Rick Jeter, here to show you my newest product: Tough Tape!

"You know," Mark said, "Sorcery is starting to really take off."

Uncle Ruckus nodded. "There's a bunch of videos and stuff out there about it. Pretty cool."

"Yeah, pretty cool," Mark said.

Tough Tape is the bestselling and most effective adhesive tape on the market!

"We're going to open up card shops for it in a couple places," Mark said. "There's a couple of conventions that want me to guest speak on it, too."

"Dang, all I heard was free tickets to Mage-Con," Uncle Ruckus said.

Mark laughed. "Yeah, maybe we can scrounge up a few of those." His tone sobered. "I'm going to have to move out to California."

Uncle Ruckus tensed. "What?"

With Tough Tape, you'll never have pieces come apart during your projects again!

"Yeah," Mark said. "They want to make a movie out of Sorcery."

The lump in Uncle Ruckus's throat felt like a wad of wet sandpaper. "That's stupid, who's gonna see a movie about a card game? Not me." He pulled his knees up to his chest and hugged them.

You can always rely on Tough Tape!

Mark's smile was somber. "You won't even go see it for free?" He nudged Uncle Ruckus with his elbow. "It might be rated R. Don't tell me you'll turn down giant CGI boobs on a movie screen."

Uncle Ruckus felt his eyes burn. Bad. "I have the internet, I don't need your crappy movie to see boobs." He pressed his sleeves against his eyes to dry them before he looked at Mark. "Cool. So, when are we moving?"

Stop the cycle of disappointment with other tape brands, buy Tough Tape!

Mark's eyes fell. "You know I can't take you with me, no matter how bad I want to."

Uncle Ruckus snatched up his backpack and stalked to the door. "Fine. I'm ready to go home."

Mark's arms hung uselessly by his side. "Buddy, listen, it's going to be alright."

"I'm in the car," Uncle Ruckus said before slamming the front door. He slumped in the front seat of Mark's Mercedes and managed to collect himself before his uncle got there.

Mark got in and didn't say anything besides a "Have a good night" to the security guard at the entrance to his gated neighborhood. They rode in silence until the car parked in front of Uncle Ruckus's dad's house.

"I know you're upset," Mark said. "You don't have to talk if you don't want to. Listen, when I was a kid, I was in this thing called Adventure Rangers. You should join. I had some of the best times of my life in my troop. I made so many great friends, and summer camp is more fun than watching you eat a whole bowl of cauliflower. Seriously. Will you at least think about it?"

Uncle Ruckus didn't look up from the dashboard of the car.

Mark kept trying. "If I could take you with me, I would. But it wouldn't fly with your dad. And your mom... You lost a mom, I lost my twin sister. Not a day goes by that I don't miss her. She'd want you to be happy. We'll still see each other, and I'll be back for your birthday! Maybe we can play Sorcery over Skype?"

Silence.

"Buddy, you know I wouldn't leave if I didn't have to. You know I love you. I know we don't get to see each other as much, but I'll always be your Uncle Mark. Nothing between us changed after your mom died."

Uncle Ruckus threw the shotgun door of the Mercedes wide and scrambled out of the car. He kicked the door shut, leaving a smear of mud across the convertible door, and stomped across the dirt yard. As always, he could smell the cigarette smoke before he opened the front door.

7

A RANGER IS BANNED

I freeze. Is Uncle Ruckus *crying*? Holy crap. "Hey, man," I say.

"Heard you drowned." Uncle Ruckus spits out the strings of his sweatshirt. "They shoulda let you drown, it's natural selection."

"Nah." I smile. "Wouldn't have been fair to all the ladies waiting their turn for a piece of Do-Over." I gesture between my legs.

Uncle Ruckus opens his mouth, but it's Turbo Cakes who speaks. "They'll be disappointed, that's a tiny piece."

Me and Turbo laugh. Since Uncle Ruckus is the only one who has actually been to our campsite, he leads the way in silence.

We stop in the middle of the site. There are eight Adirondacks built in a semi-circle around the firepit. They're like cabins with three walls and a big tarp across the front. They aren't big; there's just enough room for four bunk beds in each one. They're built over massive pits with a layer of rocks and gravel at the bottom, at least ten feet deep, and probably two dozen feet across. I think the pits are there to prevent water damage to the Adirondacks or something like that.

Uncle Ruckus squints at the nearest one and says, "Turbo, you got any Tough Tape?"

"Yeah, man, you know I do." He pulls out a giant roll of the stuff.

Uncle Ruckus snatches it out of his hand and wraps it with the sticky side facing outward around Devil Rock.

Turbo Cakes cocks an eyebrow. "Uhh, you know you're supposed to wrap it with the sticky side facing—"

"Just shut up, okay?" Uncle Ruckus keeps wrapping the tape until the entire roll is gone. He holds out the cardboard ring at the center, a tiny strip of tape is still clinging to it. "Thanks, Turbo." Uncle Ruckus holds the giant wad of tape aloft as if considering it.

I shift my feet nervously, there's nothing more frightening than not knowing what Uncle Ruckus is about to do.

He tests the adhesive with a finger and nods his head. He then sticks the same finger in his mouth, holds it up to the wind, and nods his head again. Uncle Ruckus then hefts the Devil Tape Wad up and down a few times, then finally throws the ball of rock and tape. It soars through the air and sticks firmly to the top of the Adirondack. *Thunk.* He dusts his hands and walks into the three-walled cabin, sitting down on the bottom bunk of the center bed. Turbo and I follow and sit on the floor in front of him.

"Stupid thing ruined my life," Uncle Ruckus says. "I'm fine, by the way. It's not like I care about the Adventure Rangers. I just don't want to let my Uncle Mark down, you know? He really wanted me to be in the Rangers..." He trails off.

"Yeah," I say.

Uncle Ruckus gives a half-smile. "They kicked me out."

"What?!" Turbo Cakes exclaims. "They can't do that!"

Uncle Ruckus puts a string of his hoodie in his mouth. "Yep. They can."

"Why?" Turbo Cakes asks.

"Camp is a holy place and all that." Uncle Ruckus waves his hands around as if that explains it. "Said between that and all my previous infarctions—"

"Infractions," I correct.

"Yeah, because I get in trouble a lot." Uncle Ruckus smiles wide. "I thought that sixth-grader was gonna have an infarction, though. I could almost smell him shitting his pants."

Turbo and I exchange a look. Turbo says, "You realize infarction is like a heart attack, right?"

Uncle Ruckus says, "Oh, I thought it was one of those farts that's just like way up in there, and you think it's a fart, but then you crap yourself. Details. Anyway..." Uncle Ruckus gently swings his legs back and forth. "Kid started crying. They brought me up to Admin. Momma Hackett was there with Mr. B and Camp-A-Cop."

"Camp-A-Cop was there?" I half-ask, half-laugh.

"Segway and all." Uncle Ruckus grins. "So, then they tell me I'm thrown out. I think Mr. B is still there arguing with them."

My heart drops. I draw swirls on the dusty floor of the Adirondack. "Then our week is already over? Our last week?"

Uncle Ruckus sucks in a breath. "Well, see, that's the thing."

My left eyebrow shoots up. "What?"

"To say I am definitely leaving to go to San Francisco wouldn't really be all the way, one-hundred percent accurate," Uncle Ruckus says.

Turbo Cakes's mouth drops open. "You *lied* to us? It's not really our last campout together?"

"This is so typical." I leap to my feet, nostrils flaring.

"Dude, wait, let me explain." Uncle Ruckus rises, hands out in the 'wait, calm down' position. "I had a plan."

"I don't need you to explain," I say. "This is what you always do. You're always working some angle because you're *selfish*. It's always the same with you. You take all the loot when we play *Lead Space*. You claim a whole row of seats in the van. And now you were gonna let me and Turbo bust our butts to give you the best last week at camp, but you weren't really gonna leave. That about right?" My heart pounds. My face is hot. There's no thinking. My right arm slings out and slams a windup electric lantern off the top bunk and onto the floor. Glass shatters and Turbo cringes backward. "You lied!" I shout, pointing at Uncle Ruckus and stepping forward.

"I didn't mean to lie!" he stammers.

Turbo jumps between us.

"Everything okay?" Mr. McNitt asks, standing in front of our Adirondack.

"No, Mr. McNutt, nothing is okay," Uncle Ruckus says. He slings his backpack on, grabs his trash bag full of gear, and half-storms half-skitters out of the campsite and starts up Cardiac Hill.

I watch him go, not bothering to look for stupid colors. I can control my breathing. I can control my temper. I don't need colors to help. I don't need anybody's help. Not my parents, not my so-called friends, not a wannabe troop leader. Nobody.

Mr. McNitt smiles. "What's going on, boys? Maybe the ole McTerminator can help."

I ignore the question and wait for my blood to stop boiling.

"Ruckus got thrown out of camp," Turbo says.

"Uncle," I say bitterly.

"What?!" Mr. McNitt yells, looking between us. "What do you mean Ruckus got thrown out of camp?"

"Uncle. Ruckus," I say.

Turbo tugs his creepy, long chin hair between two fingers. "He basically made a kid think he was Satan or something. Kid freaked, so they kicked him out of camp."

"That's awful," Mr. McNitt says with horror. "But he's one of our finest Rangers, and if I may be so bold, a good friend of mine. We can fix this. We just need a plan. This can't happen, it can't. This is supposed to be the best year of summer camp ever." He paces back and forth.

"I don't give a crap if they kick him out or not," I say. "He's always doing dumb stuff like this to get himself in trouble. I'm tired of covering for him. And I'm not interested in being friends with a liar."

Turbo looks at me seriously. "You're done being his friend? Come on, he might have had a good reason for lying."

"There is no good reason for lying," I retort.

Shovel saunters up to the front of the Adirondack eating a Brown Sugar Cinnamon Pop-Tart. "Sup, guys?"

"Son! I've got it!" Mr. McNitt snaps his fingers, "You're brand new here; you're perfect. Finish eating that. You're going to save Uncle Ruckus." He takes Shovel by the shoulders and herds him towards Cardiac Hill.

Turbo hesitates. "You comin'?"

I don't say anything.

"Come on. You'll feel terrible about it all week if you don't even get to say goodbye. That temper of yours has got to be calmed down by now. Even if it's not, it'll be better by the time we get up the Hill." Turbo grabs me by the bicep and gestures to follow.

Uncle Ruckus might be an asshole. But he's my asshole friend. I jog past Turbo to catch up with Mr. McNitt and hear about this genius plan of his.

By the time we make it up Cardiac Hill to get back to Admin, I'm ready to throw up. Shovel looks double ready. *I bet that Pop-Tart isn't sitting so well.* Mr. B and Momma Hackett are yelling at each other when Mr. McNitt throws open the door. Uncle Ruckus is sitting in a chair with all his gear. Camp-A-Cop is standing in the corner with sunglasses on and arms crossed, expressionless.

"Mr. B, Momma Hackett, you've got it—" Mr. McNitt gags. "You've got the whole thing wrong; you've got the wrong Ranger."

Mr. B turns to him. "What do you mean? I was standing right there."

Mr. McNitt pushes Shovel in front of him. "If you were standing right there, then you can attest it was my son who caused the scene. He's always misbehaved in school. I thought summer camp would set him straight, but boy, was I wrong."

Momma Hackett squints her eyes. "I don't understand." She turns to Mr. B, then points at Ruckus. "Why did you not say this before?"

Uncle Ruckus, always quick to save his own skin, rises and takes a deep breath before blurting out, "Shovel told me if I didn't take the fall for it, that he would beat me up."

Momma Hackett scoffs. "You mean to tell me," she points at Shovel, "that you were afraid this little boy would beat you up."

"Ma'am," Uncle Ruckus says with a face of stone, "that cold-blooded little boy is vicious."

Shovel pipes in, "I'm a devil-worshipper!"

Momma Hackett looks aghast.

Mr. McNitt starts in again. "See, Momma Hackett? I'm at my wit's end with him. The exorcisms didn't help. He drinks a glass of holy water every morning. We really thought this camp would help fix him."

Shovel rocks back and forth on his feet with a dopey grin on his face.

Momma Hackett raps her knuckle on the mahogany desk. "Be that as it may," she says, "I can't throw out this little boy on his first infraction." She rubs her temples.

"Infarction. Ma'am," Uncle Ruckus says.

Momma Hackett cocks an eyebrow and continues, "Young man." She points at Shovel and he takes a step toward her with a big smile on his face. "I have no choice but to ban you from Camp Winnebago."

Shovel's face shatters.

"You can't do that!" I yell, pushing past Mr. McNitt and Turbo Cakes. "You can't kick him out for his first offense!"

"Well, normally I wouldn't," Momma Hackett says, shuffling papers around on her desk. "But after how rotten you all have told me this little boy is, I can't allow him to stay with a good conscience."

Shovel looks helplessly at his dad and tears dribble down his face. He grabs the foil Pop-Tart wrapper from his back pocket and tries to use it to wipe his damp cheeks.

I stoop my toes right up against the desk. "You can't do that!"

An Adventure Ranger bobblehead atop the desk nods gently with a broad smile.

"Young man, I am the director of this camp, I can do what I want. What is your name?"

"Do—" I catch myself. I begin again, "My name is—"

"We helped too!" Turbo blurts.

The shock must have been evident on my face because Momma Hackett rolls her eyes and says, "Really? You, your friend, this little boy, and 'Uncle Ruckus' here all bullied that Tenderboot at the waterfront? I find that highly unlikely."

"Well, it's the truth." Turbo says. "And you can't kick all of us out."

"Momma Hackett," Camp-A-Cop's voice rumbles. His finger flicks a swift "lean closer" motion. "That young man is the boy who failed his swim test earlier today." Camp-A-Cop points at me.

Momma Hackett nods, and sits back in her chair. Her eyes seem a bit wider when they meet mine. We stare at one another for a second that feels like hours. A weird feeling creeps into my gut, it feels like it sets up a tent there for a long stay.

"Fine," she points at me. "Then this boy couldn't have been part of it. He was failing his swim test at the time. You're free to go." She does a 'shoo' motion with her hand. "As for the other three, you are sorely mistaken if you think I will not kick three troublemakers out of camp. It's the beginning of the week, and I don't need you causing trouble until Wednesday, when you do something so atrocious that I have no other choice but to call your parents. Young man, what is your name?"

"Shovel," Shovel answers.

Momma Hackett raises an eyebrow, "Your name is Shovel?" Her eyes flick to Mr. McNitt with disapproval. "You will report to Chapel tomorrow morning. Moonpie will be there to monitor your Community Service."

She looks at Uncle Ruckus and Turbo Cakes. "You two. You're old enough to know better. Go back to your campsite and pack your things. I'm calling your parents to come get you tonight. I've been running this camp for over forty years. I won't wait around to see what you do next. You're out."

"That's not fair!" I exclaim, kicking her desk.

The bobblehead nods faster with new vigor.

She looks at me, appalled. "You can join your friend 'Shovel' there for Community Service tomorrow morning. I suggest you learn to master that temper, and to refrain from lying to my face again."

Tears fill my eyes. It stings. I want to dump everything off her stupid desk. I want to smash that stupid bobblehead. But I don't.

"Shit!" I yell and stomp out the door.

Under the heat of the summer sun, my frustration surges until I'm standing in the parade field and can't take it anymore. I take off both my tennis shoes and launch them as hard as I can through the air towards Cardiac Hill. There's no satisfying crash when they hit the ground, but I feel a tiny bit better. I plop down on the ground, rest my head in my hands, and cry.

A hand touches my back. "Hey, Do-Over? It's okay."

I wipe my eyes. "It's not okay, Shovel. My friends are getting kicked out of camp. I'll be stuck here alone all week. Alone, just like at home."

"You won't be alone," Shovel says as he sits down. "I'll be here with you. We'll have fun!"

"You think we're going to have fun at Community Service? God, you *are* a stupid kid," I say.

Shovel's face contorts in pain. My temper dissipates and my heart is wracked with guilt in its stead.

"I'm sorry, Shovel. I didn't mean that. I'm just angry."

"It's okay to be angry, Do-Over. Everybody gets angry. But instead of feeling those emotions by throwing your shoes, maybe you should just try saying that. Try it." Shovel urges.

"I'm angry."

"See? Doesn't that feel better?"

No.

"Yes, Shovel. It feels better." I tear at the grass in front of me, then freeze. "We should get up. There might be bugs in the grass." *Like ticks.*

We stand, dust ourselves off, and retrieve my shoes. My once pristine white socks are now stained green on the soles and heels. But, hey, if you don't come back from camp with a few stains and scrapes, did you really go to camp? By the time I get my shoes back on, Mr. B, Turbo, Uncle Ruckus, and Mr. McNitt meet up with us in the middle of the parade field.

"Everything okay, boys?" Mr. B asks. "Well, okay relative to your physical condition."

"Yep, we're peachy," Shovel says.

Mr. B tilts his head, considering. "Well, good. Thank you for checking on your buddy, Shovel. While you boys were out here, we kept trying to improve the situation we've gotten ourselves into." He glares at Mr. McNitt, "I think a little bit more forethought might have been helpful here, but nothing we can do about that now." He turns to address the rest of us, "Momma Hackett tried calling Turbo's and Uncle Ruckus's dad to come pick them up."

"My dad is on a vegan retreat. Never thought I'd be happy to have him gone for once," Turbo mumbles.

Uncle Ruckus stays silent.

Mr. B shifts his feet, looking around at the trees as if they were suddenly very interesting. He stammers, "And Uncle Ruckus's father didn't answer."

"Typical," Uncle Ruckus murmurs.

"So, there's good news and bad news," Mr. B says.

Shovel straightens, apparently trying to look taller. "Give it to me straight, Mr. B. I can take it."

Mr. B chuckles. "Well, the good news is Turbo and Uncle Ruckus can't go home just yet. There's nobody to come get them. I can't drive them home because we need a minimum of two adults with the troop at all times."

"They get to stay!" Shovel exclaims.

"Not quite," Mr. B says. They're still kicked out. They're going home a day early on Thursday, Parent's Night. There'll be enough adults around that I'll be able to drive them home. They aren't allowed to attend any of their merit patch classes, or any official camp events."

"So, what?" I ask. "They're just like ghosts? They aren't allowed to see anybody or talk to anybody? What are they going to do all day? You should have told her—"

Mr. B raises a hand for silence. "I'm doing the best I can for you boys, Do-Over. Please believe me. Camp Winnebago admins have been very sensitive to troublemakers ever since they were unable to catch the Wafflestomper a few years ago. They aren't ghosts; we'll find activities to keep them busy. The last thing we need is a couple of bored teenage boys running around, that's when the real trouble starts. Think of them more like—"

"Outliers," Shovel interrupts.

A puzzled look crosses Mr. B's face. "Sure, if it helps to think of them that way. Like outliers. So my best advice for you boys is to just lay low for the rest of the week, and I'll drive you home on Parent's Night. Think of it like a vacation. No classes, just relax."

"I won't earn any merit patches though," Turbo Cakes says, completely devoid of emotion.

"Yeah, it makes Mark happy when I get new ones. But I guess losing one day at camp is better than nothing," Uncle Ruckus says.

Mr. B puts a hand on Uncle Ruckus's shoulder. "There's plenty of time later this summer for merit patches, don't you boys worry. Now, it's about dinnertime. You bunch must be starving. Go to the Dining Hall and get some supper. Hop to it." We nod and start to walk off when Mr. B says, "Do-Over, stay here a minute."

Turbo shoots me a questioning glance. I give him a nod.

Mr. B's mustache twitches as he talks. "You feel all right, son? I can call your parents, see if you can go home for a few days?"

I cock my head to the side and give him my best 'I'm a Teenager and Adults are Stupid' look. What is up with everybody? All I did was nearly drown during the swim test, same as every year. "Yeah, I just don't want to make a big deal about it. I'll try again next year. Maybe." I say.

Mr. B doesn't look convinced. "You're *sure* you feel all right?"

Why am I getting so much attention for failing my swim test? It's no different from any other year.

"I said, I'm fine. I just want to drop it and not bring it up again. I don't want to go home, and I don't want to talk about it anymore. I just want a good week at camp with my friends."

Mr. B gives a brisk nod.

I jog to catch up with the rest of the guys. *Jeez, I hope the rest of the week isn't this weird.*

* * *

THREE YEARS AGO...
MARCH 1ST, 2012. 5:36 PM.

Uncle Ruckus sat on his grease-stained comforter, flicking Sorcery trading cards at a trash can overflowing with Little Debbie cupcake wrappers and tissues. The daylight streamed in through his blinds highlighting all the tiny dust particles floating in the air. He flicked The Spirit Elf of the Menagerie at the trash can, and it slid off the top onto the floor with two hundred other cards he'd thrown in the last hour. A small part of him half-expected his latent superpowers to reveal themselves if he practiced long enough. In Uncle Ruckus's opinion, Gambit was the coolest X-Man by far.

BANG. BANG. BANG.

Uncle Ruckus jumped and the cards he held cascaded to the floor.

"Package."

Thump.

Uncle Ruckus stood, unable to avoid stepping on the cards that lay on the floor. His toes sank deep into the orange shag carpet, which he'd always kind of liked. He cracked the door and saw a huge box sitting there on the floor. Uncle Ruckus clawed the box closer from the confines of his room. Once it was inside, he shut the door and gave the box a swift kick to send it skidding to a stop next to his bed.

He trudged across the cluttered floor, bending Sorcery cards and crinkling candy wrappers. A cloud of dust went up as he sat down onto his bed and read the sender's name on the package: Mark Langston. Uncle Ruckus felt a twang in his heart; he scooped up The Mist Fae card his foot had been resting on and tried to smooth out the crease in it before returning his attention to the box.

Uncle Ruckus grabbed the rusty pocket knife from his windowsill and went to work on opening the box. He managed to get it open without drawing any blood.

The first thing Uncle Ruckus saw was an envelope addressed to him sitting atop a brand new Adventure Ranger uniform with the new member patches already sewn on.

8

A RANGER IS PHOBIC

The cardboard pint of milk reads *Expires: 6/2/2015.*

"So? What do you think?" Shovel jabs the milk closer to my face.

"I think," I say, swatting his hand away, "you'll be fine. But you won't be for long if you keep putting stuff in my face."

Turbo gnaws at a half-cob of corn. "You know who you could ask?" A kernel hits the table, and he flicks it onto the floor. He takes a loud sip of blue Powerade. "Dr. Cassandra."

I let out a groan. "Will you leave it? She's going to get a restraining order."

"No, she's not." Turbo Cakes smiles. "After I cut my foot in the lake, I helped her wrap it, and she said I was a natural."

"A natural dweeb?" Uncle Ruckus drops his tray to the tabletop with a clatter. "What are we talking about?"

"Shovel is afraid he's going to die if he drinks his milk," I say.

Shovel is staring at the milk carton, both hands to his forehead. "I'm just saying. If the milk expires tomorrow, but I drink it today, is it gonna expire in my stomach?"

"Drink it, and let us know tomorrow," Uncle Ruckus advises.

The food is nasty, like it is every year. I push mine around on my plate. I usually don't get desperate enough to eat it until the second day of camp. The cafeteria is loud, and there are barely enough tables to sit at. Treb walks by our table and takes his empty tray to the kitchen. He comes back, picks up his plastic cup with two hands, and stares at it with laser focus as he shuffles back to his seat. Uncle Ruckus starts to make his move, but I stop him with a swift kick in the shins.

"Ow!"

"Don't do it, dude," I say. "It'll happen, let it happen naturally. It's more satisfying that way. Plus, wouldn't you prefer it to be someone who isn't in our own troop?"

"I know, I know," Ruckus says. "I'm just itching for it. I can't stop thinking about it."

Shovel looks up from his milk dilemma. "Thinking about what?"

"Every year," Turbo Cakes sighs, "whenever somebody drops a cup in the cafeteria, everybody claps."

"Why?" Shovel asks. "Not like it's that hard to drop a cup." He moves to knock his cup off the table, but Turbo Cakes grabs his wrist.

Turbo says, "No, you don't get it. Whenever you drop the cup, it bounces a half-dozen times, sending out a distinctive, hollow echo. As soon as it hits the floor, everyone claps and cheers."

"Yeah," Shovel says. "That sounds pretty cool!"

"It's humiliating," Turbo Cakes says, empty eyes transfixed on the table. "It's a curse."

"It's pretty much the most embarrassing thing that can happen to you at camp," I say. "Happened to Turbo last year; the other Rangers clapped every time they saw him."

"Yeah," Turbo Cakes says. "Even some of the Rangers in our own troop." He gives Uncle Ruckus a sharp nudge.

Uncle Ruckus's hands creep up like he's about to clap, but Turbo's glare makes him stop.

Shovel eyes his cup. "Doesn't seem so bad, still. Just... pretend that they're happy for you or something."

"Let me ask you something," Uncle Ruckus says. "Do you think Hawkins can just imagine that he didn't fall down Cardiac Hill?"

"No, but—"

Uncle Ruckus waves his hands in a big arch. "Imagine this. You think you're alone, in the middle of taking a piss. Out of nowhere, rousing applause."

Turbo Cakes hugs himself and rocks back and forth ever-so-slightly.

Shovel considers this. "Yeah, but—"

"You don't get it," Uncle Ruckus interrupts. "Let's try again. You're sleeping in your tent. Suddenly, rousing applause."

Turbo rocks faster.

Shovel says, "We aren't sleeping in—"

"Drop the cup," Turbo Cakes grabs Shovel's collar, a wild look in his eyes. "Do it. Free me. Free me from the agony of being the last Adventure Ranger to drop a cup in the Dining Hall. Do it." He waits, but Shovel doesn't react. Turbo relinquishes the Tenderboot, then scoots away. "That's what I thought."

Shovel looks like he's about to protest again when the douchiest Adventure Ranger alive walks up to the table. Peters has almost every patch possible. There's so much lettuce on his uniform, he probably outranks most of the oldest Adventure Rangers, despite only being sixteen. His button-up shirt is ironed, his head is buzzed, and his face looks like he tried to chase a parked car.

"They decided to let you stay in the Adventure Rangers, huh?" he says to me.

I glare at him. "Hello, Peters."

"What is it they call you now? Do-Over? How appropriate, after what you pulled. Traitor." Peters raises an eyebrow at Shovel. "Tuck your shirt in, new kid."

"I'm not called new kid, I'm Shovel," Shovel says, opting to poke the dubious milk carton instead of fixing his uniform. He looks up at Peters. "Peters isn't a very creative nickname."

Peters almost smiles. "Troop 100 does not have nicknames. We believe the Adventure Rangers should keep to their roots. We go by our last names."

Turbo Cakes looks at Shovel. "Troop 100 is the military troop."

"They're the asshole troop," Ruckus pipes in, "Hawkins was Old Hawkins's last name, he went by it because he originally came from Troop 100. That's why calling New Hawkins by the same name is brutal. Because everyone who comes from Troop 100 is an asshole." He looks at me apologetically. "Almost everyone."

"I'll make you regret that this week, Ruckus," Peters smiles. Goosebumps raise on my arms.

"That's Uncle Ruckus," Uncle Ruckus says. He reaches out and slings his empty plastic cup across the table at Peters. Peters's composure falls apart, but he manages to catch the cup before it goes off the edge.

"Careful," Uncle Ruckus smiles. "You almost dropped your cup. Run along now, princess." He flicks his fingers in a "shoo" gesture.

"It's going to be a pleasure winning the Golden Plunger again this year,"

Peters says with a grimace. "For keeps. With a free trip to the best high adventure camp in the country."

"What campsite are you in again?" Turbo Cakes asks. "Oh, that's right, the same one we're in. It'd be a real shame if someone took a massive dump in one of those nice new toilets on your side of the bathrooms and the pipes got all clogged."

"Did you just threaten him with pooping in his toilet?" I whisper.

"I'm lactose intolerant. Give me a milkshake, and it'll be a doozy," Turbo promises.

Peters raises an eyebrow. "Real nice troop you joined, Do-Over." He tosses the cup at Uncle Ruckus, who catches it deftly out of the air.

As Peters walks away, Uncle Ruckus yells after him, "At least then you'll have a good use for that Golden Plunger, other than using it to please your buddies!"

Peters either didn't hear him or just kept walking.

"Good catch!" Shovel exclaims.

"All that hand-eye coordination from playing video games finally did something for me, I guess." Uncle Ruckus swirls his empty cup and takes a fake swig.

"What an ass!" Shovel yells.

"Shovel. Language," Mr. B scolds from two tables down as he pops a prune into his mouth.

"That guy is in the troop that wins the Gold Plunger every year? And you knew him? Were you in Troop 100?" Shovel asks as he opens his milk.

"Ha," I say, voice devoid of humor. "You could say that. It's a story for another day."

Shovel chugs the milk, and we all walk to our campsite in the dark. Thankfully, our place is close to the Dining Hall, which means we're usually first to get food and we don't have to walk far. Some troops walk almost a whole mile to get back to their campsite. The sun is fading behind us as we step into ours, and an idea pops into my head.

"Hang on a second, guys," I say.

We stop in the middle of the campsite, turn around, and watch the sun set behind Cardiac Hill. The first thing that pops into my head is what a shame it is that I'm not angry right now. I don't like being angry, not at all. But, standing there surrounded by the warm, fading rays of sunlight, the vivid green grass, and the deep blues chasing the sun down the horizon... That's all my colors right there. I wish the sun set whenever I lose my temper, that way it'd always be easy to calm down. Then maybe I wouldn't get mad anymore.

"Something Peters mentioned has me thinking," I continue.

"Was it the part about how he sniffs his buddies' buttholes?" Uncle Ruckus asks.

"You know, I don't remember him saying that," Turbo says, each word dripping with sarcasm.

"It's all right, Turbo," Shovel says. "I missed it too."

I shake my head. "No... The best high adventure camp in the country. That's one of the prizes for getting the Golden Plunger this year. The campout is for later this summer... So... If we won the Golden Plunger this year, we could have a second chance at a good time at summer camp. I know this week is kind of messed up, and we might not get to have that much fun... But this is our shot to fix it. Plus, it'd be a whole other week away from home this summer."

"And goodness knows we could all use that..." Turbo says.

We all nod.

"It's settled then," I say. "Let's win this thing."

A blur sprints past me into the campsite.

"Tri-Clops, come here, now!" Mr. B stomps across the camp after the fleeing Tri-Clops.

Ahh. So it begins.

Every year Mr. B has to chase Tri-Clops down to get him a shower. His mom coaches Mr. B at length before camp about how Tri-Clops has "hygiene problems." Between the hygiene issues, the large circular brown mole in the middle of his forehead, and Tri-Clops's general oddness, most of the Rangers give him a wide berth.

It's a camp-wide rule that every Ranger must shower every night. Apparently, before the rule was instituted, conditions at camp rapidly became unbearable since us teenage boys aren't exactly known for our excellent deodorant application habits.

We step into our Adirondack and Turbo picks up his knapsack full of toiletries. "I'm gonna go ahead and get in line before it gets too long," he says as he walks toward the bathrooms.

Uncle Ruckus rolls out his sleeping pad and lies down on his bunk. "I think I'm gonna relax with my favorite superhero." He pulls out a Batman comic and a flashlight, not bothering to take off his dirty shoes.

"Oh, man!" Shovel starts to inch past me toward Uncle Ruckus. "I love Batman."

I hold out my arm to block him. "I really doubt it's what you're thinking of."

Uncle Ruckus grins. "My dad subscribed to *Playboy* for like twenty years. He keeps them all boxed up in our attic, says they'll be worth a ton of money one day. He'll never notice if Issue 103 has a few pictures cut out of it. Honestly, I think Batman is way more interesting this way."

Shovel looks horrified. "You... you glued naked girls over *Batman?!*"

"I actually used Tough Tape, but yeah," Uncle Ruckus says.

I give the dazed-looking Shovel a gentle push toward the bathrooms, and without coming out of his stupor, he floats in that direction like a paper boat in a river.

Eyeing my own toiletries bag, I decide I probably don't smell *that* bad after just one day. I'll give myself the full Winnebago Spa Treatment with shampoo tomorrow. For tonight, I'll just hit the highlights.

Nearly every campsite has this thing called a bolo. The bolos are wooden buildings with concrete floors, and they are built over a huge pit. Inside, there are wooden benches with butt-shaped holes. *That* is where they expect us to do our business. In the twenty-first century for crying out loud. All manners of flies, spiders, and creepy crawlies reside within the bolos. You can't even see the bottom, and nobody dares to shine a flashlight into one. There's nothing more terrifying than feeling your cheeks dangling over that abyssal ecosystem as you pray to God that nothing lays eggs in your anus. It might be a far-fetched fear, but hey, it happened to that guy in *Alien*, so it could happen to me. Maybe. All I'm saying is, there's no way somebody hasn't gotten a disease from one of these things.

Our troop donated money so we could get a nice bathroom in our campsite to replace the bolo. Being in a troop based out of a rich private school has its perks.

I walk up to the new bathroom, which apparently has two wings. There's a line of guys in our troop; Turbo, Shovel, and Treb, followed by Mr. B standing guard at the end of the line behind Tri-Clops to enforce the showering rule. Not wanting to wait in a long line to shower, I head over to the other side—which is empty. I step inside the left wing of the bathroom. It's beautiful. Tile walls, shiny new porcelain sinks, soap dispensers, and the steam billowing out from the running showers is going to feel heavenly after a long day at camp. Hell, maybe I should have brought soap after all.

A grimy penny contrasts the white tile floor of the restroom. I pick it up. It's a wheat penny. Neat, and pretty rare. I earned the Coin Collecting merit patch not too long ago. Pretty shocking that I retained any information about coins at all; it was just as boring as it sounds. Leaning against the wall I wait for my turn in the shower while I examine the penny. It's dated 1949.

"We just can't get rid of you, can we?" Peters swaggers into the bathroom with two other members of Troop 100.

I throw my hands up to greet them. "Woody! Richardson!" I nod. "Peters."

"Got new braces. Thanks for that by the way," Richardson says.

"Sure, sure," I say, trying to sound congenial.

"What are you doing over here on our side of the bathroom?" Peters asks as he takes a predatory step forward.

"I didn't realize there were sides. I thought it was a bathroom," I say.

Mr. B calls into the bathroom. "Everything all right in there, boys?"

I push past the three of them. "Yeah, great, Mr. B. Thanks. Oh, guys?" I flip the penny toward them. "Penny for your thoughts." I instantly regret it. A shame to lose something so old and rare. All that history of days gone by in one tiny coin. But at least it was going to a good cause. A cool one liner.

Mr. B is frowning at the entrance of the bathroom. He puts a hand out to stop me and murmurs, "Not starting any fights, are we? We like having you in Troop 99; we don't want to see you go. You've had a long day today, but let's try to make it through the summer without any issues, huh? We've lost two Rangers today, let's not lose a third."

I nod at him, and he lets me go. Then I walk to the end of the shower line for "our troop's side."

"Listen, I got some great insights about where they might have hidden the flag. Are you kidding me—Tri-Clops!" Mr. B brushes past me. "Leave him alone for two seconds, and he runs off..."

Except for Tri-Clops, the shower line isn't any shorter. Ducky and the other older guys usually take long showers, so Troop 99 always has a brutal wait. The older guys always get to shower first. That's the Hierarchy of Coolness for you, I guess. Spotting a water spigot with a hose around the side of the bathroom, I get an idea.

I turn on the water and feel it with my hand. Sure, it's freezing, but even with the sun going down it is sweltering out here. It's gonna feel amazing. I shut it off, jog back to my bunk—where Uncle Ruckus is still reading his "Batman" comics, but inside his sleeping bag now—and change into my bathing suit inside my sleeping bag. I don't bother putting on my shower shoes, which I instantly regret as I tiptoe-hop down the gravel path back toward the showers. I go around the side and turn the hose back on. Two deep breaths, then I start rinsing off.

The water is freezing at first. All the hairs on my arms and legs stand up, but it's heavenly after I acclimate to the temperature. I hit the highlights: rinse my hair really well, behind the ears, armpits, feet, and a thorough rinse down the front and back of my bathing suit that my junk does *not* enjoy. I'm rinsing my hair one last time, when the water stops coming out. I stand there, staring down the hose for a second, before I whirl around and look at the faucet.

Oh, Christ. Sergeant Johnson.

Sergeant Johnson juts a nub that used to be an index finger in my face and yells in his Drill Sergeant voice, "And son, just what in the name of Sam Hill do you think you're doin'?! My God, if I still had you in Troop 100, you'da be doin' laps up and down Cardiac Hill, you hear?"

He seizes me by the arm and marches me toward Troop 99's side of the campsite. The whole way over he yells, "Scum, bottom of the barrel, that's what Troop 99 breeds! If you'd stayed in Troop 100, we coulda fixed you, boy!"

I shake my head and whip water across his dark green Leader's uniform. He releases my arm to shield his eyes as Mr. B storms across the camp, herding Tri-Clops back towards the showers.

Tri-Clops whines, "But I have to look for the flag! I have to be a hero. For king and country, Mr. B!"

"What you have to do," Mr. B pants, "is get in the shower, so your mom doesn't rip me a new one when she comes to visit on Parents' Night." He stops in his tracks when he sees Sergeant Johnson and me. Tri-Clops runs off, and Mr. B stares at us. "And just what—" Mr. B starts in.

Sergeant Johnson says, "Well, I'll tell you, Bellflower. Your boy here is sabotaging our campsite. You have no chance winning the Golden Plunger with your Rangers acting like this. Never in my life have I seen such blatant disregard for the Ranger Oath and the Ranger Law. Need I remind you that a Ranger is Cordial, Compliant, Devout, Honest—"

"So," Mr. B says, "let's give Do-Over here the opportunity to be honest. What happened, Do-Over?"

I take a breath and say, "Well, I was going to take a shower, but our line was long. There wasn't a line for the other side of the bathroom, but a few Rangers from Troop 100 came in and said that side was theirs, and I couldn't use it. I wanted to go ahead and shower so I could unpack and get ready for bed before lights out, so I decided to use the hose."

Mr. B raises an eyebrow but gives a slow nod. "Though an odd choice for a shower, it does not sound to me, *Mr. Johnson,* that Do-Over has broken any rules. In fact, it sounds like he was quite cordial to your Rangers. I'm afraid I don't see the sabotage here."

Sergeant Johnson grits his teeth and juts his knuckle-half-finger at the

Troop 100 campsite. "He had the water on, and our half of this campsite is downhill from the bathroom."

Mr. B laughs, "You don't like the fact that water runs downhill? I'm not sure that's my Ranger's fault."

"Look," Sergeant Johnson steps forward so he's chest to chest with Mr. B, who is a full head shorter than the Sergeant, "I was in Iraq and Afghanistan. If me and the guys in my platoon could make it out there in a warzone for two deployments, then I think we can make it through the week without any more issues, don't you?"

Mr. B looks up at Sergeant Johnson and meets his eyes. Even though Mr. B is shorter, somehow he is the scarier looking adult here.

"You can't play the vet card to have your way. You aren't the only one who served." Mr. B looks down at the Sergeant's half-finger. "Some of us lost a lot more than a finger out there, so I'd advise you to watch it. This is an Adventure Ranger camp, not Afghanistan. Don't lay a hand on one of my guys again."

Mr. B leans forward a little, throwing Sergeant Johnson off-balance so he stumbles backward. With that, we turn around and walk back to our campsite.

* * *

NINE YEARS AGO...
JANUARY 29TH, 2006. 2:33 PM.

"Hey, Dad," Mr. B said. "It's your son, Leslie. Terrible name, by the way, you really got me with that one. 'Leslie Bellflower.'" He chuckled. "Anyway, I, um... Appreciate everything you did for me. I miss you." There was a long pause. "I want you to know, I thought about what you said. I'll take over your Adventure Ranger troop for you. Your 'other sons' will be in good hands." A wistful smile played across Mr. B's face. "Anyway. I'll come visit and let you know how running Troop 99 goes. I love you."

Mr. B made eye contact with his father from half a lifetime away. He tapped his fingers against the top of the coffin and gave the Adventure Ranger salute to the picture of his dad. He was wearing a military uniform decorated with medals. Medals that Mr. B dreaded taking out of his father's attic, after which they would rest in his own attic indefinitely.

9

A RANGER IS INFATUATED

"And then," Uncle Ruckus says, his voice low, "the old preacher turns around and looks at the Adventure Ranger."

We all gasp. I lean closer, Turbo shrinks further into his sleeping bag, and Shovel's mouth hangs wide open in disbelief.

"He picks up the sacrificial knife from where it lay next to the goat. The preacher licks the blood off the blade with a wide smile." Uncle Ruckus changes his voice to match that of a creepy-ass old man. "'Come now, boy, come a little closer.'" Uncle Ruckus pauses, leaving us in silence for a few moments in the dark Adirondack.

"And then what happened?" Shovel exclaims.

"Shh!" Treb admonishes, then keeps on nibbling his chicken nuggets from this morning.

Uncle Ruckus continues, "So then, the Tenderboot takes a tentative step closer. Then another. Then another. With every step, he can see the old preacher more clearly. Pretty soon, the kid is close enough to hear ragged breathing. And then..."

I lean forward a little more, my feet dangling off my top bunk.

"The old preacher man picks something up off his altar and says, 'Dear Lord... thank you for this bountiful meal I am about to have...' And just as the Ranger processes what he said..." Uncle Ruckus pauses again before clapping his hands together and yelling, "*Wham*! The preacher stabs him with a fork and knife!"

I almost fall off the bunk I jump so hard, Treb stress eats a whole chicken nugget, and a whimper comes from Turbo's sleeping bag.

"And then what?" Shovel asks.

Uncle Ruckus snorts. "What do you mean, 'and then what?' He ate him!"

Shovel nods. "Oh. Yeah. Man, that was a scary story, Uncle Ruckus."

Treb finishes chewing. "Yeah, it was. Uncle Ruckus always has the best scary stories."

Uncle Ruckus smiles and takes it all in silently, something he rarely does.

"Yeah?" Shovel says, "Well, I got a really good one."

"Really?" Uncle Ruckus asks.

"Let's hear it!" Treb says.

Shovel looks around wildly. "Uh, yeah, a real good one. But I need just a minute to prepare. It's been a while since I've told it." We wait about ten seconds, and Shovel says again, "Okay, you ready to hear a spooky story?"

We all nod, except Turbo, who is probably suffocating deep within the recesses of his sleeping bag.

Shovel says, "There's a skeleton inside of you."

We all wait.

"Well..." Turbo's muffled voice says. "Yeah."

"Is that it?" Treb sounds disappointed.

Shovel says, "Yeah, but it's scary because it's true. Skeletons are scary, and there's one inside you in real life... so I thought it would make a good scary story."

Mr. B knocks against the side of the Adirondack. "9:30 boys, lights out."

"We already have the lights out, Mr. B," I say.

"You know what I mean. Don't get smart. It's quiet time now," Mr. B says, his voice receding into the distance.

"Can't believe we wasted our last minute on that story..." Treb mutters.

"It's cool," Uncle Ruckus says. "I got more for tomorrow night. Got a really good one about spiders."

"I don't like spiders. They scare me," Treb says.

"That's the point of a horror story," I say. "Don't be such a baby. Nothing in a story can hurt you. The real scary stuff is out there, in the real world." *That's where all the giant bodies of water and freaky diseases are, at least.*

"Yeah," Uncle Ruckus says, and I can hear the smile in his voice. "Besides, there's probably spiders in here right now. You're never further than like three feet from a spider. And you eat tons of spiders in your sleep every year."

Treb's voice sounds small, "Really?"

Approaching footsteps precede a voice, "I thought I told you, boys, to get to sleep."

"Sorry Mr. B," I say. "We were trying to cheer up Treb; he's afraid of spiders inside the Adirondack."

"Is that so?" Mr. B asks. He takes a deep breath and lets it out in a large sigh. "What's that movie you're always talking about, Treb?"

"*Fantasy Rifts?*" Treb suggests.

"No, that's not it," Mr. B says from the other side of the curtain across the front of the Adirondack. "The one about the little people."

"You mean hobbits? That's *Lord of the Rings*, Mr. B," Treb says. "It's about Frodo, and he has to take the One Ring to rule them all to—"

Mr. B interrupts, "That's the one where he fights off the spiders, right?"

"Yeah."

Mr. B says, "Don't be afraid of the spiders; just tell yourself you have to be like Froyo. Now get some sleep, boys. I don't want to have to come back over here."

"Hey, Mr. B?" I ask.

He sighs. "What is it, Do-Over?"

"Will you tell the Wafflestomper story?"

"Everybody keeps talking about that. What's the Wafflestomper story?" Shovel asks.

"It's a camp legend." Mr. B shakes his head. "Something that happened years ago. Another time. You boys get some rest."

We wait until he walks away.

"Did he just tell you to be like frozen yogurt?" I stifle a laugh.

"Yeah," Turbo laughs. "If you get scared, Treb, just be like froyo. Cold, delicious, and you can charge the spiders by the ounce to eat you."

We all snicker.

"I miss Dr. Cassandra," Turbo says.

"Come on, dude," Uncle Ruckus says. "Don't be gay."

"I'm very interested to hear how liking a lady makes you gay," I say, and we all laugh again. It's quiet for a long minute.

"I'm worried I don't deserve her," Turbo says. "Like, what if I can't bear her sons?"

"You can't bear her sons," Uncle Ruckus says.

"Because you don't have a chance in the world with her," I finish. "She's like twenty years older than you."

"I don't care, I still love her," Turbo mumbles as he snuggles down into his sleeping bag.

"Hey, Uncle Ruckus?" I ask.

"Yo."

"Sorry about earlier... Getting so mad and everything... What was your plan? The plan to get to San Francisco?"

He sighs. "Eh, don't worry about it. Let's just focus on getting the Golden Plunger. That's a better idea, anyway."

"I'm glad you guys are getting to stay until Parent's Night."

"Me too."

Nobody says anything after that, and sleep overtakes us one by one. In an effort to try to stay awake just a little longer, my eyes flutter open. Light emanates from inside Shovel's sleeping bag, and I fall asleep to the faint sounds of plastic tapping on glass.

* * *

ONE YEAR AGO...
SEPTEMBER 23ᴿᴰ, 2014. 5:33 PM.

Turbo Cakes loved playing snap-catch with his dad. It took all the pressure out of throwing the ball well and actually catching it. Instead, he could just focus on enjoying the time together.

Turbo whirled his arm in an elaborate throwing motion, pretending to throw something invisible straight up in the air. At the top of the throw, he snapped his fingers.

Snap.

Turbo and his dad both stared up at the cerulean sky, waiting for the invisible object to come down. After a few seconds, Turbo Cakes's dad ran a few steps forward with his arm extended.

Snap.

His dad's hand fell a few inches as if catching something and he snapped at the moment he "caught" the imaginary object.

"Nice one!" Turbo whooped.

"Thanks!" his dad said. "Now go long!" He made a big show of cocking back, then launched the imaginary ball with a loud *snap*.

10

A RANGER IS WAFFLESTOMPING

PRESENT

TUESDAY, JUNE 2ND, 2015. 6:09 AM.

"Up!" Mr. B shouts as he beats his fist against the outside of our Adirondack. "Everybody up! I want everyone out here in the next five minutes."

"I'm alive! The milk didn't kill me. I can't believe I'm alive." Shovel squeals. "And I feel fine."

I groan. Waking up early really isn't my thing. Apparently, it's not Uncle Ruckus's either, because he says, "You aren't going to be alive for long if you don't shut up." He stuffs his pillow into his face.

Turbo Cakes checks his digital watch. "It's almost an hour before we're supposed to be up for breakfast; something must be wrong."

I plant my feet on the dusty wooden floor so I don't fall back asleep. It takes me a minute to get moving, but I tame my messy, red hair and go outside in my shorts, *Lead Space* t-shirt, and flip flops. The rest of the guys in our Adirondack trickle out. Shovel wears a cheery grin that makes me wish the milk *had* killed him. Plus, since he's smiling, I can only assume it didn't make his dick fall off. He's munching on a chocolate bar— yuck, too rich for breakfast. *Where did he even find one in the last sixty seconds?*

I jump in line next to Ducky and mumble, "Are we in trouble?"

Ducky grunts at me, eyes half-open.

"This everyone?" Mr. B asks, then follows it up with, "Get your butts to the bathrooms *now*."

We all trudge to the bathrooms like we're going to the gallows. Death might actually be welcome at this point; it's too early in the morning for this.

Troop 100 stands at attention in their Class A uniforms in front of the bathroom. The sight makes my whole body wake up. What are they doing here? Our troop shuffles into a disorganized clump outside our end of the restroom, and the unmistakable stench hits me.

The scent of human feces wafts from the bathroom. I gag and cover my nose. Shovel grimaces and puts his chocolate bar in one of his many cargo pants pockets. Troop 100 doesn't waver from attention. Sergeant Johnson looks like he could kill somebody. *Uh oh.* Mr. B brings up the tail end of our troop, and the Sergeant goes and stands next to him.

Mr. B says, "Whoever did it just needs to confess, and your punishment will only be cleaning the bathrooms."

Sergeant Johnson snorts. "You'll be cleaning with a toothbrush, and I'll personally watch you lick the floor when you claim you're done!"

Mr. B mumbles, "Not helping." He addresses Troop 100. "No one stepped forward from my troop. Is there anyone from Troop 100 who wants to come forward?"

Before my next heartbeat, Sergeant Johnson pipes up again, "No chance in Hell it was one of my guys. Look at em. We're a unit. Not a one of them would pull a stunt like this." The Sergeant stares me down, and I catch the briefest of smirks on Peters's face before he gets it under control.

Mr. B juts his thumb at us. "None of my guys did it. Lay off."

"Then who did?" Sergeant Johnson demands.

There's a huge yawn behind me, and we all part like the Red Sea to reveal Uncle Ruckus stumbling toward us, still clutching his pillow to his chest. He smacks his lips a few times and gives a dazed smile, "'Sup, dudes?"

Jesus, talk about bad timing.

"What's 'sup,'" Mr. B says, eyes trained on Uncle Ruckus, "is the Wafflestomper has struck."

Never in my life did I expect to hear Mr. B say that sentence. Under most circumstances, it would have been hilarious. But the seriousness in his voice terrifies me. None of us laugh, not even Uncle Ruckus. Of course, it had to be Shovel who breaks the silence.

"Why would anyone stomp on a waffle?" the horror in his voice is evident. "They're delicious."

Mr. B's face softens. "I'm afraid there's no literal waffle. The scene in that bathroom is frightening to behold. Someone has written in... excrement on the wall. It says, 'The Wafflestomper has returned.'"

Shovel looks like he's about to speak, but Mr. B addresses the question before Shovel can ask it. "The Wafflestomper has a reputation for pooping in the showers. They never caught him, but we know it's an Adventure Ranger. He hasn't struck in a few years, so this is probably a copycat. When he's done doing his business, his M.O. is to stomp it into the drain, effectively clogging the drain with waffle-patterned scat, and consequently flooding the shower."

Shovel gags.

Mr. B says, "Ducky, get him out of here before he loses that expired milk."

Sergeant Johnson looks smug. "Weak stomach on that one, huh? My guys are tougher than that."

Mr. B whirls on him. "That 'weak stomach' has just proven he couldn't be the Wafflestomper. You're right, your guys are handling this pretty well."

He gestures to Troop 100 standing at stoic attention, and then sweeps his hand to point at us. Uncle Ruckus is holding a pillow up to his nose, Turbo is wearing a surgical mask that seemingly materialized out of thin air, and I have my shirt scrunched up against my nose. Mr. B finishes his gesture on Tri-Clops, who has jammed leaves up his nose.

"I don't know what you're insinuating," Sergeant Johnson snarls, "but it wasn't one of my Rangers. Troop 100, go perform your morning duties." With that, Troop 100 reverses and marches back toward their campsite on the other side of the bathrooms. The Sergeant sneers at Mr. B and follows his troop.

Mr. B shakes his head and gestures for us all to come closer. "Listen," he says, "I think this is a ploy by Troop 100. I don't think you guys did this. They're nervous we might win the Golden Plunger this year, and they are trying to sabotage our inspections. Let's stay focused and remember the Ranger Rules. We'll go home with that Plunger, guys."

We all nod, and he lets us go.

"Do-Over," Mr. B says.

Every muscle in my body tenses up. Oh man, he's about to accuse *me*. "Mr. B, listen," I say. "I know this looks bad for me after I argued with them last night, but I swear—"

"I don't think you did it," Mr. B cuts me off. Relief soars inside me like a bird as Mr. B continues, "Remember the community service you and Shovel were supposed to do this morning?"

The relief bird inside me implodes, and I stare at the filthy bathroom entrance—fearing his next words.

Mr. B laughs. "Don't worry, we aren't making you clean the bathrooms. I don't think poor Shovel could stomach it; he'd probably just contribute last night's dinner to the mess. I sent Mr. McNitt to get the administrators. I don't want you here when they arrive. Report to the Chapel early. Moonpie should already be there. After that, I don't want you going to your merit patch classes until we know you're feeling better from what happened yesterday."

Jeez. I wish everyone would quit talking about the lake incident yesterday.

Before I can protest, Mr. B holds up a hand. "I want you to do something for me."

Not what I was expecting. I nod.

Mr. B leans in close. "I want you and Shovel to go to everyone's activities today. See if you can find any clues about who might have done this. See if you can figure out if anyone got up to pee and saw something last night, that kind of thing."

"You want me to skip my merit patch classes to find the Wafflestomper?"

"I want you boys to have the best time possible at summer camp. Especially now that the week has started… going downhill. I'd do anything to give you guys the best week I can." He pats me on the shoulder.

"Even if that means me skipping my merit patch classes?" I ask.

"If that's what it takes," He smiles and shrugs.

"Bet, Mr. B." He looks at me quizzically. "Yeah, I'll do it," I clarify.

I go back, get ready in a few minutes, and grab Shovel, who looks slightly less green than before. Then we hoof it over to the Chapel. For whatever reason, they put it in Social Siberia; it's a good ten-minute walk until we get there.

I stop right before the Chapel and tell Shovel what Mr. B said our job was.

"He wants us to tattle?" Shovel asks.

"Yeah," I say. "But we might not, depending on who did it. Think of it like selective snitching. We don't want to get anyone we like in trouble."

"Oh," Shovel says, cocking his head. "But I like everybody."

"You like Hawkins?" I ask, raising an eyebrow.

Shovel looks torn.

"That's what I thought," I say. "Let me know if you find out anything important, but don't tell Mr. B anything unless I say so. Got it?"

He nods, and we walk into the Chapel.

It's not a *real* Chapel, exactly. It's not a building; it's just an open area in the forest with rows of benches and a big stone podium. Moonpie is reading at the podium. There's a buck eating out of his hand while he reads. An actual, grown-ass buck.

We stop in front of him. He doesn't look up or say anything. A couple of seconds go by, and the forest is eerily quiet except for the buck's munching. *This camp is so weird.*

"You look like a dirty, hillbilly Santa," Shovel says.

The buck looks up at Shovel with wild eyes, but doesn't bolt. "You look like a raccoon who skipped one too many rocks across the trailer roof," Moonpie answers as he flips a page with his free hand.

I have no idea what this means, and by the look on Shovel's face, he doesn't either. Moonpie hasn't looked up at us yet, so I ask, "What are you reading?"

"Young master Do-Over!" Moonpie says. "Nice to see you again." He holds up the newspaper. "Just reading the obits to make sure I'm not in 'em!" Moonpie chortles to himself and goes back to reading the obituary columns.

"So..." I ask, "What are we supposed to do?"

"I don't know," Moonpie says. He dumps the rest of the food in his hand on the ground and scratches his beard. "How 'bouts you and the little 'un go around and sit on every bench, make sure they're all stable." He went back to reading. The buck continues nibbling on the oats Moonpie dropped on the ground.

This is our punishment? Cool, fine by me.

Shovel and I spend the next forty-five minutes sitting, laying, crouching, and jumping on all the benches. They're all perfectly sturdy. The buck left a few minutes in, but Moonpie never looked up from reading his obituaries. Bored, I pick a bench and carve "Do-Over" into it with my pocketknife.

"My dad won't let me have my pocketknife until I'm older," Shovel says.

"Probably a good idea," I reply. "I begged my dad for mine, and when he finally gave it to me, I cut myself the first day." I laugh and shake my head as I dispel the memory. "You'll get it one day. They're pretty useful little tools."

Shovel's eyes widen. "Can I hold it? Just for a minute."

Something rattles inside me. I hate letting other people use my stuff—seems like it never goes well. "Well," I start, but hesitate when I notice how Shovel is looking at me. *Damn it.* "Okay, yeah, you can hold it for a minute." I close the pocketknife and drop it in his open hand.

Shovel rolls it around in his hand and asks, "So, who do you think stomped the waffle?"

"I don't know," I say, closing my eyes as I sit down. Peters's smirk from this morning is tattooed on the inside of my eyelids. "Probably someone from another troop trying to mess with us. Guys can be dicks like that."

"Yeah," Shovel says. "Dicks."

He offers the pocketknife back, and I tuck it away in one of my cargo pants' many pockets.

"You think it could have been Uncle Ruckus, though?" Shovel asks, genuine concern on his face.

I pause. "Yeah, I guess it could be."

Shovel lowers his voice. "Just seems like he'd be upset about everything that happened yesterday with Devil Rock. Y'know?"

Moonpie yells from the podium, "Y'all about done? I ain't getting sued for child labor laws. That's enough work for this morning. Let's go get some breakfast, boys!"

We both stand up and I dust my hands against my pants.

"This Moonpie guy seems weird too." Shovel whispers. "I've never seen a pet deer before. That's outlier material for sure."

* * *

THREE YEARS AGO...
JUNE 13TH, 2012. 6:34 AM.

Do-Over held the rod over the edge of the dock and let out his line. He didn't *want* to catch a fish. Even though they live in such a scary place, he liked fish. They didn't breathe air, and that was pretty cool. He dropped his hook into the water, watched it drift to the bottom of the lake from a safe distance, and reeled it back in. He'd probably done this two dozen times already that morning.

Do-Over started reeling his line back in when it abruptly stopped. He crouched down and poked his head over the side of the dock to see what the problem was. Staring down into that infinite murk made him dizzy. A firm hand came down on Do-Over's shoulder, which made him jump.

"Everything all right?" Sergeant Johnson asked.

"It's stuck," Do-Over emphasized with a tug of the fishing pole.

"Caught a big rock, seems like." Sergeant Johnson maneuvered the fishing pole around to try to get it unstuck, but to no avail. He tsked, "Only one thing to do." He pulled his bulky multitool off his belt and flicked the knife out.

"Is it okay if I do it?" Do-Over asked.

"Sure," the Sergeant replied. "This your first time using a knife?"

Do-Over produced his tiny pocketknife, the one his dad gave him that morning. "Yes, sir."

"I'll watch. Remember your blood circle," he said. "You don't wanna end up like me, missing half a finger."

Do-Over held out the closed pocketknife and swung his arm in front of him in a wide arc. The Sergeant took a small step back to stand outside of Do-Over's blood circle.

"Now go ahead and cut the line. Then we'll get you set up with a new hook and a bobber this time."

Do-Over pulled the line taut between his fingers and cut it.

Sergeant Johnson smiled. "Good job."

Do-Over's heart fluttered with joy at the compliment. His fingers shook as he closed the pocketknife. The tip pricked his index finger and a tiny bead of blood welled up.

Sergeant Johnson's face darkened. "The next step is learning the right way to close a pocketknife. Come along, son. Let's find you a band-aid."

11

A RANGER IS DETECTING

Mr. B steps out of the Dining Hall with a cup of coffee and a handful of prunes. "Hey, boys," he says, popping a prune into his mouth. "Moonpie, can I offer you one?"

Moonpie eyes the prune and shakes his head. "No thanks, those things'll make you poop like a goose. And from what I understand, y'all got enough of that going on as it is."

"Too true." Mr. B pulls out a manila folder and hands it to me. "That is a record of everyone's schedule. Don't lose it, but go make your rounds at merit patch classes and see if you can dig anything up. You too, Shovel. And boys? Behave." With that, he heads toward Admin.

"I'm starving," Shovel says.

"No, you aren't. You're Shovel," Moonpie laughs out.

I roll my eyes. Shovel nods with that dopey grin on his face.

We eat our sad excuse for a breakfast: Rock-hard biscuits, watery scrambled eggs, and a dubious mystery meat patty. Shovel and Moonpie both scarf it down, and Shovel keeps his plastic cup in the center of the table throughout the meal. After I'm done picking at mine, we follow Moonpie to Dam Beard to see if we can glean anything from Treb or Tri-Clops.

Dam Beard is like speedrunning the Adventure Rangers. Troops put all the new Rangers in it to try and help them rank up as fast as possible. If they do their work, they come to camp as Tenderboots and leave as Bear or even Pine rank Rangers.

Everyone in Dam Beard is about Shovel's age, which apparently means to Moonpie that he needs to talk really loud for them to understand him. Moonpie stands in front of a semi-circle of logs that all the Tenderboot Rangers are sitting on. Most of them aren't paying attention; they're admiring what came out of their noses on the end of their finger or picking at the grass. Tri-Clops falls into the first category. Treb is reading his encyclopedia. Moonpie shout-explains that Dam Beard is going to help them rank up 'real fast.' Then, he outlines the behavior system they will follow.

"See these?" Moonpie rattles a bag of M&Ms.

The reaction is instantaneous, all the Tenderboots' heads snap up. Their eyes are all transfixed on Moonpie.

Moonpie chuckles. "Whew, that never gets old. These here is chocolate. Everybody has a plastic bag with their name on it filled with M&Ms. Every time you do something bad, I take one out of your bag and eat it." He gives a toothy grin.

"We don't have time for this. We're detectives," I mutter to Shovel.

"Should we detect something?" Shovel asks.

"Yeah, follow my lead," I say, sitting down next to Tri-Clops. I keep a wary eye on his index finger to ensure it doesn't come anywhere close to me.

"Hey, bud," I whisper to him as Moonpie talks.

Tri-Clops doesn't react. Like... at all.

"Hey. Dude," I say.

Tri-Clops is still staring at Moonpie.

I give him a nudge. "Psst."

As I start to pull my arm back, Tri-Clops grabs my hand faster than I can react. I stare in horror at his booger finger that is now touching my arm. I'm so focused on the finger I barely notice Tri-Clops rear his head back like a dinosaur. Next thing I know, he is *biting* me.

I squeal and try to pull my arm back, but he has a strong hold on me. The squeal becomes a scream as I slap the top of his head with my manila folder. He won't let go.

"Tri-Clops! Tri-Clops!" Moonpie exclaims. He shakes the bag of M&Ms with Tri-Clops's name on it.

Like a trained puppy, Tri-Clops lets go and stares at the plastic bag. I yank my arm away and study it. Thank God he didn't break the skin, but I still want to soak my whole arm in hand sanitizer.

"That's five for me, boy! No bitin'!" Moonpie hollers as he pops a handful of M&Ms in his mouth.

Tri-Clops hisses at Moonpie, and we take the opportunity to slip away and head back up Cardiac Hill. Cicadas shriek all around us, and I lose myself in their orchestra to avoid focusing on how hard I'm breathing. It ain't called Cardiac Hill for nothing.

"You aren't talking... Are you mad at me?" Shovel asks.

"No, why would I be mad at you?"

"Well..." Shovel kicks a rock down Cardiac Hill. "You said to follow your lead. But I didn't want to get bit by Tri-Clops too. So, I didn't really follow directions very well. Sorry."

I laugh. "Nah, man. That's not really what I meant when I said that." I stare at the bite mark on my arm. Hopefully this doesn't make me Patient Zero for a zombie virus. Cutting it off is always an option, I guess.

"Doesn't seem like he did it," Shovel says.

"What exactly are you basing that on?" I ask. "Because getting bit felt pretty incriminating to me."

"I dunno. Seems like someone whose first reaction to a problem is to bite somebody wouldn't carry out such a well-executed crime," Shovel says.

Dang. Good point there.

"You didn't get mad, though," Shovel says.

"Yeah. I was too surprised to get mad at him," I admit.

"You should try and make jokes instead of getting mad. To decaf the situation."

I cock an eyebrow. "Do you mean: 'defuse'?"

"Same thing," Shovel says.

I almost snap at him. *No, they aren't the same thing.* Maybe a change in subject is better here. "So, who do you think did it?" I stop a quarter of the way up Cardiac Hill, huffing and puffing. I fish my water bottle from my backpack.

Shovel appears to consider this for a moment. "On Scooby Doo, it's usually the first nice person you meet. Or the janitor. Or the butler. So, try to think of the first person who was nice to you, or if Camp Winnebago has any janitors. Or butlers."

I stare at him, taking in what he just said. Thank goodness Uncle Ruckus isn't here. He'd have a heyday with this one. "You want me to try to remember the first person I ever met?" I ask.

"Well, just the first person at camp before it happened, I guess. Didn't you get in trouble with the other troop's leader?" he asks.

"Yeah. Not the first time I've been in trouble with Troop 100," I say, taking a swig of water before offering it to Shovel. He takes a long drink.

As he hands it back, he says, "Well, seems like it could be him, then. But he's an adult, and was in the army, so I don't think it would be him."

I nod. "Yeah, he's more the yelling type than the pooping type."

"What'd you do before?" Shovel asks.

"What?" I ask.

"To get in trouble at Troop 100. Seems like you and Peters know each other or something, from the way you guys were talking at dinner last night."

"Yeah, we actually used to be friends."

"What happened?"

A hollow feeling sinks deep into my chest, but I decide to tell him the truth. "I used to be in Troop 100, but I got in a fight, and they threw me out of the troop because they said I started it."

"Did you?" Shovel asks.

I meet his eyes. Shovel's head is cocked to the side, and he looks like an inquisitive puppy. I usually don't talk about this stuff, but I can tell he genuinely wants to know. It seems like he's interested in me. That feels nice, so I tell him. "No, I didn't start the fight." I grin. "You're a pretty good detective, you know that?"

Shovel beams. "Just trying to figure out if you did it or not, since you were the first person who was nice to me at camp."

That deep hollow feeling twinges inside me, and it spreads into a nice, warm feeling. I can't help but smile.

"Just trying to keep you from getting killed, my man." *Or your dick from falling off*, I think to myself. "So, do you think I did it?"

Shovel's eyes meet mine and he squints, then he relaxes and says, "Nah. You're like Tri-Clops: you solve problems with violence."

I bust up laughing. This kid has guts. "Did you just compare me to Tri-Clops?" I hold up a fist menacingly.

Shovel stares, then laughs too. "So, wait." Shovel wipes his eyes. "Where are we going right now?"

"To do some more investigating," I say. "We're going to find Uncle Ruckus."

"Found him," Shovel says.

"Huh?"

Shovel points, and I spot Uncle Ruckus and a frightened-looking Turbo crouching behind the Trading Post with a huge, black garbage bag between them. We march over there, and as we approach Ruckus looks startled.

"Oh, hey, guys," Uncle Ruckus says. "We were just—"

"Tell them," Turbo Cakes says. He looks more confident now that Shovel and I are here.

"Yeah, I saw a rare Blue Footed Booby fly by a second ago and—"

"No," Turbo says. "Tell them."

Shovel gets on his tiptoes and whispers into my ear, "Seems pretty suspicious!"

Uncle Ruckus sighs. "Okay, I'll tell them. Was going to tell you guys anyway."

Turbo shakes his head.

"I was just thinking, right," Uncle Ruckus begins, "that we should take advantage of our *situation*. Our boy Turbo over here makes for a perfect accomplice now that he's kicked out of camp too. I got all the know-how to pull off the perfect crime. And Do-Over already got the ball rolling with that whole waffle-stomping business. Nice job with that, by the way."

"I didn't shit in the shower," I say. "But what are you talking about?"

Uncle Ruckus looks left and right, then opens the garbage bag to reveal toilet paper. He closes it back really fast.

"Oh my god," I say. "Was that Golden Bum's Nine-Ply Toilet Paper?"

Ruckus nods solemnly.

"I don't get it," Shovel says.

I point at the bag. "You can sell high-quality toilet paper at double or triple the store price at camp. Nobody wants to use that sandpaper they call toilet paper that's in the bolos and bathrooms."

"That's just the start of it," Uncle Ruckus grins. "We're gonna sell it for *ten times* the store price. It's gonna be the big spit, man." He looks like he's about to burst with anticipation.

"Okay, I'll bite," I say. "How are you—"

"I'm glad you asked!" He slings a backpack off his back and opens it. It's full of chocolate.

I pick one up and read the label aloud. "'Laxative milk chocolate squares.' Oh, Ruckus. You can't."

"That's Uncle Ruckus," he says. "Once people start having some serious diarrhea, they'll pay *anything* for toilet paper of this quality. We're gonna buy a ton of chocolate bars, tape the wrappers back shut, and sneak them into the Trading Post again. We'll make a fortune once it hits their stomachs!"

My face goes red. "Yeah? And when were you going to tell us about this? Once we were shitting all over the place?"

"Come on, dude! Course, I was gonna tell you not to eat the chocolate." Uncle Ruckus holds his hands out in front of him like he's innocent.

I feel Shovel tug on my sleeve. "One second," I say holding my hand up. I turn to Turbo. "And you're okay with this?"

Turbo's voice is shaky. "Well. He told me he had a foolproof way for me to get a date with Dr. Cassandra." He strokes his weird chin hair.

Shovel tugs on my sleeve again, and I shrug him off.

"Oh, come on," I say. "Like Uncle Ruckus has any idea how to get a girl. The only date you would have gotten is one to the Infirmary with explosive diarrhea."

Turbo's face turns resolute. "It's a risk worth taking. Sorry, Do-Over."

"Do-Over?" Shovel asks. The scared tone in his voice makes me turn around. Shovel has tears in his eyes, and he's holding up a candy wrapper. The same wrapper around all of Ruckus's chocolate bars.

"Oh, buddy," I say. "You didn't."

He nods, tears coming down his face. "Am I gonna die?"

Uncle Ruckus howls with laughter, and I shut him up with a shove. "No, you're not gonna die," I say.

"I'll cut you a deal, too," Uncle Ruckus says, a smug look on his face.

"No, no deal," I say, voice full of malice. "You do this, I'll snitch, and not only will you be kicked out of camp, you'll be kicked out of the Adventure Rangers. How could you do this to him? After he stuck his neck out for you back in Admin?"

Uncle Ruckus's voice turns earnest. "No way, I didn't do it on purpose. Shovel must have grabbed one off my bunk this morning or something."

Shovel nods as more tears stream down his face.

"Then you're gonna help me fix this," I say.

"Yeah, man. That's the deal," he says. "You help me with this whole operation, and I'll help you find out who the Wafflestomper is. Things look pretty bad on you right now. If the Sergeant doesn't find out who did it soon, he's gonna start saying it was you."

"And what makes you think I can't find out who did it without you?" I growl.

"You don't have the guts to do what it takes to find out who did it. To play hardball. Think about it; if the Wafflestomper has diarrhea, their crap won't be... you know, solid enough to stomp." Uncle Ruckus smirks.

"I'll play hardball with your face if you don't help Shovel right now," I say, taking a step forward.

"Hang on, listen." Uncle Ruckus holds his hands in front of his face, keeping me at arm's length. "I'll give Shovel as much Golden Bum Nine-

Ply as he needs to get through this, *and* I'll help you find out who the Wafflestomper is. Turbo can take Shovel to the Infirmary and see Dr. Cassandra, you get off the hook, we catch the culprit, and I get rich. Everybody wins."

"Everyone but Shovel," I say. "I help you; you lay off him for the rest of the summer."

Uncle Ruckus sighs and looks at poor Shovel. "Fine. Kid, you ever heard of Sorcery: The Trading Card game?"

"Yeah," Shovel whimpers. "All the cool older kids play it. I'm not good at it, and my dad won't let me use any of his cards."

"I'll get you the newest set of cards the first day of release. Deal?" Uncle Ruckus asks, extending a hand.

Shovel considers a moment and dries his eyes with balled up fists. "With the Darkest Tides expansion too?"

"Yes, with the Darkest Tides expansion too," Uncle Ruckus says, without hesitation.

"Okay, deal," Shovel says and extends his wet hand.

They shake on it.

"First things first," Uncle Ruckus says, holding up two rolls of toilet paper. "Get this kid to the Infirmary before he explodes."

* * *

FOUR DAYS AGO...

MAY 28TH, 2015. 4:08 PM.

You have reached the voicemail of Mark Langston. Please leave a message after the beep.

Beep.

"Yo, Mark. It's me. You never called me back last week, but it's cool.

You're the big spit and all now over in San Fran, huh? That's cool. Anyways, I think I got a plan to get the money to buy a plane ticket and come see you in a few weeks. Hope everything is good and everything. Also, thanks for the Crab Runner card you printed. It's pretty cool to have a card based off a story where I drank a slushie too fast. Would it have killed ya to make the stats a little better? Kidding. Kinda. Anyway, see you soon. Hopefully. Bye."

Uncle Ruckus put the phone down and went over his math one more time. Fifty rolls of Golden Bum Nine Ply at five times the market price equals one plane ticket to San Francisco.

"I'm getting out of this hellhole and coming to live with you. Real soon. So clear your schedule, Mark," Uncle Ruckus said.

12

A RANGER IS THRIFTY

"Journey!" Uncle Ruckus exclaims as he steps into the air-conditioned Trading Post.

Journey doesn't look up from his phone. "You know the drill, Ruckus, no slushies."

"Yeah, yeah," Uncle Ruckus says before adding, "That's Uncle Ruckus."

"Whatever you say," Journey mumbles. His head snaps up, as if he just remembered something. There's a gleeful look in his eye. "Did you guys hear the second clue this morning? For the flag?"

"I totally forgot about the flag! I missed the raising of the colors ceremony on the parade field this morning. What was it?" I ask.

Journey clears his throat and speaks in an overly-theatrical voice, "The flag awaits where the elements collide." His voice changes back, "Pretty good hint, right?"

"Journey," I say, "I'm going to be honest. That does not help me or narrow things down in the slightest."

He shrugs. "Maybe tomorrow's clue will give you a better idea." Journey goes back to scrolling on his phone.

I *love* the Trading Post. Not only is it air-conditioned, but it has *tons* of snacks and pretty much any other goodies a teenager might want. I grab two Twix bars and head over to the freezer. They charge double for a Twix ice cream bar, but all I care about is eating something cold. So the trick is, you hide the normal Twix bars at the bottom of the freezer and come back for them later when they're good and frozen. We've picked up tons of tricks like that over the years.

For instance, Turbo just brings all his own snacks to avoid the overpriced Trading Post supplies. But there's one thing Turbo can't pack ahead of time. I pass Uncle Ruckus filling up a bag with all the chocolate bars on the rack and head straight for Journey.

"One Lancellottie, please," I say.

Journey tears himself away from his phone and gets to work on a masterpiece. There used to be this guy who worked at the Trading Post named Lancelot. Everyone likes mixing slushie flavors for cool combinations, but this guy was a pro. He figured out the perfect combination of all the different kinds to create something beautiful that he named after himself: a Lancellottie.

Journey brings the creation over. It's a rainbow of sugary, icy goodness. I pay the man and slurp the addictive slushie. Most summers, we drink more Lancellotties than water. Flavor wracks my taste buds. My blood would probably even taste sugary after a few of these bad boys. Rumor has it more than one kid has left camp with Type Three Diabetes all because of Lancellotties.

Uncle Ruckus sees me in ecstasy and flips me the bird. I don't even care, he's just mad because he's banned from ordering slushies at camp ever again. He dumps his chocolate hoard on the counter.

Journey raises an eyebrow at him. "This isn't going to send you into one of your crab walking tizzies, is it Uncle Ruckus?"

"Nah," Uncle Ruckus says coolly. "I can handle it."

That must have been enough for Journey, because he let him buy it all. We walk out, me drinking my Lancellottie and Uncle Ruckus with more chocolate than even Augustus Gloop could handle.

Thankfully, our campsite wasn't much further up Cardiac Hill from the Trading Post. Once we decide the coast is clear, we sneak into the site, close the tarp in front of our Adirondack, and get to work.

It takes a while to unwrap the chocolate bars in a way that doesn't destroy the integrity of the wrapper. We put them in a plastic bag and wrap each bar of laxative chocolate with the normal wrappers. We use a tiny bit of glue to seal them, and by the time we're done you can't tell they were ever opened.

I wipe my sticky fingers on Uncle Ruckus's black sweatshirt and ask, "How can we get rid of them?"

Knock knock knock.

We freeze.

I mouth at Ruckus, 'There's someone out there.'

He mouths back, 'No shit, Sherlock.'

"Boys?" It's Mr. McNitt. "Can I come in?"

I panic and say, "Yeah, come on in!"

Mr. McNitt pulls back the tarp and smiles. "What's going on, guys? Didn't feel like going to your classes, Do-Over?"

I take a big slurp of my Lancellottie to buy myself time, but Uncle Ruckus answers.

"You see, Mr. McNitt," he begins.

"Ahh, don't worry about it, *bros*, I won't tell." Mr. Mcnitt lowers himself to the floor with us, sitting 'criss-cross-applesauce' and looking like an oversized toddler. "I didn't always go to my merit patch classes as a young Adventure Ranger. What are you guys up to?"

"We found all this chocolate." Uncle Ruckus says.

"Yeah, and we can't eat it all, so we were trying to figure out how we can share it," I say.

"What's that you always say, Uncle Ruckus? 'That's the big spit!' That's cool of you guys, seriously," Mr. McNitt says, picking up a pseudo-chocolate bar.

"I'm never saying that again," Uncle Ruckus mumbles.

"Hang on, Mr. McNitt," I say before he can tear open the chocolate wrapper. "We didn't want to keep it just within our campsite. We wanted to share it with Troop 100. You know, as a peace offering, or whatever."

"Boys, that's a great idea," Mr. McNitt says. He looks at the chocolate. "Where'd you fellas say you found all this again?"

"A bush," I say. *I really need to think before I lie.*

Mr. McNitt's eyebrows shoot up. "A bush? Really? That's great! Where was it? Maybe I'll go see if I can find more chocolate."

Uncle Ruckus says, "Walk just past the fishing pier, and then go southeast. Walk straight for three minutes until you come to a bush that looks like Abraham Lincoln's head. And keep an eye out for the flag while you're looking."

Mr. McNitt grabs the bag of pseudo-chocolate bars and says, "Great! I'll drop these off in Troop 100's campsite on my way. See you dudes later." And with that, he jogs off toward their campsite.

"You have *got* to work on your lying," Uncle Ruckus says.

"I'd like to think it says a lot about me that I'm *not* good at lying," I say.

"Whatever. Nice work anyway. Now those Troop 100 jerks get what's coming to them, and we can sell them toilet paper from right next door." Uncle Ruckus stands up and says, "Be right back."

A few minutes later, he comes back with an armload of toilet paper.

I scowl, "At least leave them with *something* to use before they have to come buy from you."

Uncle Ruckus begins stuffing all the rolls of thin toilet paper under his bed. "All's fair in love and war."

"What's the plan when Mr. McNitt comes back because he couldn't find a bush shaped like Abraham Lincoln's head?" I ask.

Uncle Ruckus cackles from under his bunk. "I really doubt that'll happen."

"Huh?" I say.

He scoots back out from under his bunk and stares at me. "Abe Lincoln. He was shot in the head. *All* bushes look like his head."

Needing a break from Uncle Ruckus, I walk out of the Adirondack and spot Ducky setting up a hammock with two other older Rangers: iBall and Tyler 2 Electric Boogaloo.

"Hey, guys," I say.

They all jerk their heads in the 'whaddup' motion.

"You guys brought your hammocks, huh?" I ask and instantly feel like an idiot. Why couldn't I think of something cooler and less obvious to say?

But Ducky gives me a serious reply. "Can't sleep on those bunks. We want to sleep out in the open, in the elements. That's what camping is *really* about."

"I'm taking the Wilderness Survival merit patch class," I say.

"Yeah?" Ducky smiles. "That's one of my favorite ones. Spending a night out in the middle of the woods is the absolute goat."

"Goat," Tyler 2 agrees.

Unsure of exactly what that means, I nod and say, "Yeah, goat." It sounded cooler when they said it.

I watch them settle into their hammocks when Ducky says, "You know, you can join us if you want."

My heart leaps. "For real? I would, but I don't have a hammock."

iBall brushes long blond hair away from his eyes. "You can use my bedsheet if you want. I'm sleeping here every night; I won't need it."

"Seriously?" It takes everything in me not to grin like an idiot.

"Yeah," Ducky says. "But, uh, let's not mention this to your friends. Turbo Cakes is kind of a dork, and Uncle Ruckus is annoying AF."

"Yeah, AF," Tyler 2 says.

"Cool, no problem, yeah. I'll go grab your bedsheet, thanks. Which one is it?" I ask, practically vibrating.

"Blue," iBall answers and gives me the 'hang loose' sign.

I jog off toward their Adirondack and grab the blue sheet, then I run by my Adirondack to grab my pack and water bottle. When I throw open the tarp, I see Uncle Ruckus sitting on the floor playing Sorcery: The Trading Card game. *By himself?*

"Sup," I say, trying to get in and out as fast as possible.

"Just practicing," Uncle Ruckus says, a look of concentration on his face. "There's this Ranger at the girl's camp across the lake that's gonna come play me later."

"Good luck," I say, then jog back over to the group of older guys. I stop and look around at the lack of available trees to tie my hammock to. "So," I say, but Ducky interrupts.

"Just hang yours underneath mine."

Ducky's hammock hangs about four feet off the ground, so I tie both ends of the sheet about halfway down the same tree. That done, I crawl into my hammock. It's so low my butt grazes the ground, but I don't care. I'm getting to hang out with Ducky and his friends. Looking up, I try not to think about Ducky's hammock falling. I'd literally be crushed and die.

Ducky's form casts shade across me, so I dangle my leg outside the hammock. It touches the ground, and I use it to rock myself back and forth so the early-afternoon sun warms my skin.

I can't believe how lucky I am. I'm about to say something to try and start a conversation when Tyler 2 snores. It sounds like a dog's chew toy. I can't help but grin, nestle into the bedsheet-hammock, and drift off too.

"What is this?" Someone yells.

I blink my eyes and look around. Sergeant Johnson is standing a few feet away, staring at me red-faced with his hands on his hips.

Tyler 2 says, "What's your prob, guy?"

Sergeant Johnson ignores him and points his nub finger at me. "This poor excuse for a hammock breaks at least a dozen Camp Winnebago violations."

He stomps toward me and starts untying the hammock with me still in it. I jump up to avoid the two-foot drop when he gets it untied. I feel my face getting red, and words start spilling out of my mouth. I'm furious.

"What the hell are you doing? Piss off! What's your problem?" I yell.

Sergeant Johnson stiffens and gets in my face. "This is dangerous. Why is it you're constantly doing something wrong? It doesn't matter what troop they put you in, you'll always be a rotten Ranger; you're a disgrace."

Ducky's feet hit the ground and he puts himself between Sergeant Johnson and me, "Excuse me, *Troop Leader*, this isn't your side of the campsite. Get out of here and go back to your own site. I'm not afraid to get Camp-A-Cop involved. This is our side, and you have no right to be here."

Sergeant Johnson looks like he's about to explode on Ducky when a voice yells from my Adirondack.

"Hey! Johnson! Your childhood is calling, and it wants its behavior back!"

Sergeant Johnson turns and looks at Uncle Ruckus standing there with a huge smile plastered across his face. If a stare could kill, Uncle Ruckus would have been dead about twenty times over from the look the Sergeant gave him. After a moment, he turned to look at Ducky, then at me.

"We aren't done. Shit in our shower again, and you'll regret it," Sergeant Johnson says, then storms off to his own campsite.

"Kinda wish I was the one who shit in their shower now," Ducky says.

My heart is pounding. It wasn't Ducky, then. Time to get off my ass and catch the Wafflestomper.

* * *

TEN YEARS AGO...
JULY 4TH, 2005. 10:31 PM.

Boom.

Boom.

Boom.

Being a Sergeant in the Army wasn't easy. It meant you had to get out of bed and go deal with dumbassery whenever it arose. Sergeant Johnson rolled out of bed, put on a pair of camo cargo pants, and laced up his boots.

Boom.

Crackle.

Boom.

Fizz.

Sergeant Johnson stomped out of his tent. He was losing sleep because of these idiots, and someone was going to pay. The fireworks got louder the closer he got, so it wasn't hard to track down the hooligans.

"Heyyy, Sarge!" One of the men held up a bottle of liquor.

"I want every one of you slobs back in your bunks, effective immediately!" Sergeant Johnson barked.

"Aww, come on. Live a little," another man said.

Sergeant Johnson stormed over to him, jammed a finger into his chest, and yelled, "What did I say?" No answer. "What did I say?" Spittle flew out of Sergeant Johnson's mouth and speckled the man's face.

Sssss.

The sound of a fuse being lit came from right behind Sergeant Johnson. He whirled around just in time to see a man straighten and back away from the firework on the ground. Sergeant Johnson threw his hands up to cover his face and stepped back as the firework went off.

13

A RANGER IS SPICY

"Thanks for standing up to Sergeant Johnson for me," I say.

The lunch line winds around the cafeteria, but since none of us went to class, Ducky, Tyler 2 Electric Boogaloo, iBall, Uncle Ruckus, and I are among the first in line.

Ducky gives a half-laugh. "No problem."

"And thanks for letting me use your hammock afterward, too."

"Not a problem. Figured I'm less likely to get in trouble. No one cares what you do when you're older," Ducky says.

I spot Mr. B, Mr. McNitt, and the rest of our troop making their way across the parade field and wave. They get in line behind us, and Mr. B pulls me aside.

"How goes the investigation?"

"Okay," I say. "I don't have any great leads, but I've ruled out a bunch of suspects."

"Where's your sidekick? And Turbo Cakes?" Mr. B asks, looking around.

"Shovel was having... stomach problems," I say.

Mr. B nods, and thankfully doesn't press the subject. "Anything else to report?"

I hesitate. "Yeah. Sergeant Johnson has it out for me. He thinks I'm the Wafflestomper."

Mr. B rests a hand on my shoulder. "Don't worry, I know you aren't. We'll get to the bottom of this." He laughs. "No pun intended. Just focus on the prize. The high-adventure camp later this summer and winning the Golden Plunger for keeps. Good behavior is probably shot at this point, but we still have a chance with the Culling and finding the flag."

As if on cue, we spot Troop 100 making their way across the parade field. They're all whooping and high-fiving—and eating chocolate bars. I don't even feel guilty. Serves them right.

The camp staff opens the cafeteria doors and Uncle Ruckus laughs harder than I've ever heard. The menu in front of the cafeteria line says "Spicy Bean Burrito and Chili today!" It's perfect. I laugh too. It's not going to be a good day for Troop 100.

We get our food and sit down at the table.

"Watch my food for a minute, will you?" Mr. B asks as he goes to talk to another troop's leader.

Out of the corner of my eye, I spot Shovel sauntering over to our table with a PBJ and a glass of water. I'm not sure if he's taking it slow because of the chocolate's effects, or if he's trying not to drop his cup.

"You doing okay, bud?" I ask him.

"Yeah, it's been a bad day. First, all my stomach problems, then listening to Turbo Cakes overthink every single interaction with Dr. Cassandra the whole day. It was a nightmare."

I'm about to reply when I notice Peters, Woody, and Richardson making their way toward us. Woody brushes past me, and I walk over to Peters and Richardson.

"What do you want?" I ask.

"Oh, didn't you hear? We were awarded chocolate by the administrators. They left it right in our campsite for us. Doesn't look like you're going to be winning that Golden Plunger after all, does it, Do-Over?" Peters sneers.

I'm trying to think of a snarky reply, but Peters continues, "Penny for your thoughts, Do-Over? Oh, but it seems I don't have a penny on me. And you don't have any thoughts to spare. Enjoy lunch."

Peters and Richardson turn to walk away, and Woody bumps me as he walks past me. The whole interaction feels weird.

I sit back down and do just what Peters suggested—enjoy my lunch. Shovel and I quietly discuss potential suspects and establish a list of Rangers to investigate during the rest of the day. Mr. B comes back and helps us concentrate our efforts on the most likely culprits.

"That's enough work for now, boys. I gotta eat," Mr. B says before picking up his chili bowl with two hands and gulping it down. After two huge mouthfuls, he bursts into a fit of coughing.

"Yeesh, take it easy there, Mr. B," I say.

He chugs some water, then laughs. "That's why you should always be sure to chew your food."

Mr. McNitt sits down in front of Shovel and me. "Hey, son, feeling better?" He keeps talking before Shovel has a chance to answer. "Great. So, I went and looked for the Chocolate Lincoln bush. Couldn't find it."

I nod slowly. Just as I expected.

We finish up our meal without further incident, and everyone heads off to their merit patch classes. Everyone but Shovel and me.

"Ready, partner?" I ask.

Shovel grins, and we set off to interrogate our first suspect.

* * *

EARLIER THAT DAY...

TUESDAY, JUNE 2ND, 2015. 6:38 AM.

Momma Hackett's head drooped, cheeks resting against her palms. She looked at Camp-A-Cop. "We have a duty to these boys. It hasn't even been twenty-four hours, and we've failed them."

"We haven't failed them," Camp-A-Cop said.

"Yeah?" Momma Hackett's voice rose. "In a matter of hours, we had one kid tumble down Cardiac Hill, and another one drowned. It's a miracle they were able to resuscitate the Do-Over kid at all. Dr. Cassandra had to get out the paddles to start his heart back. Then, after all that, I'm supposed to deal with a band of devil worshippers?!"

Camp-A-Cop nodded. "Troop 99 is a mess this year."

Momma Hackett scoffed. "When Leslie said he could take over that troop after his father passed, I wanted to give him the benefit of the doubt. I'm not so sure he can handle it anymore. It might be time to disband Troop 99. They're single-handedly going to destroy Camp Winnebago. And now this Wafflestomping business? *That* is a mess. When do the sanitation guys get here?"

"They should be here by nine," Camp-A-Cop replied, maintaining his relaxed composure.

"So, until nine rolls around, we're just going to let that filth stay smeared across our new facilities? This is ridiculous. The whole point of that speech at orientation was to deter this from happening. The Wafflestomper hasn't struck in years. Why is he back now?"

Camp-A-Cop nodded. "In Troop 99's new campsite, no less."

"Something is going on," Momma Hackett said. "Find out more about the Ranger who fell down the hill. Keep the lid on that Do-Over boy almost dying in our Infirmary. But first and foremost, find the Wafflestomper. We need to stop this thing before we have more copycats on our hands."

"Yes, ma'am," Camp-A-Cop said, rising from the leather chair.

"And," Momma Hackett said, pointing one wrinkly finger out the window, "tell Johnson to lay off that kid unless he has some proof. The less anyone is poking around Do-Over's file, the less chance of this drowning fiasco resurfacing. We can't let that get out. To parents, to the media, and especially not the internet. Luckily his parents aren't the involved type, so they shouldn't ask any questions. If Do-Over doesn't stay out of the way, he and all the other Rangers can kiss Troop 99 goodbye."

14

A RANGER IS SUSPECT

"We spent the whole day talking to half the camp, and we're no closer to figuring out who the Wafflestomper is." I sink my face into my pillow, and my voice comes out muffled. "It's hopeless."

Our Adirondack is lit by an electric lantern hanging in the middle of the three-walled cabin. The bright LED light casts shadows dancing across the walls as it sways back and forth on a string.

Shovel clambers up into his own bunk. "Actually, if you think about it, we learned a lot today. I didn't know other people had their initials in their underwear until we looked through Peters's stuff."

"We need stuff that will keep Sergeant Johnson from getting me thrown out of camp," I say.

"But we crossed a lot of names off the list of people it could have been."

"Right, but how does that help us if we have no suspects left?"

The tarp in the front of the Adirondack is thrown wide to reveal Uncle

Ruckus, an LED lantern illuminating his broad grin. Frankly, it's terrifying.

"Guys," he says out of breath. "It's happening."

I sit up, throw my feet over the side of the bunk, hop to the floor, and run out of the Adirondack. Shovel isn't far behind. The gravel trail leading to the bathroom hurts my bare feet, but I don't care. This is about to be glorious.

We're just in time to see various Rangers from Troop 100 making a mad dash to the bathrooms. Most of them are doing a butt clench waddle. The few runners are simultaneously undoing their pants in a last-ditch effort to save time before they can't hold it back any longer.

Uncle Ruckus is practically hyperventilating, he's laughing so hard.

I stare at the bathroom in horror, unsure whether to join in or worry. Shovel's face is what makes me lose it. He's doing a sort of half-giggle, half-stare since the scene was probably hitting a little too close to home for him. The look on his face is priceless.

We keep our distance as the last few Troop 100 Rangers trickle into the bathroom. I can't imagine the scents and sounds coming from inside the bathroom. One more straggler runs in, and a second later a blood-curdling scream echoes from the building. We all freeze, unsure of what to do.

"Do you think someone got hurt?" Shovel asks.

Ducky sprints past me toward the scream and goes straight into the bathroom. A moment passes. Then another one. Then Ducky comes back out of the bathroom holding his nose. I don't know if the tears streaming down his face are from laughing or from the smell.

"What?" I ask, "What is it?"

Ducky wheezes out, "There's no toilet paper left! They have nothing to clean up with!"

Tears fill my eyes, but I can't stop—I've got the giggles bad.

Uncle Ruckus falls to his knees listening to the sounds echoing from the bathroom. "It's beautiful. Beautiful. More beautiful than I ever could have hoped."

I put a hand on Uncle Ruckus's shoulder. My stomach hurts so bad, I'm physically unable to laugh any more. "What about the toilet paper?" I ask.

"It doesn't seem right to sell it to them anymore, does it?" Uncle Ruckus asks.

"I don't think so either. They're suffering enough as it is. Do the right thing, man." I turn and walk back to our Adirondack, the echoes fading into the distance. So much for Momma Hackett's brand-new bathrooms...

To his credit, Uncle Ruckus came a few minutes later to return the toilet paper, but not the Golden Bum. He just gave back the cheap stuff. Soon we were all lying in our bunks.

"This is the worst day of my life," Uncle Ruckus says, completely devoid of emotion.

I prop myself up on my elbow. "Why?"

"That was the funny peak. That was it. Nothing can possibly be that funny ever again in my whole life. It's all downhill from here."

At that moment, Turbo slides the tarp open and says, "Hey, guys. What'd I miss?"

We fill him in on the night's events.

"That's hilarious!" he says. "I was helping Dr. Cassandra."

"I'm sorry," I say, "but how were *you* helping a medical doctor do her job?"

Turbo shrugs and plops down onto his bunk. "Kept her company, I guess."

"Boys!" Mr. B's muffled voice comes from the other side of the tarp. "It's that time again. Light's out."

"Hey, Mr. B?" Treb's voice sounds shaky. "I can't sleep in here. I'm afraid of spiders. Also, last night you said to be like froyo, but that's ice cream. His name is Frodo. Frodo almost died because of the spiders."

Mr. B sighs. "Don't be like Frodo then, be like the guy with the pan. The gardener. There are no spiders in there. Go to sleep. And boys? I'm on bathroom guard duty tonight. I borrowed a book from Holly to help me stay awake. Don't worry, we'll catch this Wafflestomper."

"Samwise the Brave," Treb whispers.

A soft glow emanates from Shovel's sleeping bag. *Tap tap tap tap tap.* I could be crazy, but I think I hear puppies yipping too. Turbo gives me an "I don't know" shrug before flipping over to face the wall. After that, I drift into a blissful sleep.

"Do-Over. Psst. Hey. Do-Over."

I'm awake again, but the rest of my body hasn't told my eyes yet. "What?" I groan.

"Listen, man," Uncle Ruckus says. "I gotta poop."

I crack my eyes open. "What the hell, dude? You wake me up because you have to poop? What time is it? Go back to sleep."

"It's only like two am. I haven't gone to sleep yet," Uncle Ruckus says. "I haven't pooped since I got here, and I gotta go now."

"Why can't you go by yourself?" I ask. *Jeez, I'm never going to get back to sleep.*

"I have... performance anxiety," he says.

"And having me there is going to help speed things along?"

"No, it's just," he takes a breath. "Mr. B is out there. I can't poop with him there. Plus, if he sees me, he'll instantly think *I'm* the Wafflestomper. Everyone wants to pin it on me anyway."

"Gee," I say. "I wonder why. It's not like you'd ever do anything wrong. You never scared little kids with a Devil rock. You never gave another troop laxative chocolate."

141

"For the record," Uncle Ruckus says, "it was technically Mr. McNitt who gave them the chocolate laxative. Please, dude? I have to go. I'm desperate. I'm just gonna go off into the woods and drop a deuce there, but I need you to be my buddy."

I sit up. "Amazing. You have to poop, and now suddenly the buddy system is important to you." No point in trying to go to sleep anymore, so I climb down from my bunk and slip my shoes on. I hate myself for being a good friend.

Uncle Ruckus takes the lead, and I stay right behind him until he comes to a stop.

"Wait, where are we?" I ask.

"I don't know," he replies. "I can't see anything."

"Me neither, probably because it's the middle of the night, we're in the forest, and the moon isn't out. It's almost like nature is telling us we should be asleep. Turn on your flashlight, will you?"

"I didn't bring a flashlight."

"What do you mean you didn't bring a flashlight?" I hiss.

"This is a stealth operation," Uncle Ruckus says innocently.

Great. I'm stuck in the woods with Uncle Ruckus of all people, and I have no idea how to find my way back to my not-so-cozy bunk. I give him a nudge. "Just do your business so we can get out of here."

"Okay! Okay," he says. The leaves crinkle as he moves his feet in the darkness, and then he stops moving. "Do-Over?"

"What?"

"Will you hum?"

I can't believe I'm hearing this.

"You want me to *what*?" I shout-whisper at him.

"Just hum or sing or something," he says defensively. "I told you, I can't crap with other people listening, so I need to know you can't hear me unloose the caboose."

"Fine! I'll hum something." I think for a second, then hum to the tune of *I've Been Working on the Railroad*.

Uncle Ruckus busts up laughing.

I shush him. "Just trying to keep with the 'caboose' theme," I say.

"Hey!" a voice calls. "Who's over there?"

Camp-A-Cop holds a lantern high in the air.

"Oh, shit, dude. We gotta go," I say and tiptoe-run back the way we came.

"Wait! Wait!" Uncle Ruckus calls. "I'm trying to get my pants up!"

"Stop!" Camp-A-Cop commands.

We don't listen. Instead, we sprint through our campsite in the direction of the bathroom's light. Thankfully, Mr. B is asleep in his lawn chair with a copy of *The Chamber of Secrets* splayed open on his lap. We dash past him then tuck and roll into the nearby stretch of trees.

Camp-A-Cop stops in front of the bathroom. "Mr. Bellflower. Mr. Bellflower."

Mr. B jerks awake in confusion.

"The Wafflestomper just ran through here," Camp-A-Cop says.

Mr. B looks startled. "No, that's impossible."

"Fell asleep on the job, Bellflower," Camp-A-Cop says. "Now follow me. Let's see if we can catch this sicko."

With that, they disappear into the night. We stay still until we can't see the glow of Camp-A-Cop's lantern anymore.

"Well," I say. "At least now we know: If you drop a log in the middle of the woods, it does make a sound."

"I didn't go," Uncle Ruckus whispers.

I punch him in the arm. "What were you fooling around for?" I ask.

"I can't squeeze one out that fast! Hey." He points. "The bathroom is open. Let's just go in there where I can have some privacy. I'll poop, then we can both get back to bed."

"Okay, deal," I sigh and nod.

We creep over to our wing of the bathroom and Uncle Ruckus ducks into a stall. I take a breath; it freakin' reeks. That doesn't make sense. None of the Troop 100 guys would go into our side with Mr. B on duty. I stalk around from stall to stall, just trying to do humanity a service by flushing for those who refuse to. A feeling sinks into the pit of my stomach as I come to the end of the row of stalls and stare at the shower curtain. I extend a shaky hand, pull back the curtain, and the smell hits me like a wave.

Written across the wall in human excrement reads *The Wafflestomper has returned. Enemies of The Hundred... hunted.* Someone has smooshed their feces into the shower drain. *Huh. It does look like a waffle.*

I back up and say, "Ruckus, we need to get out of here."

"Dude," Uncle Ruckus says. "Don't even start. I'm doing my best. I've been prairie-dogging this whole time, and if I could get two seconds of peace and quiet I could—"

"The Wafflestomper has been here," I hiss at him. "If we get caught in here, they'll think it was *us* who did it. Just, I don't know, pinch off whatever you got and let's get out of here."

"Did you hear that?" Camp-A-Cop's voice drifts from outside. "Sounds like there's someone inside. Could be the Wafflestomper."

"No, you know, I really don't think—" Mr. B says as they both turn the corner into the bathroom.

"I know how bad this looks," I say standing in front of the open shower with the Wafflestomper's message written behind me.

Camp-A-Cop bolts toward me, and Mr. B follows his lead. They're almost on me when a bathroom stall door flies open, and Camp-A-Cop runs into it face first. He hits the door, then hits the ground with Mr. B falling on top of him in a heap.

"Go!" Uncle Ruckus yells, pants still around his ankles as he sits on the toilet.

I take a running jump over the groaning adults and wait outside the bathroom for Uncle Ruckus. As soon as he steps out, I grab him by the sleeve and we take off running toward our Adirondacks.

"We gotta go," I say, stopping outside our Adirondack.

"Woah, bro. Speak for yourself. They only saw you, not me. I can't leave, I have all this Golden Bum to sell. I got a money-making operation to run here, and I can't afford to take a loss on it," Uncle Ruckus says.

I grab him by the collar and snarl, "I'm in this mess because of you. Because you couldn't go take a crap by yourself. Now, you have to come with me so we can fix this."

"Where are you going?" Shovel asks, rubbing his eyes and stepping out of the Adirondack.

"They caught me in the bathroom after the Wafflestomper struck. They think I did it," I say.

"Well, did you?" Shovel asks. "Seems pretty convenient they happened to find you right after the Wafflestomper struck." He crosses his arms.

"Dude," I say, "do you really think I would do it?"

Shovel stares at me for a long moment, then says, "Nah, you're not that weird." He points at Ruckus. "Him on the other hand... You said it yourself, Do-Over: he's an outlier."

"It wasn't him either," I say. "But listen, they think it was me, so I gotta get out of here. I don't know where I'm gonna go yet, but—"

"I'm coming with you," Shovel says, then ducks into the Adirondack.

I follow and whisper, "What are you doing?"

"Packing," he says and starts shoving stuff into a bag.

"Maybe we're overreacting," Uncle Ruckus whispers. "Maybe they didn't even recognize you."

"You think our own troop leader didn't recognize the only guy in his troop with long red hair?" I ask. "Okay."

"Well, you two can't just go running off into the middle of the night," Turbo Cakes says.

Great, everyone is in on this now. I look over at Turbo rolling out of bed. Thankfully, Treb is still fast asleep.

"I have a better idea," Turbo Cakes says.

* * *

TWO DAYS AGO…

SUNDAY, MAY 31ST, 2015. 8:26 PM.

"Oh, Ducky? Can we please play one more time? Before you go?"

"Goose," Ducky said, shaking his head with a smile. "You gotta know, Duck Duck Goose is no fun to play with two people. I promise, once I get back from camp, I'll bring iBall and Tyler 2 over, and we'll play a few rounds. Deal?"

"No deal!" Goose said. "I'm your big brother. I get to tell you when we play." Goose thought for a moment. "Okay. How about... When you get back, you bring friends over. Then we can play Duck Duck Goose for a few hours?" Goose's lips stretched into a toothy smile.

Ducky clipped his travel-size hammock to his backpack with a carabiner. "Sounds good, Goose."

"Goose!" Goose slapped Ducky on the top of the head and ran out of the room.

Ducky kept packing, and Goose crept into the room after a few seconds.

"Ducky?" Goose asked, tip-toeing into the room. "Ducky?"

Without warning, Ducky spun on his heels and lunged for Goose. Goose let out a squeal, but he couldn't get away fast enough. Ducky tagged him.

"You still fallin' for that one, Goose?" Ducky asked with a smirk.

"No! I'm not! I just forgot about that trick. That's all," Goose said resolutely as he plopped down on Ducky's bed.

"Boys?" Mom peeked into the room. "Everything all right?"

"Yes, yes," Goose said with a sigh. "I just got tagged, that's all."

"Sweet of you to let your little baby brother tag you, Goose," Mom said with a wink.

Goose beamed and turned to Ducky. "Hey, Duck. Since I let you tag me, maybe we could watch one more movie before you go to camp tomorrow?"

Ducky turned to his older brother. "You always ask when mom's around. Why's that?"

Mom gave Ducky a knowing grin.

"Yeah," Ducky said. "I'll watch one more movie with you, buddy. One more. Then I have to pack."

"Yes!" Goose exclaimed and bounded out of the room. "I will let you pick one, but only if you pick one I want to watch too!" His voice echoed from down the hall.

"Anything but *Iron Man*! We've seen that one too many times!" Ducky called after him.

"Thank you," Mom mouthed at Ducky.

"Oh, no," he said with a grin. "You don't get out of this. I will not be watching *Spider-Man 3* with Goose solo." Ducky threw an arm around his mom. "We're gonna watch as a big, happy family."

"All right, fine." Mom got on her tiptoes and kissed him on the cheek. "You're so good with him. You should try doing that peer tutoring thing at your school."

"I dunno, ma," Ducky said. "It's one thing when it's Goose flingin' boogers at me, because I can fling mine right back. They probably wouldn't like me treatin' other kids like that. At school, they treat them all like they're fragile and it pisses me off. They only put them in front of people for social media content and fundraisers."

"Regardless," Mom said, "you should think about it. You could do a lot of good for kids like Goose. And Duck? Thank you for being such a good little brother."

"I picked *Iron Man*!" came Goose's voice from downstairs.

Ducky and Mom groaned.

15

A RANGER IS FRAMED

Sleeping on top of the Adirondack wasn't as bad as I thought it would be. Turbo pointed out it was the safest place for me, last place they'd ever look, so we threw my sleeping pad, pillow, and blanket up. Then the guys gave me a boost. I thought I'd barely sleep, given that I could roll off and die, but I don't think I woke up once. I am pretty sore, though. Hopefully this counts for my Wilderness Survival Patch.

"We're having a meeting. Be out here in five minutes," is all Mr. B says before walking over to the Adirondack he and Mr. McNitt share.

I flip over on my stomach and scooch my way up the Adirondack roof so I can peek over the top and watch the procession. It's weird watching everyone rush around below me like that. I wonder if this is how God feels; up there in heaven watching everything unfold in front of him. He probably feels awkward. After all, just like me, He knows if He goes down to set the record straight, people are gonna be pissed. But if He doesn't go down, people are gonna be pissed. So, all you can do is watch the people scramble around and try to at least get some entertainment out of the whole thing.

"Guys," Mr. B says once everyone is gathered, "where's Do-Over?"

Nobody says a word.

Mr. B turns to Shovel. "Where's Do-Over?"

Shovel looks terrified. And who wouldn't be? Mr. B's mustache did not come to play today—there's not a hair out of place.

Come on, Shovel. Don't break.

And he doesn't, much to my surprise.

Troop 100 starts marching into the campsite, and Mr. McNitt turns to Shovel. "At least tell us if he's safe?"

Shovel gives one swift nod and cuts himself off.

"Good," Mr. B says.

Troop 100 lines up, every Ranger dressed in stained Class A uniforms. They all look pale. I smirk, their nights were a million times worse than mine. Sergeant Johnson brings up the end of the line with a smug look on his face. Camp-A-Cop is there, too.

Before Troop 100 comes to a stop, Sergeant Johnson bursts out laughing. "McMasturbator? Is that you?"

Mr. McNitt turns a dark shade of red. "You better have some strong evidence to be throwing around accusations about Troop 99."

Sergeant Johnson sobers. "Oh, I do. We have proof Do-Over is the one who's been Wafflestomping."

He reaches into his pocket and pulls out a Ziploc plastic baggie and holds it out. Mr. B steps forward to take it. I crane and squint my eyes, but for the life of me, I can't see what's in the bag.

"I don't understand," Mr. B says after staring at the bag a moment.

"Peters," Sergeant Johnson barks.

Peters steps forward, eyes unwavering.

Sergeant Johnson smiles. "Please tell the Troop 99 Leaders what transpired between Do-Over, yourself, and your friends the other night. And be assured, Bellflower, I've already punished my boys for their role in this."

Peters looks at Mr. B. "Do-Over came into our bathroom, sir. He threatened us and tossed me a wheat penny. You might remember because you stopped the confrontation, sir."

Mr. B nods and smooths his already perfectly-groomed mustache.

"Well, sir, last night at dinner, I saw Do-Over. I wanted to return the wheat penny he found, sir. I accidentally dropped it, and it fell into his chili at dinner. I was too embarrassed to tell him. Worried for his safety, I told the Sergeant after dinner, but he said Do-Over would be fine; that he would pass the penny in his feces, sir."

I replay the event in my head. I remember Woody brushing past me. But there's no way I wouldn't have noticed a penny in my food. Not to mention, I haven't shit since then.

Peters points at the baggie Mr. B is holding. "That's the same wheat penny Do-Over found on the bathroom floor, sir. The same one I dropped. Dated 1949. They found it in the Wafflestomper's... leavings. Sir."

Mr. B gags and drops the baggie.

My mind is racing a million miles a minute. I *know* I didn't crap in that bathroom. But if what he's saying is true... They're either lying or they put the penny in the wrong bowl of chili. The Wafflestomper's chili.

Mr. B stares at the penny. "And you say Do-Over originally found that penny on the bathroom floor?" He looks like he's going to blow chunks. I didn't realize how empathetic Mr. B was—he seems pretty upset they are trying to pin this on me. He straightens. "Well, how do we know you didn't plant that penny there to try and frame Do-Over?"

I fist pump from on top of the Adirondack. Get 'em, Mr. B. Ask the big questions.

"Because," Camp-A-Cop says dejectedly, "I was present when the sanitation crew pulled the penny from the Wafflestomper's leavings. Not only that, but given Troop 100's... situation last night, there's no way anyone in that troop produced anything solid. If you take my meaning."

Mr. B turns a shade paler, and Mr. McNitt steps next to him.

"So, what?" Mr. McNitt throws his hands up. "We're supposed to believe our Ranger did this because of a penny that you claim was dropped into his chili? No way this holds up with the Ranger Council or Administration." He looks at Camp-A-Cop.

"Unfortunately," Camp-A-Cop says, "it does hold up with Administration. Sergeant Johnson made a call to the Infirmary yesterday about what to do if a Ranger swallows a penny. Last night, I caught Do-Over leaving the scene of the crime. Then, I stayed in the bathroom until the sanitation crew came. We found the penny, and before it was common knowledge, Sergeant Johnson inquired about whether or not one was found. The timeline all checks out, and there's no way someone could have planted it. Whoever swallowed that penny is the Wafflestomper, and right now all signs point to Do-Over."

Mr. B takes a step backward. "I need to go lie down."

Mr. McNitt pats him on the back. "Go lay down, Leslie. I can handle this."

Camp-A-Cop says, "You have four hours to give us Do-Over. After that, we'll have to start getting parents involved. Depending on how that goes, we'll take action with the proper authorities."

A memory of Mr. B choking on his chili blurs through my head. What if Woody put the penny in the wrong chili? *Those prunes will make you poop like a goose,* he'd said.

Mr. B wouldn't frame me... Would he? He had to have a good reason. He likes me, even drives me to Ranger meetings every week. He wouldn't do this. Maybe I'm wrong. I squint at Mr. B's face, and he looks disgusted. Like he just found out he ate a bathroom floor penny. Like he betrayed one of his own Adventure Rangers and feels guilty about it.

I shrink down on the roof and curl up on my bedroll. *This is getting out of hand, fast. And they're gonna call my parents, too. I don't wanna go home. I hate home.* There's only one option to pass the time until everyone leaves. I close my eyes and drift off to sleep. The sun wakes me up an hour later. There's no one left in the campsite. They must have all gone to activities. Afraid of what the sun will do to my fragile, freckled skin, I start to come down from the roof, but stop when something a few feet away catches my eye.

I pick it up, and even though bits of leaf litter are stuck to the outside, it's got weight to it. It all comes flooding back. I remember what this is. It takes a minute to unwrap it, but once I'm done, I tuck Devil Rock into my pocket and look around. There's something else up here I hadn't noticed before: a solar panel. I shrug, then proceed to half-fall half-climb down from the Adirondack's roof.

My stomach yawls like a bobcat, convincing me to do a little gambling. I jog over to the Trading Post and saunter inside. I'm banking on Journey being out of the loop. When I step in the doorway, I give Journey the 'waddup' nod with my head. He does likewise.

"The usual?" he asks.

I nod and head over to peruse the snacks while he crafts me an icy masterpiece. It doesn't take long before I settle on a Slim Jim nearly two feet long, a box of Cheerios, and a protein bar.

Journey raises an eyebrow. "Miss breakfast this morning or something?"

I nod. "Something like that."

"Missed the flag clue again then, huh?" Journey asks.

"Sure did."

He pauses, as if preparing the greatest line in cinema history. Then says, "Seek not, great fortunes. Seek only where it all began."

"Wow," I hesitate. "That's really something. I'm sure somebody will find that super useful. It's so... detailed."

A few moments later, I drift out of the Trading Post with my loot. Although, I guess if you pay for it, it's not really loot. If I'm going to make it through the day, I'm gonna need every drop of my Lancellottie. I'm almost done with it—secluded in a stretch of trees near the Post—when I spot Turbo Cakes bobbing down Cardiac Hill. I whistle loudly to get his attention and wave him over to my hiding place.

"You know," he says, "if you wanted to get kicked out of camp, there's easier ways than crapping in the shower."

I'm about to give him a light punch on the arm, but I stop. I just don't have it in me. I fill Turbo in on my Mr. B theory. "It doesn't add up. Why would Mr. B do this to me?" I ask, picking at the bark on a nearby tree.

Turbo slowly shakes his head. His long chin hair bounces, and its curl reminds me of a beckoning, skeletal finger.

"You gotta shave that thing," I say.

He tugs the length of the hair. "Dr. Cassandra said it's cute."

"No, she didn't," I say.

Turbo makes a face. "Okay, no, she didn't. She said it's a marvel of nature. But I'm not really sure if that's a compliment or not." He pauses. "I don't know why Mr. B framed you for the Wafflestomping."

"Did you see his face?" I dig a piece of bark out from under my fingernails. "He looked horrified when he realized he ate that nasty penny."

Turbo laughs. "Yeah, serves him right. I guess."

The summer breeze floats between the trees. It's usually my favorite part about summer; the paradoxical feeling of the cool wind blowing around under the sun's heat. But I can't appreciate it right now. It tickles my skin and makes me itch all over.

"I just *don't get it*. He didn't have to let me into this troop last year if he didn't want to. He could have sent me home when I failed my swim test. He could have gotten rid of me after the whole Devil Rock thing. Why is he trying to humiliate me? Does he think I'm a bad kid?" I rip a chunk of bark off the tree and throw it over my shoulder. "Oh, and speaking of Devil Rock." I dig it out of my pocket to show him.

"Why in the name of St. George did you bring that back down?" Turbo asks.

"How could I just leave it there? It's what started this whole mess." I hold the rock up to the light.

"El Diablo!" a voice yells.

We whip around to see the same sixth-grader Uncle Ruckus has been tormenting. Half his troop is with him.

"This the guy?" One of the older boys asks walking toward me, hands clenching into fists.

I shift my feet into a boxing stance, ready for a fight. Turbo Cakes jumps between us.

"Woah!" he says. "Can't you see this is a guy *possessed* by the same entity that was tormenting you before? You can't hurt him, he's a victim!"

"Doesn't look like a victim. Don't worry, I'll beat the devil out of your friend here," the older Ranger says.

Turbo stomps down on my foot. Pain erupts from the limb and I let out an incoherent yell. I shove Turbo. He staggers over to the older Ranger.

"See?" Turbo says, pointing. "He doesn't even recognize his own friends anymore. But we can't hurt him, he's innocent. You!" He points at the older Ranger. "Take your troop and go get your Leader or a priest or something. Don't just stand there! Go!"

Nobody moves.

Shovel's voice plays in my head: *Use jokes to decaf the situation.*

Crap. I'll give it a shot. Time to play my part.

I clap once. I clap twice. Then I start cackling as I slip off my shoes. My head lolls to the side, and I put my shoes on my hands. Back in my boxing stance, I say in my best demonic voice, "Square up, mortal!" Drool leaks out of my mouth as I stomp forward.

Turbo runs at me, tackling me to the ground. "Go! Get out of here! Save yourself!"

Shoes on my hands, I swipe at Turbo and smack him on the side of the head while my other swings wildly. We keep up the façade for another few seconds, and when I peek, the troop is gone. Turbo gets off me, and I put my shoes back on. My hands reek.

"Great," I say while Turbo dusts off my back. "If they didn't have enough reasons to kick me out of camp, now I'm in the same boat as Uncle Ruckus. I should have left it up on the roof," I say, picking Devil Rock back up off the ground.

"I don't know," Turbo says. "Maybe we can use this to our advantage. I think I have a plan."

The trek over to the Infirmary takes longer than it should have since we went the long way around to avoid being seen.

"Boys!" Holly says, rising from her chair as we step inside. She comes around her desk and hugs us both. "Is Mr. B done with my book? How's camp going? Not here for anything serious, I hope?" Then she steps back to examine both of us.

"No, ma'am," Turbo says. "My friend here isn't feeling so well. I brought him to see Dr. Cassandra."

Holly grins. "You are a true Adventure Ranger, Turbo Cakes. Let me see if she's busy. Just take a seat for me."

"Remind me again what the plan is..." I mumble.

"Just trust me," is all I can get him to say.

Holly comes back a moment later. "She's ready, you boys can follow me on back."

"Look sad and hold your stomach," Turbo whispers.

It isn't hard. The long white hallway with its 'too-clean smell' makes my stomach do somersaults. Holly takes my weight, blood pressure, and sets us up in the room. Maybe it's just the stress, but out of nowhere I have to pee like a racehorse.

"Where's the bathroom?"

Turbo's eyes are glued to the *Men's Health* magazine he's reading. "Take a left out the door, it's on your right."

There's a lot of unspoken rules about the men's restroom. If there's three urinals open, you can't pick the middle one. If you pick the middle one, and another guy comes in, then he is forced to pick one of the ones right next to you. That's weird, and it'll get you marked as an outlier every time. Needless to say, I pick the urinal furthest on the right.

Looks like I missed a little bit of dirt when I gave myself that shower with the hose the other day, so I try to wipe it off my goods. But it doesn't come off. I try again with more fervor. I gotta go really bad, but I don't wanna pee with a dirty D. The dirt doesn't come off.

Squinting my eyes, my heart skips a beat when I realize what it is. Right there, attached to the end of my meat stick, is a bulbous tick full of blood.

Without giving the order, pee starts steadily streaming into the urinal and I try not to look at the tick. Oh. My. God. Maybe our interpretation was wrong. Maybe it's not Shovel's—maybe it's *my* dick that falls off. They might have to amputate or something. Can they even do dick transplants?

My dick falling off could be the best-case scenario. Ticks carry disease and who knows what else. My parents got sick from ticks. I don't want to be tired all the time like them. I don't wanna get sick. My head feels woozy. Seconds might be crucial, so I finish my business and bolt back down the hall.

Turbo looks like he's having the time of his life talking to Dr. Cassandra.

"Hey, Do-Over," he says. "This is Dr.—"

"Thank you, Mr. Cakes," Dr. Cassandra says, smiling. She extends a hand. "Hi, Do-Over. I'm Dr. Cassandra, nice to meet you."

"Hi, Doc, nice to meet you," I say. "Listen, I got a problem."

"I'm sorry to hear that, but glad to hear I'm still in business. Take a seat." She gestures to the patient's table.

I don't move. I just stand there, frozen.

"Do-Over?" Turbo asks. "What's wrong?"

I look down as my eyes start burning.

Dr. Cassandra jumps up and takes me by the arm. "Are you okay? What's wrong?" She guides me over to sit on the table.

I can't look at the doctor, so I focus on Turbo. He looks really concerned. "There's a tick. On my dick."

Turbo's brow furrows a moment, a look of shock and hurt flying across his face.

Dr. Cassandra pats me on the back. "It's going to be okay. I probably remove a hundred ticks every week during the summer. This is nothing compared to all the gastrointestinal issues we've been having all week. Turbo Cakes, do you mind stepping out of the room? This should only take a second."

Turbo rises slowly, as if in a trance. Like if he moves too fast, his whole body might crumble. His face doesn't change, he just moves to the door and steps into the hallway.

Then Dr. Cassandra says the most terrifying words a doctor can say, "You're going to feel a slight pinch."

* * *

A FEW MONTHS AGO...
APRIL 15TH, 2015. 11:30 AM.

The school cafeteria bustled as it always did at this time of day. Students hurried through the line, piling their trays high. When he was done, Mitch Frye stepped up to the lunch lady.

"Hi, Suzanne. How are you?"

"Fine, Mitch." Her wrinkled smile was warm, like fresh mashed potatoes. "So, I see you have two cheeseburgers, a side item of cornbread, a side item of macaroni and cheese, a side item of French fries, a pint of chocolate milk, one Powerade, and an ice cream sandwich. Hungry today, huh?" Suzanne-The-Lunch-Lady poked each menu item on her register's touch screen as she went.

"Yes, ma'am." Mitch smiled.

"All right, your total is going to be fourteen dollars and sixty-two cents. You don't have enough funds to pay for this, it's going to put you forty cents in the negative. I'll let you buy your lunch today, but you'll need to bring some money for lunch tomorrow." Suzanne-The-Lunch-Lady said.

Mitch dug a wrinkled check out of his pocket. "Actually, my parents wrote me this today, forgot to give it to you at breakfast. Should be enough to get me through another week or so." He flashed a grin and handed over the check.

"All right, one hundred. I'll get this deposited for you. Thanks, Mitch. Have a good rest of your day, baby," she said as Mitch swaggered toward the table of jocks.

Then Treb stepped up and displayed his tray to Suzanne-The-Lunch-Lady.

She narrowed her eyes. "Good afternoon. I see you have one pint of milk, one fruit or veggie side item, one side item, and two entrées." Suzanne-The-Lunch-Lady pointed an accusatory finger at the twin chicken nugget cartons. "Why do we go through this every day? You are allowed *one* entrée. You are on the state meal plan. That's the rules." She snatched one carton of chicken nuggets off Treb's tray and set it on top of her register. "There, now go eat your lunch."

Treb toddled out of the cafeteria without a word and sat on the floor against the wall in the lunchroom. He unzipped his backpack and pulled out his *Encyclopedia of Medieval Siege Weapons*. Fantasy was cool, but the *actual* medieval times? What could be better? With five minutes left in lunch, he finished the last bite of his meal. Eating slow was always the way Treb ate. It made the experience last longer.

Confident no one was watching, he pulled a carton of smooshed chicken nuggets out of his pocket. Treb nibbled on the goods he smuggled out of the cafeteria as he read about the effective distance of catapults.

When the lunch bell finally rang, Treb's head snapped up to seek out his target. All the other kids picked up their trays and shuffled to dispose of their garbage and stack the trays on a cart next to the trash can. Mitch Frye and the other football players got up and left their table without throwing their stuff away.

Treb closed the book and stowed it in his backpack. He ducked around students to make his way over to the jock table. He smiled. It looked like he'd have dinner tonight after all. An untouched apple, Mitch's hamburger still in its wrapper, a bag of chips, and one of the nice brands of juice boxes. It was organic. All of it went into Treb's backpack, and he hurried off to his next class period feeling a little less anxious than he did before lunch.

16

A RANGER IS JEALOUS

"Don't lie to me, Do-Over," Turbo says. "I know you put that tick there just so Dr. Cassandra would have to remove it."

We're standing by some trash cans behind the Infirmary so everyone going to and from breakfast won't see us.

"Dude. You think I put a disease-ridden insect on the most precious, valuable part of my entire body just to have the doctor *you* have a crush on pull it off with tweezers? What part of that makes *any* sense to you?"

Turbo paces back and forth. "And to think, I thought we were friends. The plan was to fake a stomachache or appendicitis or something so your parents quietly come pick you up. But then you betray me like this?"

"I. Did not. Put that tick. On my dick. How could you say that? You know how sick my parents are. You know how much ticks freak me out." I'm getting angry, but remind myself this is Turbo. He's my friend. I need to keep my temper in check.

"Well, then how did it get there?" Turbo asks with hands on his hips.

I throw my hands up and grit my teeth. "The same way bugs get any-where! It probably dropped out of a tree and got me while I was—oh I don't know—sleeping on top of the Adirondack because my troop leader betrayed me!"

"Be honest. Did you enjoy it?"

"Turbo," I say. "There is honestly no part of me that enjoyed that experience. I wish it never happened. And I'm pretty sure she wishes the same thing."

"All right," Turbo says after a minute. "But you're on Turprobation." He slings off his backpack and fishes around inside. "While you were off being a ticky little traitor..." He pauses and looks at me with a smile. "Kidding. I was off being productive." Turbo pulls something out of his pack and holds it out to me.

"A USB in a Ziploc baggie?" I hold it up to the light, "Seems like the kind of thing FBI agents swallow to protect information when they get caught. What's on it?"

"Well," Turbo says, kicking some gravel. "Let me start with where I got it. While the woman of my dreams was touching your dick, I snuck into Admin. I logged onto their computer and pulled the report about when you drowned in the lake."

"You mean when I *almost* drowned?"

"That's the thing," Turbo says. "It wasn't exactly... almost. By all defini-tions, you drowned. And... you died."

I feel my eyebrows shoot up. "Do what now?"

"But they brought you back!" He grins. "You got a do-over. You drowned, and they had to bring out the paddles and bring you back."

Flashbacks of being tasered by Michelle Obama rush to the forefront of my mind. *Huh. That makes a lot more sense now.*

Turbo continues, "They downplayed it a lot to the camp, said you just passed out from exhaustion. But the whole thing is in there, in that file."

My stomach turns over. *I died? My whole life almost ended at fifteen for a stupid Golden Plunger?*

"Do-Over?"

"I died... trying to get a clue." Rage fills me. It has to go somewhere. It has to get out. It erupts out of my leg as I topple over one of the trash cans with a kick. "I mean, what the hell?! That's why they didn't want to kick Shovel and me out of camp? They'd have to release my file?"

Turbo nods, "Yeah, but listen. I think it might have actually been a good thing."

"A good thing?" I snarl. "Me dying might have been a good thing? Just one less camper causing trouble. Just one less friend 'competing' for Dr. Cassandra's attention. Just one less son annoying his parents."

"Buddy, you know it isn't like that."

"Oh, yeah? Then what is it like?" I kick another trash can. Garbage spills out onto the gravel. "Damn it. Damn it damn it damn it." I stomp the leftover food and empty cardboard boxes into the ground.

"Do-Over," Turbo says.

I kick another garbage can and animal feed spills out onto the ground.

"We love you, we want you here."

I stop.

Turbo continues, "That's why we're all willing to do anything to keep you here. All I meant by it being a good thing was that I'm willing to bet you can use the files in this USB as your silver bullet to keep from getting kicked out this time too. Crapping in a shower our troop helped pay for has nothing on you almost dying in the lake on their watch. Take it to Momma Hackett and confess to the Wafflestomping. Then use it to bargain your way out of trouble. Threaten to sue or something."

"Yeah, but... I don't want to confess to something I didn't do," I say. Hot tears roll down my cheeks. "I'm not a bad kid. I'm tired of everybody looking at me like I am the bad kid because I got in a fight a year ago. I can't carry around the nickname 'Wafflestomper' for the rest of my life. No way, dude."

"Maybe. But not if you spin it right. You died and came back. If we talk that up a lot, maybe people will call you Do-Over the White or something," Turbo offers.

"Yeah, or zombie boy," I sniffle.

"Zombie boy is a terrible nickname; they wouldn't call you that. They'd call you Corpse Face," Turbo says.

"Gee, thanks."

"Well, if you wanna eat, you gotta come over here!" a familiar voice hollers.

Turbo freezes. "Someone's coming."

"Sounds like Moonpie," I whisper. "He might be on the lookout for me too; let's go through the trees."

We make it to cover as Moonpie and his buck round the corner of the Infirmary.

"Bigby, quit being so ornery. I'm gettin' you food." Moonpie walks over to the tipped over trash cans. "Are you kiddin' me?" He shakes his head and cleans up the garbage as the buck starts to nibble at the spilled feed. "Looks like you get extra food today. I'll be back, boy. Gonna get somebody to help me clean this up." He trudges toward the cafeteria.

"Wow," Turbo whispers. "That's so cool. He tamed a buck."

"Yeah. He's like if Snow White was a bum," I say. "I feel bad I tipped over the buck's food, though. Let's go back to the campsite. I'll confront Mr. B, and maybe find out what the deal is with him pinning the Wafflestomping on me. That sicko."

"Sounds good," Turbo says. "You've got the USB, right?"

I dig through my pockets. "I don't have it." Panic mounts inside me. "Do you have it?"

Turbo's voice rises to a squeal. "No dude, I gave it to you!"

"Well I don't have it, so where is it?"

A high-pitched whine cuts through the air followed by a loud huff and a snort.

"The hell is that?" Turbo whispers.

I peek through the trees back the way we came, the buck has its ears forward and it's frozen in that weird way prey can stand freakishly still. It's looking in our direction. Glistening in the light of the rising sun is a plastic baggie stuck through its antlers. Oh shit.

I run at the buck, intending to rip the USB from its antlers. Before I take two steps, it bolts, runs around the corner of the Infirmary, and disappears from sight.

"I want you to be honest with me," Turbo says, emerging from the trees. "Was there *any* part of you that genuinely thought that might work?"

"No," I mumble. "How did that even happen?"

"You must have dropped it and the bag got stuck in its antlers when it was eating the food," Turbo guesses.

"No worries," I say. "We'll just sneak back into Admin and get the files again."

Turbo shuffles in place. "We can't."

"Why not?"

"Because that was my only USB."

"What do you mean it was your only USB? You brought like six bags of stuff to camp and you didn't bring two USBs?"

"How many USBs did you bring?" Turbo asks.

Zero.

"That's a fair point," I sigh and sit down in the shade next to the half-eaten pile of deer food. Turbo squats next to me.

"I see three courses of action that keep you out of trouble," he says. "First, you can talk to Mr. B and find out why he did this. Maybe you can get him to confess."

"No way," I say. "Any maniac who will try to frame someone for shitting in a shower is not someone you can reason with."

"Okay, Option B." Turbo holds up two fingers. "We get a new USB somehow. And Option Three, we try to catch the buck and get the old USB back."

"I think both of those options are viable. We're responsible Adventure Rangers," I say. "Why not expect the worst and plan for both?"

"Good idea," he says. We get our stuff together and set off to find the only person in camp crazy enough to help us catch a wild animal.

* * *

FIVE YEARS AGO...
MARCH 5TH, 2010. 6:09 AM.

When Moonpie finished his pancake, he slung the extra one out the window like a Frisbee. It soared out of the Admin building and into the parking lot. The young buck tip-toed forward and craned its neck out to snag the treat.

"Get a move on, we got work to do," Moonpie said to the buck. "There's picnic tables that need fixing, the dock needs to be treated, the shack down by the climbing wall needs to be painted again."

Moonpie stacked the newspaper he had been reading into a read and unread pile, picked up the box of Honey Nut Cheerios, and poured a hearty helping into his jacket pockets. Then, he set off down Cardiac Hill

166

to start the day's work. Every few steps, he'd throw a Cheerio behind him. The fawn lagged twenty feet back, eating each morsel Moonpie left behind.

17

A RANGER IS TEACHING

It's not hard finding the only person crazy enough to help us catch a wild animal.

Uncle Ruckus waves his hands. "And you wanna know where spiders get their butt rope from? They make it from the hair on your head while you're sleeping!"

Treb, Shovel, and all the rest of the Tenderboots stare at Uncle Ruckus with wide eyes.

"Really?" Treb asks, his voice laced with horror.

"Yes," Uncle Ruckus says solemnly. "And did you know that the spores on mushrooms is how they do it and make more mushrooms? So, if you kick a mushroom and spores come off, that means it's trying to do it with you."

Shovel raises his hand. "Do what?"

"*It*," Uncle Ruckus says. "You know, like breeding."

Shovel nods thoughtfully.

We're hiding in the trees, a normal thing for us to do at this point, watching Uncle Ruckus terrorize the Dan Booners before Moonpie gets there.

Turbo nudges me. "Hey, should we like, put a stop to this?"

"Shh, quiet down," I say. "I'm learning a lot. I think."

"All right, people, I'm gonna give you some fast facts." Uncle Ruckus counts them off on his fingers. "First, if you think about someone while you masturbate, you have to pay them for their intellectual property. Second, eye contact with the ladies is a tricky thing to master. If you use too much, you're creepy. If you use too little, you're shifty. But *never* make eye contact with another guy while you're peeing at a urinal."

Treb is taking notes on a pad of paper, scribbling as fast as he can.

Shovel puts his head in his palms and moans, "Ugh, slow down, this is too much to remember."

"I have a question for the class," Uncle Ruckus says. "There's only one right answer, so think carefully. If a furry breaks their leg, do they see a doctor or a vet?"

"I don't know," Turbo whispers to me again. "It feels messed up just watching him corrupt these kids."

"*...pay them for intellectual property.*" I finish writing on my hand.

Turbo gives me a look.

"What?" I ask. "I want to do my research later and see if that's really a thing. I could be in some real financial trouble with your sister."

Turbo swats my hand. "You're a moron."

"*...and that,*" Uncle Ruckus concludes, "is where a furry goes to receive medical care."

"Damn it," I say. "You made me miss it, I was curious about that one."

Turbo rolls his eyes. "Ask Treb later, he's taking plenty of notes."

"All right," I say as I duck behind a tree. "How do we get his attention?"

"You can't just ask. That'll never work. We have to play the game his way. Like this," Turbo says, stepping out of the woods and into the Dan Boone teaching area.

"Ah, Turbo," Uncle Ruckus greets him. "Nice of you to join us."

"Professor Ruckus, I need to see you in my office, please." Turbo Cakes says and juts a thumb into the woods behind him.

"Please, call me Professor *Uncle* Ruckus. Professor Ruckus is my brother's name."

"Of course," Turbo says. "Right this way, my good man."

"Class, don't forget," Uncle Ruckus says. "Test on Tuesday."

All the Tenderboots stare wide-eyed as Turbo and Uncle Ruckus disappear into the woods.

"Do-Over! My man on the lam, what's happening?" Uncle Ruckus and I high five.

"Yeah, yeah. Listen, where *do* injured furries go if they need medical care?" I ask.

Turbo puts a hand on my shoulder. "Guys, let's focus up. Do-Over could get in some real trouble if we don't help him."

Uncle Ruckus rolls his neck and shoulders. "All right. What's the deal now, boys?"

"We have to catch a buck," I say.

Uncle Ruckus fishes a one-dollar bill out of his pocket. "Done. Simple. Easy. What's next on the list?"

I pocket the dollar. "No, like the animal."

"My dad has a .22 at home," Uncle Ruckus offers.

"No, we can't hurt it. I think it's Moonpie's pet," Turbo Cakes says.

Uncle Ruckus snaps his fingers. "I know just the guy. Well, a chick actually. She goes to the Home-Ec Ranger camp across the lake."

"How exactly is this girl going to help us catch a full-grown buck?" I ask.

"She's a Master Baiter." Uncle Ruckus says with a smirk.

"She what now," Turbo says dumbly.

"A Master Baiter," Uncle Ruckus says again, his smile wider. "Just trust me, she can help. She's smart, and she has resources."

I give Uncle Ruckus what I hope is a stern look. "Just *trust* you?"

"Yeah," Uncle Ruckus says plainly.

Turbo Cakes puts a hand on my shoulder. "It's our only option, dude."

"There's one other thing," I say. "In case catching the buck fails, we need to get a USB, sneak into Admin, and get some files off the computer in order to save my skin."

Uncle Ruckus whistles. "That's a tall order."

"Can you help us or not?" I ask.

"Yeah, yeah, calm your tits," Uncle Ruckus says. "But I wanna be totally transparent with you guys. I need your help with something too."

Here we go.

"I heard a rumor about the girl camp across the lake," Uncle Ruckus says. "Rumor has it, that when girls all get together, their periods sync up."

Turbo shifts in place uncomfortably. "Where are you going with this?"

Uncle Ruckus says, "Well, since my last scheme didn't exactly pay off, I've been trying to figure out how to make some extra cash. My plan is, we go to their camp, steal all their tampons and lady stuff, and then I can sell them the Golden Bum at an inflated price."

"You're a sick little kid, you know that?" I say.

That makes Uncle Ruckus grin. "If you polish a turd, it's still a turd. I am what I am. You guys in?"

"You're not even polished," Turbo says before looking to me for an answer.

"We're in," I say begrudgingly. "I guess. But I want to sweeten the pot, just to make sure you don't lose sight of our goal." I hold up Devil Rock.

"My baby!" Uncle Ruckus exclaims, reaching for it.

I tuck it back into my backpack. "You'll get it back *after* we've cleared my name."

Uncle Ruckus looks more serious than ever. "All right. Here's what we do..."

An hour later we are dangling our feet in the lake off the beaten path, waiting for Ducky to arrive. The plan is simple. First, we steal the St. George's Catholic Academy van. Then Ducky drives us to the nearest gas station and Uncle Ruckus goes in to get the stuff we need for a trap. Finally, we row across the lake under the cover of night while Ducky and Shovel go get the files off the Admin computer in case we fail to retrieve the USB from the buck.

"I just thought of something," I say. "How exactly are they supposed to get the files off the Admin computer without a USB?"

"Details, details. This is why you brought me on board, my man," Uncle Ruckus says, "Because I'm an expert. Just trust me, aight? We're sending Shovel and Ducky because Shovel will make us look uncool with the ladies, and Ducky will make us look bad in comparison to himself when it comes to the ladies. I've thought the whole thing out."

"Okay, you didn't answer my question," I say. "And how did you even get Ducky to agree to this?"

Uncle Ruckus shrugs. "I didn't have to work that hard, honestly. He doesn't think you're the Wafflestomper; said you were too cool for that."

That unfamiliar 'good' feeling swells inside my chest.

"Plus," he says, "I promised him a quarter of my toilet paper sales across the lake. So that probably helped."

Across the lake.

I stammer, "So... I've been thinking. Maybe we don't need to row across the lake. We could just steal the van again tonight and drive there."

Turbo shakes his head. "That's not stealth, dude. Also, the less time we spend committing grand theft auto, the better I'll feel about this whole thing."

I start to argue, but shut my mouth and stare into the water.

Turbo puts a hand on my shoulder. "I know you're nervous about getting back out on the water. Anybody would be. I mean, you literally *died*."

"Yeah, I'd appreciate it if we stopped talking about the part where I died," I snap.

"Hey, I wanted to ask," Uncle Ruckus says. "What's on the other side, anyway?"

I smile, "All liberals and no cookies."

Uncle Ruckus stares into the water. "The cookie part sounds like you went to Hell."

We all go quiet.

"Hey," Turbo says. "This is just an idea; we don't have to if we don't like it. But maybe it'll make you feel better about rowing across the lake tonight. What if we, I don't know, get our affairs in order? Or whatever. Never mind, that's dumb. Sorry guys."

I make eye contact. "No, actually. I think that would make me feel a little better." I think for a minute and stare into the water. "I'm not afraid of the dying part, not really. I did that, and it wasn't so bad. At least from what I can remember. I'm just afraid of the permanence of it, you know? Like you die, and you stay dead forever."

"Well, most of the time. But not in your case, apparently," Uncle Ruckus says.

"If I die tonight," I say, "don't give me a tombstone. They creep me out. It's just like a big rock that stays there forever and marks where you die.

That's freaking weird. And for what? Not like anybody is gonna come dig you up later... Hopefully. All I'm saying is, I don't need anybody to know where my final resting place is. Nothing good could come out of it. I can already see the 'Wafflestomper' graffiti sprayed across my gravestone."

I swirl my feet around in the water and the guys both nod. The breeze coming off the lake smells like summer, if that makes sense. For a long moment, the only sound is the water gently clambering up, then drifting down the shore in waves.

Uncle Ruckus stabs a stick into the dirt and draws boobs. "When I die, I want to be cremated."

Turbo Cakes and I both look at him, surprised at the seriousness of his answer.

"That way," Uncle Ruckus says, "you guys can bake my ashes into brownies."

Ah. There it is.

Admiring his dirt-boob-masterpiece, he adds, "Then at my funeral, pass out the brownies right before one of you gives the speech. Actually, I want Turbo to give the speech, he always nails public speaking. Give a speech about how handsome and awesome I was, but the important part, is at the end I want you to say 'I'd like to think there's a little part of Uncle Ruckus in all of us.'"

We all bust up laughing.

"Thanks guys, seriously. I don't know what I'd do without you," I say.

"You wouldn't have a ride without me," Ducky says, emerging from the trees behind us with Shovel in tow.

"Sup, Duck?" Uncle Ruckus says.

"You guys. If I don't get my twenty-five percent from this excursion, I'm flying you up the flagpole by your underwear," he says.

I don't think any of us doubt him.

Ducky claps. "Time to quit fartin' around. Let's get this over with."

About twenty minutes later, we're standing in the parking lot.

"How did you get the keys again?" I ask.

Ducky grunts. "The less you know, the better."

Fair enough.

Turbo slings the van door wide and he and I pile in. Ducky hops into the driver's seat and Uncle Ruckus, of course, manages to nab shotgun.

I curl my nose. "Do you guys smell that?"

"I'm waiting for the punchline," Turbo Cakes sighs.

"No, really, it reeks in here. Like, worse than usual." I pinch my nose.

Ducky turns around to look at us. "All right, the nearest gas station is thirty minutes away. That means a whole hour with half of Troop 99 missing. We need to keep our time at the gas station to a minimum, agreed?"

We all nod.

"Dope," Ducky says. He plugs an AUX cord into the van's stereo. It blares heavy metal as we make our getaway and hightail it right out of camp. After about thirty seconds down the gravel road, we pass a big sign that says *You are now leaving CAMP WINNEBAGO,* and I hear the first *plink* as a piece of gravel hits the side of the car.

Not this again.

* * *

EARLIER THAT DAY...

WEDNESDAY, JUNE 3RD, 2015. 9:05 AM.

With a full belly from breakfast, Shovel walked into the campsite. There were still a few minutes until he had to be at Dan Boone. Just enough time.

Confident no one else was around, he ducked into his Adirondack. Wires dangled from the corner of the Adirondack's roof, into Shovel's bedroll. He eagerly lifted the lip of the sleeping bag and was greeted by his digital babies.

"Good morning, Bubbles, Toffee, Moose, and Nibbles," he said as he gave each one a treat. "Don't worry, Cujo, I didn't forget about you." He gave Cujo some pets with the little stylus as an apology.

"Okay guys, I have to go to camp. It's this class called Dan Boone. It's for the lowest rank of Adventure Rangers, which is Tenderboot." Shovel pointed at the patch on his uniform, "See? This rank's symbol is a boot. Don't get any ideas, Nibbles, I know what you think boots are for."

Shovel dug through his backpack and got out a framed picture of himself and set it up in front of the DS.

"This is just in case you guys get lonely and miss me. I'll be back tonight though, don't worry. Gotta go, I don't want to be late!" He checked the charger one more time before he left. It looked like the solar panel he set up on the roof was doing its job. With that, he covered the picture and DS with the top layer of his sleeping bag, hopped off his bunk, and set off down Cardiac Hill toward Dan Boone.

Once he was there, he sat patiently in a circle with the rest of the Tenderboots waiting for Moonpie. Shovel aspired to earn some extra M&Ms that day, but was distracted when he saw Uncle Ruckus walking past Dan Beard.

"Hey, Uncle Ruckus!" Shovel jumped up and ran over to him. "Hey!" he said out of breath.

"Hey, Shovel," Uncle Ruckus said.

"Are you okay? You look sad," Shovel said.

"No, I'm not sad. I'm just—I'm tired."

"My dad gets tired sometimes too," Shovel said.

They stood there for a few moments in silence.

Shovel met his eyes, "Hey—"

"Didn't we just do this?" Uncle Ruckus asked as he turned to walk away.

"You interrupted me before I finished. I was going to see if you wanted to come meet my friends in Dan Boone. I bet they'd love if one of the cool older guys came over to teach them a few Adventure Ranger knots or something," Shovel offered.

Uncle Ruckus hesitated, "One of the cool older guys?"

Shovel smiled and nodded.

"Well," Uncle Ruckus grinned, "I guess I have a few things I could teach."

18

A RANGER IS CRIMINAL

We make it to the gas station in record timing. The building doesn't look as crappy as I expected, it's one of those joint gas station and fast food places.

Turbo squints at the colonel on the KFC sign. "Man, some guys just have all the luck."

The long, creepy hair on his chin twitches in anticipation.

"Keep working at it," I say. "Eventually, the rest of your face will figure out it's supposed to grow hair too, not just send it all to that one hair." I flick the hair and it bounces back and forth. "You might be able to look as good as Colonel Sanders up there one day. Or maybe, like Ruckus said, a spider will come along in your sleep and steal that hair for its butt rope."

"Uncle Ruckus. My name is Uncle Ruckus. Don't forget the Uncle." He gets out of the van and slams the door shut. "You wouldn't call Dr. Cassandra 'Cassandra,' would you? She worked hard to get that title. I worked hard to earn mine too, so I'd appreciate some respect, bozos. Besides, you wouldn't call Turbo Cakes 'Cakes' would you? That just sounds plain dumb."

"You guys call me Turbo all the time," he retorts.

"Yeah," Uncle Ruckus agrees, "because that's the cool part of your name. The cool part of my name is the whole thing together. Uncle. Ruckus." He makes a big show of interlocking his fingers. "Uncle Ruckus."

"Guys," Ducky says. "Quit messin' around. Huddle up. Turbo, here's our shopping list."

Turbo scans the list. "Uh... Are we sure this place is going to have everything on this list?"

Uncle Ruckus shrugs. "Eh, improvise if you need to."

Turbo deadpans, "A USB, net, tarp, bleach, Tough Tape, shovels, tranquilizer darts, doe in heat urine, tranquilizer gun, and a real lightsaber. Great, hopefully you don't need a license to buy a lightsaber. The manager of this place is 100% going to call the cops. And why would a gas station have doe in heat urine?"

Ducky ignores him and points at Uncle Ruckus. "You're getting the laxatives, right?"

"Woah, woah," I say. "I thought we were in agreement that we would never do that again."

Ducky puffs up his chest. "I gotta protect my investment, don't I? Period or not, I want a guarantee. This is the best guarantee I can get."

Good enough for me. I'm not arguing with Ducky.

"All right," I say, "What do I do?"

"Just keep the cashier busy. We don't want him catching onto our plan. Or calling camp to tell 'em they got a buncha rogue Rangers on their hands," Ducky says.

I feel like the guy getting paid minimum wage to work at a gas station-

KFC hybrid isn't going to give a shit, but like I said, I'm not going to argue with Ducky.

We head inside and I hit up the cashier, a leathery dude in his fifties with a bunch of tattoos.

"Sup?" I say.

"I'm not selling you alcohol, son," he says, not looking up from his book.

"No, no," I say. "I was just wondering if you sold USBs?"

The cashier raises an eyebrow. "What do you think? Does this look like a Radio Stack?"

Yikes, this guy is so disconnected from the world, he thinks Radio Stack is still a booming business. I don't have the heart to tell him about Blockbuster.

"Haha, true." I gesture towards the register. "Hey, isn't it weird how the dollar sign goes in front of the numbers?"

"Never thought about it," he mumbles.

"Well," I say, "it's just when you think about it, it doesn't make sense. You say twenty dollars, not dollars twenty. So why does the dollar sign go in front? Have you ever noticed that, because it—"

"If I can't help you, then please leave me alone. Tell your friends to hurry up," he says.

My throat catches. "They aren't my—"

"I don't care what you're up to, just buy your supplies and get out. I'm trying to read," the cashier says, never taking his eyes off the book.

Good enough for me. I peek at the cover of the book he's reading as I turn away. *Swim the Fly*. Swim? No, thank you.

Ducky is heading my way, so I step outside. The jig is up anyway. One by one, all the guys trickle back out. Uncle Ruckus is last, of course.

He salutes at the door and yells, "Long live the Colonel!" before he joins us outside.

"Way to avoid causing a scene," I say.

"Felt like causing a ruckus," Uncle Ruckus shrugs.

"Figured you'd be hungry," Ducky says, holding out a box of chicken.

Bless this man.

"What gives?" Uncle Ruckus asks. "Where's my food?"

"The only extra I got left is a couple of chicken nuggets, but they're for Treb. That kid loves chicken nuggets, so it felt wrong not getting him any," Ducky says.

We pile back in the van and Turbo covers his nose with his sleeve. "Okay, I smell it now too. You guys have showered since we got to camp, right?"

"Is that chicken nuggets?" a small voice asks.

Ducky jumps so hard he lays on the van's horn for half a second.

"Christ!" Uncle Ruckus yells and whips around.

Treb's head pokes up from the last row of seats. "Hey, guys."

"Treb?" Ducky asks, "How the hell did you get in here?"

Tri-Clops's head appears too. "We were looking for the flag. For king and country."

I cringe backwards on reflex. Kid's a freakin' biter.

"...In here?" Turbo Cakes asks.

"Well, first we came to get the chicken nuggets we stowed away in here. Then when we saw you guys coming, so we hid in the very back seat because we didn't want to get in trouble for skipping Dan Boone," Treb says. "Plus, think about the clues. Where the elements meet, bridge to the world... Sounds like a van to me."

"Wait. You hid chicken nuggets in the van?" I ask, incredulous.

Tri-Clops nods proudly, clambering over the seat to sit in the row behind me where he sat on the way over to camp. He plunges his hand into the hole where he had pulled all the seat stuffing out just a few days ago and produces a chicken nugget. He passes it to Treb, who promptly nibbles on it.

"Well, did you find the flag?" I ask.

"Not yet!" Tri-Clops shouts, "But we will! I vow it!"

"For king and country, I assume," Turbo mumbles.

"Well now that we have a total of six Rangers from Troop 99 in this vehicle," Ducky says, "I'd say it's high time we skedaddle." He starts up the van, rummages in the KFC bag, flings a box of chicken at Treb, and the van putters down the road back to camp.

As we pull back into camp, I feel like I'm going to pass out. I turn around in my seat and point at Tri-Clops. "You need to take a shower, dude. Seriously."

Tri-Clops looks up, wild-eyed at the mention of a shower, and hisses at me.

Guess that's a no.

"Uh, guys!" Uncle Ruckus sounds panicked. Why does he sound panicked? He never panics.

I turn back around and see Mr. B and Mr. McNitt standing in the gravel parking lot with their arms crossed. They look pissed.

"Oh, *shit!*" Ducky yells.

Tri-Clops calmly opens the backdoor to the van and steps out into the gravel parking lot like nothing happened. Treb clambers over the seat and scoots out the back of the van, cradling the box of chicken.

"Every man for himself!" Ducky yells. He grabs a few grocery bags, throws the van into neutral, opens the driver side door, and tucks-and-rolls out of it.

At this, shock spreads across our troop leaders' faces. Mr. McNitt runs over to the driver's side and attempts to get into the moving vehicle. Mr. B is still standing in the van's path, and part of me is convinced his mustache could stop the automobile with its secret telekinetic powers at any moment. *That* is how intimidating it is.

"Hiya, Mr. McNitt!" Uncle Ruckus yells before, yep, saluting and hopping out of the shotgun side of the car. "Scatter!" He screams as he runs into the woods.

Turbo slings the door open and jumps out with his share of the loot. I start to follow, but Mr. McNitt slams the van's brakes and the door slides shut. I clamber over the seats in an attempt to go out the back, but when I get there, Mr. B is waiting.

"Hello, Do-Over," he says.

I panic and start scooting back, thinking I can get to the sliding door before it comes to a stop, but Mr. McNitt is standing there. There's no way I can get out through the front before one of them blocks my exit. I'm trapped. I do the only thing I can think of. I slide down to Tri-Clops's seat in the second row and sit down.

"Why don't you come out, son? We can talk about things," Mr. B says.

"Yeah," Mr. McNitt agrees. "We'll go into the cafeteria and get some ice cream and figure this whole mess out."

"There's nothing to figure out," I say. "You guys are trying to get me kicked out of camp! You framed me as the Wafflestomper!" Tears well up in my eyes. "Why would you do that? I trusted you."

Mr. B slouches. "I know. I'm sorry. I didn't mean for things to go this way. You weren't ever supposed to be involved. I didn't know about the penny they planted... They must have put it in my food instead of yours."

"What was in it for you, anyway?" I yell. My face feels hot. Everything feels hot. This van is so damn stuffy. "Nothing, probably. You just wanted to get the 'bad kid' out of your troop. I'm the freaking outlier, aren't I?" I pull my knees up to my chest and bury my head.

Mr. B says, "Outlier? I don't think I follow. Listen—" He starts to get into the van too.

"Is this a good idea, Mr. B?" Mr. McNitt asks. "Shouldn't we get help or something? I don't know how to handle this."

Sobs wrack my body and I rock back and forth on the seat.

"You have a son, don't you?" Mr. B asks. "How would you treat Shovel if he was having a problem?"

Mr. McNitt goes silent.

I cry and I keep crying. I don't know how long goes by, but I keep my head buried in my arms. A few minutes later the van jostles gently and Mr. B grunts with effort as he climbs up into it. Not wanting to be near him, I squeeze my eyes shut and climb over the seat into the front row and curl up there.

"It's all right, Do-Over," Mr. B says. "I'll stay right here." He sits in Tri-Clops's seat. "I know camp hasn't been easy this year." I feel a soft pat on my shoulder. "We're going to figure this out, I promise." I cry harder at the touch and he pulls his arm back.

Mr. B stays, pauses, then says, "I'm sorry. You might not know this, but my dad was actually in charge of Troop 99 before I was. He was in the army, and ran this troop like Troop 100. He asked me to take over when he died... I know the kind of pressure dads can put on their sons. When he died, I became a dad overnight to a dozen boys. They were all different, they came from different families, they had different interests. But somehow, I was supposed to make them get along and love each other and learn how to grow up together."

Mr. B sighs, "That's not easy. I thought... For the record, I didn't do the Wafflestomping in previous years. It was stupid, but I thought doing it once could help. It wasn't my intention to hurt you. All I wanted was to unite you guys as a troop. Especially after Hawkins got hurt, I thought, 'maybe if I can give them a common goal, a common enemy, and rein in Uncle Ruckus a little bit, then maybe I could make this work.'"

"What? But we already had a common goal," I sniffle. "We all want to win the Golden Plunger."

"Do you remember the night you cleaned up with the hose?"

I nod.

"It made me so mad the way Johnson was treating you. The way he talked about you. You know how he makes a big show about that missing finger of his?" Mr. B asks.

I nod.

"Did you know he didn't lose that in combat?" Mr. B laughs. "No, he lost it trying to get his guys in the Army under control. And he couldn't do it. Lost the finger to a firework."

"Really?" I ask.

"It's true," Mr. B says. "Honorably discharged from service. He couldn't keep his guys under control, so he started running an Adventure Ranger troop. I think that's why my dad did it too, he needed a sense of control in his life."

"I feel like I don't have control over anything," I say.

Mr. B nods. "Life is like that sometimes. You just have to do your best."

"So, your best was pooping in a shower and letting me take the rap for it?" I ask.

"No, that was never my intention. I was trying to get Troop 100 to take the rap for it, actually. I had a plan. Kind of. Got messed up when all those boys came down with a stomach virus. Anyway, the point is, if we could get them out of the race, then we had a pretty good chance of winning the

Golden Plunger. Kept telling myself how much you boys would love going to that high adventure camp."

"Well that backfired, didn't it?" My voice sounds venomous.

"Yeah, it did. I messed up, and I'm sorry."

A long minute goes by before I ask, "How do we fix it?"

"We'll help," Mr. McNitt says. "However we can."

I had almost forgotten he was here.

"I'll come clean. I'll tell them it was me who did it," Mr. B says.

I shake my head. "They'll never believe it. Especially now, they'll just think you're trying to cover for me. There's only one way out of this. Blackmail. For the drowning."

"Blackmail?" Mr. B asks. "How? Do-Over, are you sure this is the right choice here? A Ranger is—"

"I don't care what a Ranger is!" I yell and beat my fist against the seat. "It's all bullshit, anyway!"

Something brown skitters across the top of the seat and I sit up with a start.

"What was that?"

"What?" Mr. B asks.

"I thought I saw something," I say. "When I hit my fist on the seat." I cautiously raise my hand, then bring it down on the seat as hard as I can.

Mr. B's face spreads into a look of sheer horror. Dozens of cockroaches flood out of the chicken nugget filled hollow seat Tri-Clops created. They flow out of the hole on the back of my seat and skitter up Mr. B's right arm. He's totally helpless, stuck in the cramped space at the mercy of the cockroaches.

"Shit! Get out of here!" Mr. B yells, waving his arms frantically and swatting at his arm.

I scramble out of the row and sling the door wide. I've never been so glad to be standing on gravel in my life. Mr. B, not as spry and agile as I am, flails around in the seat as more cockroaches flee out of their hiding place.

"Joe!" Mr. B yells from inside the car. "Get him into Admin. Help him find his medical files. I'll take care of this."

"Yes, sir!" Mr. McNitt says.

We both take off running toward Admin, and I'm not really sure why. Yeah, the cockroaches are gross, but we could probably help Mr. B. Oh well... Karma, I guess.

"What's the plan?" I ask.

Mr. McNitt is puffing air. "We go in, get on Momma Hackett's computer, email you the file, and you take care of the rest."

"Sounds good to me," I say as we stop in front of Admin.

A quick peek through all the windows reveals nobody is home. Jackpot. We waltz straight through the front door and into her office. Mr. McNitt keeps a lookout while I boot up her computer and look for my file. Everything is going great. I click the folder with my name, my real name, and dig through it. They have documentation of my behavioral record in the Adventure Rangers, history of payment, even stuff about what rank I am, but no medical records. I find Shovel's file to compare the two, his medical file is right there in his folder. What gives?

"Do-Over!" Mr. McNitt yell-whispers. "I hope you're almost done, because they're coming!"

Shit. I close everything as fast as possible, open the window, and climb through it.

Mr. McNitt is talking inside. "Yes, ma'am. Someone reported seeing Do-Over around here, so I thought it was best to guard the Admin Building. You know, to ensure he wasn't up to something. Don't worry, though, we'll find him."

.I look back toward the parking lot and see Camp-A-Cop helping Mr. B with the van. They're both holding cans of Raid and unloading the insect killer into the vehicle. RIP, chicken nugget cockroaches. Eventually, I make it back to the front of the building as Mr. McNitt is walking out.

"Did you get it?" He asks.

"Not here," I hiss. "Let's get back to our campsite and find the rest of the guys. As long as they aren't in Siberia by now."

* * *

TWO DAYS AGO…
MONDAY, JUNE 1ST, 2015. 3:11 PM.

Troop 99's Adventure Rangers stood in their social circles outside. Joe McNitt was happy to see some of the other boys were talking to Shovel. Things were obviously going well for him. He immersed himself in the *Ranger's Life* magazine sitting in the shotgun seat of the van. Nobody likes the kid with the dad who snoops around, always trying to get in on everyone's conversations. But at the same time, Joe longed to go talk to the other Adventure Rangers. He wanted nothing more than to help Shovel make some friends. He wanted nothing more than to give Shovel an incredible summer. And maybe, just maybe, seeing Shovel succeed would fill that empty place inside himself.

Joe heard his son yell something outside and he peered into the side-view mirror in horror. There was nothing to do but watch as Hawkins pressed Shovel's face against the hot trailer. He shrunk down in his seat, frozen with fear and shame. Fear that Shovel wouldn't fit in. Shame that he couldn't do more as a dad to help him. Joe McNitt remembered what that torment felt like, but he couldn't stand up to Hawkins for his son. Shovel would just take more heat for it later. Helpless and disappointed, he sat there and listened to his son squeal in pain. Surely, there had to be something he could do.

The radio in the van garbled. A Huey Lewis and the News song started playing. It made him think of a lonely night in the arcade parking lot. Joe fumbled at his pocket and pulled out his wallet, staring at the bills and plastic inside. He squinted at the Admin building and saw a row of vending machines. There's nothing snacks and soda can't fix.

After he turned off the radio, Joe heard Hawkins's muffled voice outside, "... dipshit tard-monkey."

Joe focused on the sideview mirror and saw Do-Over creep up behind Hawkins, hand raised like he planned to beat Hawkins over the head. Okay, definitely time to step in. He took a deep breath and opened the car door.

"Hey, boys!"

19

A RANGER IS DESPERATE

I point at Turbo Cakes. "You didn't. Copy. The file."

He looks bewildered. "What? Yes, I did. I put a copy of the file on the USB."

Rubbing the back of my neck, I glare at him. "I have no doubt you put a copy on the USB. The problem is, you didn't leave a copy on the computer. You took the only copy from Momma Hackett's computer and moved it to the USB. You effectively destroyed the only evidence we had that I died at freaking Camp Winnebago."

Turbo stands up. "No! *You* destroyed it. I delivered it to you safe and sound on a USB. You're the one who somehow got it tangled up in deer antlers!"

"It was a buck, not a deer!" I yell.

"Bucks are deer! Doe are deer! Fawns are deer!" Turbo's face is bright red, that chin hair is bouncing around wildly as he talks. "They are *all* deer, Do-Over! Deer is the species!"

"Guys," Uncle Ruckus says, "As much as I enjoy you guys yelling at each other instead of me, this doesn't feel productive."

"Shut up!" we both yell at him.

There's a long silence as I pace back and forth in the humid Adirondack. "There's only one option now," I say. "We have to catch that buck. And since my butt is on the line, this comes *before* going to the girl camp for your little scheme, Uncle Ruckus."

He sucks in a breath between his teeth, "Well, that's the thing. There's some stuff we need from chick camp to catch the buck. We couldn't find everything at the gas station, and some of this stuff is guaranteed at the Home-Ec Ranger camp. Also, don't forget about my friend there that's going to help us."

I groan and rub my face. I'd completely forgotten the whole reason we were going across the lake in the first place was because Ruckus had a 'friend' there that knew how to catch a deer. "Dude, what?" Uncle Ruckus asks. "No, come on man, I'm serious. We need supplies, and we need help. Trust me on this, okay?"

"Why would I trust you for a second?" I ask. "You're always working your own angle, even when you're helping us."

"Because we're practically blood brothers," Uncle Ruckus says.

"I don't think you can *practically* be blood brothers," Turbo Cakes murmurs. "I feel like you're either blood brothers or you're not."

I sit down and drop my head in my hands. "Fine. Fine, just... Fine."

All I want is a chill week at camp. Why is this year so difficult?

"Does anyone in here have peanut allergies?" a voice calls from the other side of the Adirondack tarp-curtain.

Uncle Ruckus stands up, slings the curtain open, yanks Shovel inside, and slides the tarp back into place.

"Shovel. Of course. Nice to see ya," Uncle Ruckus says. "What are you yelling about out there? Peanuts?"

"Yeah," Shovel says going over to his bunk. "Today in Dan Beard, Moonpie told us about allergies. He said that if someone has a peanut allergy, they can *die* just by being in the same room as someone who ate peanut butter earlier that day. Did you guys know that?" He pulls a Butterfinger out of his pack like it's a lethal weapon. With the precision of a scientist in a hazmat suit, he puts the Butterfinger in a Ziploc bag and seals it tight. "So, yeah, I just wanted to make sure no one had peanut allergies before I came in here to dispose of these materials." He shakes the Butterfinger in the bag for emphasis.

I start to tell him that if that was true, and one of us *did* have a peanut allergy, then we would have been dead already since we have been in the room with that candy bar for a long time. It's not worth explaining, so I keep my mouth shut.

Shovel looks like he's about to say something again, but Uncle Ruckus interrupts him. "Okay, here's the deal, buck-o," he says. "Tonight, we're going to row across the lake to the *lady* camp." When he says 'lady,' he puts this weird emphasis on it like he's trying to be smooth. "We're going to distribute laxatives, and don't worry, I'm positive you haven't eaten any this time. Anyway, gonna go to the *lady* camp for a quick scheme, and we need a lookout. Not a lookout for the ladies at the *lady* camp, I've got that covered. We just need you to stay with the canoe and make sure nobody comes, because what we're doing is super against the rules. No boys allowed at the *lady* camp," Uncle Ruckus finishes with a wink.

"Okay, cool," Shovel says. "Can I bring my new friend?"

"What? No!" Turbo Cakes exclaims. "You can't tell *anybody* about this. It has to remain a total secret; we could get in huge trouble."

Shovel's face twists in confusion, "Okay, but—"

"There's no way you already told somebody," I say. "We *just* told you. Spit it out, what's the problem?"

"Uncle Ruckus actually already told my friend," Shovel says.

I whirl on Uncle Ruckus, ready to end his life, but he throws his hands up defensively. "What?! No! I haven't told anybody anything!"

"Yeah, you have!" Shovel says. Then he turns to the tarp and yells into it, "Okay, you can come in now!"

A kid about Shovel's age wanders into the room, and—I shit you not—he is holding a puppet.

"Okay," I say, drawing out the word while I try to process this. "Shovel, what's going on here?"

The puppet looks like a creepier version of the human Muppets. It has a monocle, a beard, and a stick in its hand. It's definitely seen better days—there's holes and stains all over the thing's blue robe.

"This is my new friend," Shovel says with a smile.

We all stare, dumbfounded, and the kid stares right back.

"Does your new friend have a name?" Turbo Cakes asks.

"I don't know," Shovel says pleasantly.

"How don't you know, exactly? And is that a killer puppet? Like Chuckie or something?" Uncle Ruckus asks as he backs toward his bunk and pulls out his pocketknife.

Shovel looks at his friend. "Well, he hasn't talked yet, so that's why I don't know his name. I like him because he seems like an outlier, like us."

"So, the thing about outliers, Shovel," I say, "is some are more drastic than others. You're an outlier, but only a little bit. I'm an outlier, but only a little bit. But a kid with a puppet that doesn't talk... that's like... as outlier as you can get."

Puppet Kid stands there, unfazed.

"Well, he was standing outside," Shovel says with finality, "so he heard the whole thing, and therefore is in on the heist."

"I don't care where he came from, I can't deal with this right now," Turbo says.

"All right." I agree, because I figure a kid that doesn't talk can't snitch. "He can help you keep watch on the boat as a lookout."

"Yeah, if there's trouble, he can call for help," Uncle Ruckus snickers.

"We have one more thing to figure out," Turbo Cakes says. "We need a cool team name."

"The Buck Stops Here?" I suggest.

"For Real Doe," Uncle Ruckus says.

"Oh, Deer," Turbo blurts.

"Buck you!" Uncle Ruckus exclaims.

"Commandeer Hoof," Shovel yells.

Puppet Kid says nothing.

"These all suck," I say. "We need something cool."

"Hmm... What about Delta Tango Foxtrot?" Uncle Ruckus asks, his tone serious.

"Dude, yes! That's the most legit name I've ever heard!" Turbo Cakes says, "How did you come up with that?"

"Just came to me, I guess," Uncle Ruckus shrugs.

"Kind of a mouthful though," I say.

"Good point," Turbo says. "We'll shorten it to D.T.F. Squad. Agreed?" We all nod our assent.

Uncle Ruckus stifles a laugh.

"What?" Shovel asks.

"Eh, nothing. Just a joke I remembered." Uncle Ruckus smiles, shaking his head.

"Let it go, it's usually not worth it," I say to Shovel.

We hide out in the Adirondack for the rest of the day playing Uno.

I hide under the covers in my bunk once night rolls around and wait for Mr. B to do his rounds. We figure he probably won't care, but the less he knows, the better.

"All right, boys, it's that time!" Mr. B says. "Lights out, see you in the morning. Oh, and has anyone seen a solar panel? Admin is missing one of theirs from the camp staff's cabin."

"Mr. B?" Treb asks.

"For the love of St. George, Treb. How many nights have you been here?"

"Two."

"Okay," Mr. B says, "in your two nights at camp you are still alive and have not experienced a single spider bite."

"Well that's because I stay up at night and look for them with my flashlight," Treb explains. "But I actually wasn't going to talk about the spiders, Mr. B."

"Well, that's good," Mr. B says. "Because frankly, after discovering your little chicken nugget cockroach nest earlier today, I'm not feeling a lot of sympathy for your spider plight. Now what did you need, Treb?"

"He's scaring me," Treb says, pointing at the corner.

Mr. B swoops his flashlight toward the corner and screams when he sees Puppet Kid standing there. "Christ!" he yells. "Who the hell is that? Is that a *puppet*?"

Turbo shakes his head in a silent 'don't ask' motion.

Mr. B says, "Treb, I don't know what to do about that. I'm too tired to deal with this right now. Just, don't look at him. Goodnight, boys."

"In all fairness to Mr. B," Uncle Ruckus says, "that kid is one spooky motherlicker. He still hasn't said a word."

We hear Mr. B's retreating footsteps, and we wait another half hour to ensure Treb is asleep before we make our move.

"All right, let's go," Turbo says, swinging his legs over the side of his bunk.

"Guys?" Treb asks.

"Frick, Treb. Why the heck aren't you asleep?" Uncle Ruckus asks.

Treb nods at Puppet Kid, who is still standing in the corner with his hand shoved up the puppet's ass.

"Fair enough," Uncle Ruckus says. "He's coming with us, don't worry. You'll be able to get some sleep here soon."

"D.T.F. Squad, let's roll," I say.

There's nothing creepier than tiptoeing through the woods in the dark. Every leaf crunch sounds like the rest of the orchestra forgot their instruments and they're leaving the percussion section to play alone. Yet, we don't turn on our flashlights for fear of being caught. Once we get to the waterfront, we split up to do our pre-assigned jobs. Well, except for Puppet Kid. He just stands there with the terrifying puppet in the dark. I shudder, knowing I'll never get that moonlit image of him out of my head.

Turbo picks the lock to the waterfront shed while Shovel keeps watch. That done, Uncle Ruckus and I haul a canoe out to the end of the dock and ease her into the water.

"We got a slight problem," Turbo says. "We planned for four to come on this trip. I don't trust this thing to carry five of us across the lake."

"Hear that Puppet Kid?" Uncle Ruckus asks, "You can't come. Get your spooky puppet ass back to wherever you came from."

"Come on, guys," I say. "I feel bad kicking him out. He's kinda in this with us now."

"Is he, though?" Uncle Ruckus asks. "He could be a spy. Tell you what, if he tells us his name, he can stay."

We all turn to look at Puppet Kid.

"Ask him," Shovel whispers.

"Hey, kid," I say, "What's your name?"

Puppet Kid stares at us with a blank expression.

"Get him out of here," Uncle Ruckus says, turning to walk away.

"Wait," I say. Making eye contact with the puppet, I clear my throat. I can't believe I'm doing this. "Hello, sir. I see that monocle you have on; you must be a wizard. Erm, what's your name again?"

"Korvin the Great, pleased to meet you," the puppet says in a falsetto voice. I swear, Puppet Kid's mouth never even *moves*.

"Right when I think this week can't get weirder," Turbo says. "Fine. The kid can stay, but think about this, Do-Over: the canoe can't exceed more than four people. We're going to be out there on the lake over the canoe's weight limit. Remember what happened the last time you got in the water?" He walks away and starts stocking the canoe with supplies.

Shovel taps me on the shoulder and holds out a lifejacket. *Bless this kid.*

"Uncle Ruckus, what the hell are you doing?" I ask after buckling up my lifejacket.

He scoops a handful of sand into his pocket and says, "Just think of it as insurance, dear boy."

I shake my head and walk past him. That kid is a mystery.

"This canoe is awesome!" Shovel exclaims.

It wobbles as Turbo gets into it. "For real. We could go anywhere in this thing."

I hear Journey's voice in my head: *Beneath the bridge between elements, the gateway to the world.*

Uncle Ruckus scoops more sand into his pockets. By the water.

The flag awaits where the elements collide.

The canoe.

Seek not, great fortunes. Seek only where it all began.

Here. By the waterfront.

"Did you guys find anything? Under the canoe? When you picked it up?" I ask.

"Just a bunch of creepy crawlies," Shovel answers.

I shiver.

* * *

TWO WEEKS EARLIER...

SUNDAY, MAY 24TH, 2015. 6:36 PM.

"Don't forget to go through the camp supply checklist the night you pack for Camp Winnebago," Mr. B said. "Before the meeting concludes, I want to thank all the parents for their donations toward our campsite's new bathroom. For our last order of business, I'd like to introduce the newest member of Troop 99. He's going to be coming to camp with us in a few days, so let's be sure to give him a warm welcome. His name is—"

"Oh man, get a load of this kid," Uncle Ruckus snickered. "He looks like a total dweeb."

"I have a feeling Mr. B isn't going to let you call him 'Total Dweeb,'" Turbo Cakes said.

"Good point, we need something more covert," Uncle Ruckus said. "How about No-Nut Peanut? Because he looks like he's got nothing going on inside his head."

"Come on, give the kid a chance," Do-Over said. "You guys didn't give me an awful nickname upon first seeing me."

"Well, yeah," Ducky said, jumping into the conversation. "We called ya Do-Over because we all knew what happened; you had a story. This kid..." Ducky shook his head. "Well, I don't know. Uncle Ruckus has got a point:

he does look like there's nothing inside his head. Maybe Bucket would be good?"

"My dog's name is Bucket," Turbo Cakes said.

"Well, that's out," Uncle Ruckus said. "I like your dog. Seems cruel to the dog to name this kid after it. How smart are dogs? Like a three-year-old or something? I'm not convinced this kid is as smart as a dog."

"Or," Hawkins twisted in his chair to face the other boys, "you could name him after something *really* stupid. Like Uncle Ruckus."

"Shut up, Hawkins. Name him after something with no IQ," Ducky whispered.

"Corncob, Backrow, Yardstick, Drillbit," Do-Over suggested.

"I like where you're going with Drillbit," Uncle Ruckus said. He snapped his fingers, "How 'bout Shovel?"

20

A RANGER IS HONEST

Once we're in the middle of the lake it gets to me; that creeping feeling of existential dread. Like something is watching me from beneath the water's surface. Sometimes, the thing watching me is a bony slender thing. It would probably fling an arm out at the blink of an eye, yank me out of the canoe, and drag me all the way to the lake's depths. The creature would spin a web at the bottom, like a spider. A web made out of junk. Litter. Trash. It could be there lurking now, waiting for the opportunity to piece my bones into its web-like a jigsaw puzzle.

Tonight, though, I'm not afraid of the thin, bony monster from my nightmares. I can *feel* the thing waiting for me under the water; a massive, bulky thing. No need for stealth from this creature, no—it's big enough to drink the whole lake if it wanted to. And tonight, with our little canoe over the center of the lake, we are in the perfect position for it to open its mouth, rise, and swallow us whole.

I twitch and the whole canoe rocks. "Sorry," I mumble.

"It's cool," Turbo says. "You hanging in there?"

"Yeah," I say, thinking of the demons lurking below the surface. "I'm all right."

Turbo is sitting behind me at the back of the canoe, and Uncle Ruckus is sitting at the front. They're both doing the paddling while Shovel, Puppet Kid, and I get to 'relax and enjoy the ride.'

"The more time we spend out here, the more ridiculous I feel about this whole thing," Turbo says. "Uncle Ruckus, what's got you so dead set on trying to make a quick buck this summer?"

Uncle Ruckus, who is sitting at the front of the canoe, visibly tenses up. Glad that there's finally some conversation to be had instead of being trapped in my own mind with the lake monsters, I try to focus on that.

"I don't know," Uncle Ruckus says.

"What? How can you not know?" Turbo Cakes asks. "You're shooting for a lot of dough. Quadruple the price of Golden Bum? That's some insane profit margins. You must need it for *something*."

"There's a lot of reasons," Uncle Ruckus says. He clearly doesn't want to have this conversation, but Turbo either isn't picking up on the hints or he really wants to know. Uncle Ruckus shifts in his seat and the boat sways. "I don't like living at my house. I'd rather live somewhere else. After camp, I want to use a plane ticket or something and go somewhere else."

My heart pangs. *What?* Uncle Ruckus, no matter how infuriating he is, has been one of my best friends ever since I switched to Troop 99. Him and Turbo accepted me after I was kicked out of Troop 100. He still wants to leave? After everything that happened to us this week, I thought we'd be closer. That he wouldn't still want to go. But at least he's not lying about it anymore.

"Oh," Turbo says, "where are you guys moving to?"

Uncle Ruckus clears his throat. "No us. I told you, I lied about the moving."

"But, what about your dad?" Turbo asks.

"Who needs him?" Uncle Ruckus says, his tone bitter.

"Your dad is pretty cool, I thought?" I ask, somewhat unsure. "But you always seem off whenever you talk about going home and stuff."

"Yeah, maybe he's cool to you guys. He's always nice at troop meetings," Uncle Ruckus says.

"Yeah, he tells the best jokes. He's hilarious!" Turbo says with a chuckle.

"He's not like that at home," Uncle Ruckus stops rowing. "He's an asshole, okay?"

"Well I just don't get—" Turbo gets cut off.

"You. Don't. Live with him," Uncle Ruckus says, shaking. "Ever since mom died, he drinks, he yells, and he throws things."

"My dad yells all the time," I say. "Pretty much every time he has to pay a bill, actually. Just ignore it."

Uncle Ruckus shakes his head. "Well, I'm glad you can ignore it at your house. At my house, it's scary. I'm gonna get enough money to get a plane ticket and go to San Francisco and live with Mark. He actually treats me like I'm a person, at least."

"Yeah, your Uncle Mark was always really nice," Turbo says.

"Plus, he would bring card packs to meetings," I say.

"I'll miss you," Shovel says. "When you go."

The boat gently rocks side to side, and the water nips at me over the side.

"I'll miss you too," Uncle Ruckus says.

Shovel looks up at the sky. "Sometimes I think my dad gets too caught up in all the camp stuff. Like he forgets he's my dad and not another

Ranger. It's fun sometimes, because he acts silly. But sometimes I just want my dad."

"My dad wasn't around a lot when I was little," I say. "He was sick. I try not to blame him, because it wasn't his fault he was sick. But sometimes it's hard not to be mad at him. I know it's not the same as what you're talking about, but I guess I kind of understand." I turn around in the boat and face Shovel. "It's like neither of us had dads, but in different ways. Weird."

"Weird," Shovel agrees.

"Weird," Uncle Ruckus agrees.

Turbo shifts uncomfortably. "I feel like my dad is doing the best he can. Like with football and outside and stuff. We tried throwing football in the yard one time, it didn't really go well. I wasn't good at catching it. Or throwing. But we made up our own game called Snap Ball, it's really fun, you play it by—"

"Way to rub in how great your dad is," Uncle Ruckus says bitterly.

"Why do you have to do that?" I ask.

"Decaf..." Shovel whispers.

"What?" Uncle Ruckus asks.

"Put Turbo down like that. Obviously he's struggling with something with his dad, just like you are, and he was trying to tell us about it. But then you had to go and be a dick. Why?"

"Do-Over, decaf," Shovel says.

A high-pitched falsetto voice pipes up behind me, "Perhaps it's because Mr. Ruckus's insecurities lie within a deep-seated place of contempt for himself and jealousy of others, stemming from a lack of stability in his own home life. He has to rely on mocking superficial imperfections of others to—" Korvin the Great is cut off as Uncle Ruckus full-force throws his body to the left, and the canoe tips sideways.

"Decaf! Decaf! Decaf!"

Black. Everything is black, and wet, and cold. I can't find which way is up, I just feel myself plunging deeper and deeper into the abyss, right into the clutches of whatever Lake Monster awaits me at the bottom of the lake. If there is a bottom. I break the surface with my head up, mouth wide open, gasping for air.

"Do-Over! Do-Over!" Turbo yells as he swims over to me.

My arms are flailing, but I can't make them stop. My lungs are heaving, but it feels like I can't get air. My vision collapses in on itself and my head lolls backward as the Lake Monster wraps its tendrils around my limbs and pulls.

Hard. I'm laying on something hard. I guess it only makes sense that the Lake Monster would have a cave to retreat to—a place to bring its next meal until it's hungry again.

"Why the hell would you do that?" Turbo demands. "You know what water does to Do-Over, but you did it anyway! What is *wrong* with you?"

My eyes crack open to reveal Turbo and Uncle Ruckus standing toe-to-toe. They're both doing full body shivers, and they are dripping wet. For the first time I've ever seen, Uncle Ruckus seems to be fumbling to come up with any words to say.

"Y-you heard him! He was—" Uncle Ruckus gets cut off.

"You got antagonized by a freaking *puppet*. A puppet! The great and mighty Uncle Ruckus flipped our canoe, lost half our stuff, and risked our lives because of a puppet!" Turbo makes a wide, sweeping gesture at Puppet Kid. "All for what? For what?!"

"Well at least he doesn't have the stupid puppet anymore! He won't talk again, so it's not a problem. We don't even know this kid!" Uncle Ruckus yells back.

"You took away his voice," Turbo Cakes says so quietly he sounds like a predator on the prowl. "You of all people should know what a terrifying thought that is."

"I didn't take his voice!" Uncle Ruckus shouts. "He can talk anytime he wants!" He stomps over to Puppet Kid.

Puppet Kid is standing by the shore of the lake with water coming off him in long drips. He has his back to us as he stares across the water. Uncle Ruckus walks right up behind him and pushes him.

"Talk!" he yells. He shoves him again. "Talk!"

Puppet Kid stumbles forward, trying not to fall.

Uncle Ruckus shoves a little harder with every word. "Talk! Talk! Talk! Talk! Talk!"

Puppet Kid falls face first into the water. Feeling groggy, I get to my feet.

"Hey," my voice sounds hoarse.

"Do-Over!" Uncle Ruckus says, relief evident in his voice. "Dude, I'm so glad you're okay!" He walks over, and as soon as he's standing in front of me, I punch him in the face. Hard.

Uncle Ruckus hits the ground. I walk past him and help Puppet Kid out of the water.

"Are you okay?" I ask.

He nods.

"Stop!" Turbo yells, and I stumble forward as something hits me in the back.

I turn around and see Uncle Ruckus breathing hard, tears pouring down his face.

"What the hell is your problem?!" Spit flies out of his mouth. "Who made you king of everyone else? What gives you the right to just beat up all the problems that get in your way?"

"What gives you the right to make everyone else feel like shit?" I retort, rage flaring in my gut. "It's official; with Hawkins gone, *you're* the Troop Asshole."

Turbo marches up and gives both of us a shove in different directions. "Would both of you stop it?"

I freeze, conflicted. Uncle Ruckus is one of my best friends. I don't want to hurt him. But at the same time, he has it coming. Turbo clicks a flashlight on, illuminating the vibrant colors around me.

My red hair in my face.

Uncle Ruckus's red blood on my knuckles.

Uncle Ruckus crying in his orange lifejacket.

Uncle Ruckus's yellow swim trunks.

Uncle Ruckus's face caked in green algae.

The blue-ish purple-ish bruise swirling into form on Uncle Ruckus's face.

Oh my God. What did I do?

"Uncle Ruckus," I say. "I'm so sorry. I should have decafed."

"Save it, Turbo commands. "We have to find Shovel."

A jolt of electricity runs down my forearms. "What?" I ask. "He's missing?"

"Yeah, we all swam toward you when *somebody* flipped the boat," Turbo says. "It took the three of us to haul you back to shore since you were unconscious."

I imagine octopus tendrils wrapping around Shovel's chest, dragging him toward a wide mouth with rows of jagged teeth. When I look back at the lake, Puppet Kid is pointing. A tiny blond head bobs up and down in the water. My feet register what I'm seeing before the rest of me does, and I run toward the lake.

"Do-Over!" Uncle Ruckus yells, but I'm already in the water.

My head goes under the surface and I try to mimic what other people do when I swim. My arms windmill in long strokes, and when I need air, I bring my head up and take a gasping breath. Legs pounding through the surface of the lake, I feel like a machine, even though I probably look about as graceful as a chubby kid swimming the butterfly.

After doing this for about fifteen seconds, I'm exhausted. When I stop to look around, I see Shovel floating a few feet away, staring across the lake.

"Hey," I say, gasping for breath. "You good, bro?"

Shovel nods, and sniffs loudly. "Yeah," he croaks. "I'm okay..." He looks into the murky depths. "My Nintendogs drowned."

We float there, staring down into the lake. I consider telling him about the Lake Monster, but I opt not to. Doesn't seem like the right time. Seeing Shovel handle the shitty situation so well, my own uneasiness starts to subside. After a few minutes bobbing around in the water, I even feel comfortable. Maybe it's like what Mr. B was telling Treb about the spiders. If they were going to bite him, they would have done it already. If the Lake Monsters were going to make me their next meal, they would have done it already. A Nintendo DS and Nintendogs cartridge wouldn't be enough to satisfy them. Probably.

When Shovel and I get back to shore, the group is solemn. Silent. Puppet Kid is most quiet of all.

Turbo slaps me on the back and says, "That was cool, man. You beat your fear."

Uncle Ruckus stares down at his shoes and doesn't say anything. I glare at the top of his head. *Should I yell at him? Punch him again?* He killed Shovel's Nintendogs.

I embrace him. Uncle Ruckus collapses into me, sniveling with tears rolling down his face. He snots all over my shoulder, but I don't mind. I pull him closer. I want to ask him what he's thinking about, but I don't. He pulls away after a while and says, "Thanks." We collect everything we can out of the water. Some stuff floated, but some of the essential stuff like the

Nintendogs didn't. Once we're done, we line up at the water's edge and watch the canoe drift into the distance.

We do a twenty-one-gun salute by spitting into the water. There's only five of us, so we each get to spit four times. Shovel does the extra spit at the end by himself.

"Okay," he says, smacking his lips. "That does it for Bubbles. We have to do that four more times for Toffee, Moose, Nibbles, and Cujo."

Uncle Ruckus gives me a pleading look that says, "Do we have to?"

I pick up a salvaged bottle of water, take a sip, swish it, spit, then pass the bottle down our row. We were all out of spit, so it seemed like the best approach. Three bottles of water later, we finished.

"Now what?" Turbo asks.

I say, "The buck stops here." Dang. Even though it's nighttime, I wish I had sunglasses to put on as I said that. Coulda been badass.

* * *

SEVEN YEARS AGO…
DECEMBER 29TH, 2008. 4:36 AM.

Saturday mornings sucked. Do-Over was so excited to watch cartoons that he woke up before they even came on. So he'd get up, pour himself a bowl of cereal, and watch the only thing on so early in the morning: Tough Tape infomercials.

The cartoons went off around noon, and there wasn't much to do. Another bowl of cereal and a peanut butter sandwich later, Do-Over was bored. He glared at the brand-new copy of Super Mario II for the Game-Boy, a game he'd gotten for Christmas. A game that came out forever ago that was re-released on every new console because old people kept buying it. His stomach roiled looking at the game. Instead of tearing into the package of the game he already had, he left it in that precious plastic. GameStonk offered more money for trade-ins if the game was still in the wrapper, even if it was only fifty cents.

Instead, he turned to Legos. Do-Over had a massive box of ever-growing Legos. Not the boring bright blue and red cubes, but fantasy ones. He had four different dragons: Silver, bronze, gold, and black. They had gemstones that, when inserted on their throats, would glow if you turned them clockwise. Do-Over had two different armies, a silver army and a gold one. He always liked using the silver army, because the gold side was always pompous and cruel. They were the bad guys.

He set to work on building two castles, though the gold army's castle was always superior. Do-Over liked being the underdogs—the silver soldiers. They weren't really the underdogs though, not with four dragons on their side. Building the castles was easy. The sets came with walls that clipped together, so it never took long setting up to play.

The eight-year-old worked tiny axes into tiny Lego men hands over the next hour or so. There was only one piece missing from the game: The Boss. This oversized golden colossus always gave him trouble. The Boss would need his helmet off for this battle, after all he was the leader of the golden army. Problem was, Do-Over always had a hard time pulling the helmet off. He checked the time—3 PM. His parents *still* hadn't gotten up.

With all the stealth a child can muster, Do-Over crept down the hall and tip-toed into his parent's room. Right up to his mom's side of the bed.

He nudged his mom. She didn't stir. She was laying on her side. He rocked his hands back and forth, back and forth. After a minute or two, she woke up and held her hand out. Do-Over wordlessly placed The Boss in her hand. She pulled his helmet off and handed the pieces back. Satisfied, he slipped back out and stood in the living room, ready for battle.

Whoops of joy warbled outside the sliding glass door, and Do-Over peered outside. He saw another boy his age swinging a stick wildly as he charged down the pavement. His parents—fit, lean, and smiling—easily kept pace with him. The dad broke into a run at the boy and swept him into his arms. He held the giggling child tight against his chest, leaving the boy's tan belly exposed. The mom seized her chance and lunged at her child.

She buried her face into his soft tummy and blew out air. The sound ripped through the air and Do-Over laughed as the boy outside squealed with delight. The man lowered his son to the ground and the child took off running. Do-Over made eye contact with the mom and she waved. Do-Over waved back, a warm feeling welling up inside. After ten more seconds, the family disappeared down the street and out of sight.

Do-Over turned back to look at his Lego marvel. The battle was ready to begin, and here he was...

Alone.

The warm feeling inside coiled and writhed; it didn't feel good anymore. It thrashed about inside him and made his face hot. It made him feel tingly, like tiny jolts of electricity shooting down his arms. It made Do-Over *mad*.

He turned, reared back, and slammed his foot into one of the massive Lego towers he had built. The castle exploded into a cacophony of sound, crashing into a wall with a clatter. Noise rang in Do-Over's ears. He stared down the hall, hoping his dad would wake up. Hoping he would march out and yell at him for waking them up. Hoping for just a little bit of attention.

But his dad didn't wake up. Do-Over crept back to his parent's bedroom, ready to confess to his recklessness. His parents didn't stir. He stood in the doorway, watching their chests rise and fall as they slept, sunlight muted by dark navy curtains.

21

A RANGER IS JOINING

"What's the Home-Ec Rangers for, anyway?" Shovel asks as we trek through the woods.

"Bunch'a chicks painting their toenails and cooking stuff," Uncle Ruckus says as he ducks under a branch.

Turbo looks up from his map and compass, his head lamp temporarily blinding us. "That's not all."

"Yeah? What else do they do?" I ask.

Turbo looks down at the map again and says, "Okay, you may have a point. It was kinda just a cash grab after the Adventure Rangers was founded. They started it in a different time, back when girls were only supposed to cook and clean and stuff. Dr. Cassandra gets riled up when she talks about it."

"How come?" Shovel asks, stepping over a rotten, fallen log.

Turbo doesn't look up from the map. "Well because the Home-Ec

Rangers didn't change with the times. They still do that stuff; girls don't get to do anything when they camp except bake."

"You sure know a lot about being a Home-Ec Ranger," I say.

"Because my sister *was* one, Do-Over," Turbo says, his voice thick with venom.

"Ooh. Turbo's sister: My favorite topic." Uncle Ruckus rubs his hands together.

We emerge at the edge of the woods, looking in on the most modern campsite I've ever seen. There were rows and rows of massive tents. Not only that, but they had mini air conditioners blowing cool air into them. Soft lights dance inside some of the tents... *They're watching movies?!*

A female voice from behind us says, "You bunch are a long way from your campsite."

We all whip around and see a girl who stands a few inches shorter than me. The next thing I notice is her nose. Random, I know, but it's small and shiny and perky. Like a hedgehog. Her dirty blonde hair is in a ponytail. I don't know a lot about girl hair, but even I can tell that the braid has seen better days.

"Don't move," she says, pointing something at us. She takes a few steps closer. "Are you Adventure Rangers?" I start to say something, but she interrupts, "Woof, you guys reek. Yep, you're Adventure Rangers." Electricity crackles to life at the tip of the object she's holding. It's a taser.

Uncle Ruckus runs toward her before anyone else can do anything and throws his arms around her. I freeze, unsure of the best way to incapacitate this girl without *actually* hurting her.

"Banders!" Uncle Ruckus yells.

Giggles dance through the air and the girl slaps at him. "Okay, okay, that's enough. Can I taze any of these nerds?"

"Nah, they're cool," Uncle Ruckus says, then squints at Puppet Kid. "I think."

"I'm Rose," she says. "Rose Pander, but I like Banders."

"Works for me," I say. "I'm Do-Over. This is Shovel, Turbo Cakes, and," I think for a moment, "I don't actually know this kid's name. We call him Puppet Kid."

Banders slings a backpack off and paws through it. "You guys hungry? I stole one of Laura's strawberry shortcakes for you guys, but I ate half and decided it wasn't that good, so I threw the rest away. Oh, but I found this weird doll by the lake." She flops it onto the ground by her pack and continues, "Cindy's red velvet cake is honestly top notch though, so here's the rest of it if you guys want it. I only ate half. You're welcome. Oh, and here's what I made today in Cooking Class: Peanut Butter and Gummy Worm sandwiches. I call it the Banders Special. It's all I ever make in Cooking Class—I'm never gonna get that stupid patch. Buncha idiots around here. They don't know genius when they taste it."

Puppet Kid creeps forward, then dashes for the 'weird doll' Banders found. *It's Korvin the Great!*

After Puppet Kid slides his arm into the water-logged doll, Korvin sighs, "Ahh. M'lady. I'll be forever in your debt. I thought I'd be lost at sea for the rest of my unnatural life. I'll never be able to read the tale of Odysseus the same way." Puppet Kid is wicked good at this. I can't even see his mouth move when Korvin talks.

Banders points the taser at Korvin. "Call me a lady one more time, and the weird doll gets it. Get your hand out of that thing's ass, it's cruel and unusual."

Puppet Kid gives a sideways look at where his hand becomes Korvin.

"Where did you find that thing?" I ask.

"Oh, I've been watching you guys from across the lake ever since you set sail. Saw the whole thing. Boat flip, the fight... Thought I could try and help recover some of what you guys lost." She chomps down on a peanut butter and gummy worm sandwich.

"How were you guys communicating? Smoke signal?" Turbo asks.

"Try text, moron." Uncle Ruckus says.

"Oh, I'm sorry," Turbo retorts, "I guess I'm the only one who actually *tries* to follow the rules at camp."

I chuckle and take a bite of the sandwich. She's right, it's amazing. I can't help but stare at Banders. She's not what I expected out of a Home-Ec Ranger.

"This cake is delicious!" Turbo exclaims.

Banders smacks it out of his hand and it sails into the woods. "The sandwiches are better. Plus, Cindy's a bitch, so..."

"Is she mean or something?" Shovel asks through a mouthful of sandwich.

"All of 'em are." Banders spits into the darkness.

Uncle Ruckus grins. "I met Banders during a Sorcery tournament at the mall. She's the best Bleeding Ghoul deck player I've ever met."

Puppet Kid bites into his sandwich as Korvin speaks, "Sorcery you say, my lady?"

Banders glares at the puppet. "Watch it. Don't test me. I've got a lighter in my fort with your name on it, doll face." She jumps up. "Oh, yeah. You guys should come see my fort." Then she walks away.

Uncle Ruckus stands up, hauling his backpack with him, and takes off after her. Shovel crams the rest of his sandwich into his mouth, then scampers behind them.

"I don't know if I like her," Turbo mumbles as he gets to his feet. "I was enjoying that cake."

I flash him a smile. "She seems great so far."

Banders's fort is easily the coolest thing I've ever seen. It's half-rock overhang, half-treehouse, half-tunnel, all in one. She's decked out the whole thing with amenities from her tent.

"...and this is my archery tower," she continues a tour I wasn't paying attention to. "It's where I launch projectiles at my enemies. Mostly I use it to spit on counselors when they try to make me go to activities and throw pinecones at Olivia when she tries to bring me food and water. How many times do I have to tell her? Drop it and run! Yeesh."

"Your Castle of Solitude is one to behold. The secrets this place must contain..." Korvin the Great says in awe.

"This is pretty cool," I agree. "You got a war council room?"

She gives me a 'duh' look and leads the way through a side tunnel into a cave lit by a TV displaying static. "This is where I plan my pranks on Alenna. She's my roommate in the tent I'm supposed to be sleeping in. Sometimes she tries to get me in trouble with the counselors. She probably won't bother us; she hasn't come to bug me ever since I put hot sauce on all her pads."

"You did what?" Shovel asks.

"Alright, time to change the topic," I say. "I'm not giving Shovel *The Talk* tonight."

"Listen, Banders," Uncle Ruckus says, "if you can help us get everything we need, I'll get you any ten Sorcery cards you want. Does that deal still work?"

"Nope," Banders says cheerfully. "No deal."

"Uh," Uncle Ruckus clears his throat, "Well, then what do you want?"

"I want to be an Adventure Ranger too," she says.

"Well, you can't be an Adventure Ranger," Uncle Ruckus says. "You're a girl."

"Yeah, so?" Banders demands. "I'm sick of everyone in this stupid camp using that stupid excuse. *You have to act like a lady.* No mud fights, burping, or anything else protected under the Constitution apparently. Being a girl is stupid. So, I quit." She kicks her feet up on a rock and leans against the cave wall.

"Aren't they trying to merge the Adventure Rangers and the Home-Ec Rangers?" Turbo asks.

"I think I heard something about that," I nod.

"Yeah, the Home-Ec Rangers won't do it. Wanna know why?" Banders asks. She whips the taser out of her pocket and presses a button and the electricity crackles to life. Then she drops the taser.

Korvin picks the taser up in his mouth, and Puppet Kid peers at it. Korvin spits it out and says, "It bears markings of the Home-Ec variety. Might the lords and ladies of the Home-Ec corporation be benefiting from this taxation?"

"Probably, doll face, I don't know," Banders says. "We gotta buy all kinds of stuff: special cooking equipment, special dresses, and then this year they add a Taser merit patch and make us all buy their special tasers for the stupid class."

Turbo leans over to me and whispers, "I get her point, but do we really need her help? I know Uncle Ruckus said she had the resources and know-how to help us build the buck trap, but I don't know about her."

Banders stands in the middle of the cave with the taser on, inching her tongue ever closer to the live prongs on the end.

"Deal," I say.

Her tongue zips back into her mouth. "What? Really?"

Uncle Ruckus licks his lips. "That's a tall order, Do-Over. I don't know how we're going to change the rules of a whole corporation. Not to mention, they'll do headcounts. They can't have an extra kid."

I grin. "We don't have to change the rules. Plus, where else would we find an arsenal of tasers?"

It was a simple matter getting Puppet Kid to wear the Home-Ec Ranger uniform. We explained to him that if he wanted, he could stay here and play with his puppet all day. All he had to do was make an appearance every once in a while and throw pinecones at people who came to get him.

"Smite all thee who approach with the cone of the pine. Your command is heard, my liege." Korvin the puppet does a little bow.

"Perfect," I say. "Banders, how does that Adventure Ranger uniform fit?"

"It's all mellow, bro," she says in a too-deep voice.

"You really don't have to talk like that," Uncle Ruckus says. "Just talk like your normal self and everyone will assume your voice is like that because your balls haven't dropped. Like Turbo."

Turbo shoots Uncle Ruckus a spiteful glance, but doesn't say anything. He gets picked at enough by Uncle Ruckus to know if he keeps his mouth shut, then the teasing will stop.

Banders clears her throat to practice, "Hi, everyone. I'm Uncle Banders, and my balls haven't dropped. I'm the big spit."

Her impression of Uncle Ruckus is spot-on, and he stands there in shock, listening to our laughter rebound off the cave walls. Finally, someone to give that kid a taste of his own medicine.

"All right," I say. "Banders, lead the way. It's getting late, so let's get the supplies and get out of here."

Most of our materials for the trap didn't survive the journey. We did salvage a few things, but not enough for our original plan to work. Luckily, in addition to a seemingly never-ending supply of peanut butter and gummy worm sandwiches, Banders was full of good ideas. The first place we decide to raid is the Home-Ec Rangers' Self-Defense Tent. After a few minutes of tip-toeing past tents where *Keeping Up with the Kardashians* is playing, we find it.

There are rows upon rows of tasers inside. Any kind of taser you can imagine, they have it, and they're all branded with the Home-Ec Ranger logo.

"Is that a *cattle prod?!*" Uncle Ruckus asks. He sounds choked up, like he could cry tears of happiness at any moment.

"I'd stay away from the Sack Zapper 9000," Banders advises. "You aren't trained on how to use it, you aren't responsible enough to use it—and most pressing of all, you aren't intelligent enough to use it."

"Fair enough," Uncle Ruckus says, retracting his hand and sounding disappointed.

"Korvin would have loved it here," Shovel says with a somber tone. "These are like lightning spells."

Banders opens a pillowcase and starts filling it up with tasers.

"What should we be doing?" Turbo hisses in a whisper voice.

"Stick to the plan," Uncle Ruckus says. "We split up and find the supply tent. Steal all the feminine products you can find. We're gonna get rich or die trying."

* * *

THE DAY BEFORE...
TUESDAY, JUNE 2ND, 2015. 4:36 PM.

"Laura!" KC squealed. "You've outdone yourself this time! This is the *best* strawberry shortcake I've ever had. Be sure to save the extra cake you made for Parent's Night on Thursday. It's just delightful."

Laura beamed. "Thanks, Ms. KC. I made it just like you told me."

Banders straightened. It was showtime. If she could finally get KC's

219

approval, she could get her Cooking merit patch. Then, at long last, she'd be just like the other girls. She'd fit in and then they'd invite her to their slumber parties.

"And..." KC checks her clipboard, "Rose. Oh, delightful!" She smiles, "You've baked something for once. What do we have here?"

Banders smiled sweetly. "It's a lemon cake."

"Ooh, I'm excited," the camp counselor said. "How nice to see you come out of the woods and join us for once. Maybe you'll finally be able to earn that Cooking Patch." She sliced a generous helping of the tiny cake with a spatula and scooped it onto her plate.

Banders flinched. *Does this bitch not understand how long it took to get it to look that pretty?*

Balancing a massive chunk of the cake on the spatula, KC heaved Bander's hard work into her mouth... and started coughing. Cake splattered against the tent walls, the bright yellow a stark contrast to the pink canvas.

"What *is* this?!" KC rubbed her tongue with a napkin.

Banders felt small. "It's a lemon cake. Only, the recipe didn't ask for that much lemon, so I thought it was a mistake, because it's a lemon cake. I thought it should have more lemon..."

KC gagged, which seemed like overkill. It wasn't *that* bad. Probably.

Laura sneered. "Looks like you won't be getting the Cooking Patch again."

On Banders's other side, Cindy shrugged apologetically.

KC bent over a trash can, and Laura exploded into laughter.

There was only one logical thing to do. Banders grabbed her pack and a plate with one of Cindy's red velvet cakes on it, stacked Laura's other strawberry shortcake atop it, and bolted out of the tent. As soon as she was hidden by the trees, she slowed. Banders picked at the cakes as she walked.

They *were* pretty good. So, she dumped Laura's cake onto the ground. Served her right.

That's how she ended up sitting and eating half a red velvet cake in her super-secret hidden fort. She retrieved her phone from its hiding place and texted Uncle Ruckus. *Sup, bitch? Come get me from Home-Ec camp across the lake. I wanna kick your ass at Sorcery again.*

22

A RANGER IS SHOVEL

We rendezvoused back at the canoes after we stole the goods. I felt a little bad about not saying goodbye to Puppet Kid and Korvin, but honestly, I don't think he cared. He seemed like he was having a great time. Banders set us up with a new canoe, a big lime green one made of fiberglass. She's already filled the boat with the supplies she stole: a pillowcase full of tasers and a bag full of fireworks.

"My uncle works at a quarry. He gives me all the fireworks kids hide out there to try and make their demolition bigger. Did you guys get what you came for?" Banders asks.

Shovel proudly holds up a box labelled *Feminine hygiene products. Private!* "It was way easier than we thought it would be! They labelled the box for us!" he says.

"Yeah, we found it in one of the counselor tents," I say. "Turbo and I stood watch outside—"

"And then I snuck in and grabbed it!" Shovel says, beaming.

Banders asks, "Did you guys look inside?"

"Nah, I wanted to get in and out as fast as possible," Shovel says.

Banders clicks off her headlamp and says, "Okay, now reach inside and hand me the contents."

"Why'd you turn off the light?" Uncle Ruckus asks

"Dramatic effect," Banders says. It sounds like she's stifling a giggle.

"Woah," Shovel says. "What is this thing?"

The headlamp clicks back on.

I'm momentarily blinded by the light, but my vision readjusts after a moment. I burst into laughter, and so does everyone else after a second. Everyone but Shovel.

"What?" He asks. "What is this thing?"

He waggles the eight-inch-long pink d—

"Dude, no way!" Uncle Ruckus wheezes as it flops back and forth in Shovel's hand. "Is that a d—"

"A Bilbo!" Turbo blurts.

Uncle Ruckus and I give him a confused look.

"It's a Bilbo. That's what it's called. Right guys?" Turbo gives us a glare that says *go along with it or die.*

"I don't get the joke," Shovel says. "Is this like one of those cosplay things? It's like a weapon or wand or club, right?" He swings his arm in wide arcs and Turbo jumps back.

"Keep that... Bilbo away from me!" Turbo yells.

"Yeah, wouldn't want to penetrate Turbo with it," Uncle Ruckus says, sending Banders to the ground she's giggling so hard.

Shovel looks around, clearly uncomfortable. "Whatever, you guys are being dumb," he says. "You bunch of outliers." He pretends he's about to throw it into the woods, but Banders manages to cut off her laughing.

"No, wait!" she yells, and Shovel hesitates. "We can use it for my plan."

"Okay, fine," Shovel says, putting it back in the box. "But I still don't get it."

"Like I said, I'm not giving you *The Talk*," I say. "But, I do highly recommend you wash your hands in the lake."

Some handwashing and a few minutes later, we're all in the boat rowing back to Camp Winnebago. It doesn't take long to get back across, not with everyone rowing this time. But the closer we get, the surer I am that there's a figure standing on the end of the waterfront dock.

"Do you guys see that?" I ask.

"Yeah, who is that?" Turbo asks and squints his eyes.

"Oh, shit," Shovel says.

My throat catches. It's Mr. McNitt.

We drive the canoe straight into the shore Viking raider style. Me and Uncle Ruckus jump out and pull it a few feet onto land so it doesn't float away. Uncle Ruckus crouches and starts filling his pockets with sand again.

"What are you doing?" I hiss.

"Just trust me," he says with a wicked grin.

"I'm gonna be honest with you, because you're my friend. Out of everyone on this entire Earth, I trust you least."

Uncle Ruckus shrugs.

"Dad?" Shovel calls, climbing out of the boat and clutching the box with the bulging plastic Bilbo inside. I really hope he doesn't open that, because it's going to be tough to explain.

"What are you doing out here?" Mr. McNitt demands. "I was so scared! It's the middle of the night!"

"I'm sorry," Shovel says. "I didn't mean to scare you. It's just, we have to help Do-Over. But don't worry, we have a plan—"

"Did you know," Mr. McNitt cuts him off, "that there is nothing scarier than checking on your son and seeing he's not in his bunk?"

"Dad, I'm really sorry," Shovel says.

I feel uncomfortable, like I'm intruding on something I shouldn't be privy to. But I can't move; I just stand there frozen in place next to Uncle Ruckus.

"Why didn't you tell me?" Mr. McNitt asks, the pain is evident in his voice. "I've always tried to be close to you. I always wanted you to feel like you could talk to me about anything."

"It's just," Shovel pauses, "it feels like you always try so hard to be friends with everyone. Like you want to be an Adventure Ranger too. It doesn't feel like you're my dad, or like I can go to you when I'm in trouble."

"Son, you can always come to me when you're in trouble. I know I haven't done a very good job of protecting you. I've turned a blind eye to some things I maybe shouldn't have. When I was younger, I got bullied too, and that hurts to admit. All dads want to be invincible, but we're not." Mr. McNitt sucks in a breath. "I was trying to protect you, in my own way. I remember when my dad tried to make me stand up to my bullies. Or the times when my dad stood up to my bullies for me. It just made everything worse, every time. Eventually, I quit the Adventure Rangers because I couldn't take it."

"It's okay, Dad," Shovel says, his voice trembling.

"No, it's not okay," Mr. McNitt says. "This week would have been miserable for you if Hawkins hadn't fallen down Cardiac Hill. And I would have let it happen. I'm not going to do that anymore. I'm going to stand up for you, son. I'm going to be better than my dad was. I'm not going to fight your battles for you, but I'm going to be better than I have been."

Shovel falls into Mr. McNitt's arms and they hug. Tight. I wish my dad hugged me like that. They stood like that for a long time. Until a sweeping beam of light focused on them from Cardiac Hill, and we all hit the deck.

"Did you find them?" Camp-A-Cop's voice yells.

Shit. Shit, shit, shit. After all that, *this* is how we go down?

Mr. McNitt hesitates then says, "Yeah! I found one of them!" He walks over to Uncle Ruckus and whispers, "Put your hood up. Play along. Don't worry." Then, he yanks Ruckus up by the scruff of his shirt and pushes him over to Camp-A-Cop. "Yeah, found this one! Looks like he was trying to vandalize. No sign of my son, though."

I lift my head and see Uncle Ruckus flash me the 'okay' sign behind his back, followed by a 'shoo' motion.

"Shovel, Turbo, Banders, grab all the stuff you can and shove the canoe back in the water. After that, we're going to army crawl into the woods," I say.

Banders grabs my arm. "What about Uncle Ruckus?"

"He has a plan," I say. Mr. McNitt is dragging Uncle Ruckus up the beach as Camp-A-Cop approaches them. "I think."

We reach the woods just as Camp-A-Cop reaches Mr. McNitt and Uncle Ruckus. We hunker down in the bushes and watch, wondering if Mr. McNitt is about to betray us.

"This the one?" Camp-A-Cop grumbles.

"Sure is," Mr. McNitt says, shaking Uncle Ruckus by the scruff of the neck. "I don't recognize him though."

"What's your name, boy?" Camp-A-Cop asks.

"They call me," Uncle Ruckus says in a slow, measured tone. He hesitates a moment as his hands sink deeper into his pockets. "The Sandman." And with that, he flings two handfuls of sand into Camp-A-Cop's eyes.

"Aghh!" Camp-A-Cop screams, clutching his eyes.

"Ah, nooo, my eyes!" Mr. McNitt exclaims half-heartedly, shoving Uncle Ruckus in our direction. I don't know how anyone ever thought he had the chops to be an actor with performances like this.

"Can you see him? Can you see him?!" Camp-A-Cop screams, blindly grasping at the air in search of Uncle Ruckus.

"I can't see a thing!" Mr. McNitt yells, shooing Uncle Ruckus, who cackles as he sprints toward us.

"Okay, that was kind of badass," I admit.

"Probably not what Mr. McNitt had in mind, but it'll do," Turbo agrees.

Uncle Ruckus grins, and Banders says, "All right, boys. Lead the way, let's go catch this thing. Where are we going to set this trap?"

I hadn't actually thought this far ahead. My mind reels for an intelligent answer, but I'm too exhausted to think.

Shovel says, "Let's head to the Chapel. It's far enough out of the way that other people shouldn't find us, but also a place we know the buck is familiar with."

"Shovel," Turbo says, sounding surprised. "That's actually a pretty good idea."

"Nice one, man," Uncle Ruckus agrees, and Shovel's face lights up into a broad grin. I'm glad for the kid.

* * *

A YEAR AGO...
JUNE 3ʳᴰ, 2014. 7:32 PM.

"Everyone, I call this Troop 100 meeting to order," Peters announced. "Now, you all know the rules. You have twenty minutes to build a fort with your team. You can use sticks, trees, boulders, whatever you can find. But as soon as you hear this whistle," *tweeeeeet*, "the game starts. Any questions?"

No hands.

"All right, in that case, get to building everyone! Time starts now! And remember, once you bleed, you're out!"

All the members of Troop 100 scattered in all directions, frantically making teams as they spread out. Peters, Richardson, Woody, and Walker stuck together.

"I know the best spot," Peters said. "Woody, Richardson, go collect rocks. Remember, nothing larger than about half the size of your fist." He smirked. "But you can probably go a little bigger. Walker, you're with me."

Peters and Walker head over a few feet into a cluster of boulders still within the boundaries of the game.

"Let's get a roof and some cover going, that's the most important part," Peters said. The pair spent the next twenty minutes building up walls and a roof around the massive rock formation.

"Dang, guys, not bad," Woody remarked as he approached carrying dozens of rocks in the front of his shirt. "You guys seen Richardson?"

"Nah, but he better hurry," Peters said as he checked his watch, "because the game starts now."

Tweeeeeet!

Thwack!

Instantly, a rock slammed into the shelter, causing the whole thing to shake, but not fall.

"We're under attack!" Woody yelled.

"Defend Fort Walker, you morons!" Walker shouted as he ducked into the shelter.

"Fort Walker?" Peters asked. "That doesn't seem fair."

"All right," Walker said. "We could call it Fort Stinky Peters."

Peters rolled his eyes. "Very funny."

Rocks continued to pelt the outside of the fort with a steady *thwack, thwack, thwack.*

"Jeez, you think they'll ever run out of ammo?" Walker asked.

"Look!" Woody yelled. "It's Richardson!"

Richardson ran through the battlefield. He ducked between the projectiles with a backpack full of rocks. Unfortunately, he just wasn't fast enough, and one of the flying rocks sliced his cheek open.

He threw his hands up and called, "I'm out!" Blood streamed down his face.

The rocks stopped falling around him after a few seconds. Before exiting the battlefield, he slung off his backpack and sent a meaningful look to the rest of his group. A look that said, *You losers better win.*

"All right," Peters growled. "Time to go on the offensive." With a battle-scream that sounded more akin to a hobbit than a warrior, Peters stood and started throwing rocks.

Thwack, thwack! "*Aghh!*"

Walker offered up a steady supply of ammunition and Peters's arm worked like a machine throwing rock after rock at anything that moved. The enemy's onslaught gradually slowed as their own ammo and troops decreased.

Thwack, thwack! "*Aghh!*"

Thwack, thwack! "*Aghh!*"

Peters was unstoppable. He sent a stream of bloody Rangers shuffling out of the playing area with their hands up in surrender. "Woody, stay on lookout. The enemy is weak, so they'll be getting desperate. They might try something ballsy here."

"Sir, yes, sir!" Woody said.

"Walker, you better have a damn good reason for it if I run out of rocks," Peters said.

"Sir, yes, sir!" Walker said with a grin. "I'll be proactive and think of a good one now, sir!"

Just as Peters predicted, the enemy tried something ballsy. A lone Tenderboot Ranger darted out of his hiding place and made a beeline straight for the bag Richardson left behind. Walker handed Peters a rock. He took aim. *Thwack! "Aghh!"* The sixth-grader collapsed to the ground in a heap.

Shaky, the boy stood up and patted his shoulder where the rock hit him. No blood.

"You're out!" Peters called. "Walk off the field."

The boy looked at the bag of rocks again, expression confused. "I'm not bleeding," he yelled.

"Christ, give me another rock, Walker. This kid doesn't know when to quit."

The boy stood in the open, waiting to hear Peters confirm whether or not he was out. *Thwack,* followed by a loud screech this time. The Tenderboot knelt and grabbed his knee, tears streaming down his face. Still no blood. He rocked back and forth as he howled in pain clutching his knee.

"No blood," Peters grinned. "Guess he's still not out. Give me another rock."

"Come on, man, it sounds like the kid is done for now," Walker said, sitting behind a boulder. "Leave him alone. Let's go get his team and win this thing."

"No," Peters growled. "If he wants to play my game and have the audacity to argue with my rules, then he's going to get what's coming to him. Give. Me. Another. Rock." Peters held his hand out, and Walker gave him another rock after a moment's hesitation.

Thwack!

"Stop! Please!" the boy screeched, his hand holding his forehead where blood flowed freely.

Walker peeked over the top of the fort. "All right, he's bleeding. He's out."

"I don't see any blood," Peters said. "Give me the biggest rock you have."

Peters held out a hand, but no rock came.

"I said," Peters turned to face Walker, "Give me another—"

He was cut off as Walker punched him in the nose. Blood spurted from it. "Shit! I think you broke it!"

"You're out," Walker said as he flicked a pebble at Peters.

23

A RANGER IS TAZED

Even though we wanted to build the trap, catch the buck, and be done with this whole mission, Team DTF was exhausted by the time we made it to Chapel last night. Shovel all but collapsed onto a bench and went straight to sleep. Turbo laid out a sleeping bag, which he shared with Uncle Ruckus. Banders clambered up into a tree and fell asleep there. *She's weird. I like it.* I wound up sleeping on the ground beside Shovel's bench, the same one we carved our names into. I kept my distance from the Bilbo box Shovel placed under his bench.

When we wake up it is all business, and we set to building our buck trap. None of us had ever actually *built* a buck trap before. Hell, most of us hadn't built anything except for in Minecraft before. But, we have to try. Using the materials Banders brought, we combine our initial plan for the buck trap with her idea. And, we create something beautiful.

Our original idea was simple, but tried-and-true on television. We were going to dig a pit and cover it with leaves and sticks, then put food for the buck on the top. Then, just like in the cartoons, the beast would fall into the pit and we could just pluck off the USB and get the heck out of dodge.

We dig the pit, put the sticks and leaves on top, and then sprinkle the doe in heat urine—which miraculously survived the journey—across the trap, hoping to attract the right horny buck. This done, Banders distributes the tasers.

"Why do we have tasers again?" Turbo asks.

Uncle Ruckus flicks his taser on and off, staring at it in awe. I'm afraid. Uncle Ruckus should *never* be handed a weapon this flippantly.

"Because," Banders says, pulling something out of her backpack. "We're going to tie them to this beauty." She holds up a net.

"Okay," I say slowly. "I don't get it. This kind of feels like overkill."

"You really don't get it, do you?" Banders asks. "You want to entice a horny animal into a pit, then expect to just take the USB and escape?" She shakes her head. "It's just not that simple, my young Do-Over. That buck is going to be *pissed* when it's stuck down there. It could be dangerous." She flicks her taser and electricity hums in the air, "That's why, if we can immobilize it, it's way safer and better."

"I have a lot of ethical problems with this," Turbo Cakes says.

"Yeah, plus, it's Moonpie's pet," Shovel adds. "This seems cruel."

"You guys brought me on to help you," Banders says. "Do you want to help your friend? I say it's best to immobilize the beast. So, are you going to let me do my job or not?" Nobody says anything, so she plops down on the ground and starts tying the taser into her fishing net. We all follow suit, and it takes another half hour before we've got all the tasers tied in and turned on with Tough Tape holding down the triggers. They hum with a dull crackle that promises pain.

"All right," Banders says. "Now we just have to set up the fireworks to scare it into the right direction."

A twig snaps in the distance. There's a snort and a huff. It sounds like a big animal. Like maybe a buck with a life-changing USB caught in its antlers. *I hope.*

"Hurry," Banders hisses. "Throw the net over the leaves and hide!" We haphazardly drag the net with the buzzing tasers over the leaf-pit and retreat to a hiding place in the bushes. *I'm getting really tired of hiding in bushes.*

The buck takes a cautious step out of the woods, its nose working furiously along the ground. Somehow, it's bigger than I remember. But there it is, with my USB dangling from its antlers. It takes a cautious step forward until it reaches the edge of the pit. The beast dips its head down lower. I hold my breath.

And just like that, the USB slips off its antlers. My heart races. We did it. We got the USB, now we just have to retrieve it and I can blackmail my way out of trouble.

The buck takes another step toward the pit, its antlers scraping against the net near one of the buzzing tasers. Then it takes another step, its antler going under the netting and the horn disappearing under the hole we dug. Then the buck takes another step.

And crushes the USB under its massive hoof.

"No!" I scream.

The buck flings its head up, suddenly on alert. Its antler catches the netting, and the entire thing flips onto the buck's antlers. It shakes its massive head, but it just tangles the net and live tasers further. None of the tasers are even touching it; they're stuck in its horns.

The buck snorts and blows out air as it focuses on me. It stomps one massive hoof against the ground, lowers its head, and charges.

In case you've never been chased by a horny—literally and sexually—super buck with electrified antlers, let me just say this: it's fucking terrifying.

"Scatter!" I yell, but my friends are way ahead of me. Banders scrambles up a tree. The rest of Team DTF sprints into the woods.

I try to duck around a tree, but the buck swipes its head and manages to chap my ass with one of its tasers. My eyes squeeze shut as my whole body goes rigid, and suddenly I want cookies. My body convulses with electricity.

"Hey!" a voice yells.

Is that Shovel?

"Hey, you big dummy!"

Yep, only Shovel's insults are that weak.

I crack my eyes open and see the buck standing in front of me, staring right at Shovel. To his credit, the kid looks like he means business. His face is scrunched up like he just found out it was the Taser Buck that killed his Nintendogs. The only thing is, he's holding a huge pink Bilbo in his hand. He swings the Bilbo around like nunchuks and it flops lazily back and forth in his grip.

The buck snorts, but Shovel doesn't let up. He keeps sweeping the Bilbo in front of him in wide arcs and taking slow, deliberate steps toward the buck. The huge mammal stomps its hoof and lowers its head, antlers and tasers aimed right at Shovel. The Tenderboot Adventure Ranger swipes the pink Bilbo back and forth, faster and faster, but the Taser Buck doesn't back down. He's almost a foot away from the thing when Banders leaps down out of her tree and yells *"Waaaa!"* The sound startles Shovel, and he throws the Bilbo at the Taser Buck.

The Taser Buck's antlers skewer the Bilbo's base, and it dangles in front of the buck's eyes. It throws its head up to the sky and shakes from side to side, trying to escape the new threat, but doing little more than causing the offending object to wobble back and forth. Banders pulls Shovel backwards as the Taser Buck rears up on its hind legs, turns, and bolts off into the woods. The Bilbo thumps against its face with every gallop.

Turbo and Uncle Ruckus creep out of the woods and stand with us. We stand there in stunned silence staring off in the direction the Taser Buck went.

Uncle Ruckus pats my shoulder. "Bro. You've had a shit week. Talk about a crazy last day at camp for me and Turbo."

I fall to my knees looking at the USB. *We failed. They're going to kick me out of the Adventure Rangers for something I didn't even do. No more friends, just sitting in my house all summer long playing the same video games while my parents sleep their lives away. No Golden Plunger. No more adventures. No more misadventures.*

I clench my fingers into fists. My eyes burn. I don't want to sit here and cry in front of my friends. I'm pissed. I should do something about it. I get to my feet, stare off into the direction the Taser Buck went, and sprint into the woods.

My friends yell after me, but I don't care. This shit isn't fair. It's not fair at home. It's not fair at camp. Nothing about life is fair, and realizing that just fuels me more. My arms and legs pump like pistons as I dart between the trees at full speed. I pass trees scored by antlers, busted tasers, and broken branches. I can feel my body losing energy. I'm hungry. I'm tired. But I'm too mad to stop. I don't know what I'm going to do when I catch up to the Taser Buck, which startles me. I slow down to a walk. *What am I doing?* I'm not going to hurt that stupid animal. It's not its fault. It wouldn't be fair to blame it on the Taser Buck.

I stop, breathing hard, and stare at the thing in front of me on the ground. My friends catch up with me a few seconds later, Shovel and Turbo Cakes heaving as they try to catch their breath.

"Hey, dude," Uncle Ruckus says gently.

I don't say anything, I just point at the object on the ground.

"Oh my God," I say. "Shovel's dick fell off."

"Shovel's dick fell off," Turbo Cakes echoes. "The puke puddle was *right*."

Me, Turbo, and Uncle Ruckus laugh at our inside joke.

"You did it," Shovel pats me on the back. "You decafed the situation with humor."

We all stare at the damaged, pink Bilbo. Nobody moves.

"You guys are pretty weird," Banders says.

Shovel picks up the Bilbo. "Duh." It droops to the side. "We're outliers."

* * *

A YEAR AGO...

AUGUST 24TH, 2014. 4:49 PM.

Walker knocked on his parent's bedroom door. "Hey, Dad? Can I come in?"

A groan came from inside. "Yeah, come in."

Walker cracked the door and eased it open, trying to be as quiet as possible. "I found a new Adventure Ranger troop I'd like to join, if that's okay."

His dad swung his legs over the side of the bed, as if every movement was a monumental effort. "Sure, son, whatever you want." He groaned and rubbed his eyes, "Do I need to take you? What time is it?"

"It's almost five," Walker said.

His dad laughed. "Wow, I managed to sleep the whole day away!" He slid his house shoes on. "Where is this new troop?"

"It's okay," Walker answered. "You don't have to take me, I found a ride. They meet at that private school. St. George's Catholic Academy."

"Oh," his dad said. "I've heard good things about the new troop leader they got a few years ago. Supposed to be a great guy, really cares about his Rangers. Sure you don't want me to take you?" He yawned.

"No, that's all right," Walker said.

"All right. I'm going to rest my eyes for a few more minutes," his dad said and slipped back out of his house shoes.

"Okay. Night, Dad," Walker said. He crept out of the room and pulled the door shut.

Walker went outside and stood in the driveway until a big white van pulled up. It read *St. George's Catholic Academy* across the side in glossy red letters. Stranger danger popped into Walker's mind. What if it isn't an Adventure Ranger troop, but a disguised pedophile ring?

Big white van, strike one. Catholic, strike two. The driver smiled and waved as he rolled down the window. The guy was middle-aged with a big, black mustache. Strike three. Walker was about to bail when he saw three other guys sitting in the back of the van.

"Hey, there!" the man said, squinting at the address on Walker's mailbox. He looked down at a paper in his hand. He hesitated. "Are you Brent Walker?"

"Yeah, that's me," Walker said. "This the ride for Troop 99?"

"Sure is," the driver said, reaching across the console to open the passenger door. "First time riders get shotgun!"

"Cool." Walker grinned, and he climbed into the vehicle.

"Mr. B, nice to meet you," the driver said as they shook hands.

"Yeah, nice to meet you too," Walker replied. He did a quick glance at the boys in the back. There was a sneery-looking skinny dude in the very back row, and the other two sat in the second row. One had greasy, unkempt hair, a face riddled by acne, and wore a sweatshirt. The other one was a little shorter, and he kept fingering the beginnings of a tiny black hair on his chin. He wore a pristine Class A khaki Adventure Ranger uniform.

"Hold up," the one with the acne said. "You're Walker? Like from Troop 100?"

Walker smiled. "Yeah, guess I got a reputation. Don't worry, I'm not gonna pound your face in."

Acne kid cocked an eyebrow.

Walker pointed, "Aren't you the kid that's banned from drinking Lancellotties at Camp Winnebago?"

Mr. B put the car into drive. "Look at that, you two already know each other! I'm not worried about you in the least, Brent. I've heard good things about you from the summer camp staff. Heard you can't swim, too. That aside, I think you're going to fit right in with this troop."

"Not without a nickname," the uniformed kid said.

"Let's call him Dick Face," the older boy in the back said.

"Really creative, Hawkins," acne kid said, tone dripping with sarcasm.

"Well, how do you pick nicknames? What are you guys nicknamed?" Walker asked.

"I'm Turbo Cakes, that's Uncle Ruckus, and the one in the back is Hawkins," the uniformed Adventure Ranger said. "Nicknames usually just kind of happen, we don't really have a process."

"Weren't you the kid that killed somebody in Troop 100, and they kicked you out?" Hawkins asked.

"Hawkins," Mr. B said, casting him a warning glance in the rearview mirror.

"Haha, nah. I didn't kill anybody. I did kind of get in a fight, so they kicked me out," Walker said.

"We could call you Face Breaker," Uncle Ruckus offered.

"Oh, yeah. *That'll* help him fit in," Turbo Cakes said. "How about New Game? Like when you lose at a video game and have to start a new run."

"I feel like that's going to be weird once he's around for a while though, since he won't be new for long," Uncle Ruckus said.

"Oh, yeah. We wouldn't want to pick a weird nickname. *Uncle* Ruckus," Turbo Cakes said.

"Besides," Hawkins said, "He probably isn't going to last long in Troop 99 anyway." Mr. B shot him another look in the rearview. "But," Hawkins said, drawing out the word. "Everybody deserves second chances, right Mr. B? So why not call him Do-Over?"

Silence hung in the air.

"I actually kind of like that," Walker said.

Turbo Cakes smiled, "Do-Over it is."

24

A RANGER IS ARRESTED

PRESENT

THURSDAY, JUNE 4TH, 2015. 12:11 PM.

"You sure you want to do this?" Turbo Cakes asks.

"Well," I say, "since I'm about to starve to death, and I really have no other choice, yeah, I do."

"We got your back," Shovel says.

"All the way," Uncle Ruckus adds.

"What kind of food do they have in there?" Banders asks.

I sigh. "Okay. Let's do it."

We emerge from the trees and walk across the parade field to the Dining Hall. Other Rangers who are socializing point at us and whisper in hushed tones. I imagine it's something to the effect of, "*Look! There's the guy that died, then became the Wafflestomper, then called down a cockroach plague, then got tazed in the ass by a buck!*" Almost to the Dining Hall, I catch a snippet of conversation.

"...giant pink, veiny..."

I look at Shovel so fast I almost give myself whiplash. He's proudly carrying the Bilbo around like it's no big deal.

"Shovel!" I whisper-hiss. "Get rid of that thing!"

Shovel looks hurt. "No way! It saved your life. We owe it more than just dumping it in the trash."

More Rangers are pointing and laughing at us now. If we go into the Dining Hall with that thing, our lives might as well be over.

I stick out my hand. "Give it to me!"

Shovel hugs it closer, protectively. "No."

I can feel all the eyes on us. "Dude, I promise I'm not going to get rid of it. Okay?"

Shovel narrows his eyes. "Ranger's honor?"

"Ranger's honor," I promise, and Shovel hands it over. I take it from him, and we huddle up against the side of the Dining Hall.

"What's the plan, exactly?" Turbo asks.

"Give me your belt," I say.

"No way!" Turbo Cakes says. "I won't be in complete Class A uniform!"

"If you don't give me that belt right now," I say, holding up the Bilbo, "I'm gonna shove this up your Class Ass uniform."

That sends Uncle Ruckus into a fit of giggles. Turbo begrudgingly takes off his belt and hands it over. Uncle Ruckus stops.

"Uh, guys?" he says. "No pressure, but Camp-A-Cop is coming this way. He looks pissed."

"Shit, shit, shit," I say. "Okay, you guys make a wall around me and Banders. I'm about to solve two of our problems at once."

I take the belt's prong and push it through the hole in the Bilbo's base where the antler went through.

"Ready to be an Adventure Ranger?" I ask.

"Ohhh man, this is going to be *awesome*," Banders says, trying not to laugh.

She wraps the belt around her waist and fastens it with the Bilbo still on the prong. The belt sags under the weight of the enormous pink phallus, but it stays on.

"Hello problem—I mean, hello officer!" Turbo Cakes shouts. "What seems to be the problem?" Then in a hushed voice, "Guys, he's almost here. Hurry up."

"A—all right," I stutter, making eye contact with Banders after staring at her new appendage. "Now just..." I do a pants-stuffing motion.

"Nice try, Do-Over," she says. "You're not seeing my goods today. A little privacy please."

I turn to face the other way, trying to stand between Uncle Ruckus and Turbo to occlude as much of Camp-A-Cop's view as possible. Banders unzips her pants behind me.

"Stupid dick, get the hell in there," she mumbles.

Uncle Ruckus opens his mouth.

"Not a word," I say. "Not a single word."

Camp-A-Cop stops a few feet away from us. "Hello, gentlemen," he says. "I am hoping there won't be a problem here, but we do have a few things we need to clear up. If you'll come with me, please."

"Damn it, go in, go in!" Banders whispers behind me.

"Is your friend al—"

"Who? *Him?*" I say, making sure to nudge both Uncle Ruckus and Turbo. "Oh, yeah. He's fine. Don't worry about him, anyway, what do we need to clear up?"

"Well," Camp-A-Cop says in a deliberate tone, "first there is the issue of the Wafflestomping. I'm assuming your friend, Uncle Ruckus here was your accomplice in that. Not to mention Turbo Cakes and Uncle Ruckus aren't supposed to go *anywhere* on camp property without supervision." He eyes Shovel. "You know, your father has been quite worried about you."

"Come on, come on, come on," Banders whispers. I turn my head a little to see her arm working violently back and forth. Christ. This looks *bad.*

"And you, back there," Camp-A-Cop says as he looks over my head. "I don't recognize you. I'll need you to come with me as well."

Banders lets out a huge sigh of relief. "Ahh! Thank you, yes! Finally!" Her pants make an audible *zzzpt* as she zips them up and turns around. "I had to piss so bad!" We turn and look at her.

My eyes instantly dart to her thigh, where a large bulge starts at her crotch and extends halfway down to her knee in a distinctive shape.

"What in the—" Camp-A-Cop says.

"Our friend," Uncle Ruckus says. He catches my glare. "*He* has been really stressed. He wanted to follow the Can't Come at Camp rules, so he didn't want to take care of business in the shower. As you can see, he's," Uncle Ruckus coughs to hide a laugh, "very well endowed."

Camp-A-Cop's expression is pure rage. "All of you. Admin. Now."

Turbo takes the lead. Banders does a funny waddle the first few steps she takes, but she gets the hang of it after a while and starts walking normally. Camp-A-Cop follows close behind us. Shocked silence hangs in the air. We march back across the parade field, around the Dining Hall, and into Admin.

"Sit down," Camp-A-Cop commands before going back into Momma Hackett's office.

We do. The wooden chairs are discolored from the hundreds of sweaty Adventure Ranger butts that have sat there over the years. Rangers in trouble, Rangers in pain, or Rangers like us, that have no idea what they're doing. Uncle Ruckus chews on his sweatshirt string. Turbo meets my eyes. He looks worried.

"We're going to be all right," I say. "I promise."

Turbo nods and then rests his face in his palms. The too-long, curly chin hair juts out from under his hand. Feeling self-conscious, I poke around my own chin with my fingers. Smooth. Damn, no silver lining there.

The door opens and Mr. B steps inside, followed by Mr. McNitt.

"Dad!" Shovel exclaims. He leaps out of the chair and into his dad's arms.

"You boys all right?" Mr. B asks. We all nod. "Who is this?" he asks, looking at Banders.

Uncle Ruckus clears his throat. "My time to shine. When we first uncovered the secret government lab, we—"

Turbo Cakes put his hand over Uncle Ruckus's mouth. "This is Banders. We left Camp Winnebago to row across the lake to the Home-Ec Ranger camp to go get Banders because Uncle Ruckus knew her and thought she would be able to help so we had to trade an Adventure Ranger for her and she did help us after we stole a Bilbo and a bunch of tasers to make a trap to try to catch the buck with the USB that had Do-Over's medical files on it so we could blackmail Camp Winnebago but then Uncle Ruckus assaulted Camp-A-Cop and later on Do-Over got his butt tazed and we didn't get the USB but we wanted lunch and Banders had to put the Bilbo down her pants so everyone will buy that she's a boy." As he finishes, Turbo sucks in so much air he sounds like a balloon deflating in reverse. He looks dizzy.

Mr. B's face is blank and slack jawed. "A... Bilbo?"

Momma Hackett's door opens, and Camp-A-Cop says, "In."

The McNitts go in first, followed by my friends. Mr. B and I take up the rear.

"What's the plan?" I ask.

"I don't know," he admits. "But I promise you aren't going to go down for the whole Wafflestomping thing."

We crowd around Momma Hackett's desk and Camp-A-Cop stands in the corner.

Momma Hackett looks around the room, staring at each and every one of us. When it's my turn, I feel terrified. It's probably what it's like for a fawn getting stared down by a wolf. My balls feel like they are trying to retract back up inside me. Just when I'm about to break our eye contact, she settles on Banders.

"I know the rest of these troublemakers," Momma Hackett says. "I don't know you." Banders looks like she's about to speak when Momma Hackett holds up a hand. "And, I don't *want* to know you. Whatever you've done, just leave. Consider finding yourself some better friends. I don't want to see you in here again. Understand?"

Banders nods.

"Good. Now get out."

Banders turns, shrugs at me with wide eyes, and slips out of the room.

"Now, for the rest of you," Momma Hackett says with a sigh. "What am I supposed to do?" She looks at me. "I can't have Adventure Rangers defecating in my newly renovated bathroom showers. Do you want us to go back to bolos?"

I shake my head.

"Me neither. They're filthy. They stink." She looks at Uncle Ruckus in his splotchy black sweatshirt. "Speaking of stinks, you need a shower, young man. Now, I am to understand that you helped Do-Over with the

Wafflestompings? After I let you stay most of the week? And, our camp officer tells me you assaulted him by throwing sand in his eyes? And you!"

She looks at Turbo Cakes. "You're supposed to be the best of them. You were privy to all their wrongdoings? You were an accomplice, and even helped them plan some of their little schemes? Well, Camp Winnebago is missing one of its canoes. It's not going to pay for itself."

She turns her attention to Shovel. "I have never had a new Ranger wreak so much destruction. *This* washed up on the shore of our Waterfront this morning, along with some other questionable items." Momma Hackett places a waterlogged Nintendo DS on the table. It has a label across the top that says *McNitt*.

A steady stream of tears slide down Shovel's face.

"Now, I can see that you're sorry," she says more gently. "But if we catch you polluting our lake again, there will be serious consequences. Consider this your final warning. You may leave. Mr. McNitt, I advise you keep a closer eye on your son."

Mr. McNitt nods, places a hand on Shovel's shoulder, and they leave the room.

She points at the three of us. "You three are banned from Camp Winnebago indefinitely, and you can bet your bottoms the Ranger Council will hear about this. I'll see you three are stripped of your ranks and do my darndest to see you kicked out of this organization. And you," Momma Hackett says with distaste. "You are the worst Adventure Ranger Troop Leader I've ever encountered. I had high hopes for you. Your father had a marvelous track record of graduating boys at the highest rank. In your years since, you've not managed a single one."

Mr. B narrows his eyes. "I will not be lectured by you regarding my father. My father ran Troop 99 like a platoon. Those boys didn't enjoy their time as Adventure Rangers. I know, because I was one of them. It was miserable. All I have done since volunteering my time with the Adventure Rangers is try to cultivate a safe, loving environment for each and every one of my Rangers. My boys. We're supposed to be teaching them to be independent—we're supposed to be graduating men, not boys with elite ranks. *Men.* How can these boys become men without love? I drive all of these boys to and from Adventure Ranger meetings every week, because their fathers won't. They're either too tired, too busy, or just don't give a damn. Fathers like that don't raise men. Treating them like soldiers won't make them men, it will make them grey. Grey people with no personality, no aspirations, and no creativity."

Mr. B leans forward over the desk and continues in a deathly-low tone, "Now, have these boys misbehaved? Yes. They have. I will see to it that they are punished appropriately. We will make reparations where necessary to Camp Winnebago. But you leave that to me. Getting these boys kicked out of the Adventure Rangers will not teach them a lesson, it will not punish them. It will damage them. Rob them. Is that what you want? To take these boys away from the only sense of place they have? I spoke to each one of them privately. They tell me they did not shit in your showers—which *we* funded, I'll remind you. I believe them. So, you better go start looking to point the finger elsewhere, because I will not stand by and watch Johnson play puppet master to dismantle my troop."

Silence. Mr. B and Momma Hackett look like wax figurines. It would be impossible to tell they are real people if not for the perspiration collecting on their foreheads. I become aware that my eyebrows are raised high on my head. I try to lower them slowly back to their normal position, just in case doing it too fast makes a sound. Turbo is breathing heavy next to me as he tries to force enough air in and out of his nostrils to stay conscious. The silence drags on, with small sniffles from Uncle Ruckus sounding like gunshots in the room. I'm about to start counting the seconds when Momma Hackett sits back in her chair.

"I will look into the shower matter. Your boys can build a new canoe for Camp Winnebago. I leave it to you to decide their punishment for skipping their merit patch classes. To be clear, if one of your boys attacks any staff member of this camp again, there are no more chances; I'll call the police. If any of your boys partakes in fighting at this camp, I'll call the police. If they are caught stealing, damaging, or so much as sneezing on camp property, I'll call the police." Momma Hackett's face hardens. "And if you ever talk to me in that tone again, the rest of Troop 99 will no longer be welcome at Camp Winnebago. In addition, I'll be sure I mention your behavior to the Ranger Council during your next review. Are we clear?"

"Crystal," Mr. B says. "Out, boys."

Without a word, we about face and wordlessly shuffle out of the room. A lightbulb goes off in my head and I bump into Mr. B as I turn.

"What are you doing?" he whispers, "Let's get out of here."

"Okay, one second," I say. "I forgot something."

I meet Momma Hackett's eyes. My gaze flickers to her smudgy, red, pastel-like lipstick. I make slow, deliberate moves. The way a zookeeper does in a lion's cage. I reach across the desk, pick up Shovel's DS, turn, and leave.

* * *

A FEW MONTHS BEFORE...
APRIL 16TH, 2015. 2:39 PM.

Uncle Ruckus shook his opponent's hand, smiled, and gathered up his things. This new Cirque du Beast expansion was pretty gnarly. The main idea behind the deck was killing off as many of your beasts as you can in the early stages in order to increase your Ringmaster's attack stat. Just when the other player thinks they are about to win, you play your Ringmaster and one-shot them from full health. It was an infuriating deck to play against, the only counter to it being a Kingfisher rush deck, which *nobody* played because it lost against every other matchup.

He hesitated before placing the last card in his deck. It was the Crab Runner, one of Uncle Ruckus's favorites, and one he helped Mark design based on a story from one summer at Camp Winnebago. Ridiculous times. The best times. Uncle Ruckus smiled.

"Yeah, keep gloating," his opponent mumbled.

"Huh?" Uncle Ruckus looked up.

"Is this really fun for you?" the other player asked. "You get every rare card just because your dad or whoever made this pay to win game. You shouldn't feel good about winning with a deck that takes no skill." The other player didn't make eye contact, just kept methodically packing up his things. "Besides, you're going to get wrecked in your next match." Then he stood up and walked out of the card shop in the mall.

What was his prob? It wasn't easy being the big spit. Bitches be bitter. Uncle Ruckus went to look at the bracket. One match left, and if it was anything like the last nine matches, it would be a breeze. It wasn't about the prizes for him; Mark got all the Sorcery merch he wanted, and as many cards as he wanted. For Uncle Ruckus, it was about feeling talented at something other than making milk come out of his nose or being able to crab walk at high speeds.

According to the bracket, the next match was at table four. He walked over, sat down, laid out his card mat, and began setting up. His opponent sat down across the table, but Uncle Ruckus didn't look up. There wasn't much point in trash talk, not when you're the best. Instead, he shuffled his deck three times, placed it in the middle of the table, and waited for his opponent to cut the deck however they liked.

"No chance I'm touching that deck," the feminine voice across from him said. "I know you're playing a Cirque du Beast deck and there are way too many chicks with their tits out in the art. I'm not risking catching an STD from your cum-stained cards."

Uncle Ruckus flicked his head upright to look at his opponent. It was a *girl*. A girl playing Sorcery. *Holy shit.* He wiped his palms against his jeans and his face flushed red. "It's actually anthropomorphic animals that get me going, not the chicks," Uncle Ruckus said.

"Ooh, a furry. Hey, quick question: When I'm done wiping the floor with you, are you going to go to a vet or a hospital?" the girl asked.

"What makes you think you're going to win?" Uncle Ruckus smirked.

"Because," she said, "the Cirque du Beast expansion came out like a week ago. Everyone and their *mother* is playing that deck. I bet you most of all, since your weird uncle made this game and you get all the cards."

"Yeah, but you're coming from the loser's bracket. I haven't lost a game yet today," Uncle Ruckus said.

She laughed. "Yeah, the game I lost was against some basic deck noob."

Uncle Ruckus raised an eyebrow at that. "How do you lose to a basic deck?"

"Because," she said smoothly drawing her hand, "I'm playing a King-fisher rush deck. Made sense to counter the Cirque du Beast flavor of the month, just a shame Kingfisher loses to basically every other matchup out there."

Uncle Ruckus froze. *Shit, this is going to be a tough match.*

It wasn't. It was over in minutes, because it was a massacre.

The card shop owner came by. "Uncle Ruckus, you win the first round?"

Uncle Ruckus shook his head, and the card shop owner's eyebrows shot up in surprise. "Oh. Well, I'm excited to see the next two games play out."

There weren't two more games. There was one, because Uncle Ruckus lost again. The card shop owner seemed ecstatic that someone other than Uncle Ruckus won for once. He even gave the girl an extra pack of Sorcery cards in her prizes.

"You're pretty good," Uncle Ruckus admitted.

"Nah, I just prey on the ideations of sheep," the girl said, tearing into her card packs. She held up one of the cards from a Cirque du Beast pack. "The heck is this thing?"

"That's Crab Runner, he's one of my favorite cards. I helped design him."

"Really?" the girl asked.

Uncle Ruckus nodded.

"That's pretty cool... Um. What the heck is it? I've never seen anything like that in a circus. And what's with the rainbow coming out of his mouth?" She squinted at the card.

"It's... um..." Uncle Ruckus hesitated. "Well, it's a long story. It's something that happened with a slushie at Adventure Ranger camp a while ago."

The girl leaned forward. "You're an Adventure Ranger?"

"Yeah," Uncle Ruckus laughed. "Pretty lame, huh?"

She stuck out her hand. "I'm Rose."

He shook it. "Uncle Ruckus."

Rose wrinkled her nose. "That's weird. I like it. Why do you go by that?"

"That's kind of a long story, too," Uncle Ruckus grinned.

"Well, I'm a Home-Ec Ranger," Rose said.

"That sounds like fun." Uncle Ruckus tried to feign enthusiasm.

Rose rolled her eyes. "It's the worst. You guys get to do all the fun stuff like fighting and hunting and stuff. We just bake, clean, repeat. It sucks ass." She dug through her backpack, found a sharpie, wrote something on the Crab Walker card, and flung it across the table. "That's my social media handle. Let's play some Sorcery Online this weekend. If you turn out to not be a serial killer, then maybe you can come rescue me from Home-Ec Ranger camp this summer. It's right across the lake from the Adventure Ranger camp. Anyway," she said, slinging her backpack on, "it was nice pub stomping you and your reputation with the worst deck in the game. See you later, Uncle Dingus." She strode out of the card shop.

Uncle Ruckus picked up the vandalized Crab Walker card and read the word written there: Banders.

25

A RANGER IS GRATEFUL

After Admin, we all went and ate a well-deserved lunch—even Banders, who was waiting for us outside instead of returning to the Home Ec. Rangers camp. Taking care not to drop any cups, we ate in silence, mostly. Not talking made the meal worse. There was nothing to distract from the crispy burger patty, the greasy green beans, and the crunchy pudding. I'm not confident, but I think the food at Camp Winnebago violates the Geneva Convention. When we finished polluting our bodies with camp "food", we stepped out of the refrigerator-temperature Dining Hall and into the summer heat. We were probably about halfway across the parade field when Uncle Ruckus broke the silence.

"This is a repeat after me song!" he yells from the head of the pack.

Turbo and I exchange a look and play along. "This is a repeat after me song!"

Uncle Ruckus cups his hands around his mouth, yelling at the top of his lungs, "My troop leader, he's the best!"

Banders and Shovel join in too this time, "My troop leader, he's the best!"

"He's so cool, who would have guessed?"

I grin and look at Mr. B in time to see him slap a hand to his face.

We all yell back, "He's so cool, who would have guessed?"

Uncle Ruckus yells, "My troop leader, he's so green!"

"My troop leader, he's so green!" We repeat back.

"Because we peed in his canteen!"

If Uncle Ruckus is involved, the jokes inevitably turn to potty humor.

"Because we peed in his canteen!"

Uncle Ruckus clears his throat. "My troop leader, he's got class!"

We look at each other nervously. "My troop leader, he's got class!"

"His face looks like a bulldog's—"

"That's plenty, thank you, Uncle Ruckus," Mr. B says with a grin as he shakes his head. "But let's be clear, boys." His expression sobers. "You are going to build the best damn canoe. You are going to stay out of trouble. And we are going to do our best to win that Golden Plunger. Do you understand?" His mustache twitches.

We all nod.

"Good. I've got some good news for you boys..." Mr. B says, then turns to Banders to add, "and girl? I still have to decide what to do about you." He turns back to look at the rest of us and smiles. "Hawkins is coming back for the last day of camp!"

Shovel whimpers and the rest of us groan. Well, except Banders, she just looks confused.

Mr. B's face hardens. "Boys, I know you haven't gotten along with him, but he is a member of this troop. He'll be back tonight, and I expect a warm welcome for him."

To which we respond with a disheartened chorus of, "Okay."

"I'm hungry," Banders says, unbothered by Mr. B's announcement. "That meal was practically dog food."

"Well, I've got some good news about that too!" Mr. B says.

"I don't think I like your definition of good news," Shovel mumbles.

"It's Parent Night!" Mr. B announces as we step into camp.

"Jesus Christ," Uncle Ruckus says.

"Screw that," I say.

"We're going to eat the parents?!" Shovel stops dead in his tracks.

"With the right seasoning," Banders makes an 'okay' sign with her fingers, "there's no way they could be bad."

"Do you all ever get tired of being overdramatic?" Mr. B sighs.

"Me? Overdramatic?" Uncle Ruckus puts his hand to his forehead and crumples to the ground as if he fainted.

In a singsong voice, Mr. B says, "We're making Choco-Tacos and Hobo Sacks."

Uncle Ruckus's head jerks up. "Really?" He springs to his feet and dusts his pants off, "Bet. Hobo Sacks are the big spit, Mr. B."

Now Banders looks as worried as Shovel. She says, "I was just kidding about the cannibalism thing earlier. I'm not eating any part of a hobo, especially not his—"

"It's not made out of people," Turbo says flatly. "It's aluminum foil with butter smeared on the inside. You throw in some chicken, vegetables, whatever you want. Wrap the whole thing up, throw it on the fire, and ta-da! You've got a meal in no time."

"They're actually pretty good," I admit.

"They will be, but first we need ingredients. Grab a couple of other Rangers and head back up to the Dining Hall for our Parent's Night rations," Mr. B says as he settles into his camp chair.

"You couldn't have told us when we were up there ten minutes ago?" I ask.

"Nah, I gotta wear you boys out," Mr. B says.

"What are you gonna do?" Uncle Ruckus asks.

"Start the fire," Mr. B says, pulling his bucket hat down over his eyes and settling back in the chair.

"Grown-ups." Shovel says, shaking his head.

We round up Treb and Tri-Clops to come help us get the supplies. We're about to head up when I notice Ducky and the other older guys laying in their hammocks.

"Hey," I stammer, "wanna come help us?"

"With what?" Tyler 2 Electric Boogaloo asks.

"And will there be chicks?" iBall asks.

Ducky doesn't move, a content expression on his face.

"Uh," I hesitate. "Does Turbo count?"

"I think we'll pass," Ducky says without opening his eyes.

"Ha ha, yeah, that's cool," I say turning to leave. "Oh, did you hear the 'good' news?"

"What's that?" Ducky asks.

"Hawkins is coming back tonight."

Ducky cracks one eye open. "Really?"

"Yeah, his leg looked bad whenever we saw him. Kinda surprised he's gonna be back already. Maybe the pain meds will mellow him out."

Ducky closes his eye and smiles. "I think he's going to be more friendly from here on out."

Goosebumps erupt down my arms. What was *that* supposed to mean?

The distress must be evident on my face, because Ducky clarifies, "Just because he'll probably be in a lot of pain and all. You know?"

I nod, stammer something about going to get the food, and start up

Cardiac Hill with the others. Uncle Ruckus and Turbo are bickering about something, but I don't feel like joining in. My mind wonders, for the first time, if Hawkins tumbling down the hill just minutes after we arrived at camp was truly an accident or not.

"Hard to get excited about Parent's Night," Shovel says, huffing and puffing.

"Yeah," I breathe. "Turbo and Uncle Ruckus have to go home, and most of the parents don't even show up. Because that's what parents do."

We continue up the hill in silence, mostly to conserve oxygen. But also because that's what guys do. The group pauses at the top of the hill to rest.

"I'm downright twitchy," Uncle Ruckus says.

"Just take care of it in the bathroom," Turbo says. "That's what I've been doing."

"Not a chance," Uncle Ruckus says. "Not after the adventures we've had in the bathroom so far."

"What are we talking about?" I ask.

"Something called Trail Fever," Shovel says. "But I don't think I get it."

"Me neither," Treb says.

"They're talking about spanking the monkey," Banders says.

"Oh," I smirk.

"Huh?" Shovel asks.

"You know, choking the chicken. Spending some quality time with Jill," Banders says.

"Wait, how do you know about Jill?" Turbo asks, sounding horrified.

"Jill and I happen to be quite close," Banders says with a wink.

"Wait, who's Jill again?" Shovel asks.

Uncle Ruckus holds up his left hand, fingers extended, and a devilish grin spread across his face. "Meet Jill."

"Oh, I get it. Trail Fever is when you make up fake people because you're sad and lonely." Shovel leans in close to Uncle Ruckus's hand and mock yells, "Hello, Jill! It's nice to meet you!"

Uncle Ruckus tries to swat Shovel in the face, but the younger Ranger pulls back before the hand can make contact.

I laugh. "Actually, he's not that far off with the lonely bit." I hold up my own left hand, "See, your thumb and forefinger make the J. Your middle finger is the I, and the last two are the L's."

"Oh, that's clever!" Shovel says, then pauses. "But I still don't get it."

"They're talking about masturbating," Banders says flatly. "Their definition of Trail Fever is when a guy hasn't seen a cute girl in a few days, so ugly girls start looking cute."

"Yeah, like Dr. Cassandra," Uncle Ruckus says.

Turbo punches him in the arm.

"In my case," Banders says, "Trail Fever is when you haven't seen a cute ANYONE in days."

"Anyone?" Shovel asks, sounding hopeful.

Banders tousles his hair. "You're cute, buddy. Just in a different way."

Shovel beams.

We reach the back door of the Dining Hall, where Journey stands with a clipboard. He checks Troop 99 off the list and loads us up with supplies. Chicken, potatoes, onions, carrots, rice, that kind of thing. We also score some butter, seasoning packets, pudding, fruit cups, and two jugs of milk. Troop 99 has an old trick for getting more food out of Parent Night at Camp Winnebago. After we get everything the camp is required to give us, we stand off to the side and send a younger kid, Treb in this case, to go back and ask if that's *all* the food we get.

It's surprising how much more food we score just by asking. Treb is by far the best at it, too. Probably because he's such a scrawny dude. We end up with our rations and a little wagon full of other miscellaneous items like just-add-water-eggs and off-brand bags of chips. There are no expiration dates on anything. It's possible we aren't getting as good a deal as we think.

Tri-Clops and Treb start in on the bags of chips as we make our way back down the hill. There's some dark, twisted part of me that wants to jump in the wagon full of food and ride down Cardiac Hill. Sure, I'd die, but it would be the most epic exit to life anyone has ever had. Of course, I could end up like Hawkins. But that could almost be a blessing when I consider some of the other alternatives. I shudder. What got into him, thinking he could run Cardiac Hill? Ducky's face flashes across my mind, and I replay our earlier conversation in my head.

Would Ducky really do something like that? I mean, sure, Hawkins is a total dick. But he could have died. He was bullying Shovel earlier, but Ducky doesn't seem to care about Shovel *that* much. Not enough to potentially kill a dude over. I wonder what sent him over the edge.

"Yo, Shovel," I call, lagging back behind the group.

Shovel draws back, leaving Tri-Clops and Treb to continue their conversation about the airspeed velocity of an unladen swallow.

"What's up, Do-Man?" Shovel asks.

I cringe. "Nice try, but let's just stick with Do-Over."

"Yeah, you're probably right," he says.

I pull out the waterlogged 3DS. "Check it out."

Shovel's eyes go wide, "You saved it from Momma Hackett! How in the world—thank you!"

"Well, don't thank me yet," I say. "I think it's a little messed up from its dip in the lake. If I were you, I'd snag some of the rice from the food supply and put the 3DS in it. I think the rice helps suck water out or something like that. I don't know if it'll make it work, it's just something I've heard—"

Shovel throws his arms around me and I stop walking. He doesn't say anything, just hugs me tighter and tighter.

"I know, buddy. You're welcome," I whisper, hugging back.

* * *

EARLIER THAT WEEK...
MONDAY, JUNE 1ST, 2015. 4:32 PM.

Ducky's stomach acid felt like molten lead roiling around inside of him. He replayed Hawkins pushing Shovel up against the hot trailer. That made his temper flare. But what made him most angry was Hawkins's words. Ducky turned around and saw the rest of Troop 99 sitting down in the parking lot to enjoy some snacks.

"Huh. Huhuhuhu," came iBall's stilted laugh, soon joined by Tyler 2 Electric Boogaloo.

"What's so funny?" Came Hawkins's nasally voice.

Ducky swallowed his rage. Hawkins was dumb, even for sixteen. He'd at least give him a chance to rethink what he said.

"Who knows with them," Ducky said, throwing an arm around Hawkins. "You guys go ahead to the campsite. I wanna tell Hawk here about the time Donnie DiAngelo tried to run Cardiac Hill."

Tyler 2 and iBall didn't even notice, they simply kept walking down Cardiac Hill as they guffawed at whatever lame joke they were sharing.

"I've heard this one a million times," Hawkins said as he ripped off a piece of beef jerky and offered it to Ducky.

Ducky chewed the piece of meat and talked around it. "I like you, man. You're a funny guy." He pulled Hawkins closer into something more akin to a headlock than throwing an arm over his shoulder as friends.

Hawkins laughed nervously. "Thanks. Cool comin' from you and all."

"Yeah." Ducky tucked the jerky into his cheek and spoke again. "Thing is, don't you think you might have gone too far with the new kid back there?"

Hawkins sneered. "What, with that little tool? Aww, come on, man. Didja see his face? Chunker was begging for it. Anybody that obnoxious has gotta be put in their place sooner or later."

Ducky patted Hawkins. "I'm glad ya think so. We think alike, you and I." He drew in a deep breath. "But, uh, you ought to apologize to the kid, I think. I'm all for giving each other shit, but let's not go overboard again, huh?"

Cardiac Hill started steepening even more now, the pair took small steps to control their momentum.

"I mean, yeah, I guess I could," Hawkins said.

"Is there anything you wanna say to me?" Ducky asked.

Hawkins looked puzzled. "About what?"

"I didn't like some of your language."

Hawkins's body tightened up like a rabbit who just spotted a predator. "What?" He laughed, but it came out short and stilted. "You talking about the retard stuff?"

"I think you know that I am," Ducky said smoothly.

"I didn't think you were that soft," Hawkins said. "Word like that gonna bother you? Come on. My dad says it all the time. He says it's a medical condition. No reason not to use it. 'Sides, there's worse words. I heard you say fuck the other day."

"Guess I did, didn't I?" Ducky asked.

"Yeah, you did. And that's a real bad word. That's the only word my dad won't let us use," Hawkins agreed.

Ducky squinted at him. "Wanna know what I think?"

Hawkins nodded once.

The pair took even smaller steps as Cardiac Hill continued to steepen. Ducky took a deep breath. "I think that's bullshit. Sure, it's an ugly word. But who says it's a bad word? Somebody. How'd you get here? Somebody fucked. Why are we talking right now? Somebody fucked up. I love the word. It's applicable to all kinds of situations. You can even use it instead of saying 'very.' You could say: I'm fucking tired. Or, right now, I could say: I'm fucking mad. Wanna know why I'm fucking mad?"

Hawkins didn't nod this time.

Ducky lowered his voice, "Because the somebody who fucked up is you, Hawkins. Fuck means as much as you want it to. The difference is, fuck doesn't discriminate against anyone. We'll all do it one day. Well, except for you. Unless you pay somebody," he conceded.

Hawkins shrugged off Ducky's arm. "Look, dude. I get it. You're mad because I said 'retard.' It's not a bad word either. All right? It's the same thing as saying somebody is fucking dumb. So, in Shovel's case, he's fucking dumb. That's all I meant."

Ducky's heart rate picked up at the sound of the word, but his voice remained level. "You've met my big brother before, right? Goose. Loves Marvel."

"Well, yeah," Hawkins mumbled.

"So, you think he's fucking dumb?" Ducky asked.

"No, man... But... Like..." Hawkins stopped walking. "Your brother *is* retarded, right? Like, that's what the doctors or whatever would call it."

"My brother is a person. You're testing my patience here," Ducky said. "Now, I'd like you to stop using that word. I don't like it. It makes me feel bad. It makes Goose feel bad. You aren't a doctor, and you don't mean it the way doctors do. You mean it like an insult. You said it yourself, you meant it like 'fucking dumb,' right?"

"Oh, come on, dude." Hawkins shook his head, "This is a load of crap.

You can't censor me. You can't tell me what I can't say. It's freedom of speech, dude. You can't make me stop saying stuff you don't like."

"You're right," Ducky said. "You can say whatever you want. But just because you can say whatever you want doesn't mean there won't be repercussions. I'm going to ask you one more time not to say it. Please."

Hawkins scoffed and started back down Cardiac Hill. "Nah, man. You're being retarded."

The rage in Ducky's stomach surged, and he shoved the bully. Hawkins tumbled down Cardiac Hill.

26

A RANGER IS TRANSFORMED

Parent Night. We're all different, but at the end of the day, we're all part of this weird family called Troop 99. Parent Night is like meeting new in-laws for the first time, or your new step-parent's family. It's awkward because new people enter the scene that aren't normally part of it. There's an established rhythm in families, and sometimes there's a different rhythm between sides of the family.

Take Ducky for instance. Looks like a badass Blackbeard 'roid-wrestler. We look up to him, but we also try to stay out of his way and not antagonize him because I'm pretty sure he could beat up Chuck Norris, Terry Crews, and Conor McGregor all at the same time. Yet, his family gets here, and his whole demeanor changes. He kisses his mom on the cheek. *He kissed his mom. On the cheek.* Everybody stares as he does it. It's like watching an elephant pet a cat. You know the elephant isn't going to hurt the cat on purpose, but you're amazed to see the massive creature stroke the cat so gingerly with its trunk. If my parents had shown up, I would have kissed my mom on the cheek after watching that.

Not only that, but then there's watching how Ducky interacts with his brother, Goose. I've met Goose before, so I kind of knew what to expect. Uncle Ruckus is different in a bad way. He's weird and can be a jerk. Goose is different in a different way, and it takes a minute to figure out how you're supposed to treat him, but watching Ducky interact with him helps remind me every time.

"Duck, duck, duck!" Goose yells, punching Ducky in the arm with each word after he's done greeting their mom.

Ducky rubs his bicep, makes a big show of winding up a punch, and then does the same to Goose. "Goose, goose, goose!"

"Didn't even hurt!" Goose proclaimed with a grin.

"Hey, Goose," I say, walking over to them.

Goose's eyes go wide, "Doodoodoo!" He punches me in the arm three times.

"Ow." I rub my arm, that actually hurt. "Googoogoo," I say as I punch him back equally as hard. Goose is just another one of the guys.

"Ow! That hurt!" Goose exclaims, then smiles. Ducky gives an approving nod.

"Watchya been up to since the last time I saw you?" I ask.

Goose considers, then says, "*Iron Man.*"

Ducky and his mom nod gravely with empty eyes, which makes me laugh. "Yeah, that's definitely one of my favorites too, man."

"Nice to see you again, Do-Over," Mother Goose says. "Are your parents going to make it tonight?"

"I think they both work night shifts tonight, so they'll probably just sleep instead," I say.

She frowns. "Doesn't your dad work in a bank?"

"Yeah, it's a twenty-four-hour bank," I lie.

"How interesting," she says, her tone genuine. "I didn't know they had those."

"Y—yeah," I stammer, committing to my story. "It's a new thing they're trying out, I guess." I look around, desperate to find someone to save me. "Anyway, good talking to you guys, I'm going to go make sure Shovel isn't burning the Hobo Sacks."

I turn to walk off and hear Mother Goose turn to Ducky and say, "They're burning a hobo's *what*?"

"Jack of all Spades," I say, addressing Shovel.

"Huh?" Shovel asks, looking up from poking a tin foil package resting on the hot coals.

"Never mind, just trying something out," I say and crouch next to him. "How did the rice trick work?"

"I don't know," Shovel says, fishing something out of his pocket. "How's it looking?"

Bless his heart. He'd taken cooked rice, put it in the bag, and put the 3DS in with it. I don't have it in me to tell the poor kid. I put on a smile. "You'll have to let me know how it goes!"

"Where's your family at tonight?" Shovel asks.

"Probably too tired to come. It's okay, though, they can't help it."

I take Shovel by the elbow and we go sit around the fire to dig into some Hobo Sacks with everyone else. They turned out pretty well. Although, anytime you smear butter all over aluminum foil and wrap food in it, it'd be challenging to mess up—which is exactly why it's the safest meal for us to prepare on Parent's Night.

"Can I talk to you for a second, Do-Over?" Turbo asks after I take the last bite of my sack. "Privately."

We shuffle away from the rest of the group and step into our Adirondack.

Turbo whirls around to face me once we're inside. "What's the plan?"

"The plan for what?"

Turbo throws up his hands. "The plan for keeping Mr. B from taking me and Ruckus home."

"*Uncle* Ruckus," a voice says.

"Holy shit!" I jump about a million feet in the air.

Uncle Ruckus unzips his sleeping bag and sits up in his bunk.

"Jesus, Ruckus, what were you doing in there?" I ask.

Uncle Ruckus makes a show of looking around inside his sleeping bag. "First of all, I don't see Jesus in here. Second of all, it's Uncle Ruckus, not Jesus Ruckus. Although, from what I understand, Jesus did cause quite a ruckus a few times here and there." He fishes a Batman comic book out of the sleeping bag and puts it under his pillow. "As for what I was doing in there," he winks, "you don't want to know."

He stands up and stretches. "Anyway, it shouldn't be all that hard to avoid Mr. B tonight. He doesn't want to see us go home, and he doesn't want to have to leave camp. We're probably fine; we'll just hide when the time comes. We got bigger fish to fry, anyway."

"Such as?" Turbo asks, sitting down on the floor criss-cross-applesauce.

"First, and foremost, I'd like to announce that I still need to take a dump. Second, did you guys hear the final part of the clue about the flag? Mr. B said it was '*The ties of brotherhood, of song, and of pledge come to the camp flag.*' How the hell is anybody supposed to find the flag with lame ass clues like that? Thirdly, I'd like to know exactly how you gentlemen plan on helping me earn enough cash to buy my plane ticket to San Fran. After all, you guys messed up the laxative plan. *And* the feminine hygiene plan. Fourthly—Holy shit, is that *Hawkins*?" Uncle Ruckus points behind us.

It's him. His dad pushes his wheelchair through camp, the gravel jostling the chair and making Hawkins flop around as he tries to stay in it. He has a big, blue cast going from his toes to his thigh. *Oh, I'm not missing this for the world.* I grab Turbo by his uniform collar and haul him up from the ground. Uncle Ruckus leaps from his bunk and we all bolt toward the fire.

Hawkins's dad is shaking Mr. B's hand when we walk up, "Thanks for taking him back. Never thought my son would be dumbass enough to try to run down Cardiac. You think you raise a kid better than that, you know?" He gestures toward Shovel, his dad, and Banders, then lowers his voice, but not by much, "Say, who invited the queers?" He laughs, slaps Mr. B on the back, and turns back toward the fire.

Hawkins looks like shit. He's got scabs and bruises covering his face and arms. I can't believe he's *back*. He doesn't say anything—he just looks tired the way he's slumped over in his wheelchair. I look from Hawkins to his dad and back to Hawkins. Poor dude. There's a sick irony here. My dad isn't really part of my life, and I feel like I'm worse off because of it. Hawkins, on the other hand, could probably use a little less influence from his dad. Shovel is staring at Hawkins, too. His eyes are wide, and the look on his face is somewhere between horror and sadness.

"Who you callin' queer, you crusty dehydrated doggy dick?" Banders asks.

Hawkins's dad bursts out laughing. "I like this one. Girly looking though. What are we eating, gang?" He gingerly pulls a Hobo Sack off the coals with his fingertips and unwraps it. "Let's see what you retards cooked up for tonight."

Silence.

Except for Goose, who is prattling on to his mom about who would win in a fight: Thor or Captain America. Ducky rises from his seat. He

269

does it real slow, like it's taking a monumental tax on his body to do so. Tyler 2 Electric Boogaloo and iBall leap to their feet, looking anxious. They each put hands on Ducky's arms and start frantically whispering to him. Mother Goose is staring past Ducky with a pained expression.

Mr. B steps forward, takes the half-unwrapped Hobo Sack off Hawkins's dad's lap and puts it back on the fire. "That one isn't done yet. And now that I'm counting, I think we cooked just enough extra for Hawkins. I don't think we have enough for you too."

Hawkins's dad rises but doesn't look Mr. B in the eye. He just stares at the big black mustache. "Well, that's pretty rude. Don't you think?" Hawkins's dad asks. "Maybe you'll share yours with me, then." He moves toward Mr. B's food.

Ducky starts to take a step forward, and his friends struggle to keep him in place.

Mr. B holds his arm out to block his way and murmurs, "It might just be best for everyone if you leave."

"What'd I say? What'd I do?" Hawkins's dad asks. "What, suddenly I'm not welcome? You fags get your feelings all hurt 'cause I called you retards? It was just a joke, man, lighten up."

Ducky steps forward as iBall and Tyler 2 struggle to restrain him. Mr. B stares Hawkins's dad in the eye, while Hawkins's dad stares Mr. B in the mustache. All while Goose audibly considers the effectiveness of a shepherd's staff as a weapon.

"Snoogums! Snoogums, baby!" a voice calls. A big woman with her arms full of snacks waddles down the path.

"Mom!" Tri-Clops squeals and runs toward her. She can't hand Tri-Clops all the junk food fast enough and he clambers to snatch as many bags of candy as possible. Nobody else reacts to her arrival.

"We need to do something," Turbo says. "This is about to get really out of hand."

Uncle Ruckus shrugs. "I'm all out of pocket sand."

Decaf the situation before somebody gets hurt. Tri-Clops's mom holds the only thing that might help. Time to find out if the stories from last year are true. I sprint over to her and say, "Hi, Mrs. S. Thanks for the snacks." I grab one of the two Lancellotties she's balancing in her hand, and the other one tumbles to the ground, splattering rainbow across the dirt. My eyes linger on the fallen Lancellottie. *Red, orange, yellow, green, blue, indigo, violet.*

iBall and Tyler 2 are losing their grip on Ducky. He's making deliberate, measured steps toward Hawkins's dad. I dash back to my friends and hold the drink out to Uncle Ruckus.

He looks up at me with panicked eyes and takes a step back. "Dude, no. I can't. No way."

"It's the only way," I plead. "If Ducky gets away from them, you know what'll happen." I hold out the beautiful, sugary abomination that is a Lancellottie.

Uncle Ruckus sighs, swipes the drink, and sucks it down. Slowly at first, but after a second or two he's inhaling the stuff. The entire thirty-two-ounce drink is gone in a matter of seconds. Turbo and I salute Uncle Ruckus. He salutes back. Then we run toward Mr. McNitt.

"Hi, uh, Mr. McNitt? We need to get out of here. Right now."

Mr. McNitt doesn't take his eyes off the two men standing toe to toe. "You think? I don't know, I was wondering if I should step in and say something. Things feel pretty tense. I was thinking I might try to help defuse the situation."

"Uh," I say, pulling on Mr. McNitt's hand. "I'd say the situation is only going to escalate from here."

I point at Uncle Ruckus who is twitching like crazy. He vibrates so much he drops the Lancellottie cup, which makes a hollow echo as it hits the ground. Uncle Ruckus trills his tongue in a low tone. Mr. B is the first one to break the stare down, but it has nothing to do with masculinity and everything to do with self-preservation. Hawkins's dad is totally oblivious and stares at Uncle Ruckus slack-jawed.

The trill grows louder and the pitch goes up slowly but surely. Uncle Ruckus unbuckles his pants, throws them around his ankles, and steps out of them. Then he pulls his black sweatshirt over his head. Only his tighty whities remain. Tri-Clops, seeing that Uncle Ruckus isn't wearing clothes, strips down too.

"I thought you guys were cool," Banders says, "but this is starting to feel cult-y."

"Climb a tree," I say.

"Huh?" Shovel, Mr. McNitt, and Banders all ask.

I grimace. "We probably have thirty seconds. Maybe less. He can try to stay on target, but he probably won't be able to. It's like Dr. Jekyll and Mr. Hyde—he's about to *change*."

Turbo and I clamber up the nearest tree with the help of a picnic table. Banders, Shovel, and his dad follow suit. Mr. B takes a step back as the trilling grows louder. Ducky seems to take notice of it for the first time too, and stops struggling against his friends. I can't hear what he says to Goose, but his lips look like *watch this* and he points toward Uncle Ruckus.

"Behold," I say, "From Uncle Ruckus to El Diablo."

"*Dios mio*," Turbo mumbles.

The trilling stops. Uncle Ruckus, now El Diablo, lays down on the ground.

Tri-Clops throws his arms up and shrieks, "For king and country, Mr. B!" Then he sprints into the woods.

The legend goes that when Uncle Ruckus was little, he wanted nothing more than to join the circus. He tried juggling, knife throwing, tightrope walking, snake whispering, even accounting, but none of it took. Until he stayed up late one night and watched *The Ring* for the first time and discovered he *did* have a talent. That talent is crab walking.

El Diablo snaps his arms into position and lifts up his body.

"Sweet Christmas!" Hawkins's dad exclaims.

"May God have mercy on our souls," Turbo says.

Then El Diablo crab runs at Hawkins's dad.

"Cut that shit out!" he yells, flinching backwards but standing his ground.

El Diablo's head dangles upside down until he's a few feet away from his target. Then he raises it to look up at the sky and a rainbow geysers out of his mouth at the bully's father.

"What the—" Hawkins's dad starts, then stumbles over his feet and falls.

El Diablo flips over and empties the rest of the thirty-two-ounce Lancellottie, and the other contents of his stomach, right onto the man's chest.

Turbo salutes, a tear rolling down his cheek. "A technicolor tribute to Walt Disney."

The deed done, El Diablo flips onto his back and begins reverting back to a vomit-covered Uncle Ruckus. Mrs. S has been screaming the entire time. Hawkins's dad stands up and pukes, stumbling toward the bathroom. Sergeant Johnson sprints out from around the other side of the bathroom and smacks into the fleeing man.

"Is everything okay? I heard scr—" Sergeant Johnson looks down at his now filthy uniform, promptly throws up, then they both run into the bathroom.

Ducky, Goose, and Mother Goose howl with laughter. Goose yells, "Who's retarded now?!" and he and Ducky high five.

"Oh... my... God..." Banders says. "The Crab Walker card. It all makes sense."

"We can never do that again. Never." I hold up my pinky and Turbo wraps his around it.

"Never," he agrees. "Now let's collect our fallen hero."

* * *

A FEW HOURS AGO...
THURSDAY, JUNE 4TH, 2015. 5:03 PM.

It was nice, sometimes. He did this occasionally at his house, too. Put some earbuds in, close the curtains, and hop in bed. Tons of blankets and pillows stacked on top of him. It felt like being between the worlds, being crushed by the mattress and feeling the steady weight above too. There was something peaceful about it.

As much as Uncle Ruckus loved hanging out with his bros, sometimes he needed a minute. It wasn't as good at camp since he only had his sleeping bag, but it would have to do. It had been a wild few days, and he needed these few minutes to relax.

And of course, it had to be Turbo's worried voice to bring him out of his trance.

"What's the plan?"

27

A RANGER IS CULLING

Mrs. S helped catch Tri-Clops and get him dressed again, but she went home after. Hawkins's dad cussed everybody out and stormed up Cardiac Hill, leaving a rainbow drip trail behind him. Ducky's family is the only one that stuck around. Not much of a Parent's Night, but that's typical for us.

Dr. Cassandra ended up coming down to check out Uncle Ruckus. Turbo was thrilled, and he helped her clean up Uncle Ruckus and get some food and water in him. He was feeling better before long, and we all ended up sitting around the fire roasting marshmallows.

"I just can't believe I got to see the Crab Walker in action," Banders says. "First thing I'm doing when I get home is making a Cirque du Beast deck."

"First thing I'm doing is going to bed," Mother Goose says rising to her feet. "Thank you all for such a delicious meal and for your hospitality."

"I probably need to get going too," Dr. Cassandra says.

"Thank you," Goose says as he plays with his mom's hair.

"Thanks for coming," Mr. B says. "It was great having y'all. Sorry about... earlier."

"Me too," Hawkins says. It's the first thing he's said since he got here.

Goose looks up and smiles. "It's okay."

Hawkins straightens in his wheelchair. "I'm sorry to everybody. I'm sorry for my dad. I'm sorry for being a jerk before." He looks at Ducky. "I'm sorry."

"We forgive you," Shovel says.

"Yeah, and besides," Uncle Ruckus says, "no sweat about your dad. You don't get to pick your parents, and sometimes they're dicks."

"And sometimes they try their best, but miss the mark," Mr. McNitt adds.

We all sit there for a minute in silence. Then, an empty paint bucket clatters to the ground out of nowhere. Shovel, Banders, Treb, and Dr. Cassandra jump. The bucket has 'BAMA' written across the side in red, and there's a corncob painted on it.

"Damn," Ducky sighs. "I forgot the Culling and Parent's Night were on the same night this year."

"Does somebody want to explain what the hell is happening now?" Banders asks.

"the Culling," Ducky says. "They'll explain this year's rules when we get there. But that looks like a Culling Card to me."

Mr. B nods at the camp schedule. "It's tonight. I hope you boys are well-rested. It's the Alabama Troop this year, so that certainly looks like a Culling Card from them. Whichever troop is in charge of the Culling has to leave a 'calling card' to give the other troops a hint about what this year's event is going to be. But I'm not sure what paint and corn could mean. Doesn't matter. Let's win this Golden Plunger."

Holy crap, the Golden Plunger. I had almost forgotten about it. Our chance for another campout.

"Has anyone found the flag yet?" I ask.

"If they have, they haven't come forward with it," Mr. B says. "They might be waiting until the last minute so we all waste time looking for it. We've had enough sitting around, anyway. Duck, pick your crew."

"They're a sorry bunch," Ducky says, looking around. "But, I'll take iBall, Ty 2, Do-Over, Uncle Ruckus, and the new girl."

Banders rolls her eyes. "My name is Banders. Don't call me the new girl. Just think of me as one of the guys."

"There's another problem," Mr. B says. "I'm taking Uncle Ruckus home tonight, so he can't compete."

"Look around, Mr. B," I say with a grin. "There's no extra parents left here. You can't leave."

Mr. B says in a gruff voice, "Do-Over, you realize Dr. Cassandra is more than capable of helping Mr. McNitt watch the troop while I'm gone, right? And you've just reminded a member of Admin that Turbo and Uncle Ruckus are supposed to be going home tonight."

Shit. I deflate.

Dr. Cassandra glances at Turbo, who looks heartbroken. She sighs, then puts her fingers in her ears. "Lalalalalalalalalala…"

"Of course," Mr. B grins. "If it'd help our chances of winning the Culling, and thus the Golden Plunger, I wouldn't mind waking up early in the morning to take those two home."

Turbo pumps his fist and mouths 'Yes!'

"Now y'all get going. Before I change my mind." He lowers his hat over his eyes.

I lean over to Shovel. "You cool, man?"

"Huh?" He asks cheerfully.

"With not getting picked."

"Oh, yeah. I don't even know what it is, but I'm excited to stay here and see if my game works later tonight!" Shovel holds up the DS in the steamy bag of cooked rice.

I laugh. "Okay, just checking. Anyway, be seeing you."

"See ya."

Ducky kisses his mom on her head, does the 'up high, down low' routine with Goose, and then we set off down Cardiac Hill with the decorated paint bucket to answer the call.

"Okay, so earlier when half your troop was getting naked you guys said this wasn't a cult," Banders says.

"Uh huh," I say.

"And then a paint bucket flew into our camp. And you guys acted like it's normal."

"Uh huh."

"But it's still not a cult?" Banders asks.

Uncle Ruckus burps. "Jeez, it still tastes like Lancellottie. Yeah, so, the Culling is more or less organized hazing. They take a bunch of Rangers out into the woods, make em do some bullshit in the name of adventure, and the only troop that doesn't suffer is the one running it—which is the Alabama Troop this year."

"So we have no idea what to expect?" Banders asks.

"Not exactly," I say. "We can base it off previous years. I've never done one though."

"Okay, so what can we expect?" Banders asks, agitation evident in her voice.

Uncle Ruckus and I exchange a look. "We dunno."

Ducky chimes in from the front of the pack. "That's because when you participate in the Culling, you aren't allowed to talk about it to the uninitiated." He scratches his beard. "But we can talk about it with other people who have been through them before. Tyler 2, remember what it was like last year?"

Tyler 2 Electric Boogaloo shudders. "Salem Troop, bro. They're something else."

iBall shook his head. "Who thinks of that stuff? Straight creepy vibes. Go into the woods, dig your own grave, and spend the night in it."

"Wouldn't have been so bad if it was just that," Tyler 2 says.

"You had to stay in the grave once it's dug," Ducky says. "They waited until we fell asleep and started messing with us. Played creepy music through speakers in the trees—kids singing, whispering—that kind of thing. Then if you somehow managed to fall asleep, it got worse."

"Remember when you fell asleep?" iBall laughs.

"No, I forgot," Ducky says sarcastically.

"They put a frick ton of red dye in there while he was out cold, ran a hose to it, then started filling it up," iBall says. "Then you woke up and thought it was blood, and you scre—"

"Point is," Ducky interjects, "they do some whack stuff depending on the troop in charge."

"So," Banders says, "what do you think the Alabama Troop will make us do?"

"Make out with our cousins, probably," Uncle Ruckus laughs.

"Hard to say," Ducky admits. "But we're about to find out."

We stop at the bottom of the hill where the waterfront begins. There are rows of lanterns leading to the dock where figures stand in a line. My palms sweat as we approach the lake. Upon closer inspection, which I instantly regret, I notice the figures are wearing nothing but camouflage speedos. They painted the rest of their bodies from head to toe with camo. They looked like they were auditioning for *Apocalypse Now*.

"Feels *culty*," Banders says in a singsong voice.

"Beats baking," Uncle Ruckus mumbles.

"Damn straight, skippy," Banders says.

"Stop," a voice commands, so we do. "You have responded to the Culling, Ducky of the Troop 99. Do you understand the risks and rewards involved?"

"Yes," Ducky says without hesitation.

"Does the rest of your crew?"

"Yes."

"Hold up, no we don't," I blurt.

"Dude, just because Turbo isn't here doesn't mean you need to fill in his role as group pansy," Uncle Ruckus says.

I stare out at the water. Why else would we be down here if it wasn't to get in the water? I feel my breath coming in faster and faster, but it feels like I'm moving less air than usual. In short, I'm losing my shit.

"Calm down, bro," Ducky says. "It's gonna be okay. I picked you because you can handle this. Take deep breaths. I'll be right back." He walks over to one of the figures and whispers something, and the other figure follows Ducky back.

"It's okay, Do-Over," the nasally voice says. "Momma Hackett sent me with them to make sure things don't get out of hand in any way. We have a first aid tent with food, water, and nurses out at the Culling location."

"Journey?" I ask, then look down. I instantly regret it; there's just enough light to see his speedo and get scarred for life.

"Yeah. The Culling is a camp thing. Sure, it walks the line a little maybe, but it's not dangerous or anything," Journey says.

"I know," I say, standing taller. "I just haven't been picked before, and I don't know much about it. Just want to make sure there was more regulation than a Troop 100 Rock War is all."

Ducky claps me on the back. "I'll look out for ya. Don't worry, we'll win."

"Hang on, sorry, what exactly do we get if we win?" Banders asks.

Journey makes a face, but it's hard to tell what kind, because, you know, camouflage. "I thought every Adventure Ranger would know about the Golden Plunger."

"Oh, yeah, haha," Uncle Ruckus says putting an arm around Banders. "He's pretty forgetful, but he knows all about the Golden Plunger."

"Yeah," Banders says, trying to play along, but her voice is full of uncertainty, "the Golden Plunger, duh."

"It's always Troop 99," Journey shakes his head. "All right, Troop 100 is coming down Cardiac. We'll have to skip the rest of the pleasantries. Leave the Culling Card, get in a boat, and row for the red light across the water."

The six of us clamber in the boat. There's three paddles, so Ducky, iBall, and Tyler 2 Electric Boogaloo all grab one and start rowing us across the lake toward the glowing red light. It's pretty creepy, honestly. In *Space Odyssey 2001*, the red light was bad. Why would this one be different? There's a light in *The Great Gatsby* too, I think. We had to read it for school one summer. I didn't actually read it, but Spark Notes talked about green lights across the water a lot. I'm pretty sure everybody died at the end of that book. For this reason, glowing lights—especially those across bodies of water—have a negative connotation in my head.

"Let me get this straight," Banders is the first one to break the silence.

It pulls me out of my train of thought and makes me startlingly aware of the fact that, yet again, I have found myself floating in a little boat in the middle of the black lake.

"We are delving into the wilderness, losing sleep, and risking life and limb... for a plunger."

"Don't say it like *that*," Uncle Ruckus says. "the Golden Plunger is a symbol. It's like the Statue of Liberty or something... But better."

"Or," Banders says, "it could be a symbol of how boys are stupid and gullible. You go to camp, jump when they say jump, be on your best behavior, and do a bunch of bull crap, all because they spray-painted a plunger gold and told you it was special."

"Yeah," iBall says, "sounds about right."

"Don't forget the free trip to a high adventure camp," Ducky says.

"You guys are dumb," Banders trails a finger across the water's surface.

I grin. "You're not wrong."

Everybody goes silent. I sink back into my thoughts and stare at the spooky red light drawing ever closer. Red lights *usually* mean to stop, and yet here we are, rowing ever closer toward what might as well be a big red flag. But even better than a red flag, it's a red light. You can't spot red flags in the dark.

I convince myself the red light is a Terminator with an eyepatch on. When we actually make it to the shore, it turns out it's just a big LED with a plastic red lens over it. I'm relieved it's not a Terminator, but a little disappointed, because that would have been way cooler. Plus, if I die to a Terminator it means I don't die by drowning. Call me crazy, but I'd rather be ripped apart by a robot.

We're about to walk past the light and up the trail when I hesitate. "Hey, Uncle Ruckus?"

"Hmm?" He grunts.

"How good is Troop 100's pathfinding skills, you think?" I ask, staring at the extension cord hooked up to the light.

Uncle Ruckus grins an evil grin. It's terrifying in the red light.

"You scare me sometimes. Oh, that reminds me," I say as I fish around in my pocket. I pull out what I was looking for and toss it to him.

"*My baby!*" Uncle Ruckus screams. He cradles Devil Rock like an infant.

"Thanks for helping me get out of trouble," I say.

"What? What's that?" Uncle Ruckus holds the rock closer to his ear. "You think I should thank Do-Over for returning you to me? But, how?" He pauses, then his eyes slide to the extension cord. "Well," Uncle Ruckus says, "if you say so, Devil Rock." Uncle Ruckus reaches down and unplugs the extension cord, plunging us into darkness.

"What the heck, man?"

"Not cool, broseph."

"Uncle Ruckus, I'm going to crush you."

"Wait, guys, it's cool!" I say. "This'll give us a leg up on Troop 100."

"Hmm," Ducky says. "Not bad. I like how you guys think. We'll show those pricks."

Our eyes adjust after a while and we all stumble up the path in the dark together. It's not a long walk, probably about five minutes or so before we reach the top. We step into a clearing at the top of a cliff overlooking the lake. I'll give it to Banders; it straight up looks like a cult gathering.

The rest of the camo-painted Alabama Troop stands in a semi-circle. There isn't a single other troop in sight.

"That Troop 99?" a voice with a thick country accent asks.

"Sure is, how long until we get this thing started?" Ducky asks.

One of the figures hawks and spits off the side of the cliff. "Starts at nine, lasts the full eight hours 'til five AM. The other troops all showed and prepped. 'Cept Troop 100. Not like 'em bein' late."

"All right, well, let's prep," Ducky says.

First, they had a paint bucket with three batons in it.

"What's this?" Tyler 2 asks.

"Take 'em," the Camo Dude says.

"What happens if we take them?" Ducky asks, his voice full of caution.

"Fine, don't take 'em," Camo Dude says.

"No," Ducky blurts, "we want them."

Ducky, Tyler 2 Electric Boogaloo, and iBall each take a baton.

Next, we are taken to a table with six plastic bottles.

"Drink," Camo Dude says.

"Like hell," Banders says.

"Nah, I know this part," Ducky says. "They do this every year. It's Lightning in a Bottle, a concoction of Red Bull, Monster, 5 Hour Energy, and Coke."

Uncle Ruckus sighs. "It has Coke? Makes me think of Mr. McNitt. Miss that guy already."

"Down the hatch, boys," Ducky says, and he chugs the whole thing.

"This feels dangerous," I say, but drink it anyway.

Ducky almost trips halfway to the next station. "Yo, Banders. Hold this for me." He hands her his baton. "Gotta tie my shoe. I'll catch up."

We step up to the next table and Camo Dude says, "Present your batons."

iBall, Tyler 2, and Banders hold out their batons. Camo Dude takes each one, ducks down behind the folding table he's standing behind, and comes back up with three huge guns.

"Woah, woah," Tyler 2 says, "We don't want any trouble."

Camo Dude laughs. "You'll be wantin' these. They're made special, modified by our troop. These paintball guns shoot faster, hit harder, and carry more ammo than anything else on the market."

Ducky jogs up. "Sweet guns." He reaches for one, but Camo Dude pulls it back.

"No, only the ones who had batons git weapons," Camo Dude says.

"Oh, that's a cute trick," Ducky mutters. "What do the rest of us do?"

"Follow me," Camo Dude says.

While Banders, iBall, and Tyler 2 learn how to use their weapons, we head to a different table.

"What are your sizes?" Camo Dude asks.

We tell him and he produces three giant yellow and green foam costumes. Why do bad things happen to good people?

A few minutes later and the three of us are standing there dressed as cobs of corn.

"This is so demeaning," I say, watching Ducky try to stuff his beard into his too-small costume.

Uncle Ruckus looks himself up and down. "I don't know, I kind of like the way it hugs my curves."

When the other three arrive they double over. They're all wearing bright red head bands and camo shirts that say: *Mothershucker.*

"Yeah," I say over their laughter, "because you guys look so awesome."

Camo Dude grins. "One more thing."

He takes us to two boxes full of shoes and tells us to find our sizes. One box is labelled *Cobs* and the other box is labelled *Mothershuckers.* We sit down and put on the shoes. There's nothing different about them.

"I don't get it," iBall says.

"Stand up," Camo Dude orders.

iBall stands up and the sound of banjos erupts from his shoes.

Badadingdingdingdingdingdingdingding.

iBall sits back down and it stops. "Righteous."

I put some weight on my shoe and the sound of popcorn blares out of my shoes. "You have got to be kidding me."

"As you might'a guessed," Camo Dude says, "this is a fancy game of hide an' seek. Troop with the least amount'a paint on their corn wins. Mothershuckers can't shoot each other, only cobs. If you take off your shoes you're disqualified. If a Mothershucker tags a Mothershucker, the shooter is out. Only other rule is you have to stay on this island. Game starts in," he checks his watch, "ten minutes. Good luck."

"This is sadistic," I say.

"Aw," Banders says. "Does someone feel sad because they don't get a big scary gun?"

"Focus up," Ducky says. "We have like ten minutes to come up with a game plan. How do we want to play this?"

"We could try running and gunning," iBall says.

"No good," Banders says, "Everyone will be listening for popcorn popping. We'll just be screwing ourselves."

"Did he say island?" Uncle Ruckus asks.

"Yeah, I think we're on Thief Nick Island," Ducky answers.

"This is where they bring Rangers for the Wilderness Survival merit patch. Anybody know a good place to hide?"

"Oh, yeah," iBall says. "This is where Trylinair Point is, right? Just a little ways, away."

"Good idea," Ducky says. "They are some caves around there. We could post up in one. Let our Mothershuckers cover the entry points and hide the cobs in the back?"

"Not bad," Tyler 2 agrees. "We can also jump off the cliffs if we need a quick escape."

"Sounds like we got a plan then," Uncle Ruckus says.

Troop 100 huffs and puffs up the hill behind us.

"Five minutes to spare. Cuttin' it close!" Camo Dude calls.

"Ready?" I ask my friends, ready to spring to my feet. My blood feels electrified; probably all the caffeine.

"Let's shuck some corn," Banders says.

We all get to our feet and a chorus of banjos and corn popping plays. Ducky takes the lead and we sprint toward Trylinair Point.

* * *

FIVE YEARS AGO...

FEBRUARY 5ᵀᴴ, 2010. 6:33 PM.

"Hi there, uh, I must admit I am a little out of my element here," Mr. McNitt chuckled. "I want to buy a game for my son. His birthday is soon."

The clerk didn't look up from his computer. "Get him Grand Theft Hotties."

Mr. McNitt glanced at the cover. "I'm not sure he's old enough for that quite yet. He's a sensitive boy."

The clerk raised an eyebrow but said nothing.

"You know what? Never mind, I'll just pick something out," Mr. McNitt said.

He perused the wall of games. There were *so many* to choose from. Games with guns, games with dragons, games with demons, games with plumbers—but none of them seemed like the kind of game his son would like. Just when he was ready to give up and go buy clothes instead, a grinning dachshund caught his eye.

Mr. McNitt walked over and looked at the game. He'd had a dachshund when he was a boy, and he loved it very much. This appeared to be a game where you took care of dogs. It would be cheaper than buying him a real dog, that's for sure. Besides, this would be good practice for having a pet in the future. This game seemed like the type a sensitive boy might like to play. He reached forward and took it off the shelf.

28

A RANGER IS SHUCKED

Badadingding-popopop-ding-poppop-bada-poppop-ding-pop-ding-pop!

It gets annoying really fast. We can barely hear each other over the sound of our shoes. After running for a few minutes, we take a quick breather—in, you guessed it—some bushes. For once, I don't mind wearing the corn suit. Should help keep the ticks out, or at least that's what I tell myself. The Mothershuckers are on their knees keeping watch while us corn lay down gasping for air. Ducky was built for strength, not endurance. Uncle Ruckus and I, well, we aren't even built.

"What's the time, iBall?" Tyler 2 Electric Boogaloo asks.

"No real names," iBall says. "This is a stealth operation. If we use names, *they* might figure out which troop we are and target us. Call me Little Dog."

"Okay," Tyler 2 says, "then call me Elmo Mouse."

A series of shots rings out in the trees behind us and we all snap to alert.

"I'm gonna go check that out, try and paint some Cobs. Stay here, guys," Tyler 2 says.

"You got it, Little Dog," iBall says.

Tyler 2 gets to his feet. Banjos blare then recede into the distance.

Badadingdingdingdingdingdingding...

"Tyler," Banders says. "You know Elmo Mouse is the worst nickname I've ever heard, right?"

"Bro." Tyler 2 looks hurt.

But I can't get into the fun of it. I'm too busy thinking about those cliffs—our backup plan for escape. What the heck am I gonna do if my choice is either leap off a cliff into the potentially monster-infested death lake or be pelted by superpowered paintballs for the next eight hours? My anxiety has steadily risen, probably in part due to the mass amount of caffeine I ingested with the Lightning in a Bottle.

"Talk to me about these cliffs," I say.

"Not much to say," Ducky wheezes.

"Well, how do you know where it's safe to jump?" I ask.

"We lost a lot of good men to trial and error," Ducky says, and I can't tell if he's serious.

"Yeah?" I ask nervously.

"That's why we named it Trylinair Point. Trial and error," Ducky says. "Oh. You have a thing about water, right?"

"It's not a *thing*," I say. "It just makes me... nervous."

"Well, it *sounds* like a thing," Ducky says.

"It's a thing," Banders confirms. "I've seen it."

Dingdingdingdingdingdingdingdingbadadingdingdingdingding.

We all freeze; nobody moves. The banjos get louder.

Dingdingdingdingdingbadadingdingding!

Someone sprints through the brush, and Tyler 2 and Banders open fire.

Papapapapapap!

The banjos stop as the person plops to the ground, "*Guys, it's me!*"

"Little Dog?" Tyler 2 asks without lowering his weapon.

"Oops," Banders says. "We pet the wrong dog on this one."

iBall looks down and sighs. "It's all right, it's open war out there. Everybody is firing on everybody. There's Mothershucker on Mothershucker violence, and I'm worried a troop might have followed me."

"We should get out of here then," Banders says.

Ducky moans.

"Remember, if we get split up, we try and meet in one of the caves," Banders says.

Dingdingdingbadading.

We all leap to our feet and the shoes blare their respective sounds. iBall takes the lead this time, and we keep sprinting down the path. It's slow going between the bulky suits, the rocky terrain, and the odd tree root sticking out of the ground. Paintballs whizz past us.

"They're gaining!" I scream.

"Almost.... There!" Ducky puffs.

Moments later, we burst into a clearing, and what is presumably Trylinair Point. I freeze, unable to go closer to the cliff edge. Ducky looks at me, recognition in his face.

"It's going to be okay," he says. "You guys take cover in one of those trees. We'll lead them away."

I nod. Uncle Ruckus, Banders, and I climb as high as we can in a cedar tree and let our legs dangle so our shoes don't make any noise.

"And remember!" Ducky screams over the sound of his shoes popping. "Run faster if you hear the banjos!"

Three Mothershuckers burst out of the trees from the way we just came. I can barely make out what they're saying over the sound of the shoes.

"Well, well, well," Peters says; Richardson and Woody at his heels. "Troop 99. Where's the rest of your cobby little friends?" He raises his gun and points it at Ducky.

Tyler 2 lunges in front of Ducky. "You can't shoot a Mothershucker!" he yells.

Peters rolls his eyes, turns, and shoots Woody in the chest.

Pop pop! "Oof!"

"A heads up would have been nice!" Woody exclaims. "Damn, they really did mod the heck out of these things. That hurt."

Peters's face morphs into shock. "Troop 99 just shot one of our Mothershuckers in cold blood. Guess all bets are off!"

Peters raises his gun again, and Woody and Richardson follow suit. They open fire.

"Ducky, go!" iBall yells, escorting him in a 'Get down, Mr. President!' maneuver.

Tyler 2 gets *plastered* with paint as Troop 100 fires off a relentless barrage. Ducky leaps off the cliff, Mothershucker guards in tow. Troop 100 sprints to the edge and fires down on them for about twenty seconds. Then, they sit down on the edge and their shoes go silent.

"What's the move?" Richardson asks.

"Simple. We wait for them to swim to shore, listen for their shoes, then head in that direction," Peters says. "I don't care if another troop wins the Golden Plunger, I just don't want it to be 99."

About three minutes later, faint banjos and popping started playing in the distance.

"Perfect, let's go," Peters says with a wicked grin.

We wait in silence for a good ten minutes after we last hear banjos.

"Caves?" Uncle Ruckus asks.

"Caves," I agree, and start to climb down. I put some weight on a branch with my foot and I'm instantly met with *popopopop*. I lift my foot back up. "Shit, sorry."

"We need to be careful," Banders says. "I don't even think it's safe for me to walk around if people are shooting Mothershuckers too. This is gonna suck, but I think we go on our hands and knees. Or slide on our butts."

Getting down from the tree is tedious since we can't put weight on our shoes, but we manage. Back on the ground, we get on our butts and scoot like our lives depend on it. I alternate between scooting and crawling to keep from scratching up my hands and knees. More importantly, I don't scoot the whole way because I don't want to tear myself another asshole. Paintball gunfire rings in the distance, but we don't hear banjos. We stop at the first cave we find.

"It's *freezing* in here," I shudder.

"Let's take inventory," Uncle Ruckus says. "What do you guys have on you?"

My pockets are empty. Banders pulls out a peanut butter and gummy worm sandwich—shocker. Uncle Ruckus pulls out a pocketknife, a roll of Tough Tape, some Ziploc bags, a granola bar, and Devil Rock.

"All right, most important thing," Uncle Ruckus says. "Which one is the poop corner?"

"It's a cave," I say. "There probably aren't corners. And you haven't taken a crap yet? *Still?*"

"No," Uncle Ruckus shifts uncomfortably, "but there's something stirring in my loins. And I don't think it's the kind of thing that's usually supposed to be stirring in your loins."

"Too much information," Banders says. "But, listen, caves are really dangerous. Hug a wall, and let's go around it really slow. And be careful of drop-offs. It'll be good to know what's in here in case we get found, that way we know if we should run or hide."

Banders and Uncle Ruckus start at opposite sides of the cave and work their way around it until they disappear into the darkness. I assign myself the job of keeping watch. Unfortunately, the cave is cold. And wet. And I need to pee like crazy. I don't want to pee into the cave because it'll run down onto my friends. I don't want to get in the water to pee either. If I were an imaginary Lake Monster, I would probably strike when someone is most vulnerable—when they're going to the bathroom. Just saying.

The Ziploc bags catch my eye. *Hmm. That could work.* I grab one, unzip my pants, tuck my knees into my shirt so nobody can tell what I'm doing, and get to business. Banders and Uncle Ruckus return just as I'm finishing up.

"Nothing to report, really," Banders says. "Just some bugs and bats."

Frick. I seal the bag and zip my pants.

"Yeah, nothing to report here either," I say.

I maneuver the bag up next to my stomach so I can pull my knees out of my shirt. The bag is warm against my skin; it feels nice. I remember it's my pee, and I'm instantly disgusted by myself.

"You okay?" Banders asks. "You seem freaked out." She sits down next to me.

"Yeah, no, I'm good," I say, nodding to assure her.

"You know what always makes me feel better when I don't feel good?" she asks, reaching behind her. She pulls out the peanut butter and gummy worm sandwich and offers me half.

"Thanks," I say, then take it and scarf it down.

Uncle Ruckus sits down on my other side and says, "Yeah guys, no worries, I'm good. I don't need any of the sandwich. I'll just eat this delicious granola bar. But I appreciate the offer."

"Oh, whatever," I say. "If you had a sandwich, you'd eat it in a heartbeat rather than share it with us. Selfish."

Uncle Ruckus looks taken aback. "Do-Over, you've gone and hurt my feelings. All I ever did was—" he sniffs, "was love you." His voice shifts like he's talking to a baby. "How can I help cheer you up?" He snaps his fingers. "Oh, I know. Whenever I'm sad, the thing that helps me most is... a tickle fight!"

My heart leaps into my throat and I unleash a scream of defiance. I hurl myself backwards and throw up my hands to fend off Uncle Ruckus's attack, but it's not enough. He dodges my defense and goes straight for my stomach. Warmth spreads across my belly. I stop trying to defend myself and lay there. Suffering.

Uncle Ruckus freezes. "What the— Dude, you're wet. What are you covered in?" The smell hits him and he shrinks back in horror. "Did you just *piss* yourself?!"

Banders's laughter rebounds off the cave walls as she rolls around on the ground.

My face feels hot. "No, dude. I peed in a bag!" I pull it out for emphasis. "See?"

Uncle Ruckus's expression shifts from horror to amusement. "Well, well, well. Look who's cuddling a bag of liquid now. Taking a page from old Uncle Ruckus now, are ya? Using your pee to keep warm; that's not a bad idea."

Banders laughs harder.

"You can't even say *a word* because you can't even take a shit in the same room as someone else!" I yell.

"You can't *what?*" Banders's laughter intensifies.

"It's true!" I say. "And you know that rock he had in his pocket? He talks to it and uses it to scare the younger Adventure Rangers."

She squeals with laughter, which was apparently the last straw for her, because her giggle cuts off. She looks at us with a stoic face and admits, "I peed too."

We crack up together this time, then decide it might be best if we take a quick dip in the lake. After all, we don't want to sit in a cave smelling like urine for the rest of the night. After removing her shoes, Banders takes a running leap into the water, and Uncle Ruckus does the same. I feel nervous, so I take it slow. I'm still in costume, since it'll be easier for the authorities to find my body when I drown if I'm wearing bright green and yellow. I slip into the lake and doggy paddle around. We listen to the sounds of paintball guns firing. Two cobs and a Mothershucker floating around in the water, safe in each other's company.

"Thanks for rescuing me from Home-Ec camp," Banders says.

"Thanks for saving me," Uncle Ruckus whispers.

I don't know what that means really, but I reach out and give him a squeeze on the shoulder. "Sorry about your plane ticket money," I say.

"Oh," Banders says. "Your toilet paper scheme didn't pay off?"

Uncle Ruckus shakes his head. "I don't know what I'm going to do. I can't stay at home. I miss Mark... I miss my mom." His voice breaks. "What if I can't beat this?"

I meet his eyes. "Sometimes you can't beat your problems, and that's okay. You don't have to be strong enough to beat them, because you're always strong enough to withstand them. At least until things get better. Besides," I say, "you've got all of us. We're here for you, buddy. You're a little shit, but we love you."

"You don't get to pick your family. But you do get to pick your friend-family. We'll be your fremily." Banders smiles.

Uncle Ruckus smiles back. "I'll be your fremily, too."

We float there for a long time, looking up at the stars.

"You know what?" I say. "I think I got scared of the water because of this one time at the beach and I almost drowned when I was little. The water pulled me under and seaweed wrapped all around me. I had nightmares about drowning by some huge sea monster every night for years. And thinking about it now, I realize I kind of psyched myself out. There was nothing to be afraid of, I just kind of overthought things. Maybe you're overthinking things with Mark. Maybe you don't have to buy a plane ticket. If you really want to go to San Francisco, just talk to him. Really talk to him, don't just be a dickhead like usual."

"You might be right. I'll try it," Uncle Ruckus murmurs. "I just... miss my mom. I never talk about it. And I don't talk about how my dad changed. We're guys, you know? We have to be tough. But I don't feel tough. Maybe I should try talking to Uncle Mark about missing my mom. I guess she was his sister, same way she was my mom. What if it's as simple as a conversation?"

My eyes burn. "I get that. I feel like maybe if I talked about stuff more, with my parents and friends and everything, that maybe things would turn out better. You don't always have to have a scheme, and I don't always have to punch my problems. Sometimes it works better if you think it through in the moment and be rational."

"Yeah," Uncle Ruckus laughs. "You could probably stand to resort to your fists a little less."

My cheeks burn.

"But you're doing better lately!" he says.

Badadingdingdingdingdingding!

"Oh shit," Banders says. "Talk time is over. We gotta get back in the cave before they shoot so much paint up our assholes that we're crapping rainbows for the next two weeks."

"Eloquently put," I say.

After swimming back to the cave, we huddle together. Not in the pee corner. Banders sits with her gun trained on the entrance of the cave. The banjos don't come close again, and we all fall asleep.

* * *

THREE YEARS AGO...
OCTOBER 21ST, 2012. 7:30 AM.

"All right, handsome, time to wake up! Time for school!" She waited. The lump in the bed didn't move. She drew the Super Soaker filled with ice water from behind her back and crept across the orange shag carpet. "Honey!" she sang, but the boy laid asleep under the covers, unmoving.

In her left hand she held up the lid to a plastic storage tub. Her son had caught her off guard before when she got too close, but not this time. This time she had a shield. She crept ever closer until she was a few feet from the bed.

She used her sweetest mom voice. "Babe, time to wake up."

Still no movement. He deserved everything that was coming to him. She smiled and pulled the trigger. Water gushed out from the Super Soaker as she swept it up and down the length of the motionless form—but nothing happened. No screaming, no cursing, no running. She realized too late, *It's a trap.*

"See you in hell!" Uncle Ruckus leaped out of his closet brandishing not one, but two Super Soakers. He sported full rain gear as he unleashed a torrent of water from each weapon and soaked his mom to her bones. She laughed hysterically and dove into the bed and under the covers to try and defend herself, but it was no good.

Sure, Uncle Ruckus was soaking his bed. This would just have to be a Pyrrhic victory. He didn't let up on the triggers until the guns ran out of water.

"Menopause has made your mind feeble, old woman," he gloated. His mom's laughing doubled, and Uncle Ruckus's eyes narrowed. "What's so funny?" Uncle Ruckus felt his rain hat being swept off his head and was doused with ice-cold water. He turned in place to face his dad, whose laughter boomed throughout the house. He had an empty bucket.

"Age and tenacity will always beat out youth and enthusiasm," his mom said.

Uncle Ruckus reached down the front of his pants, pulled out the mini squirt gun hidden there, and fired a pathetic barrage of water upon his defenseless father. His dad squealed and bolted out of the room with Uncle Ruckus in hot pursuit.

"I'm coming, babe!" his mom yelled down the hall after them, eyes gleaming with joy. "Right after I reload at the bathroom sink. Try and corner the little shit so we can tickle him!"

29

A RANGER IS REDEEMED

'And we all fell asleep.' Yeah, right. Lightning in a Bottle is no joke; we ended up staying up literally the entire night. I wish I could say we played Uno, but we didn't. We sat in a cave, soaking wet, and made fun of each other until morning. It was the best time I've had at camp so far.

Unfortunately, morning came right as we started to get sleepy. A loud bell rang at sunrise and the paintball gun sounds ceased. We made our way around Thief Nick island and toward the sound of the bell. We were the last ones to make it back, and we arrived to a gruesome sight. While every person was covered in paint to an extent, no one was worse off than Troop 99's own Ducky, iBall, and Tyler 2 Electric Boogaloo. They looked like they'd been playing on a paint slip-and-slide all night.

We sidle up to Ducky and listen.

"Right," Journey says. "This wasn't as clean as we would have liked. I know there was some genuine misfires and accidents out there with Mothershuckers shooting other Mothershuckers. But, there was also some deliberate rule breaking." His eyes narrow and dart between Troop 100 and us. "However, it's indisputable that there is one troop who rose above the rest." He gestures toward mine and Uncle Ruckus's clean cob costumes. "Troop 99 wins the Culling!"

Ducky swoops us all in a giant bear hug and we jump up and down cheering. *We did it.*

"Yooooo," iBall says, "the whole night was worth it now!"

Peters flips us off and Ducky growls at him. Like, actually growls.

"Maybe we should go see how everybody back at camp is doing," I say as I grab Ducky by the kernels and tug him backwards.

He relents, and we hop in our canoe to head back to camp.

"Just so awesome, bro," Tyler 2 says as he rows.

"For real. We got a real chance of winning now," iBall says. "We got absolutely plastered by paintballs all night long while you guys hid like legends and came out totally clean. Nice work, you guys scored us the dub."

Ducky smiles. "Yeah, you guys did all right."

Uncle Ruckus fists bumps me, and I can't help but grin. *We* did it. We made it happen. It's an amazing feeling.

"Stay focused," Ducky says. "Stay alert. We have had terrible behavior all week. We still have to find the flag to have a real shot at the Golden Plunger. We don't have much, but we got a shot. Let's not blow our lead."

I want to win so badly. I think back to the beginning of the week when we were all going crazy over the Golden Plunger. I was really hung up on winning, largely due to thinking Uncle Ruckus was about to be gone. But, even knowing he's not leaving for real, I want to win it. Because this week I've had the best times at camp just hanging out with my friends. It's not about the Golden Plunger itself. It's about the chance to get to do it all over again at a high adventure camp with my best friends. Dying, laxatives, running from the law, a Taser Buck... That stuff was awesome. And none of it was about a Golden Plunger.

Once we reach land, we get our stuff together and trudge up Cardiac Hill. We beeline for the Dining Hall since everyone would be at breakfast right about now. Like a bunch of zombies, we meander through the masses and join the rest of our troop.

"How'd it go?" Mr. McNitt asks.

"We won," Ducky says as he shovels spoonfuls of gravy into his mouth.

"Nice work," Mr. B says. "That's one guaranteed point in our favor out of three. Let's see if we can't stay sharp and find that flag today. Hope you boys got some sleep last night," Mr. B says.

"Not even a little," Ducky picks red paint out of his beard. "They did awesome last night, though," he nods at us.

"Guys!" Shovel squeals and comes up to hug us in turn. "How was it? Was it cool? What happened?" Then in a lower voice he says, "You guys aren't gonna believe what happened last night."

"What?" I ask.

"I had the best night *ever.* Hawkins let me play a game on his phone! And then my dad gave me my own pocketknife, look!" Shovel holds out a tiny Swiss army knife. "And then, we played charades all night. What did you guys do?"

We look at each other and Banders says, "We shucked some corn."

She starts going into detail, explaining the previous night's events, but I notice a wheelchair out of the corner of my eye. Hawkins is balancing his food tray on his lap as he tries to wheel his way through the crowd and over to our table. *Maybe I should go help him? He apologized after all. Was even being nice, sounds like.* His cup tips forward and tumbles off the tray. The cup turns end over end, the translucent plastic catching the light as it falls. There is nothing anyone can do at that point.

The cup hits the ground and the hollow echo resounds inside my chest as it resonates through the Dining Hall. The whole room goes silent as the cup bounces around on the ground a dozen times, then goes still. Before anyone can say anything, Shovel grabs his cup of juice in his right hand and Turbo's cup of milk in his left hand. Then, he sends both cups hurtling toward the floor.

Even though the cups are full of liquid, the effect was the same. The juice and milk slosh together on the floor in a disgusting combination, and the twin cups boom throughout the Dining Hall. Hundreds of Adventure Rangers and Leaders stare in stunned silence.

I grab Shovel's arm and hiss, "Why did you do that? He was such a dick to you."

Shovel looks taken aback and murmurs, "He said sorry. And he's in Troop 99. He's just an outlier like the rest of us."

The whole room explodes into laughter, pointing at Shovel, apparently forgetting about Hawkins. Shovel did something no one had ever done in the history of Camp Winnebago. He dropped *two* cups. There would be no living this one down, *ever*.

The sound is too much. It fills my ears and sends jolts of anxiety coursing up and down my limbs. I feel angry and frustrated. How can I make them all shut up? I can't beat them all up. My vision turns red; there's no colors to look for. Helplessness flares inside of me. My eyes flick around the room. I want to hit something. I want to fix this. Shovel doesn't deserve this.

A tear rolls down Shovel's cheek and he shrugs. "Hey, at least they're laughing. That's what decafing a bad situation is all about."

Uncle Ruckus and Turbo step up next to me, each with a hand on either shoulder.

"Do-Over?" Turbo asks nervously.

And then, my eyes settle on one spot in the room. And I have an idea.

"Follow me. I need your help." I start walking, all the while the rest of the room continues their raucous laughter.

"Uhh, Do-Over," Uncle Ruckus says. "Are you thinking straight? I know you tend to get a little physical when you get mad, but I'm not sure how that's going to help us here."

"Just trust me. I can't ask you to participate in what I'm about to do, but if it feels right, I'd appreciate the help," I say, more confident in my decision than ever. I weave in and out between tables and Rangers until I reach my target. I put my hands on the dining cart. "Ready?"

Turbo Cakes and Uncle Ruckus stare back with wide eyes, but they nod and put their hands on the dining cart too. Then, we push. The entire dining cart tips over with a crash, sending hundreds of plastic cups tumbling to the ground. I thought it was going to be horrifying, but it was beautiful.

There were so many stupid rules to fit in, and we just broke the biggest one in the biggest way possible. Don't drop a cup in the Dining Hall.

The Dining Hall descends into madness. Right away someone flings a gravy-covered biscuit that hits me square in the forehead. I peel it off my face and send it sailing back in the direction it came. *Oh, man. It's over now.* Everyone starts throwing food and dozens of voices yell, "Food fight!"

"Come on!" I drag my friends toward the door.

We burst through the front doors and run into none other than Camp-A-Cop.

He raises his eyebrows and gestures at the chaotic Dining Hall. "You boys do this?"

We don't answer. We take off running, heading around the back of the Infirmary, only to stop in our tracks. Moonpie takes a bite out of an actual

Moonpie and then offers a bite to his best friend in the whole world. A best friend we know as The Taser Buck.

The Taser Buck looks at us with recognition in its intelligent eyes. It takes the rest of the Moonpie from Moonpie's hand and chews deliberately as the old man tries to disentangle the tasers from its antlers. The Taser Buck lowers its head, and it charges.

Just then, Camp-A-Cop comes appears wielding a can of pepper spray. "I'm sick of your tomfoolery!" he shouts and blasts a stream of the stuff as he turns the corner.

He misses us, but the Taser Buck runs straight through the stream of pepper spray. The poor beast's head whips from side to side in misery.

"What'd yee do?" Moonpie exclaims.

Mr. B appears right behind Camp-A-Cop with Shovel and Banders in tow.

"Boys?!" Mr. B yells, his mustache twitching.

Moonpie tackles Camp-A-Cop to the ground and they begin to wrestle.

"Oh, for the love of Saint George," Mr. B shouts and takes off running to break up the scuffle.

"Banders, Shovel, come on!" Uncle Ruckus shouts as we turn and run the opposite direction and round the corner of the Infirmary with Turbo in the lead.

Turbo, despite his name, is not very fast. None of us are, to be fair. Banders was faster than the rest of us, and she should have been in the lead. But luckily for Turbo, he had a head start on her. It's lucky because Turbo was the first person to round the corner. And when he does, Turbo runs smack-dab into Dr. Cassandra.

Turbo isn't especially tall. I'd be willing to bet on most days, Turbo wishes he was taller. But after today, I don't think Turbo will ever want to grow another inch. Why? Because it just so happens that Turbo Cakes is the *perfect* height. He is just tall enough so that his face is cushioned by Dr. Cassandra's breasts when he runs into her.

"Boys!" Dr. Cassandra shouts, stumbling backwards. "I heard a ruckus out back and I came to see what was going on."

The look on Turbo's face is priceless. It looks like all of his three functioning brain cells are trying to keep him breathing, and none of them are working on communication.

"A ruckus?" Uncle Ruckus asks. "Can you describe the ruckus?"

"I thought I heard..." Dr. Cassandra hesitates. "Is that a buck with tasers attached to its antlers? And... Moonpie! Who is he fighting?" She darts around Turbo and heads into the fray.

"Get your crap together Turbo, we gotta move!" Banders yells, and we all take off running again with Turbo Cakes in tow.

* * *

MOMENTS LATER...
FRIDAY, JUNE 5TH, 2015. 8:21 AM.

Holly yawned. Besides the inevitable phone calls from worried parents and a few upset tummies, it had been a relatively quiet week in the Infirmary. Would have been even quieter without that Turbo Cakes kid toddling around after Dr. Cassandra all week. She closed her book and picked up the seventh and last volume in the series. This was her own little tradition every year. Reread her favorite books from when she was a kid while she worked the Infirmary desk at summer camp. Just one more to read before the end of the day. Doable.

"You son of a—"

"For king and country!"

"Fight like men, you cowards!"

She sat up in her chair and peeked out the blinds. Her heart almost stopped at the sight on the parade field. A buck with *tasers* and netting tangled in its antlers spun in distress. Camp-A-Cop and Moonpie rolled back and forth on the ground as Troop 99's Leader and Dr. Cassandra shouted at them to stop. On the other side of the field, the Hawkins boy held up lunch trays in a Spartan-esque fashion as a young Ranger with dark hair wheeled him across the field. Another boy with a birthmark in the center of his forehead chucked spoonful after spoonful of mashed potatoes at their pursuers. More and more Adventure Rangers spilled out of the Dining Hall like a disturbed ant colony.

Holly sat in stunned horror. She debated if she should call the police or don a rain poncho and join the fray. After a moment's deliberation, she knew what she needed to do. She closed the blinds, sat back in her chair, and began the last book. This seemed like someone else's problem.

30

A RANGER IS MISADVENTURED

What would any reasonable group of teenagers do when faced with that kind of heat? We hid in the woods. And why not? It was the last day of camp, all we had to do was survive until our parents came to pick us up. Mr. B was going to drive Turbo and Uncle Ruckus home anyway, so what's the harm in hiding out all day so they can stay a bit longer? We sat around playing Egyptian Rat Trap, Uno, and Texas Hold Em by the lake for the rest of the day. Uno, being the game that Turbo's morals were most at ease with, was what we played most.

"When do you guys think we should come out?" Turbo Cakes asks in a quavering voice, laying down a blue four.

"Turbo, Turbo, Turbo," Banders tsks. "Haven't you ever been in big trouble before?" She plays a wild card. "Red," she says.

A heartbeat later, Turbo answers, "No, not like this."

I play a red skip card and give Uncle Ruckus a big smile.

"Bitch," he mumbles, holding only two cards in his hand.

Shovel lays down a red two and says, "Wait, so what should you do when you're in big trouble?"

Turbo lays down a blue two, "Don't listen to this bunch, that's for sure..."

"Okay, well here's a simple rule of thumb when it comes to big trouble: hide your ass off." Banders sits back and slaps a green two onto the pile of cards. "Uno," she says.

I consider the cards in my hand. A green eight, a green reverse, and a yellow six. "You see, young Shovel," I say, fingering the green eight. "To the unexperienced, it might seem stupid to hide when in such big trouble. In reality, it's genius."

"You don't know the first thing about big trouble. The only thing you're experienced in is kiss ass with Mr. B," Uncle Ruckus snorts.

"Just for that," I smile sweetly and flip Uncle Ruckus the bird. Then I play my green reverse card, the turn goes right back to Banders.

"Oh, you dick," Uncle Ruckus seethes, clutching his last two Uno cards even tighter.

We all focus our attention on Banders and her last card. She stares a hole into the card, then looks up. "Point is, Shovel: If we hide, they'll end up being super worried about us. Then, when they finally find us, they'll be so relieved we're safe that they won't even remember what we did!" She slaps down the last card, a green one. "Suck it, bitches."

"You did that. Way to go, Do-Over," Uncle Ruckus says.

"How long do you think it'll be until they find us?" Turbo asks. "I don't think I brought enough mosquito repellent for all of us to stay out here multiple days."

"Oh, whatever will we do?" I ask in a mocking tone.

"Okay, fine. Enjoy more ticks on your dick. I'll enjoy itch-free, malaria-free bliss all on my own," Turbo says defiantly.

"I'm not worried about malaria right now," I say. "I'm worried about the Taser Buck finding us again."

"Come on," Banders says. "You aren't afraid of a little deer, are you?"

"Uhh, point of importance," I say. "Little deer killed Mufasa. Disney conditioned me to be terrified from a young age."

The wind picks up and sunlight litters the ground as the leaves above rustle in protest. It dies off a moment later, and a heavy silence fills the spaces between the trees.

"I miss the snack days," Uncle Ruckus says.

"What do you mean?" I ask.

"You know," he says, "back when you were young enough that your mom made you snacks after school. You weren't too old to drink Capri Sun and eat Lunchables. The snack days."

"Wait..." Shovel says. "I won't be allowed to eat that stuff when I'm as old as you guys?"

"Not if you want to be 'cool,'" Turbo says.

"Can I tell you guys something?" I ask.

Nobody answers.

"I still drink Capri Sun. They're still awesome."

Banders clears her throat, her voice sounds scratchy, "Yeah, me too."

Uncle Ruckus scrambles to his feet, scattering playing cards across the forest floor.

"Hey!"

"What the hell?"

"We aren't doing this," Uncle Ruckus says. "We don't need the snack days. Screw it. Boys, we're not too old for snack days. Especially not Shovel."

"He scares the shit outta me when he talks like this," Turbo says.

"No, guys. I'm serious," Uncle Ruckus says. "We aren't too old for Uno, snacks, or having a good time at camp. Shovel, why did you come to camp?"

Shovel thinks for a moment. "Well, I guess to earn some merit patches. Maybe rank up past Tenderboot?"

"I'm not a miracle-worker," Uncle Ruckus says. "You're probably going to leave this camp as a Tenderboot still, I'm going to be honest. But maybe you can leave here with a few merit patches. We can at least do that much before the big bonfire tonight."

"You... want to help me?" Shovel asks.

"I mean, it's the least we can do, right guys?" Uncle Ruckus asks.

"Yeah," I say. "To be fair, you kind of got roped up in all our bullshit. You didn't get to do any normal camp stuff, huh?"

"Not really," Shovel admits. "But are there any merit patches I can earn before we have to go to the bonfire?"

"Sure there are," Uncle Ruckus says. "Turbo, pass me your Adventure Ranger Handbook."

"Why do you just assume I have it with me? What, do you think I just carry it around at all times?" Turbo protests.

Uncle Ruckus holds his hand out.

Turbo sighs, digs around in his pack, and passes the book to Uncle Ruckus. He flips through it and reads off some of the merit patches, "Fingerprinting, Fire Safety, First Aid, Fishing... there's a ton of easy ones in here. Dude, no way! There's one for *Art*. The only requirement is to 'make something you're proud of.'"

Shovel grins, grabs a stick, and jabs it into the dirt so it's sticking straight up.

"That's beautiful," I say.

"Truly captures the essence of *art*," Banders says.

Turbo chokes up and says, "The post-contemporary metaphorical resonance of the facture contextualizes the accessibility of the piece. The disjunctive perturbation of the biomorphic forms visually and conceptually activates the exploration of montage elements."

Uncle Ruckus stares at him. "Why do you have to ruin everything?" He turns to Banders. "You still got your phone on you?"

"Sure do," she says.

"Take a pic of this bad boy. That way we have proof to show Mr. B that our mans is an *artist* deserving of one Art merit patch."

Shovel stares at his sculpture in awe, "Thank you guys so much."

"Oh, we're not done there," Uncle Ruckus says. "Turbo, how much time do we have until it's time for the bonfire?"

Turbo checks his watch. "Looks like we have about two hours."

"All riiight!" Uncle Ruckus exclaims. "Let's see how many merit patches we can help Shovel get in two hours. You guys in or out? In or out? In or out? In or out?"

Banders stands up and we both join in with the chant and put our faces closer and closer to Turbo's with each chant.

"In or out? In or out? In or out?"

"Okay! Okay! Sheesh, fine," Turbo stands up amidst the lean-to rubble and dusts himself off. "The ethics of half-assing Shovel's merit patches with him are dubious at best, but I'm in."

We all hoot and clap him on the back.

I look down at Shovel and smile at him, extending a hand. "In or out, bud?"

Shovel beams. "In. All the way, bro."

He takes my hand, and I haul him to his feet.

"What's the plan?" he asks.

There's no plan. Which ends up being half the fun. We go down the list of merit patches and do the ones that sound easy. Or half-asseable.

"Aha! American Business, this'll be easy," Uncle Ruckus says as he fishes something out of Turbo's pack. "Sell me this pen."

Shovel takes the pen. "Um. It'll help you write stuff?"

"I'll take it!" Uncle Ruckus shouts. They get a picture together with Shovel handing him the pen and smiling with a thumbs-up.

"Oh, look," Turbo says. "There's one for 'Pets.' But it looks like you have to take care of a pet for several months in order to get it..."

A silence falls over us. *RIP virtual dogs.* "Wait," I say. "How long did you play that game with the dogs?"

"Hard to say exactly how long, but... I had them for a long time," Shovel sniffs.

"Good enough for me," Uncle Ruckus says. Shovel digs out the water-logged game and gives a somber smile while Banders takes his picture.

She hands off the phone to me, "Here. There's some stuff I need to do before the bonfire."

"Stuff?" I ask.

"Not so loud," she says, gesturing to our friends as they flipped through the Adventure Ranger Handbook. "Just going to make tonight a little more interesting for everybody. Besides, I didn't bring these along to let an opportunity like this go by." She pats her backpack.

Before I have the chance to ask what else she brought along, she takes off into the woods back towards camp. *Godspeed, Banders.*

We went down the list. Shovel earned the Emergency Preparedness patch by posing with Turbo's pack full of gear. He got Geology for posing with a rock. I don't even know what kind of rock it was. Before today, I didn't even know there *were* different types of rocks. We took a picture of Shovel staring at a ladybug for Insect Study. We took a very blurry picture of Shovel chasing a squirrel for Mammal Study. We took a picture of Shovel staring at a tree for the Plant Science patch. We even got him the

Fishing merit patch. Granted, the fish was dead when we found it. But nobody needs to know that detail. I'm convinced we could have gotten him even more, but before we knew it, it was time for the bonfire. I threw my arms around Turbo and Uncle Ruckus and we started back toward camp.

"Thank you, guys. For everything," Shovel says. "This is the best week I could have asked for."

"You don't need to thank us for messing up your week," Turbo says.

"No, I mean it," Shovel replies. "I had a really good time. Um... Are we friends now?"

I laugh. "Of course, we are."

"Oh," Shovel says. "Cool. So, how about Turbo Cakes's nickname?"

Uncle Ruckus sighs, "He was doing so well. I hate that we have to kill him now."

"On second thought, I don't need to know that bad," Shovel says. "Where did Banders go again?"

"Smooth topic change," I say. "I dunno, she said she had something to do before the bonfire. I didn't want to press her about it. What if she was talking about *girl stuff*?"

We emerge from the woods smack-dab in the middle of Cardiac Hill and descend in silence. Probably because nobody wants to say something wrong about the girl stuff and look stupid. It's dark when we finally walk into the amphitheater where the bonfire is usually held. The amphitheater is Greek-style with a huge semi-circle of benches up high around a stage on the ground. Despite the whole camp being there, an uncomfortable silence hangs over the air. Everyone stares at us from the rows of benches above. It's impossible to figure out where we're supposed to be in the sea of khaki and forest green uniforms. Banders waves from the crowd along with the rest of Troop 99, and we go sit with them. *Thank goodness.*

Mr. B leans over and murmurs, "You know this looks bad for us, right? You start a food fight, pepper spray Moonpie's deer—"

"It's a buck," Uncle Ruckus interjects.

"And actually, *we* didn't pepper spray it. Camp-A-Cop did," Turbo adds.

"Needless to say," Mr. B says. "Momma Hackett has made it clear to me that Troop 99 is no longer welcome at Camp Winnebago in future summers."

My heart sinks. "I'm really sorry, Mr. B. We didn't mean to get the troop banned."

"I know you didn't, son," Mr. B says. "Did you at least happen to find the flag while you were M.I.A. this afternoon?"

"No. We didn't... But we did help Shovel get a couple of merit patches."

Mr. B smiles. "That's good enough for me."

Thhpt. A shiver goes down my spine. I'll never be able to unhear the sound of Momma Hackett prying her lipstick smeared lips apart. She speaks into a bullhorn, "Now that *everyone* is here." She glares in our direction before sweeping her eyes over the crowd. "Camp Winnebago, welcome to the last bonfire." The crowd erupts into cheers. Journey makes big 'quiet down' gestures with his arms behind Momma Hackett. "At the top, I'd like to ask whoever *borrowed* our solar panel to please return it before going home." Shovel wiggles on the bench next to me like he can't get comfortable.

She continues, "I know I speak for everyone when I say this has been a very exciting week. Certainly, this week has been a perfect example of why Camp Winnebago can no longer handle the Golden Plunger competition."

Her tone turns harsh. "You boys turn into heathens. When Journey, Dr. Cassandra, Officer Bryant, and myself sat down to figure out which troop had the best behavior this week, we had a truly difficult time. It saddened me deeply. We weren't trying to figure out who had the best behavior. You've all behaved terribly. We had to make the decision on who had the *least worst* behavior. You're Adventure Rangers!" She shouts in the bullhorn, causing the whole crowd to cringe back. "You're supposed to be well-behaved. To stand out amongst your peers doing good turns as leaders of your communities." She shook her head. "That being said, Troop 100 wins best behavior for the week."

Troop 100 erupts into cheers. Journey once again makes exaggerated 'quiet down' gestures from behind Momma Hackett. They gradually settle down. I catch Peters's eye and he smirks. *Jerk.*

"Which leaves us in quite the predicament..." Momma Hackett continues. "Troop 99 won the Culling. Troop 100 won best behavior. But the flag has yet to be found. Administration toyed with the idea of calling the whole thing off given the way the camp has behaved this week. We also considered outright disqualifying Troop 99 and awarding the prizes to Troop 100." Troop 100 gasps collectively. "However, in the spirit of the Adventure Rangers, we don't believe that would be fair. Despite their ill manners this week. Being an Adventure Ranger is fundamentally about community, service, and the ties of brotherhood. This is the one area Troop 99 has excelled this week. They are a tight knit group. A true Adventure Ranger troop." Mr. B sits up a little straight next to me. "And for this reason, they are not disqualified."

"Which brings us to our issue." She says it like *isssyou.* "How do we decide who wins the Golden Plunger? Journey?" She gestures behind her, and Journey disappears backstage. He doesn't reappear. "Journey, please simply get the Golden Plunger and return." Journey reappears, walks up to Momma Hackett, and whispers in her ear. Instead of whispering in return, she says into the bullhorn, "You fool, it's sitting on the table back there."

Journey whispers again.

"Yes, I'm sure it's on the table," Momma Hackett says, exasperated. "Go look again."

"Sounds just like my mom when she asks me to get something for her," I mumble.

"Right? Like, just go get it yourself," Turbo replies.

"Ha. Yeah, guys," Banders says. Her voice is wavering. Jumpy, almost. "She should just get it herself." She never takes her eyes off Momma Hackett.

Journey returns empty-handed, with a shrug.

"Well, then," Momma Hackett says. "It seems someone has misplaced the Golden Plunger." The crowd gasps. "Perhaps it is fitting. No troop has truly earned it this week. It is fitting that no one get to keep it. But there is still the matter of the all-expenses-paid trip to the high-adventure camp taking place later this summer. Since Troop 99 and Troop 100 are the only two troops who have fulfilled requirements for the Golden Plunger, they will compete in a tiebreaker."

"What's the tiebreaker?" somebody shouts.

Momma Hackett glares toward the source of the yell, "Would Troop 99 and Troop 100 please send one representative from their respective troops down to the stage?"

We all lock our eyes on Ducky.

"What, me?" He asks. "Nah." He points at me. "You got this, boss man."

"Are you sure?" I stammer. "You probably have a better chance of winning whatever the tiebreaker is than me."

"I believe in you. You've given everything for this troop this week. Hell, you died, dude. Nah, you're the man for the job. You got this." Ducky stands, points at me, and chants, "Do-Over! Do-Over!"

The rest of our troop catches on and chants with him. "Do-Over! Do-Over! Do-Over!"

Banders grabs my arm. "Whatever you do," she says, "do not stand on that stage when they light the bonfire." Everyone continues chanting as they shove me out into the aisle. I wobble down the stairs, clamber up onto the stage, and stand next to Momma Hackett. Journey does his signature waving motion to try and get everyone to quiet down.

"Real star in your troop, aren't you?" Momma Hackett murmurs, voice laced with sarcasm.

My retort catches in my throat when I see the representative from Troop 100 deftly climb onto the stage. Peters. Of course.

"You ready to get this over with, Do-Over?" he asks as he rolls up his sleeves. "What's on the agenda, Momma Hackett?"

She pulls the bullhorn up to her mouth. *Thhpt.* "We had several ideas for the tiebreaker. Wrestling, a one-man skit, knot contest, who can light the bonfire fastest..." I flick my eyes up to look at Banders. Her face is twisted with worry and she gives a half-shake of the head. "However, it is late. The week has been long. And I think I speak for all of us when I say, I'm ready to go home. Drumroll please." Everyone stomps their feet back and forth. It sounds like a stampede. I glance at Peters out of the corner of my eye and hear Scar's voice in my head. *Long live the king.*

"The tiebreaker... To win the all-expense paid trip to the high-adventure camp later this summer... An opportunity for Troop 100 to refine their Ranger skills... An opportunity for Troop 99 to get in more trouble together... The tiebreaker will be..." Momma Hackett does a 'cut-off' motion with her hand and the drumroll stops. "Rock, paper, scissors. Best two out of three."

Silence.

Journey steps up next to me, waving his arms to try and get the crowd hyped, but it only yields scattered claps from the parents in the crowd.

"Rock paper scissors?" Peters asks. "Lame."

"Hush," Momma Hackett says, then turns to Journey. "As soon as there is a clear winner, light the bonfire. We'll sing a few songs, then we all get to go home. Finally." Journey nods. "Gentlemen," she says into the bullhorn. "Assume the position. Standard rules. Rock beats scissors. Scissors beats paper. Paper beats rock."

Peters and I nod then face each other. Left palms up. Right hands in rock position.

She booms, "Rock, paper, scissors—"

Peters changes his rock to paper.

"Shoot!" Momma Hackett concludes.

I change my rock to scissors. Whoops and cheers go up from Troop 99.

"Not fair!" Peters shouts, his face flush. "I didn't know we were going on shoot!"

Momma Hackett gives him a questioning look, "That's how the game works. You always go on shoot." She pulls the bullhorn up to her mouth. "First point goes to Troop 99! Get in position. Rock, paper, scissors... Shoot!"

On shoot, I don't change my hand. I keep it in a fist for rock.

Peters hand blurred into paper again. "Ha!" He boasts, "I knew you'd try something like that."

Momma Hackett says, "One point to Troop 99, one point to Troop 100! Next point decides it all. Get in position. Rock, paper, scissors... Shoot!"

My heart pounds. Sweat drips down the center of my back. It's super itchy, but I don't scratch it. *Scratching is weakness. Just like paper. Peters has picked paper every time so far. Time to win this thing. One more trip with all my buddies this summer. We'll do it right this time. Win this for Uncle Ruckus. For everybody in Troop 99.*

I throw scissors.

So does Peters.

"A tie!" Momma Hackett exclaims. The crowd groans but chatters in anticipation. She turns to Journey, "Get ready to light the fire on this one." He holds a lighter to the base of the woodpile. "Get in position... This one is for all the marbles. Rock, paper, scissors... Shoot!"

My fingers twitch. My knees wobble. *For all the marbles? What does that even mean? Focus, Do-Over. What is Peters going to do? Anticipate. The rock fight. He'll pick rock, it's too perfect for him not to try to win on rock. Which means...*

I throw paper.

So does Peters.

"Another tie!" Momma Hackett exclaims.

The crowd gets louder. There are random cheers from the audience.

"You got this, Do-Over!"

"Knock 'em dead, Peters!"

"Get it over with!"

"All right..." Momma Hackett says. "Last one. This one is the tiebreaker. Get in position. Rock, paper, scissors—"

A shrill scream comes from the woods and we spot Tri-Clops sprinting towards us, naked as the day he was born, waving something back and forth. "I found the flag, Mr. B! For king and country!"

"Troop 99 found the flag!" Momma Hackett exclaims. "They win the Golden Plunger and the trip to the high-adventure camp!"

Journey's face lights up with alarm and he flicks the lighter. Trusting Banders, I turn and sprint off the stage. I dive off and land on a tree root. Pain shoots down my hip. *That's definitely going to bruise.* I look back just in time to see Journey lower the lighter to the bonfire's base. Yellow flame erupts as the woodpile catches. Then blinding light erupts from the bonfire. A thundering *boom* fills my ears. Then *pop pop, pop pop, fizzle!* Vibrant color lights up the sky with ribbons of reds and sparks of blue.

* * *

A FEW MINUTES BEFORE…
FRIDAY, JUNE 5TH, 2015. 7:09 PM.

Beneath the bridge between elements, the gateway to the world.
The flag awaits where the elements collide.
Seek not great fortunes. Seek only where it all began.
The ties of brotherhood, of song, and of pledge come to the camp flag.

Tri-Clops wandered up Cardiac Hill to the Trading Post. It was closed, but unlocked. He let himself in, made himself a Lancellotti, and left. He wandered down to the waterfront, sipping his rainbow drink all the while. He walked to the end of the dock and saw a box turtle in the water. Eager to share with the creature, he poured the remainder of the Lancellotti into the lake. The turtle swam away from the sugary drink, so Tri-Clops hopped into the water to help guide it to the sugary goodness.

The water was still warm this early in the evening. By the time Tri-Clops resurfaced, he'd lost track of the turtle. He swam along the underbelly of the dock, almost back to shore. There was something hanging—a roll of cloth. He snatched it and swam the rest of the way back to shore. With the breeze blowing it felt much colder outside of the lake. Shivering, he stripped down naked and left his Adventure Ranger uniform in a sopping heap on the ground.

He unfurled the cloth and upon it read: *Official Camp Winnebago 2015 Flag*. It was signed by Momma Hackett.

Tri-Clops's eyes grew wide. He looked up Cardiac Hill and whispered, "For king and country, Mr. B."

31

A RANGER IS FIRED

PRESENT

FRIDAY, JUNE 5TH, 2015. 7:15 PM.

Fireworks blast out of the blazing bonfire in every direction. Some people dive onto the ground, some flee to the woods. The only people still standing is my troop, jumping up and down and cheering like idiots. As Mr. B tries to herd everyone away from the bonfire, Banders, Uncle Ruckus, Turbo, and Shovel leap over benches like hurdles until they make it down to the stage. They haul me to my feet and drag me towards the woods.

The last thing I see before we disappear into the trees is Tri-Clops standing in front of the colorful bonfire. He faces it down, feet shoulder-length apart, displaying the flag above his head. "I did it, Mr. B! For king and country!"

My hip throbs with a dull pain from my stage dive, but it fades after we walk a few hundred feet. At least that's one thing checked off the bucket list. I feel like it would have been way better with people to catch me. We steer towards the waterfront as if our brains are all on the same autopilot setting.

Uncle Ruckus howls with laughter. "That was *amazing*. Banders, that was you, right?"

She smiles and says, "Where did you guys think I was going? We didn't need the fireworks for the Taser Buck trap, and I sure as hell wasn't going to let that opportunity go to waste."

His face sobers. I swear, a single tear rolls down his face, and he puts one hand on her shoulder. "That was beautiful. Thank you."

"I just hope no one got hurt," Turbo says. The silence is deafening. I hadn't even considered that.

"But it sure was cool, huh?" Shovel asks.

"Yeah," I say. "It sure was cool."

"Dude!" Banders says, punching me square in my non-existent bicep. "That was the most intense game of Rock, Paper, Scissors I've ever seen. You were gonna whup his ass on that last one."

"You totally had it," Uncle Ruckus agrees.

"But I'm still glad Tri-Clops came through for us," Turbo says.

We hop the fence to the waterfront, take off our socks and shoes, and sit at the edge of the dock with our toes tracing the surface of the lake. Screw you, Sharktocrab.

Banders slings her backpack off and pulls an oblong shape wrapped in a pillowcase out of it. "There's something else." She removes the pillowcase.

"The Golden Plunger?" I pull it from Banders's arms and cradle it in my arms like I'm auditioning as Mary in a stable for a Christmas play. "What? How? I don't—"

"Bro, they just had it *sitting* there on a table in the amphitheater. I guess they left it there to give out once the ceremony started..."

I stop listening and stare at the Golden Plunger. The thing we've spent the last week trying to earn, trying to redeem ourselves for, the thing that's put a rift between all of the Adventure Rangers at camp. The thing that will give us another campout together. I shake my head.

"We can't keep this," I say. "It's too hot. If they find out you took it, they might take away the rest of the prize."

"What are we supposed to do with it then? We can't put it back," Turbo says.

"We must cast it back into the fires from whence it came," Uncle Ruckus says.

I look down at the weight in my hands. The Golden Plunger.

"We should have a sendoff," I say. "Our own, I mean. Our own closing bonfire for the crazy week we've had. Who's in? We can get Shovel the Fire Safety merit patch while we're at it."

"Listen, Do-Over, buddy," Uncle Ruckus says. "Ya makin' me nervous here. I know we had the whole Mount Doom reference, but you don't *actually* want to destroy the Golden Plunger, do you? We just got it."

"I know, I know," I say, "And I appreciate it. But it doesn't feel... *right* keeping it. I think it's better this way. Nobody gets the Golden Plunger for keeps. Besides, like we were saying earlier, pretty soon we aren't going to be kids anymore. We're about to start high school. The snack days are over. This dumb thing has caused so much trouble. It's time we say goodbye."

Banders chimes in, talking like a surfer dude, "Yeah, man, it's just like, the Golden Plunger is just like a unicorn, man, you can't just like hold it in the palm of your hand, man. Nobody gets to keep a unicorn."

I give her a playful shove. "Come on, you know what I mean. I think we've done a lot of growing up this week. Not all the way, obviously. But still. I feel like we owe this week the symbolic goodbye it deserves. Am I right?"

They all agreed. It didn't take long to collect enough sticks to lash together and make a miniature raft that bobbed atop the lake's surface. I place the Golden Plunger on the raft.

"Banders, if you'll do the honors," I say.

She moves forward with a lighter in her hand.

"Wait," Uncle Ruckus says. He fumbles around in his sweatshirt's pocket and pulls out Devil Rock. He sets it down next to the Golden Plunger.

"Me too," Shovel says and drops his waterlogged DS on the raft.

Banders laughs. "Well, guess my troop leader wouldn't want this thing back anyway, with a hole through it." She flops the pink Bilbo down onto the raft.

Turbo Cakes turns bright red. "Well, I guess if you guys are all growing up, then I want to grow up too." He fishes a crumpled note out of his pocket and tosses it onto the raft. "It's a love letter. To Dr. Cassandra." He clears his throat. "I, uh, just don't think we're good for each other anymore. It's a mutual thing."

Everybody chimes in their assurances.

"Sure."

"Course it is, buddy."

"It couldn't have worked out."

"That's not all, though," Turbo says. "Anybody got a knife?"

"I do, I do!" Shovel says, whipping out his pocket knife.

We all jump backwards to avoid being shanked on the last night of camp.

"Sorry," Shovel says sheepishly and hands it over to Turbo Cakes.

"Turbo," I say, "what are you doing with that knife, my guy?"

"Something I should have done a long time ago," he says in a gravelly voice. He reaches up with his left hand, grimaces as he draws out his chin hair to its full length, and slices through it with one clean cut.

"Oh my God," Uncle Ruckus says.

There wasn't even enough time for stunned silence as Turbo breaks down crying. "I knew I'd regret it," he sits down on the ground in sobs.

Uncle Ruckus sits down next to him and gently rubs up and down his back. Shovel sits down next to Turbo and rests his head on Turbo's shoulder.

"Banders, will you do the honors?" I ask.

She nods, lights the tinder on the raft, and steps back. I give the raft a soft nudge and it sails out into the night. We sit down around our friends.

The first to break the silence, of course, is Uncle Ruckus, "See you in Valhalla."

"You know," Turbo chokes out. "I didn't even think about the environmental implications. We just littered in the lake while simultaneously contributing to carbon dioxide emissions with the fire. We're causing global warming right now." He sobs harder.

He's just emotional over the chin hair, I mouth at the concerned-looking Banders.

"Think on the bright side," Shovel offers. "By contributing to global warming, it's like we're avenging the Titanic. No more icebergs."

After a few moments, I can't even tell there's a raft at all. It just looks like fire dancing across the lake's surface. Maybe the Vikings had the right idea with this kind of thing. I look around at my friends. None of us have had it easy. Just a bunch of outliers who don't fit in with the rest of the world. People who don't have relationships figured out yet. People who don't know who they are yet. We'll get there. We'll make it. If this week has taught me anything, it's that friends, that human connection we feel, is the reason why we can make it through anything.

* * *

THAT NIGHT…

FRIDAY, JUNE 5TH, 2015. 8:23 PM.

Puppet Kid sits and stares at the sky. There were fireworks an hour ago. *Weird.* He checks his watch for the millionth time that day. Puppet Kid was excited when that chubby kid with the Brown Sugar Cinnamon Pop-Tart asked him if he wanted to hang out, but he was ready to get back to ventriloquist camp now. After all, there were still six weeks left.

Puppet Kid checks his watch again and gets the sinking feeling that nobody is coming back for him.

ACKNOWLEDGEMENTS

Thank you to this book's earliest readers: Becky, Cassie, Coach Knight, and my English 464 class.

Thank you to this book's most dedicated readers: Kaeli and B.K. Bass. This book was a dumpster fire before you two got your hands on it.

Thank you to Camp Buck Toms, Kellie, Katie, Mrs. May, Brian, Dana, Trey, Cole, Vance Link, Don Calame, and the wrong Jonathan Glenn.

Thank you to all my English teachers. Except the one who banned me from the library for reading too much. And the one who accused me of not reading Manal Omar's autobiography in the 7th grade.

Thank you to everyone who was in the Boy Scouts with me. I was a terror. I blame hormones.

Thank you to my parents and the Dieter family for supporting me and encouraging me to chase my dreams.

Thank you to my friend, Jason Louro, for believing in this book.

Jackson Dickert has disappeared. He left a note that said he isn't coming back until he rides a manta ray. We believe him. This guy means business. Keep up with his misadventures at **www.jacksondickert.com** or on Twitter **@SwagXMcNasty**. Yes, that is his real username. Yes, he refused to change it.

Campfire Publishing is a subsidiary of Campfire Technology, a fast-growing startup that helps writers imagine, plan, and tell their stories. Since the founding of Campfire Technology in 2018, more than 100,000 writers have used its software to plan and write their books. In 2021, the company founded Campfire Publishing, a publishing house that uses modern technology to revolutionize the way wonderful stories are discovered and distributed. *The Quest for the Golden Plunger* is Campfire Publishing's first novel, though more are in the works for 2021 and beyond.

We hope you enjoyed *The Quest for the Golden Plunger*. You can learn more about Campfire Technology on our website at **www.campfirewriting.com**.

Made in the USA
Middletown, DE
03 August 2022

70507259R00201